Chapter One
September 1980

Millie was sitting in the library with her head down surrounded by books when Miss Sparrow found her. "Millicent, you're needed in the office." She paused before saying on a quieter note, "I fear you need to brace yourself for bad news."

Millie gathered her books and haphazardly pushed them into her bag. Her heart felt heavy. She guessed it was her father. Last year he'd been admitted into a nursing home after a devastating stroke. Miss Sparrow tapped on the office door. Not waiting for a reply, she pushed it open. "Millicent Marlow, Mrs Davis." Miss Sparrow left Millie standing in front of the chancellor, who was head of Saint Hildegarde's University. Millie was twenty-one and in her final year. She was a happy, easy-going girl, well-liked by her friends, and her dedication to learning made her a popular student. In appearance she was small in every way and wore her thick brown hair short, which framed her face in a flattering way.

"Yes Mrs Davis. You wanted me?"

"Millicent, sit down please." Millie sat. "Is it my father?"

"No, Millicent, it's your mother. The police are on their way. They will aim to get you to the hospital as quickly as possible."

"Mum? What could have happened to my mum?"

Mrs Davis's eyes seemed to soften with her voice. Millie leant forward to hear. "Millie…" There was a pause. "Millie, your mother was found wandering in the village with a head wound. The first thought was she'd been attacked, but it seems she was kicked by her horse this morning. It appears she's suffered a nasty headwound. I fear her condition has deteriorated. A police escort will be here very shortly. You might like to go to your room and gather a few bits and pieces."

1

"No thank you. I will be fine. I shall probably return here tonight. If I decide to go home, I have things there."

Millicent sat in the police car quietly. She didn't engage with the policewoman who tried to converse with her. Her mind was going wild, imagining what would happen to her if her mother died and her father was left alone in a nursing home. She was fearful the scenario would impact on her plans to travel next year with her boyfriend, Simon. The police car had its blue light flashing and every now and again it sounded the siren. They made the two-hour journey to St Richard's hospital in record time. They were still too late. Mrs Marlow had died twenty minutes ago. "Is there anyone we can get to sit with you?" Millie shook her head. She was in shock. Her mother dead. It didn't seem possible. She only spoke to her two days ago. She'd been out to lunch with a friend. She'd sounded so happy. Tears didn't come. Her voice was void of emotion when she said, "my father is in Rose Cottage Nursing Home. It's only…"

The policewoman touched Millie's shoulder, "we'll take you there."

Once Millie was in the back of the police car again, she was asked if she needed transport back to the university. She shook her head. "Thank you, but I'll be okay now."

The policewoman went with her into the nursing home despite Millie saying she'd be fine. Millie signed in the visitor's book and was greeted by the matron. "Millicent. Your father's been told. His mother's visiting, she's with him now. I am so sorry."

"His mother?" Millie looked confused. She had never had grandparents. It had always been just the three of them.

"Yes. Mrs Marlow. Doris. Your grandmother?" It was obvious the confusion on Millie's face made Matron falter under the scrutiny of the policewoman. She added for confirmation. "She always visits your father on a Tuesday."

Millie didn't say anything. She looked towards the policewoman, nodded, and smiled. "Thank you for your help. I shall be fine now."

She walked with purpose towards the stairs. She heard her name being called, but ignored it, walking faster. Millie didn't knock on her father's door, just pushed it open. A plump woman in her late seventies looked up from the bent figure of her father. She was trying to get him to drink from his beaker. The woman said, "Millicent."

Millie was annoyed but tried to hide it. Her voice betrayed her feelings when she said, sharply, "how come you recognise me, yet I had no idea of your existence?".

The woman didn't seem fazed by her outburst. "Photos in the room. It didn't take too much guessing." The voice had an air of wealth and was well pronounced.

Millie ignored her and moved over towards her father, despite the woman's close contact. "Dad, it's me, Millie." She picked up his good hand and held it to her lips. Hugh Marlow raised his eyes to his daughter and a big solitary tear fell down his cheek. Millie gave way to her own bottled emotion and knelt between her father's legs, resting her head on his chest and sobbed. The woman who was supposedly Millie's grandmother moved away and sat on the bed. There was no compassion in her voice when she said, "tears don't change anything. Get yourself together. Hugh doesn't need this."

Millie was angry now. "He's not Hugh to me. He's my dad."

"Really, is that what they've led you to believe all these years?"

Hugh Marlow started making noises in his chair. Millie turned on the woman, "Stop upsetting him. What is the matter with you?"

"You are a bastard child. He took your mother on when she had nowhere to go. My son was engaged to a nice young girl of means when his head was turned by your slut of a mother."

Hugh Marlow was becoming very agitated and the noises coming from his twisted mouth were alarming.

Millie was very able to hold her own. For a young woman of twenty-one her vocabulary was not lacking in strength. There were no hysterics or bad language. She held her father's hand and looked right at the woman, saying, "please leave us. I want some time with my dad…"

Doris laughed, "You weren't listening, were you? He's not your father."

"He's, my dad. He's brought me up and I love him, and he loves me."

"Oh, you do, do you? Well, if that's true you can take your beloved father home. Home is where he wants to be. There's nothing to stop you now. Your mother's gone. She was the fly in the ointment. Didn't want him impinging on her life now he's no more than a vegetable. After all he did for her. That's what…"

"Stop!" Millie's voice was raised but controlled. "Stop being so cruel. Mum would have taken him home if it were possible. Dad wouldn't have wanted it either. He needs care. Anyway, it's not possible now. Who would look after him?

Doris placed her hands on her plump hips. She spared no thought for the fact that Millie had lost her mother less than an hour ago and Hugh his wife. She blustered on; her voice full of aggression. "Haven't you heard of live-in carers?"

4

Millie couldn't believe this woman was for real. "Why would you suggest such a thing? Dad's happy here. Well fed, clean and warm…"

"Pathetic, that's what you are. Shallow like your mother. Open your eyes. No one wants to end their days like this. Stuck in a room. A number on the door. He's still in his fifties. A relatively young man to all these fuddy-duddies."

Millie looked at her father, who had gone quiet. She got closer to him. "Dad?" she whispered. "Dad would you like to go home?" Millicent was asking the question but didn't know the first way forward if the outcome was that this woman was right. Hugh stared at his daughter and nodded. Millie dropped her head, defeated. "Oh, dad."

Millie's head spun with questions. She wanted to know if he had always wanted to go home. She wanted to know if her mother had known his wishes. She wanted to know the history behind her existence and who her real father was. There were so many things, but no answers. Her father didn't have the words to express himself anymore. The door closed and Millie realised Doris had left without a goodbye to either of them.

Unperturbed by the recent happenings, she said, "Dad, I hear you. I don't know how, but I will sort out your coming home. There's a lot to organise. I feel I'm fumbling in the dark. I'll need to get you assessed for your needs and hire someone to be a carer…" Millie stopped rambling. She picked up her dad's hand and held it to her lips. "Dad, I love you. You are my dad. Now mum's gone you are all I have." She waited for a reaction. Nothing. Just two big hazel eyes stared back at her. "Dad, you do understand, don't you? Mum has gone. She had an accident today."

Hugh nodded again and tears fell down his face for a second time. Tears were not unusual these days. Since his stroke he was prone to this emotion. If he laughed, it normally ended up with him crying. Millie put her own grief aside for the time being. "Chin up, dad. You're coming home. You made it clear that's what you want."

She kissed his wet cheek and said goodbye. Her heart felt heavy as she closed her father's door. So much to happen in just a few hours. Her mother had died. She had met a woman, who was supposed to be her grandmother, who didn't want to acknowledge her as such, and the man she'd looked upon as her father was not a blood relative if what this Doris had said was true. Millie couldn't and wouldn't let her mind think of Hugh Marlow as anything but her dad. She would though dig into her background and see where this rumour had come from and if there was any truth in it.

Millie caught the bus, making her mind up to stay at home tonight. The day's events were too unsettling. She felt she needed time to think. Think about how she would arrange getting her father out of Rose Cottage and back living in his own home The Four Willows.

*

Doris put down her bags and opened the front door. Her head buzzed in thought. *What a day. Who would have thought it? Davinia dead and the child, brazen as you like, standing before me looking so like her mother I could have slapped her.'*

She called out to John that she was home but there was no answer.

She found him sitting in the newly built conservatory listening to the radio with ear plugs in, watching the football on television with no sound. His obsession with sport drove Doris mad.

"John!"

He raised his hand in acknowledgment but put a finger to his lips warning her he was listening.

The sheer frustration of the day had her flicking off the television, something she never would have normally done.

"Doris! What do you think you are doing? Put that back on."

"No, John. Davinia's dead. Dead. I met the child today. You would have thought it was Davinia herself standing in front of me reading me my rights."

John took out his ear plugs. "What happened?"

Doris flopped in the chair exhausted by the twists and turns of emotions. "Accident with her horse. She died within the hour of being in hospital I believe." She took a tissue from her sleeve and blew her nose. "It was awful seeing our Hugh cry. How could he still love her after she dumped him in that home?"

John reached out and placed a hand on his wife's knee, sensing her distress. "Was the child polite to you?"

Doris ignored the reference to the child that had caused her so much trouble even though she'd never met her until today. Doris said quietly, "at least I know now he understands everything I say to him. Watching him as I have done, sitting in his chair week after week dribbling like a child with a bib on, unable to walk or talk… I hate to say it and I never thought I would say it, but it would have been better if he'd died today instead of her."

John got out of his chair, "I'll make you a cuppa, you look like you could do with one." Doris smiled weakly. She hadn't managed to tell John how spiteful she'd been. The more she thought about it the more she wished she could rewind the meeting. It was the memories and shock that had clouded her better judgement and gave rise to bitterness.

Once the tea had warmed her, she said tentatively, "I haven't been wholly honest with you, John." She waited for a reaction, but he only paused, holding the earplugs in his hand. He looked over his

7

glasses waiting for an explanation. She added, "I said something that was unforgivable to the child. Well not child. She is a woman in more ways than one."

John placed the earplugs in his lap and said, "out with it. Come on let's hear what you said."

"Oh, John, you will think me spiteful. I don't know what came over me. I…"

"Spit it out, you'll feel better."

Doris put her cup in her saucer and placed it on the tray. "I told her Hugh wasn't her real father. I said he'd married her mother…" She paused before adding "Oh, John, I called her a slut."

"What the child?"

"No! Davinia, silly. I called Millicent, a bastard child."

The colour drained from John's face, "Jesus, Doris, you don't do things by halves."

Tears fell down Doris's cheeks with the relief of telling her husband how cruel she'd been. Between sobs she told him how Hugh had reacted. "He understands everything we say, John. That was obvious. If you could have seen his leg jigging in frustration at not being able to defend the girl. Then when I verbally attacked her, I said if she really loved him, she'd take him home. It was a ridiculous thing to say. I just wanted to be spiteful, make her feel bad towards her mother, but no, she got down and asked Hugh if he wanted to go home." Doris looked at her husband to make sure she still had his attention. He was still watching and waiting. "You won't believe it, he managed to convince her that that is what he'd want. Grunting and shaking his head. She got more response from him in those ten minutes than I've had for this past year. I honestly believed he was a cabbage. You've heard me say it."

"Love don't be so hard on yourself. If the girl's taking him home as you say, time will tell as to the suitability of the situation. She's at university, isn't she?" When Doris nodded, he added, "well the care won't fall on her shoulders, or ours. It will be down to the girl to sort out the nursing. Then there's the horses too. She'll either have to sell them or they'll need a stable hand. It's a lot for a young girl to manage and organise at a distance. Don't worry about it, Doris, it probably won't happen."

"But, John, if she takes him home, I'll not see him again. I've just got used to having him back in our lives."

"Your life, Doris, not mine. He burned his bridge a long time ago."

John turned the television back on and put the earplugs in his ears. The conversation was over.

Doris still had things to air but didn't push it. She was pleased to have been able to admit her nasty tongue had got the better of her. She gathered up the teacups and put them on the tray. Going through to the kitchen her mind was on Millicent. *'What an able young girl. She had to be in her twenties. Same sort of age as her mother when she'd stood in our front room beside Hugh. Our son telling us he was calling off his engagement to Sylvia as Davinia was carrying his child and they were going to be married by special licence next week. I knew even then it wasn't his.'* Memories flooded back. The heated conversation. Things that were said. Unforgivable things. Hugh had struck John and they hadn't spoken since. John had not even relented when Hugh had the stroke and was admitted into Rose Cottage Nursing Home. Her husband was a stubborn man. His last words to Hugh had been 'don't you ever darken this doorstep again. As far as we're concerned you are six feet under the ground.'

Doris emptied the tumble dryer and started folding the washing into neat piles for ironing and what could just be put away. Her mind was on other things. *'It might have been easier if I hadn't heard on the grapevine of Hugh's stroke. Left them all to it.'*

Doris thought back to the rows her proposed visit to their sick son had caused. In the end John had relented, but he'd forbidden her to speak to Davinia should their paths cross. With confidential phone calls to the nursing home, she realised Davinia didn't visit her husband every day. He got a Sunday visit and sometimes Wednesdays. This had angered Doris at the time and her heart went out further to her son. Not the son who had walked out of their house in anger, but the little boy he'd been. Her youngest child, the baby. She'd had two sons. Mark was the elder by five years and now lived in Singapore. He married a Singaporean girl. They have three children of their own. Life had dealt a cruel blow to Doris and John. Distance and feuds had ostracised them from their boys. Seeing her son, Hugh today with Millicent was proof enough that she hadn't been forgiven for harsh words twenty odd years ago. She had been wasting her time visiting him weekly. Not only that, but she'd caused a regular Tuesday atmosphere in her own home, upsetting John with the weekly visit.

Chapter two
The Four Willows – October 1980

It had been six weeks since Davinia Marlow had died. Millie had always been an independent child and had grown into a very capable young woman but missed her mother more than she thought possible. The funeral had been a quiet affair and Millie was pleased to see her supposed grandmother had not attended. She was also pleased she hadn't seen her since the day of her mother's accident. Her true parentage still niggled away at her. She tried hard to let it go, but of an evening or in the early hours of the morning it would play on her mind. She didn't have anyone to ask. Her father had nodded furiously when she had asked him if she was really his. She knew he was not the best person to give her an honest answer.

They were a family. He was the man she'd called daddy, dad, and father for as long as she could speak. Whatever was real didn't matter. Millie just wished the seed of doubt that had been planted and disturbed her sleep would go away.

November 1980

Plans had been made for Hugh Marlow's care and Monday he would be moving back home. Millie wouldn't be there. She was back at university. A good care package had been put in place along with a mature lady, Alice. She had come highly recommended by the stable hand, Duncan. It was arranged that Alice would live in so Hugh wouldn't be on his own. So many changes for Millie to adapt to. Duncan had been employed by her mother to help with the upkeep of the garden and horses and her father's stallion had been sold a few weeks after his stroke. Millie wondered how he would feel when he realised his Master Black was absent from the stables that had been built into their garden when she was ten years old. Millie knew her father was mute now,

11

but felt sure once he was home he would want to see the horses. They had been his love, passion, and pastime.

Saturday 1ˢᵗ November

Millie was dressed in a pair of faded jeans, a thick woolly jumper, and a pair of cowboy style boots. Her short hair had grown over the weeks and made her face look softer. The ballet classes she had attended as a child gave her a beautiful posture and confidence oozed from her. She had dressed for warmth. Stephanie was throwing a firework party. She had become Millie's best friend in her first year here at university.

Millie heard Simon calling her name. He had been her boyfriend for the past three years. Time had made them comfortable with each other, so much so he was like the brother Millie had so yearned for in childhood. She grabbed her jacket saying, "coming."

Simon had let himself in and met her on the stairs. His eyes swept over her body. "Do you know how good you look?" He kissed her. "Shall we go later?"

Millie laughed and let herself be kissed again, saying, "come on, you know we can't be late. You're in charge of the firework display and I'm giving out the punch."

"Why does she have to make everything so regimental and organised? Why can't we just go and mingle."

Millie pulled at his arm, refusing to be tempted to take the stairs back up to her room. "Let's go. It's not for us to wonder. You were the one who said you were happy to play firework master, and I said I was happy to spoon drink into glasses... come on let's do our bit, it makes Stephanie happy. It is her birthday after all and you know what she's like, all her plans will go out of the window once she starts on the baccy." Millie grabbed the small, wrapped gift box off the side and the bottle of sparkly. Hand in hand they made their way across the green to catch a bus. Stephanie didn't do things by half. It was going to be a long night.

The windows were lit up like Christmas trees. Guests were already dancing to the music that blared out and could be heard in the street. "Complaints tonight, I reckon."

Millie snuggled up to Simon for warmth. He was a good six inches taller than she was and she fitted under his armpit like a piece of jigsaw. "I don't think so, she said she's invited the street."

"There's always one. You wait and see. Especially when I let those rockets off at midnight."

Giggling, they pushed open the door. The warmth and the smell of food and cannabis filled the air. Millie found Stephanie in the kitchen putting vol u vents on to a plate. She embraced Millie like she hadn't seen her for years. Millie knew she was already stoned. "For you." Millie gave her the little gift bag and bubbly.

It got put on the side, unopened. Millie didn't need to hand out any drinks it was already a free for all. Simon went outside to see what the plans were for the fireworks. A bonfire was in full flame with people sitting in chairs placed round it for warmth.

In the early hours of the morning, Simon and Millie made their way back to hers. They had missed the last bus and found themselves walking home at just gone three. The two of them had had too much to drink and even though neither smoked the wacky baccy they had breathed enough of the air to be a little lightheaded. When Simon said, "marry me, Mills." She laughed out loud as if he had told a hysterical joke.

He dropped down on one knee despite the wet grass, "I'm serious, Millie. I want to marry you. I love you. I have for so long now. Please, please say you will?"

The laughter died on Millie's lips for a second, only to start up again as she looked at his earnest face. "Get up you silly donkey. I can't marry you. We have plans remember."

"You can. We can. We can do whatever we want. Marry me, Mills." When he pulled out a box and flipped open the lid, Millie knew he was speaking from the heart. This had been planned.

"Simon, Simon, Simon."

He looked at her pleadingly, "is that yes?"

Millie felt tearful. The sad, trying events of the past few weeks seemed to come to the fore and spill over with his genuine display of love. "Don't cry, Millie. Just say yes."

"I want to, I really do, but..."

"No buts, Mills, let's just do it."

"Not now, Simon. Life's complicated for me at the moment. Let me settle dad in. See what happens at home." Tears fell freely down her cheeks and Simon clambered to his feet gathering her up in his arms, cradling her like a child. He kissed the top of her head. "Don't say no, Mills. Please, don't say no. I'll ask you again. Later."

They made their way back to her student accommodation together, Millie tucked under Simon's arm. "We were made for each other, Mills, I know we were."

Chapter Three
February 1981

Millie had gone home to The Four Willows every weekend for the past six weeks. Simon's constant pleas for her to stay had fallen on deaf ears. He refused to go with her, telling her he would be bored. Millie knew the truth was he didn't like seeing her father as an invalid. Neither did she, but felt duty bound.

Her dad was happy. That, she was sure of. He now spent his days in a reclining armchair, watching programmes on the television that he would have once called rubbish before his stroke.

Millie had organised the builders in to turn the upstairs into separate living accommodation. It had been a relatively easy job. Two of the four bedrooms had been turned into a kitchen dining room and the work had been completed just before Christmas. Upstairs was going to become live-in accommodation for Alice, which would become a part of her wages. The nursing home had been expensive, but day-care was also proving a money pit. Millie now had power of attorney and had been alarmed at how her parents finances were dwindling. Her father's business, Marlow's estate agents had been sold before her mother's death and Millie had used a lot of the money to fund the conversion. Alice seemed to like the idea of moving in as part of her pay. This suited them both.

Things were coming together at home at last, but Millie knew things with Simon were far from normal. She loved him with all her heart, but what had happened last year had taken its toll on their relationship. She made up her mind that now was the time to put things right between them.

There was so much hype about the new lady in Prince Charles's life, Lady Diana Spencer and the forthcoming wedding. She was beautiful. Her face was on the television, in magazines and newspapers on a daily basis. This all seemed to remind Millie of the distance that had grown between herself and Simon. She couldn't help feeling gooey eyed and romantic herself as she looked at Shy Di as she was being called. It really did seem like a fairy tale. For Millie, these days Simon's proposal felt like it had been a foolish drunken moment. A looseness of the tongue. She would have let herself believe that completely, but for the little ring he had produced in a box. How she wished she had slipped it on her finger. Promised him there and then she would marry him. She told herself over and over, *'of course I'll marry him. We're inseparable.'*

Valentine's Day was fast approaching. Millie was secretly hoping Simon would ask her again. She was determined now with these thoughts that she would put things right between them. They needed to start laughing together, instead of the boring agony aunt talks she had been prone to over the past weeks.

Tuesday 10th February 1981

Millie was walking to the college carpark when she spotted Stephanie. She called out to her, "Stephanie, wait up." Millie started to run towards her friend. "I'm going to buy some bits in the town. Do you want to come?"

"No, sorry. I have heaps of work to catch up on."

Millie was surprised. Perhaps she had been going home so often she was losing her friends too. "We'll get a frothy coffee. I'll treat you."

"I really can't Millie. I've got to get my dissertation in by Friday. I'm well behind with my work. I'm not like you, don't have to try."

Her friend's words stung. "Hey that's not fair. I have a lot on my mind with home at present and my work is taking second place. I'm struggling too."

"Yeah, well can't do today. Sorry." Millie watched Stephanie walk away without a backward glance, her bulky figure apparent in her tight jean skirt and puffer jacket. Stephanie was a good-looking girl, despite her wild auburn hair that wouldn't stay flat. It was her eyes that got her noticed. They were strikingly dark. The lashes too.

Millie opened her car door and forgot about Stephanie. She turned the stereo on and pushed a cassette in the deck. It was Abba. The music washed away any uneasy feelings.

Once back in her room, Millie unpacked her toiletries and had a shower. With her wet hair wrapped in a towel, she phoned Simon and asked if he fancied going for a drink this evening. Millie wouldn't normally go out mid-week, but at the weekend she had gone home again. Simon's constant refusal to go with her hurt, but she knew her father's condition was alarming even to her own eyes. She guessed what Simon said was true, he probably would be bored, and being home was depressing. The house was losing the familiar smell of home and had started to smell clinical.

Millie was surprised and pleased when he said, "I could do. Where?"

"The Paperchase?" This was a youngsters' bar, noisy but full of atmosphere. Millie had things on her mind. She wanted to air them with Simon, but now wasn't the time. She felt they needed some fun."

She was surprised again when Simon said, "can't we go somewhere quieter. It would be good to talk."

Millie agreed. She had been hurt by Stephanie's offish behaviour to her earlier. She still couldn't understand why, so if Simon wanted quiet time to talk, it would be good to get things off her chest.

She replaced the receiver. They were meeting at The Springs. A hotel with a quiet lounge.

When he knocked on her door rather than just walk in, goose pimples went up Millie's arms. "What's got into you? Knocking before you come in."

"I wasn't thinking. It feels like ages since I've been here."

Millie tried not to sound cross when she said, "that's unfair. It's been weekends. I'm always here. You've been busy..."

Simon interrupted her. "Let's not fight. Come on. You look amazing."

Simon always said nice things to her. Mollie did look amazing and she knew it.

Once they were sat together in the hotel lounge, both with a glass of lager in front of them, Simon's tone of voice said it all. "I've been wanting to speak with you, Mills. It's just..."

Millie sensed what he had to say was going to be upsetting. She interrupted him. "Please don't hurt me with words, Simon. I've had a gutful of it lately. What with one thing and another."

Simon reached for Millie's hand. "Mills, I do care a great deal for you, you know that, but things have changed between us. I've changed, I..."

"No! Nothing's changed. I've been wrapped up with sorting out my dad's care. It's done now. I'll be here more, I..." Millie was talking fast but Simon hung his head, shaking it in a negative way. "Don't Millie. Don't. Whatever was between us is no more. I hate doing this, but I want a fresh start."

"Why?" Millie let the tears fall. She couldn't hold them back. This was one blow too many. "You only asked me to marry you a while back. What could have changed."

Simon wrung his hands together. "Mills, can I just say I'm sorry. I'm really sorry."

"Is there someone else. Is that it?"

When he hesitated to answer, Millie knew. "Oh, my God. You've been cheating on me. That's what this is all about. Guilt."

"I… Mills, it's not what you think."

Millie was desperate. She couldn't bear to lose Simon as well. "Simon, I understand. Okay? She paused briefly, "don't finish what we have for a fling. What with all the crap that's been going on in my life of late, I get it. Honestly, I do. Please…"

"No, Mills, no. I don't want forgiveness, I don't want you to beg either. I just want you to let me go. We're over."

"Who is it? Whose turned your head." Simon didn't say anything. He continued to look at his hands, his drink staying untouched on the table. Millie raised her voice. Hurt made her lose control. Heads turned when she said, "tell me for fucks sake. Who's stuck the final knife in my heart when I'm already trying to breathe."

"Don't do this. Please." Simon stood up as if to leave. Millie began to cry and beg him not to go. She didn't care that people were staring and a hushed silence had fallen over the hotel room. A very smartly dressed man approached them. His uniform told of his position in the hotel. "Would Sir kindly take the lady outside." He hesitated a fraction before adding, "please."

Millie stood, "NO!" she shouted. "No Sir won't fucking take me anywhere." The penny dropped. It all became crystal clear to Millie. "He's screwing my best friend." She turned her angry hazel eyes to him. They glistened with tears. "That's it isn't it? You're screwing Stephanie. It all fits." Simon tried to take Millie's arm. She shrugged him off. "Leave me alone. I don't care if I never see you again, either of you. You deserve each other." Millie pulled on her coat and shouted, "I hate you Simon Few, and I'm bloody glad I didn't agree to marry you. You little Shit!"

The man in uniform escorted her out of the room and into the fresh air. "There you go missy. Obviously upsetting for you, but…" Millie shrugged him off not saying anything. What she had just heard and discovered had shaken her to the core of her heart.

Millie wanted to go home.

*

Millie didn't know how, but she had driven back to The Four Willows that same evening, crying all the way with her cassette of love songs blaring from the car stereo.

She sat this morning red-eyed with her father trying to do The Telegraph crossword with him. He couldn't speak but he seemed to enjoy her company, and she was sure he was following the questions. Millie squeezed his hand. "You can do all these can't you dad? I bet you are bursting to tell me the answers." Millie gave way to tears. Still holding her father's hand, she said, "I'm sure you're wondering what I'm doing home." She pressed her lips to the veiny top of his hand. "My world seems to be shaking by its roots, dad. Mum dies, I meet a grandmother who says she isn't my grandmo…" Millie didn't get to finish. Hugh started jigging his knee up and down. The grip of his hand tightened, and his eyes seemed to double in size. Millie took her hand out of his grip and stroked his head like you would a dog to soothe it. "It's okay, dad. I know. I'm sorry. It's just everything in my world that was safe seems to be crumbling around my feet or has crumbled. The final straw is Simon. Simon's finished our relationship. He's seeing Stephanie." As she looked at him to check he was following, fresh tears fell from her face. She wiped at them with her sleeve. "Yes, dad, Stephanie, my best friend. I'm gutted. You won't believe it." Millie was going to tell him about the proposal he had sprung on

20

her when he had begged her to marry him, but changed her mind saying instead, "what was it mum used to say? Better find out sooner rather than later that he's a wolf in sheep's clothing." Despite the sadness, Millie laughed. "It didn't go like that, did it dad? But the gist of it's there." Millie stood up as Alice, the live-in carer came in with a mug of coffee. She smiled saying, "there you are, Hugh, nice and milky with two sugars. Just as you like it." She turned her attention to Millie and asked. "Can I get you one?" Millie shook her head. "No ta. I'm going out for a ride." She leant over and kissed her dad's head, folded up the newspaper and turned the television up, leaving him watching the screen. His eyes followed her as she slipped on her wax jacket and went into the garden. Millie didn't hear Alice telling Hugh that Duncan was mucking out the stables.

Chapter Four

Duncan was stroking Champagne's nose and blowing gently on her face. "You're a real beauty you are." He mistook the footsteps for Alice. He thought she was bringing him a cup of coffee like she sometimes did. He was surprised to see a pretty face peering over the stable door. "Well, hello." His eyes swept over her body. "Dressed like that I'm taking it you must be Millie. I'm Duncan, Duncan James."

His introduction was ignored. Millie's tone was clipped. "Who did you expect?" Millie knew she looked good in the wax jacket and jodhpurs, but his flattery fell on deaf ears. She said, "I've come to ride Truffle. I'll take my mother's horse out this afternoon."

"Well, I was hoping for a cuppa, but I'm happy to ride Champers for you. We could ride over the copse. It's a lovely morning for it."

Davinia had always called her horse Champers for short but hearing the name on this young man's lips annoyed Millie. "Thank you, but no thank you. I can manage just fine." She sounded sharp and unfriendly. Trying to soften her words, she added. "Alice is just making coffee. I suggest you go across and grab a cup. I can manage here."

Duncan said, "will do." Without a backward glance in her direction, he pushed his hair out of his eyes and pulled the wavy ends out of his collar. Doing his coat up as he went.

Millie watched him go. He was tall like Simon, but everyone looked tall to Millie. Everything else about Duncan was different. His eyes were a soft blue, like the sky on a warm day. Simon's were green. The outdoor work Duncan did, gave him a rosy complexion, but what was really striking about him was his round baby face and the slight indent of a dimple in his chin. He was also wearing a gold band on his left hand. Millie told herself it was unimportant; she was finished with men. Her heart had been broken into a thousand pieces one way and another. So, from now on it was going to be all about her.

She tacked up Truffle and swinging her leg over the saddle she trotted out of the garden onto the path that led to the copse. *'Duncan was right. It's a lovely day for it.'*

*

At the house Duncan stood in the kitchen and chatted with Alice. "She's a frosty fish, isn't she?"

Alice lowered her voice. She put her finger to her lips before saying, "I think there's trouble. Boyfriend. There were tears this morning. I caught the tail end of it."

"Had you met her before?"

Alice offered Duncan another biscuit, "Yes, she did the interviews."

"She didn't interview me. Mrs Marlow took me on. This is the first I've seen of her. I tell you, looks are deceiving."

"You've just been unlucky with her. She's really nice. Down to earth. I guess she's just hurting at the moment. She's lovely with her father. You can tell she genuinely cares for him."

"Well, he's lucky he isn't getting the rough end of the stick like she gave me."

"Go on you silly bugger. Your Sindy would be miffed if she thought you were upset by a little brush off this morning from an attractive young lady. Especially in her condition. How is she by the way?"

"Pregnant. Fat." They laughed together. Then on a more serious note he added. "Sindy has high blood pressure. Her mum's come to help with the boys today. Paul's easier because he's at school all day, but Jack needs to be taken and picked up from playschool and he's lively. He's awake before sunrise. It's taking its toll on her, and me. I shall be glad next month when the baby's out."

Alice pushed him in the arm. "You make it sound like something that's cooking. I tell you they're a lot less trouble when they're in than out."

Duncan gave his empty mug to Alice. "Thanks for that. I better go and make sure the tack is all ready and waiting for the mistress of the house's return. He left to the sound of laughing.

The Four Willows

Duncan came cycling up the drive at just after eight. Millie had both horses in the horsebox ready for a hack. They were going to Slindon to ride up over the downs. Millie had made her peace, apologising for taking her own problems out on him.

Out of breath, he said, "sorry, Millie. Sindy needed help with the boys. Her mum's gone home, and Jack woke up feeling awkward. Nothing you asked him to do seemed to sink in. Which I might add is nothing unusual."

"Kids! Rather you than me."

Duncan laughed. "You say that now, but one day."

An easy silence settled in the truck as Millie towed the horse box behind them.

Galloping over the Downs was exhilarating and Millie felt good. Happier than she had done for weeks. Losing Simon still hurt. She was lonely without his company and love. Nights were the worse and she cried herself to sleep. Simon's betrayal had broken Millie. He'd been part of her life since the beginning of Uni. Life had seemed one long party back then. She'd still managed to make reasonable grades in her exams. Stephanie hadn't done so well but scraped through. Millie's second year had been a more focused year and despite sharing her time with Simon, she achieved excellent results. This year was proving emotionally trying in every way possible. Just when she thought nothing else could go wrong, this happened.

Millie shared her heartache with Duncan as they sat eating the picnic lunch she'd packed for them. It was nothing special. A couple of cans of Coke and a Marmite roll each. It was enough.

"Not much of a friend if you ask me." Duncan wiped his mouth on his sleeve, belched and apologised.

Millie laughed. "She was. In the early days that is."

"I'd punch her lights out."

Millie was shocked. "What you'd really hit a woman?" Her father had always been such a gentle man. She couldn't remember a time when he ever smacked her, and she was sure there were times when she'd needed it.

Duncan smiled. "No, I wouldn't hit a woman, but I know if a man tried to take Sindy from me..." He paused and added, "why, I swear I'd kill him."

Millie kicked the soil with her riding boot. "Ladies don't behave like that." She hesitated. "I don't know what I'll even say to her when I see her. I was so angry on Tuesday. I could have killed them with my bare hands..."

"What even though you're a lady."

Millie pushed him in the arm. She didn't like the scrutiny. Losing Simon was still raw. "Tell me about you. How did you meet Sindy?"

"We went to school together, primary, junior and secondary. We used to walk from the village."

"Did you always like her, even back then?"

"Not really. She was just my friend's kid sister. Then... I don't know where the years went but she grew up. She came to a disco at the village hall. She was sixteen. I was seventeen. I was working on a milk round back then. She caught my eye. She looked lovely. She had on one of those frocks that when you spin, they flare out. Her hair was tied in a ponytail like a schoolgirl, but the face paint told another story. I couldn't take my eyes off her. I asked her to dance. Smoochie one. We kissed and five years later she was pregnant. We married quickly and six years on we're about to have our third child. I'm no longer a milk man but an odd job man come stable hand for the very wealthy Marlow daughter."

They both laughed at that. "You are funny. Where do you live?"

On Parson's Green. We live on the council estate at low bottom road. You probably don't know Parson's Green?"

Millie ignored the question. "Do you have brothers, sisters?"

"I have an older sister called Susan, but no one calls her that. We call her Peg. It used to be Peg leg because she has one leg longer than the other. Cruel really, but that's kids for you. She wears one of those boots. You know the ones that have a built-up sole. That didn't help the mickey taking either. The fights I used to get into defending her."

"That's horrible. Poor girl. I would never call her Peg on principle. She would always be Susan if I knew her."

"Trouble is she wouldn't know who you were talking to now. She's Peg. Not Peg leg anymore thank goodness, but the taunts are probably always there in her head. Never married either. At thirty-one I suppose you'd say she's on the shelf."

Millie stood up and brushed herself off. "Come on, let's get these horses back in the box and head home. I'm going back to Uni tomorrow." Millie touched Duncan's arm. "Thank you for today. I'm struggling at the moment, and my insides feel permanently like they're tied up in knots. The ride's helped. Blown the cobwebs away." She smiled at him before adding, "and your company.

Duncan bowed, mockingly. "At your service mam. With what has happened to you this year you have every right to be a little lost and tied up emotionally."

Millie pushed Champagne into the box. The horse resisted and sidestepped with annoyance. "Go on, Champers. There's a girl." Once Millie had both horses side by side feeding on a nose bag, she said, "lost, Duncan. I've felt more than lost." She wanted to tell someone her doubts of her parentage, but not now and not with him. It just didn't feel right. It was still too raw to share with anyone.

*

Millie parked her car in the university car park. A wave of sadness washed over her and for no reason nerves gripped her stomach, which made her feel sick. The walk to the dormitory seemed long. There was no one around, but it felt like eyes were watching her from everywhere. She could feel the pity.

She closed the door of her bedroom and threw her bag on the bed. Paula had been in the kitchen and seemed pleased to see her back. She'd attempted to say sorry about events. Millie had held up her hand halting the conversation. Tears threatened.

She should unpack the few items she had stuffed in a bag on her hurried exit last Tuesday, but she was determined to get some work done and catch up on missed lectures. She grabbed the duffle bag that held her books, pulled a large blue folder from the bookcase and headed for the library. This was a place Millie felt at peace. She loved it here.

"Millie?" The voice was too familiar.

She looked up to see Stephanie standing opposite her desk. Her face was pale, and she looked nervous. "Millie, please let me explain."

Millie had become so engrossed in writing an essay that she hadn't realised anyone had entered. Seeing Stephanie was like a knife in her stomach. "I've got nothing to say to you, except I'm busy." The pain in Millie's voice was reflected in her eyes.

"Millie, please. I…"

"Either you go, or I'll go."

"I'm sorry. Really sorry. We didn't want it to…"

Millie stopped her by saying. "You just don't listen do you. It's over between us, all of us. What do you want? My blessing. Is that what you came here for?"

Stephanie sat at the desk. Her face ashen. "Please, Mills, let me…"

Millie was on her feet now. She had gathered her books and shoved them in her duffle bag, tucking her folder under her arm. "Stephanie, you're welcome to him." She left without looking back.

Millie's hands were shaking as she made herself a coffee. Once in the security of her room she gave way to tears.

Chapter Five
Peg James

Peg made her way home. She was dirty and smelly. Working at the egg farm was not the most glamourous job, but she was grateful for the income. Her hip ached. The heavy clumsy built-up boot she wore helped with her limp, but walking up and down the rows of chicken cages collecting and sorting the cracked eggs and sizing them on trays into large medium and small, by the end of the day, it wasn't only her hip that ached.

When she heard a wolf whistle, she didn't even turn her head. No one whistled at Peg. She'd been ridiculed all her life for having one leg shorter than the other. Christened Susan Jane James was lost in primary school. There she had been taunted for her big boot and funny limp. Trousers weren't allowed to be worn by girls, so she stood out as different.

Learning didn't come easy to her, so she was seen not only as an invalid but as what they called a thicko. The taunts. She could still hear them. "Peg leg with the wooden head." The times she'd cried all the way home. Then as the years went by, she built a shield around herself and to the outside world it looked like their comments fell on deaf ears.

Here she was thirty-one years old and still living at home. The only time she'd ever kissed a boy was when she'd found herself as the booby prize in a game the children were playing. She was the forfeit. That had hurt too. She'd been held down while Peter Sammond had kissed her. She could still visualise him spitting on the ground after the event and wiping his lips with his sleeve like they were covered with a horrible tasting sticky substance. When she got home her mother had scolded her for her dirty frock. The memories of those painful years still brought a cloud over Peg's world.

Duncan had married Sindy when he was twenty-three. This had been another blow for Peg. She had been making plans to leave home herself. She'd seen a live-in position as a companion. It was in the Lady magazine. Scotland, Aberdeen. She'd liked the idea of travelling. Seeing a different part of the world. Getting away from here. Perhaps even becoming Susan and not Peg. It didn't happen. It wasn't only her brother's shame of bringing a pregnancy before marriage home, but her father had been diagnosed with a brain tumour. This had meant she couldn't leave. Her father died shortly after Duncan's wedding. Peg became companion to her mother, Martha, whose tongue could be as cruel as the school children in the playground.

She was brought out of her reverie when she heard someone chasing after her calling, 'wait up'. Peg turned to see one of the builders who were working on the new builds. One hundred and eighty houses were going up where there had once been an orchard.

"Didn't you hear me whistling to you?"

Peg's heart thudded in her chest. Her cheeks felt hot and her armpits moist. "I didn't realise you were calling to me." She eased her weight off her heavy boot, "what do you want?"

"It's your lucky day, my love. I was hoping to take you out for a drink tonight."

Peg just stared at him. She couldn't believe what she was hearing. He was a good-looking chap too. Before she could think of something that sounded half sensible to say, he asked, "well?"

Her face felt like it was on fire. "Yes. Yes, I'd love to." She rubbed her hand down her dirty light jacket. Feeling the need to explain her appearance. "I'll have to change. I've been working on that smelly farm all day."

He laughed. Held out his hand and said, "Sidney. I'll meet you in The Blue Cow at eight. Is that enough time to freshen up?"

Peg smiled at him. She'd not had feelings like this before. Her heart was banging inside her chest like a bass drum and her legs felt weak, so much so she thought she might collapse on the floor in front of this gallant knight in shining armour. "I'm Peg. That's what people call me anyway."

"Call you?" He looked puzzled. "What's your real name then?"

"Peg will do. I'll see you at eight. Blue Cow. Looking forward to it." Peg hurried away grateful for the long trousers she wore that hung low over her boot. She couldn't possibly have told him about her leg. Not then. She'd maybe tell him tonight.

Once in she called out to her mother. "I'm in, mum." Peg filled the kettle to make tea. This was a habit she did five days a week. She put a mug of tea on a small tray and a couple of biscuits for her mother. Peg didn't have anything today. Nerves jiggled in her tummy with anticipation of what the night ahead might hold. These feelings had taken her appetite.

"I'm going to run a bath. You can have that bit of pork pie with a salad tonight. I don't want to cook."

Martha took the mug, looking over her glasses at Peg, "what do you mean, you aren't cooking. Course you're cooking and eating with me. You always do."

"Not tonight. I'm meeting a friend. In the pub."

"What friend, you don't have friends. You never have."

Peg put her hands on her hips. "For God's sake, mum, anyone would think I'm committing a crime the way you're looking at me. I am going out. Out for a drink. No, I don't have friends, but it looks like I have one now."

"Who is she?"

"What makes you think my friend's a She?" Peg wished she hadn't said that. The last thing she wanted was the Spanish Inquisition, but her mother said, "it has to be a She. No one would look at you twice smelling like a sewer and limping along like a lame duck." The comment shook any confidence Peg had achieved from Sidney's earlier attention. Feeling deflated she left Martha with her tea and went upstairs to run a bath.

Peg busied herself wearing a dressing gown and her wet hair wrapped in a towel. The salad was put on a plate and given to her mother in silence. Peg washed and dried the dishes and not a word was spoken between them. Her mother was a champion at sulking. Peg had given up ages ago trying to talk to her when she went into one of these moods.

Once in the safety of her room, away from her mother's steely gaze, Peg dried her shoulder length hair. It was wavy and blonde like her brothers. She had the same blue eyes but her father's sharper nose. Duncan was the one with the cute baby looks.

The long, flared trousers Peg wore to hide her boot were not in fashion anymore. All the youngsters were wearing tight leggings and baggy colourful tops. This was out of the question for Peg. She wore instead, a long ankle length floral skirt with a pale pink t-shirt. She looked very acceptable until you looked at her feet, but it was the best she could do. For the first time in years her face was made up with foundation, blusher, mascara, and eyeshadow. The end result was pleasing. A quick spray of musk perfume, Peg felt feminine.

"Cheerio, mum." Peg grabbed her overcoat off the peg and closed the front door. She hadn't gone into the lounge to say her goodbyes. She couldn't have taken the criticism and mocking over her appearance. Peg was struggling with the nerves that jiggled in her stomach like a bag of kittens.

The pub was lit up with lights. There were still paper hearts in the windows, a reminder of Valentine's Day last week. Peg was early. She didn't want to walk in the pub looking for Sidney. There was no sign of him outside either. She leant up against the side of the wall watching and waiting for his appearance. The evening was cold, and daylight had long gone.

Peg checked her watch in the artificial lighting coming from the pub and a lamppost. It was gone eight and no sign of him. She was cold and felt ridiculous standing outside like some prostitute. She told herself she'd give him ten more minutes. Just when she convinced herself she'd been set up, the pub door opened. "There you are. I was beginning to think you were standing me up." Peg nearly collapsed with relief. "Sidney! I've been waiting for you."

He laughed. "What out here? You must be crazier than you look."

The comment stung, but she told herself he was joking. She was far too sensitive to cruelty.

Once inside they sat by the fire in the corner. She asked for a port and lemon. She didn't know if she liked it, but it sounded grown up. "Tell me about yourself." Sidney looked at her enquiringly. He seemed genuinely interested. Peg held her glass in her hand. The first sip of her drink told her she didn't like port and lemon. "There's nothing to tell."

Sidney brushed her hand with his finger, which sent tingles like electricity up her arm. "You look lovely tonight, Peg. I've watched you for weeks walking home from the farm. Tell me about your job, where you live. Your family. Anything."

Peg attempted to sip her drink again and tried not to shudder as her taste buds sensed the alien liquid as it slid down her throat. It tasted like medicine. "You tell me about you."

Sidney sat back in his chair. Taking a swig of his beer he said, "I live in Liverpool. I am here working for Barlott's Building firm doing the electricity on the new builds. I like rugby, but don't play. I like pretty women." Her eyes met his and he winked at her. She felt her cheeks grow warm. Embarrassed by this rare attention, she looked down.

"You really are shy, aren't you? I could believe you've never been out with a man before by the way you just looked at me."

Peg held her breath and gulped a good mouthful of the offensive drink. It seemed to be helping her nerves and warming her insides. Her voice came out in a whisper. "I haven't. I live with my mother." Peg told him how she had hoped to move away, but life dealt a bitter blow. Once she started explaining. her childhood, the taunting and how she was called Peg because of her leg and before she knew it, it felt like she had told him her life story. "I'm sorry. I've prattled on a bit. It must be the drink."

He looked uncomfortable. Peg thought she'd said too much. Perhaps he didn't like the thought of having a cripple for a girlfriend. The silence from him was too much for Peg. "I understand. Thank you for taking me out. I've enjoyed it."

"Where are you going?"

"I just thought…"

Sidney reached across the table and held Peg's arm saying, "that is the saddest tale I think I've ever heard. Your name is Susan. Susan. What is wrong with your mother to let that name become lost in such cruelty."

"Well, you must have guessed my mum's not the kindest to me. I know though that it comes from fear of losing me. She knocks my confidence all the time, so I don't believe in myself."

Sidney said, "it's working. It's got to stop. Yes, you have a short leg, so bloody what. You really are an attractive woman. Seeing you tonight, you're better than you look walking home from that egg place you work at."

"You're just being kind. I know I'm nothing special, but I made a bit of an effort for you."

"Peg…I mean Susan. You are so lovely. you look lovely. Believe me."

Peg blushed again. "Please call me Peg. Susan doesn't sound right to me." She surprised herself when she reached across and touched his hand, "Thank you for this evening. I really must go now because I have to help my mum get ready for bed."

"She's only got arthritis. It's a bone thing isn't it? Surely she can get herself into bed."

"No. No she can't. It's not only arthritis. It's a rare form. Her bones are misshapen with the condition, but her muscles are wasting too. I really do have to go."

Sidney stood up with her. Helped her on with her coat and said, "I shall walk you home."

"I won't be able to take you in. She will be in a right old mood because I have been out. I couldn't bear it if she were rude to you."

Sidney put his arm across Peg's shoulders and pulled her close. She felt instantly warmer. It felt good to be liked. She really did feel Sidney liked her too.

Chapter Six

March 1981

Sidney had gone home to Liverpool to visit his children. He did this every weekend. He had a girl of ten years and a son of eight. Peg looked forward to Sunday evenings when he returned. She couldn't help but feel disappointed when Sindy went into labour Sunday morning and Duncan brought the boys round for Peg to mind. She knew she wouldn't be able to see Sidney later today.

Having a relationship had done wonders for Peg. She seemed to glow, making her appear quite striking. Both Duncan and Peg had taken after their mother in looks with the fair hair and blue eyes. Only their eyes lacked the hard steely look that life had given Martha James.

Jack ran in to the kitchen. He looked cold and his anorak was undone. "Auntie Peg, auntie Peg hide me. Quick Paul's coming." She opened up the larder and told him to crouch down under the shelf.

Within seconds Paul appeared. "Have you seen Jack?"

Peg looked as if she was filling the kettle to make tea. "I think he went into the lounge with nana Martha." He flew through to the lounge only to be chastised for letting in the cold air and being noisy. Peg took silent pleasure out of annoying her mother in a backhanded way. Jack came out of the larder and ran back out into the garden, calling as he went. Paul tore out after him, leaving the doors open.

Martha's moans were ignored as Peg hurried to answer the phone. She hoped the baby was here and Duncan would be picking up the boys. A warm sensation went over her body when she heard Sidney's voice. "I'll be home at about four. Shelley has a bug, and it looks like Alan's going to follow suit, so I took them back to their mum early. Any chance of seeing you earlier." He lowered his voice, "I've missed you."

"I've missed you too. Trouble is Sindy is in labour and there is no way I can leave the boys with Mum. She's pulling her hair out with them running around as it is."

"Can't I come there?" He attempted to laugh. "I could meet the old dragon, couldn't I?"

Peg lowered her voice. "I'd like nothing more, but it's mayhem here. Let's leave it until tomorrow. One day won't hurt us."

Martha could be heard in the hall as she raised her voice at her grandchildren. Peg laughed. "See what I mean? She's like a bear with a sore head at the best of times. Having the boys has added to her disgruntled view of life."

Peg replaced the receiver and went in to sort out the boys.

Martha raised her eyes at Peg and said sarcastically. "I bet that was lover boy. Been home to his family and has come back to his bit on the side."

"Mum why do you have to be so cruel. I told you Sidney has children. He goes home to see them. It's important. I understand."

"Gullible that's what you are. I tell you, girl, men are all the same. Look at your father. He was as bad. Once away from home, the wife's forgotten. You're being used. He's going home to a wife and family. I bet my life on it."

"Not in front of the boys, mum."

Martha ignored the warning. "Open your eyes. If he didn't have a wife, he wouldn't be looking at someone like you now, would he? Limping along like a wonky donkey. I tell you he's playing away from home. He's just filling a gap. I only hope it's not the gap between your legs, girl. I'm too old to have any more trouble brought home here on my doorstep. I don't want to be saddled with a bastard living here under my nose."

Jack said, "bastard, bastard." Paul giggled.

Peg took hold of their hands and with her own visibly shaking, said, "nana Martha said basket. She doesn't want to be left holding a basket. Too heavy for nana Martha. Now let's make some orange squash and get a biscuit. I'll read you both a story from a book your daddy used to read." The two boys giggled together in the kitchen. Peg knew she hadn't fooled them.

Martha's shouts from the lounge calling for help had Peg turning a deaf ear. Since she'd started courting Sidney, looking after her mother had become a bigger chore than it had been. At this very moment she hated her.

Monday 2nd March 1981

Duncan stood at the door of the Four Willows. His eyes shone with pride and his voice was alight with joy "It's a girl, Alice. She's lovely. So tiny. Smaller than the boys. A mass of dark hair too. Sindy's tired. She was born at three thirty this morning." He couldn't keep still. Excitement oozed from him.

"Congratulations." Alice hugged him to her. "I'm pleased for you. Have you told the boys they have a sister?"

"Yes, I phoned this morning. Peg's keeping them today until I finish up here. Paul's at school and Jack's at nursery this morning, so hopefully they aren't causing too much havoc. I'm hoping Sindy will be allowed home later today as well."

Alice's voice changed. "How's Peg? I heard tell she's courting."

Duncan smiled. "Yes, yes she is. Some chap on the new builds. I don't suppose it'll last."

Alice looked uneasy. "Do you know anything about him?"

Duncan picked up on Alice's concern. "Why, Alice, what do you know?"

She stood in the doorway not wanting to make eye contact. "It's only hearsay. I'm not one for gossip."

"Spit it out. What's on your mind?"

"You know what I'm going to say. It's Peg. She's looking so happy of late. There's a spring in her step." Alice stopped. Apologised for her poor choice of words. "You know what I mean. Love makes us bloom, especially in those early weeks."

Duncan had a feeling there was more to this. "So?"

"Oh, Duncan. I don't want to be the one to tell tales. It's just…" Alice paused. She really did hate repeating. "I heard this fella only asked Peg out for a dare. My nephew's working on the same site. I couldn't bear it if he were leading her on. She's such a good girl is our Peg."

Duncan kicked a stone. "I tell you, if he's playing her for a fool, I'll fucking kill him." Duncan quickly apologised for his language. "It'll destroy her, Alice. She's so loved up you can almost smell it on her."

"I know, lad. I know. I hope I'm wrong, but you know how talk gets around."

"I do, Alice, I do. I had a gut full of poisonous talk as a boy with my mother being the biggest offender. I don't go in for gossip. I like facts."

"I wish I hadn't said anything. You were so happy with your news and I feel I have spoiled the moment."

"Oh, you couldn't do that. A girl. I wanted a girl. She's perfect too."

Alice laughed. Pleased the tension had eased. "Every child is perfect. Go on, go and get your jobs done and pick up your little ones."

Duncan tipped the last of his coffee in the pot plant at the door. "Any news from Millie?"

"She phoned again yesterday to check on her father. She said to tell him she wouldn't be home again this weekend. Busy with college work. She sounds unhappy, I think..." Alice stopped, laughed and took the mug from Duncan's hand. "Go on, off with you. I have too much to say for myself these days. Give my love to Sindy. I shall like a cuddle when she's up for visitors."

"I'll be bringing her here to show her off. Do you think the old man would like to see her? Might make a change."

"Less of the old. "He's younger than me."

Laughing, Duncan walked away calling, "cheerio for now."

Duncan thanked Peg for having the boys. Alice's comment was still niggling at the back of his mind. "How's lover boy, Peg?"

Peg smiled. "Wonderful. I shall see him later."

Martha called from the lounge. "Stop filling her head with nonsense. He'll be gone in the summer. Won't give her another thought. She's being used."

Duncan raised his eyes at Peg. She put her finger to her lips. "Give my love to Sindy. I shall be over to see the baby as soon as she's settled."

40

"Bring this Sidney with you. I'd like to see who makes my sister look absolutely ravishing."

Peg's face lit up with joy. As she laughed, she said, "get off home. I'll bring him with me. Promise."

Peg watched her younger brother go down the path with two little boys skipping beside him, asking questions about the baby." Paul was saying he wanted a brother. This had Jack saying the same. Duncan ruffled their hair and opened the car door for them. They scrambled into the back, giggling.

Sindy was sitting in the armchair feeding the baby. They had named her Charlotte. When both boys ran in to see her, Sindy smiled at their excitement. "Steady, boys." Paul stroked his sister's mass of downy dark hair, and Jack kissed her cheek. "I like her mummy. She's the best."

Sindy smiled at the boys. "You're all the best. When she's finished her feed, you can hold her."

Duncan and Sindy went off to bed just after nine when Charlotte had had her last feed. They had her in the carrycot at the bottom of their bed. "Sleep while she sleeps. That's the idea."

Sindy smiled. "I can't believe we could be so lucky. A little girl to finish our family."

"She's beautiful too."

Monday 16th March 1981

Duncan had been boasting to Alice daily for the past two weeks about how good Charlotte was. Today was no different, only that he had her with him. He'd dropped the boys off at school and had pushed the pram the mile and a half to the 'Four Willows'. Alice said she'd watch the baby for him while he dealt with the horses.

She took Charlotte out of the pram wrapped in a pink crotchet blanket. "Will she be alright. Does she need a feed or anything?"

"No, she'll be just fine. She's fed every four hours. She takes her feed, she's winded, changed and put down to sleep. Honestly, Alice, she's the model baby. Easier than either of the boys were."

Alice smiled down at the baby sleeping soundly in her arms. "She's certainly beautiful. You go off. I'll show Hugh."

Duncan watched as his daughter was taken through to the house. He'd been hoping Millie would have been home. He so wanted to show off his latest addition. He hadn't seen her since they went over the Downs together with the horses. That was nearly six weeks ago.

"Hugh, I have a little visitor for you." Hugh looked up at Alice. "It's Duncan's little girl." Alice liked to sit and talk to Hugh like this. He seemed to listen to her tales of village life. "You must have known Duncan's mother, Martha? Martha James, she lived on the council estate, Bicknell Close. She still does for that matter." There was no response from Hugh. So, Alice kept talking. "Martha married Dickie James and had the girl with the short leg. She's Duncan's sister." Alice leant over showing him the downy hair and pink cheeks poking out of the blanket. "There she is. She's like Duncan. You know, Duncan. He sees to the horses. Your Davinia took him on. Fond of him she was. I can still see…"

Hugh's leg twitched up and down and he rocked his body in his chair pushing at the baby with his good arm.

"Steady, Hugh she's only a few weeks old. I thought you might like to see her. I'll put her back in her pram until Duncan has finished seeing to the horses."

Alice went back to Hugh once she had the baby settled. She was horrified to see tears falling freely down his face. "Hugh, Hugh. What's all this for? Memories of your, Millie. Your own little girl no doubt." She wiped his eyes and told him to blow his nose. She held out the handkerchief and he took it with his good hand. Trying to cheer him up she said. "You know what? Easter will be here before we blink. Your Millie will be home then I'm sure." Alice wasn't sure about anything, but she wanted to take Hugh's mind off his upset. "Let's see what's on the other side of this television. Alice flicked through the channels. "I bet when you were in the estate agent business looking over properties pricing up, you saw some sights." She knew she was waffling, but she didn't care. "There's nothing on. Only rubbish. Let me get you one of your talking books. You know the ones Millie organised for you from the library. She's a good girl." Tears started to fall down his face again. Alice knew tears were a side effect from his stroke, but she didn't like it. He could and would cry at anything. Alice dried his face and went back to the kitchen to check on baby Charlotte.

Duncan returned smiling, within the hour. "I've finished now. Well, all I'm going to do." He pulled back the blanket so he could see his daughter. She was still sleeping. "Did the old man like her?"

Alice smiled. "Memories. There were tears."

Duncan brushed the baby's face with his little finger. "I'm not surprised. She's so gorgeous I cried when I first held her. She'll break some hearts when she's older, I bet." He took the brake off the pram saying, "I better get her home. She's due a feed in half an hour."

Alice took a final peep at her and said, "the movement of the pram will keep her sleeping."

She watched Duncan stride away at a good pace. You could see he was proud. It seemed to shine from him as he walked with his head held high.

The postman handed Alice the post. There was only one letter and a leaflet. She instantly recognised Millie's neat handwriting. *'This will cheer him up.'*

"Hugh, cup of tea for you and a letter from your girl." He didn't hear her. He was listening to the talking book she'd put on earlier for him. Alice waved the letter in his eye line and he took out the ear plugs one at a time with his good hand. The lopsided smile told her he understood. "Yes, Hugh, it's from Millie.

She opened the letter and sat opposite him with her own cup of tea on the side table.

Dear Dad,

Life here is manic. I just handed in a project which will go towards my final results in the summer.

I can't get home until Easter. It's only four weeks away. Then I shall stay for the holidays.

I hope you are well, and everything is going to plan with the carers. I am sure Alice would be in touch if anything were amiss.

I expect Duncan's wife has had the baby now. I have a feeling it will be another boy. They'll end up with a football team. Duncan wanted a girl. We don't always get what we want. I wonder if you hoped I'd be a boy, dad? If you did you never let on. I was always your little girl. Not anymore. All grown up. Making my own mistakes now.

One of the girls that shares the dormitory has broken her arm. Went partying midweek and fell down the stairs. She is a quiet one usually, so I am guessing the drink went to her head. I wasn't invited. I guessed Simon was going to be there with Stephanie. Not quite over that pain yet. I'm getting there, so don't worry about me.

I went out at the weekend. It was a quiz night. We called ourselves The Know-alls and it turned out we knew nothing. We were rubbish. Coming in second to last. I did win a bottle of Champagne on the raffle. So not all was lost.

Dad I hope you are feeling happy. I haven't got a lot to write. I'm busy with work and getting ready for my finals.

I look forward to seeing you on the tenth of April all being well.

Love Millie. XX

Hugh reached out with his good hand and took the letter and held it tightly, screwing it up in his clenched fist. "There that was nice news, wasn't it?" Alice helped him put his earplugs back in his ears and switched on his story. She gathered up the cups and left him to his story, clutching the letter.

Chapter Seven
Hugh Marlow

Hugh sat staring ahead with the letter still crumpled in his good hand. *'My, Millie. Always my Millie. God if I could strangle my mother I would.'* With these thoughts came tears. Hugh let his mind remember.

'Sixteen I was. Straight out of school. I had wanted to work at the book shop. They'd offered me a position as bookkeeper. My father nearly went ballistic. He saw it as a failing that both his sons had chosen to work elsewhere instead of heading for the family business. I didn't have the backbone to stand up to him like Mark, my brother. He was five years older. I'd always looked up to him. I was just as heartbroken as mum when he left for Singapore.

It was a wet morning in July 1951 that I went to work for the family firm. Marlow's. I was given instant hierarchy and placed in the office. If you could call it that. It was cold, dirty, and miserable. Adverts, women, and memos were stuck on the brick painted wall to remind us of things to do. The ashtrays were overflowing, and you could smell the stale habit in the air. I hated it. I hated my father.

By the time I'd been there six weeks the walls were free of adverts and ladies posing. I had an appointment and phone book with important numbers and a memo pad of things I had to remember to do. My so-called office was swept clean, ashtrays emptied, and my bench was tidy. I made a bad job bearable.

The years slipped by and before I knew it, I was twenty-one. Mum wanted me to have a party. I'd absolutely refused. I was a loner. I believed she only wanted a party to bring Mark home for a visit. He hadn't been back for nine years. All the while I dreamt. I dreamt of getting out of this hell hole and working for myself.

Property had started to interest me. I told myself over and over, one day I'll be an estate agent. My shyness had held me back. I guessed to be an estate agent you would have to speak to people without stammering like a schoolboy or blushing like a teenager.

Still more years went by. I was still jack of all trades, master of none. Fearful to speak out of turn. Butt of many jokes at the yard. Then my mum's friend's daughter got married. I was twenty-eight. The jibing I took about not snapping her up when I had the chance. I used to lie in bed and say to myself, 'chance? When did I get a chance to have Sylvia?' She was three years older and seemed so much more worldly-wise than me. I don't believe she even thought of me in that way. I used to be frightened to speak to her let alone ask her out.

Sylvia hadn't been married two years when her husband was killed in a road accident. Pushed by both of my parents I managed to ask her to the cinema. It had seemed a good place to take someone when you had no conversation. Sylvia had made the first moves in everything. She had reached out for my hand. Kissed my cheek goodbye. Slowly I got braver and the following year I asked her to marry me. I think in my parent's eyes that was the first thing I'd ever done right.

Then I saw Davinia. It had been New Year. She was the same age as Millie is now. Twenty-one. I'd gone outside to get a bit of fresh air and there she was, holding a glass of bubbly. I can still see her. So alive. Full of fun. Laughing with the crowd that had gathered at the fountain, waiting for the bell to ring in the New Year. This was tradition. I couldn't move. I was transfixed by her charisma. I watched like a dazzled rabbit as she threw her head back in laughter as one by one people started to jump in the fountain. I lost count of the times she was kissed. I envied every one of them.'

Hugh looked down at the letter in his hand. How had he let himself be bullied? All those wasted years. Thinking back to that night he first set eyes on Davinia made him smile. His good side of his face twisted awkwardly with the paralysis caused by the stroke. If anyone had been watching him, they could be forgiven for thinking he was in pain.

'I had become more confident in myself since becoming engaged to Sylvia, but still too shy to approach Davinia and ask for a kiss like everyone else was doing. My mother's annoyed voice broke the spell I was under. She'd stood calling from the reception area. I'd gone back to the hall where auld lang syne

was being sung. I joined hands in the circle. There were kisses going on around us, but I'd missed the initial chimes of New Year mesmerised by a young girl I didn't even know the name of.

Three weeks later I met her again. I'd decided to go to the new swimming pool that had opened up in the town. I'd always liked swimming as a child, and there she was giving out hanging baskets and bands at the entrance window.

I didn't want to just hand over my money, take my basket to put my clothes in and the wrist band. I wanted to speak to her. I smiled and asked if I could join as a member. I got one of those winning smiles of hers. She told me it wasn't that sort of pool. You wear the band on your wrist and when the colour is called, it's your turn to get out. I asked if there were exceptions for members. She laughed then and told me we don't have members. It's a good idea though. That's how it began. I went swimming every evening after work and soon learnt that she didn't work on a Tuesday or a Thursday evening. The more I saw of her the more infatuated I became. My chance came when I went late to the pool. She was there at the window. She even commented on my late arrival. This had pleased me that she'd noticed. I told her that work was busy. This hadn't been a lie. She didn't ask me what I did. When I got out of the pool and left, the little window she peeped out of giving baskets was closed. Initially I was disappointed, but there she was waiting out in the car park. She was standing by the entrance. It was March and in daylight you could tell spring was on its way, but by evening it was dark and cold. I couldn't just drive past. I'd got quite comfortable speaking to her every evening when she took my money and gave me my basket and band. I wound my window down and asked if she was okay. She'd laughed and said she'd been stood up. God knows how I managed it, but I got her to get in my car and let me take her home. No funny business. She thanked me as she got out and said she'd see me tomorrow.

I took her home more often than not after that. Leaving my swim later and later. Neglecting Sylvia.

Then one night I said did she fancy going for a drink. My palms were clammy on the steering wheel, my armpits were sweating, and I was convinced she could hear my heart thudding in my chest. She said, yes. Behaving like an idiot, I repeated what she'd said. Yes? She'd laughed nodding repeating herself. I laughed too.

Once we were sitting in the little snug, she told me about herself. Her mother had died in childbirth and for the first six years of her life she'd been brought up by her grandmother who she called Mottie. When Mottie died, she'd been sent to live with an aunt and uncle. She said she'd been happy there. There were three boys. Her cousins. Then when she was eighteen, she came here to live with her father.

She asked about me. I told her I worked at Marlow's, the building firm, and suppliers. I added I was in the office. It sounded better. I was pleased at my confidence, but guessed it was the brandy easing my nerves. She asked if there was any lucky lady waiting for me at home. I laughed then. The referral to lucky lady made me feel good. I'd told her just my mother. I then said what happened to this lad that stood you up the other night. She'd looked in her lap and said, not lad. Man. Like you. Mature. Only you're nicer somehow. We were both lying in our own way.

I was loving the compliments. My confidence was growing by the minute. She hesitated before telling me that she'd been seeing a married man. Hurriedly she told me she hadn't known originally. When she found out she was already in love, or thought she was. I still didn't tell her about Sylvia. I didn't want to think about her anymore. I wished I were single. I just didn't know how to get out of it.

Our Monday evening drink became not only a regular event, but the highlight of my week. The more I saw Davinia the more I wanted her.

When there were tears a few weeks later, she told me she was having this chaps child. I'd been shocked. I still hadn't slept with Sylvia and she'd been married before. I wanted to. It just didn't happen. I put the absence of sex down to her going home to live again with her mother. Here was Davinia, crying. Still a child in my eyes, having a baby by a married man. What was she going to do? She said it over and over. I told her there and then I'd marry her. Her eyes had widened in disbelief. The more she protested, the more I wanted it. I had to tell her about Sylvia. I was honest then. Told her how I was bullied into working in the family business. Bullied into marrying Sylvia when her husband died, and how I'd seen her at the New Year's dance and fallen in love instantly. The rest followed. She kissed me. I knew then it didn't matter what obstacles got in my way, I was going to make an honest woman of Davinia and love her until I died.

Tears fell down Hugh's cheeks with the memories. The fight in his family home. The name calling. His mother had called Davinia a slut. Hugh and his father had fought. Fists too. He'd been ordered out of the house. Davinia's father had taken Hugh in even though he had no job and no home. Three months later they were married and Hugh was the manager of an estate agent and they were living in a large spacious flat over a bank. He'd never been happier. When Millie was a year old, Hugh had his own firm, and they'd bought a sought-after property 'The Four Willows' in a select part of the village. Life had come good for Hugh in more ways than he could ever have envisaged.

Alice appeared with his lunch. "Let me take Millie's letter. I'll put it up here on the mantlepiece." Alice straightened it out. "Look at it you've almost crushed it to death."

It was silly talk, but Alice liked to keep chatting to Hugh. She was sure he liked it. "After you've had lunch, I'll read the local news to you. There's a bit in there about the village pub being taken over by a Mr Lal. A family from Pakistan wishing to turn it into an Indian restaurant. There's a bit of an outcry over it." Alice put a large bib like cloth round Hugh's neck and said, "I'm not surprised, are you? That little pub's been part of this village since the sixteenth century." Alice took her place in front of Hugh, perched on a stool. "Here you are." She loaded the spoon with shepherd's pie and gave it to Hugh to feed himself. This had been on Millie's instruction. She had said her father must try and hang on to the skills he still has and do things for himself where he can. Alice did as she was told but found the process slow and tedious. It would be so much easier to just fill his spoon and pop it in for him.

Chapter Eight
March

Things were difficult for Peg at home. Sidney wanted to spend more and more time with her but having to see to her mother's needs made this difficult. The care that Peg had given her mother willingly had become a chore. One which Peg was becoming increasingly resentful. She knew it was down to Sidney's attention. She wanted to spend all her spare time with him. She loved him completely and couldn't remember ever feeling so happy. Even her mother's sharp tongue, nasty insinuations and cruelty couldn't take the joy away from the feeling of being loved.

Peg had made herself a new skirt. Long skirts were not in fashion, but it was a way for Peg to hide her big boot. Wearing long skirts was acceptable, long flared trousers were a no no. The fashion was still tight leggings and baggy tops.

Peg checked her appearance in the mirror. The floral skirt she'd made looked feminine. The skinny top accentuated her tiny bosom. She'd had her hair cut and the new feathered style suited her. She could hear her brother, Duncan downstairs and called to him.

His face appeared round her bedroom door. He smiled. "Oh, look at you. Where are you off to?"

"Out with Sidney. We're going to the pub. There's a band playing tonight. I won't be out long. You know what mum's like for wanting to get to bed at ten. She's worse now I'm seeing someone."

"Peg, don't be so hemmed in by mum. She can do more than she lets on. I popped in the other morning. She was coming down the stairs on her own."

"Really? She tells me she has to use the commode in the day because she can't make the stairs."

"Well, that's when it suits her. The Avon lady that keeps her up to date with all the gossip was calling round. She turned up with mum's order while I was still here. I guess mum didn't want the aroma of Richard the third in the room."

Peg laughed out loud at his choice of words. "Thank you for the thumbs up. I tell you she is becoming increasingly difficult every time I so much as want to leave the house. Unless it's for her or work of course."

Duncan put his arm around Peg's shoulder and kissed her head. "Being in love suits you. Come and see us. Charlotte's amazing. She sleeps seven hours through the night and she's only just three weeks old.

"Come on, let's go downstairs and face the dragon together."

Peg laughed again. She loved Duncan. She always had. There had never been any jealousy between them or not that she could remember. When Duncan had been old enough to understand his older sister was being bullied and made fun of, he did his utmost to protect her. Often coming off worse.

Martha looked up as her two children entered the room. "What are the smiles for. You ought to be me sitting here day in and day out. Not seeing anyone only her." Martha pointed at Peg showing dislike on her face.

Duncan straightened his shoulders. A sign that told Peg he was annoyed. "Her? Peg you mean. Peg who helps you every single day with less than a thank you. I tell you, mum, if I was at home, you'd be in a nursing home by now. Peg isn't allowed to live."

Martha almost spat with anger. "Allowed to live. She's out Monday to Friday with that builder chap. God knows what he sees in her. Probably what she puts…"

"Shut up, mum. Shut up. I've told Peg how you can get up and down the stairs on your own when it suits you, so on my birthday you need to brace yourself because Peg will be coming to my party and she won't be home all night." Duncan looked at Peg. "Put that in your diary. Tell Sidney too. I shall expect you both."

Martha went to say more but Duncan got in first. "Just shut up for once unless you can say something kind."

"She'll get hurt. Mark my words. Then who'll pick up the pieces. Me."

Peg gathered up the cups and put them on the tea tray and went into the kitchen. She didn't wash them up, but called out 'cheerio' and closed the back door behind her.

*

Sidney was already in the pub propping up the bar. Without a thought Peg pushed the door open and stood behind him putting her hands over his eyes. How much she'd changed in six weeks. "Umm I wonder who this can be?"

Peg punched him playfully in the arm. "It could only be me. Surely?" Sidney kissed her. "I only want it to be you. That's the difference. What are you drinking?"

"I'll have a white wine with a splash of lemonade." In the six weeks Peg had taken quite a fancy to wine. Port was never touched again.

The band were setting up in the area they'd cleared. Sidney grabbed a table reasonably close with a good view. "Tonight, you are going to dance with me. No arguments. I'm going to hold you in my arms, and we are going to move round and round in circles as if we are the only ones in the room."

Peg looked uneasy. "Sidney, I can't dance. Honestly. I'll tread on your feet and make you look as ridiculous as I feel."

"You're going to dance with me Peg. I need to make as many memories as I can. I'm going to miss you terribly when I have to move on from here."

Peg's heart sank. She wanted to tell Sidney to stay. Get work here. Just go home at weekends for his children's access. The words stuck in her throat. She didn't want to look too desperate, but she was. Hearing those words on his lips had cast a big shadow over the evening. She drank her wine too fast and ordered another. This time without the lemonade. If she were going to dance with this heavy boot, the alcohol would give her the much-needed Dutch courage.

Peg became relaxed and the evening enjoyable. It was nearly ten o'clock. Her mother liked to be in bed by now and if Peg was late things would be more awkward than usual. Tonight, after Duncan's revelation that their mother could come downstairs on her own, made Peg's mind up that she was not going to hurry home anymore.

The band were fun. They introduced each song they sang and encouraged people up to dance. Peg hadn't taken to the floor yet but enjoyed watching the different styles of dancing taking place.

The lead singer tapped the microphone. "We're nearing our last songs of the evening. Get your lady up on the floor for a few smooches."

Peg let herself be taken to the floor. She wrapped her arms around Sidney's neck, and he held her waist. The first was a rendition of the song, 'Torn between two lovers' and the next was an Elvis song, 'Can't help falling in love with you.' The last song had Sidney singing softly to Peg as he danced her round the room. "You're once, twice, three times a lady, and I love you." Peg looked into his eyes and they kissed there and then on the pub floor. She felt like one of the teenagers she was surrounded by. "I love you too, Sidney. With all my heart."

Sidney whispered into her hair. "Let me love you, Peg. Like a man loves a woman."

Peg wanted to lie with Sidney more than anything. Where, was the problem. She didn't want her first time to be in the back of a van. Peg would struggle to get away from home for a night in a hotel. Sidney brushed his hand gently over her head. "I'll come to yours. You put your mum to bed. Flash the lights on and off in the lounge when the coast is clear, you can let me in the back door."

Peg told him how she might have gone with this idea, but for Duncan's revelation.

 They took a slow stroll back to the council estate where Peg lived. The light was on in the front room. "Mum's still up. She'll be spitting blood that I'm so late."

"Peg you're thirty-one years old. Help the old bat upstairs. Then come back out with me. We'll go back to mine. You'll have to ignore the teasing from the guys." Sidney was staying in a caravan with two of the brickies.

Peg wanted to, but found herself saying, "I can't Sidney. I just couldn't. Not knowing the lads were in the van listening. Laughing. It's just not me. I'm sorry."

Sidney squeezed her hand. "It's alright. I understand. I'll sort something. I want you Peg and it's driving me crazy."

Peg took Sidney back to her house and kissed him in the porch. Normally she let him walk her to the end of the twitten out of the sight and sound of her mother's evil eye and tongue.

Sidney's voice was husky when he said, "I love you, Peg. Really love you. You must remember that."

Peg thought she would cry. All the conversation this evening had felt like it was reminding her that their relationship was coming to an end with the building work. Peg held on to him. "No one's ever loved me before. No one."

"I'm sure that's not true. What about your dad?"

Peg shook her head. "No. Dad was a ladies man. He had a roving eye. There were more arguments in this house over his lady friends than I care to remember. I feel this is why mum is so …" Before Peg could finish a tapping could be heard on the window along with Martha's voice. This broke the magical moment. Peg opened her bag and fished round for the key. Her hands were shaking.

Sidney took the key from her and together they entered the house. Sidney strolled over to Martha's chair. "Martha, I believe. Sidney." He held out his hand as an introduction, but she waved it away saying, "this is all your fault."

Sidney didn't seem fazed. Turning to Peg he said, "make us all a hot drink. It's time I got to know your mother."

Martha James glared at Sidney. Her blue eyes that both Duncan and Peg had inherited, sparkled with anger. "I don't want a hot drink. I've been waiting to go to bed for over an hour. You never said you'd be late."

"Oh, mum. You should have gone on up."

"How dare you. That would suit you, wouldn't it? If I fell on the stairs."

Peg handed Sidney a mug of hot chocolate putting her own on the side. "Mum, you know Duncan told me tonight you're well able to go up and down the stairs if it suits you." Peg paused waiting for a reaction, when there was none, just a stony silence, Peg reminded her, "the Avon lady? Duncan came round and you'd been upstairs to the…"

"Shut up, girl. I might be an invalid, but I want some of my movements private."

Sidney tried to lighten the situation by making a joke. "We all have to go, Martha. Even the queen."

She turned in her seat to focus on him. "I'd like you to go. You're disgusting. You're not welcome here. I'd like to go to bed and…"

Sidney ignored the order. Winking at Peg he said, "your mother wants to go to bed. I'll wait for you down here."

Peg tried to sound sympathetic. "Mum it might be wise if you take a sleeping pill tonight to settle you down. You're getting yourself in a right old tiz-woz."

"No! No, I don't. They make me all woolly headed the next day. Just put me to bed. Say goodnight to him and I'll go up."

Feeling brave with Sidney beside her. "Mum, we are going to say goodnight when you're in bed…"

"Oh no you're not. Not under my roof. Have some pride, girl. He's playing you for a fool. You're talk of the village." The silence felt deafening with the accusations. Neither Sidney nor Peg said a word. "There that's told you. The Avon lady as you call her. She keeps me up to date with you all. I know what's going on everywhere. He" Martha pointed with her finger. "He! Has a wife and family back home. You need to take those rose-coloured glasses off and see the wood for the trees."

Peg looked at Sidney. His face seemed to have lost its boozy flush and he looked quite ashen. "Sidney this is my mother. You can see why I have no confidence. This has been my life."

Martha hit her stick on the floor impatiently. "Enough. Enough of this nonsense. I want to go to bed. If you want to make a fool of yourself with this…" She didn't finish. Sidney stood up and said, "I'd like to say it was a pleasure to meet you, but you're the one with a tongue for lies." Peg grabbed his arm as he made to put his coat on. "Don't go, Sidney. I'll be down in a minute. Please don't…"

Martha was on her feet now. Needing no usual assistance to stand. "Have some pride, girl. Come on get me to bed."

Peg took her mother's arm and guided her to the stairs. She looked behind her and pleaded with Sidney silently to wait.

Sidney was still waiting for Peg. She tried to apologise for her mother, but he put his finger over her lips. "Don't let her ruin this moment. He wedged a chair under the handle of the lounge door. "Just in case the old bat thinks she'll come down." He took Peg in his arms. The kisses deepened and clothes were removed. Sidney made his way down her body kissing every inch of her, saying the sweetest things she'd ever heard. Peg forgot about everything. All that mattered was here and now. Her short leg was insignificant too. She felt beautiful and loved for the first time in her life.

Chapter Nine
April – Simon Few

Simon entered the pub with Stephanie holding his arm. They'd quarrelled earlier but the suggestion of a drink and getting out had eased tensions.

"You get a table and I'll get the drinks in."

I'll have a white wine." Simon raised his eyes at her. "Just a small one. Please?"

He didn't want to row again so held up his fingers to show her just how small it would be. While standing at the bar his eyes scanned the room. They settled on Millie. His heart quickened at the sight of her. She looked thinner. Her cheek bones were more defined. It suited her he thought. What concerned him were the black shadows under her eyes. He guessed he was the cause. How he ached to turn the clock back. It was all too late.

When he'd told Millie, he was calling off their relationship and she'd begged him not to and that she could forgive him, he'd been sorely tempted. Over these past weeks he'd had to keep reminding himself why he had to stand by Stephanie and not cave in. It had been a shock when she'd dropped the bombshell, she was pregnant. What had been a couple of weekends madness while Millie went home, had turned into what felt like a life sentence. He couldn't walk away from Stephanie now. There was no way he would let a child of his suffer at the hands of a stepfather. As a child himself he'd had no choice. His mother remarried when his father left. He'd been six years old. He not only suffered at home; he had to suffer the vicious tongue of his stepmother on school holidays. His young life felt like he was in the way wherever he went. There were no safe places. School was the closest he came to being wanted. He'd relished and grown at the praise given by his teachers. Maths being his best subject.

Millie looked away, breaking eye contact. She leant over and spoke to one of the girls. He wanted to go over and kiss her like he used to and watch her eyes light up with a smile as she stood on tiptoe to kiss him back. The barman asking him what he wanted, brought him back to the present. He looked across at Stephanie. She'd seen, he could tell. She'd followed what had caught his attention and the looks she was giving him now could kill. His stomach turned over again. This time it wasn't because of the pull of wanting Millie, it was the prospect of another showdown. The arguments were becoming more and more frequent. They were always Millie related too. Now this.

He carried the small white wine and beer to the table she'd sat herself at. "There you go." He forced himself to say 'love.' It was wasted. "She's over there. I know you've seen her. Ogling, you were."

"Not now, Stephanie." Simon sat so he couldn't be seen by Millie's table of friends but was sure he could feel eyes boring into his back like daggers. Simon changed the subject and talked about a job he'd applied for. An accountant's position in an engineering firm. The pay was excellent. He just had to pass his final exams this year. The plans to travel with Millie were all gone.

Stephanie and Simon were going home to meet her parents for the Easter weekend. They would tell them they'd be grandparents at the beginning of August and about their planned registry office wedding in June after their exams. He didn't relish the meeting, but knew it had to be done.

Stephanie excused herself saying she needed the loo. Once she was out of sight he swivelled round. Millie had gone. He'd not seen her leave. His mood was low these days, tonight was no different.

'God, Millie, I miss you.'

*

Millie knew it was Paula knocking on her door. She didn't want to speak to anyone. "Not now, Paula. I'm tired."

Millie poured herself another glass of wine and downed it in one. The tapping increased. "Millie, please. He's not worth it."

Tears fell down Millie's face unashamedly. Seeing Simon with Stephanie had been incredibly painful. She'd tried to tell herself she was getting over him, but tonight she knew she was kidding herself. Paula tapped again. Millie opened the door and fell into her friend's arms. "Oh, Millie. What are we going to do with you?"

"I need to go home."

Paula sat with Millie on the bed, cradling her in her arms like she was a baby. "You have one week, just one week. Then it's Easter. Don't miss out on Monday's lecture. You've only just caught up from your last absence."

"I can't stay here. It hurts so bad."

Paula stroked Millie's hair. "I know. I know it does. Time Millie. Time will heal."

Paula stood up. "I'll make you a coffee. You can't go home tonight anyway. You're pissed!"

Millie half smiled. "Are they still in the pub?"

"No. The minute old fish face went to the loo; Simon was looking over at our table. You could see he was upset you'd gone."

Fish face is how Millie and Paula referred to Stephanie. It was childish but seemed to help.

"Don't say he was upset, Paula. I know and you know he's made his choice."

Paula hesitated at the door. She took a deep breath and Millie felt unease at what was coming next. "I don't want to be the one to tell you this."

Millie was instantly defensive. "What?"

"Millie, this is only hearsay."

"Yes?" Millie stared at Paula. Her eyes red and swollen from the tears she'd shed.

"Stephanie's pregnant. That – Millie - is why he isn't knocking on your door begging for forgiveness."

If Paula had thought this would make Millie feel in any way better, she was wrong. Millie lay back on the bed and curled herself up like a hedgehog trying to shield herself from the pain. "Leave me alone."

"But…"

"No, Paula. Please. Please just leave me."

Millie stayed rolled up in a ball. This was the worse news ever for Millie. She knew Simon was lost to her now. Forever. He'd told her the tales of his young life living with step-parents. He'd sworn over and over that no child of his would suffer like he had. The finality of her relationship was staring her in the face. The pain it brought was excruciating.

Chapter Ten
Easter

Millie had been home nearly a week. Her father seemed to sense the sadness she bore. He reached out with his good hand and tried to communicate with her. His eyes shone with concern and tears. "I'm alright, dad. Tired of lectures. I'm ready to quit."

Alice came in with the bottle for Hugh to urinate in. Before Millie could leave them to the privacy they needed, Alice said, "you're looking tired, lass. Thin too. I'm glad you're home for a while. We'll sort her out won't we, Hugh?"

Hugh said nothing. Just stared teary-eyed at his daughter. Trapped in his silent world, but not missing a trick. All this love, kindness and concern brought tears to her own eyes. Millie couldn't face breakfast. She went out to the stables. It wasn't quite eight o'clock. Duncan's bike was there though. Placed up against the fence.

He was grooming Champagne but looked up as Millie walked past. "Morning. You're about early." Millie didn't usually ride until ten. "Restless that's all."

Duncan popped his head up and leant on the stable door. He stopped smiling when he saw her tears. "What's going on?"

"Don't take any notice of me."

Duncan came out of the stable and put his arm around her shoulders. "Millie. No one cries for nothing. Is it that bloke? You know the one at uni."

With the mention of Simon, fresh tears spilled down her face. "You're a good-looking girl. He must be blind to have let you go."

Millie blew her nose on a tissue. "I know you mean well but you don't understand."

"I do. You came home to look after your dad, and he played away from home. You might not think it now, but he's the loser."

"There's more to it than that."

Millie brushed the tears away with her sleeve as a child might. All these actions made Duncan want to hold her. "What I know now makes it all the more painful because I know I've lost him."

"Come here." Duncan threw caution to the wind and cuddled her into him.

As he embraced Millie, she gave way to the emotions she'd been trying so desperately to hold under control. She sobbed and sobbed. She had to admit to herself it felt good to let it all go. It felt good to be held.

What she didn't realise were the emotions she was stirring in Duncan. He held her to him tightly. He could feel her tiny frame and bony shoulders as they heaved with the sobs. "Millie. Oh, Millie." He had the urge to kiss her head. He was so close to her he could smell the shampoo she'd showered with this morning. His own heart seemed to ache for her sadness. "Shall we ride this afternoon? You'd like that. We could go back over Slindon. That was fun, wasn't it?"

He was rambling. He wanted her to stop crying. It was making him weak. Since Sindy, he'd never thought about other women. At this moment he wanted to lift her chin up and drop his head down so their lips met. When he thought for one reckless moment, he might just be brave enough, Millie pulled out of his arms. He missed her instantly and wanted to hold her again. These feelings were wrong. He knew that, but they were exciting. Millie was an attractive young woman. He'd noticed that the first morning he set eyes on her, but it wasn't until today that he realised he had feelings for her. He wanted her.

She thanked him and opened Truffle's stable door. He could hear the shuffling of hooves as she moved beside her horse. Whispers could be heard as she spoke softly to it. Duncan didn't know how he went back into Champagne's stable and continued where he'd left off. He ached to hold Millie again. Telling himself he was mad wasn't helping at all. She hadn't agreed to a ride. He knew it was wise, but he couldn't help feeling disappointed. There was nothing to keep him here once he'd put Champagne out in the paddock. He would have to go home. He kept telling himself this, trying to get his train of thoughts back on his wife and children.

Millie tacked up Truffle and walked her out. The sun was shining. It felt warm. The gardens were a mass of daffodils and the lawns needed mowing but were a gorgeous green. She pulled herself into the saddle and walked her over to Champers stable. "Are you coming?"

Duncan smiled at her. "That's better. You're lovely when you smile." He pulled the bridle off the hook and started to tack up Champagne. "Steady, girl." When he had the horse tacked up and ready for a ride he said. "You didn't fancy Slindon?"

"No, let's just ride over to Dell Quay. It's a nice morning."

Millie asked him while they were riding what her mother had taken him on for. She aired her concerns of jobs she'd noticed around the house and the garden that needed attention. "The lawns need mowing. The guttering on the side of the house needs cleaning out. The rain was pouring over the top the other night. I think they must be blocked."

"Your mum hired me as a stable hand. I liked her. I did other jobs too if she asked. I'm more than happy to take on the garden for you as a permanent position."

"I wondered if you wanted a more permanent position. Like a caretaker. You'll be paid monthly all year round. Now Alice is living in the flat upstairs it makes sense to have someone she can call if anything goes wrong."

Duncan laughed as the two horses walked side by side. "Alice would call me anyway, without me being the caretaker."

"I'm sure. she would, but I want to give you the position."

When they got to Dell Quay they dismounted. Millie tied her horse on the farmer's five bar gate and sat on the grass. Duncan followed suit and sat beside her. Millie was unaware of the feelings Duncan was struggling with at the closeness of her.

While she sat with him, she told him about Simon and the latest news that there was a baby. He'd laughed it off saying, "He still might come back to you Millie. If he doesn't love your friend, a baby won't hold him there."

"That's where you are wrong. Simon was damaged as a child." She told him Simon's sad life story living with a stepfather and holidays spent with a stepmother. "Up until I heard about the baby, I guess I thought there was a chance he would come to his senses and beg my forgiveness." Millie attempted to laugh. "I used to rehearse what I would say to him in my head. It'll never happen now. He will stay with Stephanie if it kills him. He won't let anyone bring his baby up and suffer as he did."

"I think you're better off without him."

Millie felt tearful again but managed to hold the emotion back. "It's easy for you to say that, but I love him. We had so many plans. We were going to travel this summer. Go off for a year." Millie brought her legs up under her chin. Her voice became wistful. "I guess it isn't just Simon. I miss him. I know I'm hurting, but it's so much more than just Simon. Losing mum. Dad being home. It's a responsibility I can do without."

Duncan pooh-poohed this saying, "Alice does most of the care. The agency sends someone to help her in the mornings and evenings. It seems to me it works like clockwork."

"I know but I feel responsible."

"Why? You're away most of the time. Travel. There's nothing to stop you."

"I know. I know all you say is right. It's just that the house and dad… they always seem to be on my mind. Everything is down to me now. I couldn't be on the other side of the world. I would worry there might be a problem."

Duncan took a breath and said with true feeling. "I'm not joking when I say this. I'd give my eye teeth to travel. I'd love to come with you. I really would."

This did make Millie laugh. "In your dreams. You've too much baggage… and you wouldn't be able to get away even if you wanted to."

"I'm just saying, that's all. Not being able to have things doesn't stop wishes."

Millie stood and started untying Truffle. "Dreams, Duncan. They're just dreams."

"Call it what you like. I'm being honest with you. I'd like to travel."

Millie mounted. "There was me, thinking the attraction was travelling as my companion." She was flirting, she knew it, but it felt good. She noticed Duncan didn't comment as he mounted Champers.

*

68

Once they were back at The Four Willows, Duncan untacked Champers and wiped her down. He walked her in the fenced off area of the garden where Truffle had been put. Millie was hanging over the fence watching her horse. Duncan said he was going home for some lunch and if nothing had been planned at home he'd come back and cut the lawns.

As he rode his bike home, he told himself over and over again he was behaving like a silly schoolboy with a crush.

He found Sindy at the sink with their budgie, Borgie in her hand, trying to wash him with cotton wool. "Hi love, what's going on here then?" When she turned to face him, her eyes glittered with tears and anger. Her cheeks were flushed. "Jack!"

"What's he done now?"

"Poured glue over the budgie. Look at the poor thing he can't even open his beak." Borgie was named after Bjorn Borg the tennis player. It was Sindy's budgie and she'd brought it with her when they married. Duncan looked at the helpless little thing in Sindy's hand and was fearful it just might die. It seemed to be struggling to breathe. "I'll go and talk to him."

"You're wasting your time. He says he doesn't know why he did it. I tell you Duncan, it's behaviour like this that leads to serial killing in later life."

Duncan kissed Sindy on the side of the cheek. "Don't be so dramatic. He's four years old. He doesn't understand."

Duncan went upstairs where he found the boys building a tower with Lego. "Jack. What have you done to Borgie?"

The little boy looked sullen. It was obvious he'd already been in trouble. "I dunno."

"You've stuck his feathers and his beak with glue. Why?"

"I dunno."

Duncan picked him up and put him on his knee. "How would you feel if someone did that to you? Stuck your arms and legs down so you couldn't move and filled your nose and ears up with glue so you couldn't hear or breathe."

The little boys eyes glistened with tears and his bottom lip quivered. "I dunno."

"Borgie might die. He's struggling downstairs. How will you feel if you have hurt mummy's bird so much, he goes to heaven with Grandad J?"

"Paul said it would stop him flying away. That's all."

Duncan held the boy close as he cried. "I don't want Borgie to die. Mummy won't like me at all."

"Hey, hey, soldier. Mummy and daddy will always love you."

"No. Mummy loves Charlotte now. I'm not her baby anymore."

Duncan put him down on the carpet so he could look right at him. "It doesn't matter how many babies we have. We only have one Jack, one Paul and one Charlotte. You're all ours and you're all special. We're a family."

Jack seemed to forget about Charlotte and favouritism. His eyes were big in his head when he said, "will Borgie live?"

"You stay here with Paul. I'll help mummy with the first aid."

Duncan looked at Paul. He too looked sheepish. "you know telling Jack to do that was wrong, don't you?"

Paul nodded but didn't look up.

Duncan said no more. He knew it was a case of six of one and half a dozen of the other. "Stay up here until I call you. Mummy needs to cool down a bit." Both boys nodded their heads up and down, pleased at being let off so lightly. They'd already had a whack with the wooden spoon across their bottoms.

Sindy was in tears when Duncan went into the kitchen. The budgie was dead. He took her in his arms. The action reminding him that only hours ago he was holding another woman, having ridiculous thoughts. He held his wife close whispering words of comfort. "I think Jack's feeling it a bit with the new baby too."

Sindy's anger at Jack had gone. Replaced with sadness at losing her budgie. "What are we going to do. How are the boys going to understand that Borgie's dead?"

"Leave it with me. Tell them I've driven the bird to the vets." Duncan rarely used the car. He cycled everywhere. It made sense as his jobs were all local.

As he started up the engine, he realised with the saga of Borgie, he still hadn't told Sindy the good news about being offered a full-time position at the Marlows. It would cheer her. In the winter months when people didn't need their gardens tended, he had to scratch around for indoor work and last year things were so tight Sindy had to take a cleaning job three mornings a week.

He pulled up outside Mr Haller's. He bred and showed budgies as a hobby. Duncan had made the large aviary that stood in the garden three years ago. It had been a good little earner. Cash in hand. There was only one problem, Mr Haller didn't have a green bird for sale. "Please…there's lots of them in there. It really has to be green."

Mr Haller took his flat cap off. "Sorry, no can do. I've plenty of blues but can't do green."

In desperation Duncan took a young ten-week-old blue budgie home in a small box.

Both boys ran out to the car as he pulled up outside the house. "Did the vet fix him, dad?"

"Yes, but he had to re-feather him. He said don't ever do that again as he won't survive another plucking."

Not another word was said about the gluing incident. The blue bird was a hit with the boys and when they put their hands in the cage trying to get the bird to sit on their finger like Borgie had done, it ran along the perch away from them. Duncan laughed out loud lightening the situation. "He's frightened he's going to get another glue job done on him." Even Sindy laughed. She was taken with the young bird. "You'll have to rebuild the bird's trust."

He was no longer Borgie, but Billie Blue.

Once the boys were in bed and Charlotte had had her night feed, Duncan told Sindy about being taken on at the Marlows full time. "I'm going to be given a weekly wage of a hundred and twenty pounds. That's going to help in the winter. You won't have to go back to the Houndley's to clean."

Sindy was delighted. Her eyes shone with excitement. "Duncan we could buy the house. Maggie Thatcher is giving people the chance to buy their council houses. If you have a set income coming in and we can prove it, we can buy this house at a discount."

Duncan's foolish crush on Millie was forgotten with the prospect of doors opening to them.

Chapter Eleven
Sidney Rounds

Sidney replaced the receiver and was just about to open the door of the telephone box when he caught sight of Peg. Her cheeks were flushed. She looked dishevelled and dirty. The limp was apparent in her hurry to catch him. The effort caused her to call out. "Sidney! Wait."

Sidney ran a hand over his face. He'd just had a run in with Minnie, he didn't want to see Peg now, but he had no choice but to wait. He forced a smile on his face. The first thing Peg did was apologise for her appearance. Sidney wasn't too bothered about the state of her, what he couldn't stand was the smell of those blessed chickens.

He remembered that smell when he had first called out to her for a date. How he wished now she'd said no. He wished he'd never got caught up in the silly game of being dared to do something. He'd never intended it to go further than one drink, but when she'd told him her sorry tale of how everyone mocked her, he'd felt shamed. The sad life she lived made him cringe at his own cruelty. At the time she'd seemed so desperate for friendship, he hadn't the heart to not see her again. Trouble was he had fallen for her. She was the sweetest, kindest person he'd ever met. She'd bloomed too. She was quite a looker. Even the long frocks she wore to hide her big boot were a style of her own. It suited her.

"Hi love. Alright?"

"Yes. You?"

He knew she was looking for an explanation as to who he was phoning. What was one more lie. "I was trying to follow up on a lead on a job closer to you. I've got to wait and hear."

Her face lit up making him feel a bigger cad than he already was.

73

"Come on. I'll walk you home. You can make me a cuppa if that old bat of a mother of yours will allow it."

Peg laughed. "Look at the state of me. I bet you could smell me a mile off too."

"You are a sight for sore eyes I might tell you. Every minute away from you is a minute wasted." She took his hand and he wondered when he learnt to be so smooth. He'd never spoken like this to Minnie or any other woman for that matter. Peg had brought out the best in him.

Peg pushed open the back door. Her mother was listening to some programme on the radio. There was no response to Peg's hello. "Shush!" That was all she got. How Peg put up with her mother, Sidney had no idea.

"Sidney's here. I'll make tea. We'll have ours out here in the kitchen."

Peg filled the kettle with water and switched it on, leaving Sidney in the kitchen. She went upstairs to change and freshen up a bit. Martha turned on her the minute she entered the lounge. "What are you doing bringing him here for?" There were no whispers, and she knew Sidney would be listening.

"Sidney is my boyfriend, mum. It's time you accepted…"

"Don't be so ridiculous. How old do you think you are? You're acting like a silly teenager. You need to wake up to yourself. He's playing away from home. He's a man. I've told you before, he's like your father. Can't keep it in his trousers."

Sidney despised the old woman. He was thankful Peg ignored her and went on upstairs. When she appeared again, she'd changed out of her work things and into a track suit. It wasn't flattering like the long skirts she wore, but she was clean. He could smell the toothpaste and soap on her as she moved around the kitchen putting biscuits on a plate. "I'll just give this to mum, and then I'll be back, and I'll be all yours." He watched her go into the lounge. He hated the old woman for her sharp tongue and hurtful insinuations, but he knew what he had in store for Peg would hurt her more than that old woman ever could.

Sidney drank three cups of tea and ate too many biscuits. He kissed Peg on the doorstep. He loved her. He knew he did. He would pick her up later. They would go somewhere quiet. They had been making love every possible chance they got for the past five weeks. Peg was so inviting and warm. All the things Minnie wasn't. He made love to her when he went home of a weekend. He had to. He didn't want to cause suspicion. The sad thing was that even though they didn't see each other all week, Minnie wasn't waiting for him like Peg. Years together had reduced their response to each other's advances and lovemaking had become a duty rather than love and desire.

Sidney's appetite had gone. When he got back to the caravan, he grabbed his toilet bag and went over to the shower block. As the water poured over his head, he asked himself over and over how he was going to get out of this mess.

'I should have told Darren to go and take a run and jump when he said I wouldn't dare ask the woman out who limped along like a cripple. I'd seen Peg most afternoons when she finished work. She had seemed an odd bod. When Darren said I bet you couldn't get her to go out with you, I'd risen to the bait.

I can see her now standing outside the pub, frightened to come in. Everything about her back then had been subservient. She was three times the person these days. What's more I love her. I love her and I want her, but I can't have her. I've lived with Minnie since she got pregnant with Shelley, Alan came two years later, nearly eleven years ago. We're comfortable together but the romance has gone. I spend so much time working away these days. Going further and further afield. There've been other women but no one like Peg. Oh, God, I wish I'd never set eyes on her. How am I going to tell her? She now thinks I'm *looking for work closer to home. When she asked what I was doing in the phone box how could I have told her that I was wishing my partner a happy birthday. That I'd been telling her I'd be home tomorrow and to get her glad rags on. We were going out. These days my whole life seems to consist of pacifying situations with lies. I'd already rowed with Minnie over the Easter break. I told her I could only do the weekend and had to be back on site on the Monday. She'd not liked it. It's a Bank Holiday she'd pointed out. More lies were spieled, and she'd swallowed them. Every bloody one of them. Now I've got to make it up to her by doing something special for her birthday. Trouble is my heart is here. I want to be with Peg. I wish I never had to go home again.*

Sidney groaned inwardly. *'The kids That's my Achilles heel. How could I leave them? Live so far from home. Minnie would be spitting blood. She's no Peg. She's a fiery one.'*

Sidney felt sick. He was like a Jekyll and Hyde these days. Guilt had him making an extra effort at home, but the love and lust he felt for Peg had him wanting to be here all the time.

'What a bloody mess. What a bloody, bloody mess.'

Chapter Twelve
May 1981

Alice Saunders

Alice woke in the early hours of the morning. She could hear the dawn chorus. Her life to date had been a happy one and despite things on her mind, she was content with her lot. She'd never married and had remained living at home with her parents, Daphne and Barry. When Barry died Alice and Daphne had done many fun things together. Alice had loved her and still missed her. Daphne had always looked youthful for her years, and her outlook matched her appearance.

Despite having never married and no children, there had been an abundance of friendship and freedom for Alice.

This job, looking after Hugh, had come at the right time. Her mother had died five years ago. Alice had left her job at the chemist's and gone to work for the West Sussex County Council as a home carer. Something she would never in a million years have considered when her mother was alive, but she'd fancied a change and at fifty-two she felt it was high time for it. What was more, she loved the work more than she could ever have envisaged. So, when Millicent Marlow advertised for someone to live in and care for her father last year, the job had seemed the answer to her prayers. She wasn't unhappy, but she was beginning to feel the house she had grown up in was far too big for just one person. Alice kicked the duvet back. Having a good stretch and yawn, she moved over to the window and drew back the curtains. This flat Millie had had converted was perfect. It meant her wages were decreased somewhat, but she didn't care. There were no bills to pay. Everything was included. Even her meals. Alice had been given the trust and freedom to take from downstairs what she needed up to the flat for her own use. What more could she want?

There had been no mortgage to pay off on the house she'd grown up in. Her brother had been left her parents savings and life insurance money and Alice had been given the family home. Now she'd sold the house, she knew she'd come out of the settlement a little better and was a wealthy woman in her own right.

She asked herself when Duncan brought the boys or the baby up to see her, had she missed out? She didn't think so. She'd had men friends and lovers, but no one to really make her want to give up her freedom. She always felt lucky. Never having to ask permission to do anything or give an explanation if she was late for any reason. She could holiday where and when she wanted to. In these latter years, her mother had accompanied her, and Alice had loved that too.

There was one thing bothering her at present. Keeping her awake and causing her to wake early. Peg James. Alice knew through her nephew that this Sidney from Liverpool was playing her for a fool. Instinct told her to keep her mouth shut. When she'd hinted to Duncan a few months back about her fears for Peg, she wished she'd said nothing. Alice wasn't one for gossip. She heard lots of tales and talk of things that went on in the village, but she was discreet.

This talk on Peg was worrying her though. Alice was very fond of the young woman. Always had been. Being born disfigured had brought many trials. She'd not had it easy. Then when Duncan married and her father died shortly after, Peg had been left saddled with her bitter, crippled, cruel mother.

Alice went downstairs in her dressing gown. It wasn't six o'clock yet. She peeked in on Hugh but knew by the sound monitor he was still asleep. She made herself a cup of tea and took a few biscuits back upstairs to bed with her. Still troubled by thoughts of Peg.

'I don't like feeling like this. One of the joys of being alone is not having to worry about anyone but myself. I've let myself become involved because of Duncan. Living here and seeing him every day has made me feel like part of his little family. Then there was Peg. I'd been delighted when he said his sister was dating some lad on the building site. I'd mentioned this to my nephew who was a plasterer on the same site. I knew he would know of the lad. He'd laughed. Said it was all a dare to see if she would actually go out with anyone if she was asked. He said they'd dared Sidney because he was always whistling at the ladies as they walked past. He'd drawn the short straw and his forfeit had been to ask the lame duck out. I was saddened by his cruelty. He was only eighteen though, no excuse, but it takes a while to grow up. I did tell him off for his choice of words. The youth in him had him smiling, saying not mine, theirs. Another sign of youth. They have an answer for everything.'

Alice thought about Peg. She'd seen her a few months back, walking home from work. *'Happiness radiated from her. Love gives you that radiance, Peg seemed to shine like a beacon.'*

Alice couldn't lift her spirits. This was going to be a bad show. She was actually frightened how the young woman would take the news that her romance had been a prank, a silly game, a bit of fun at her expense. To Alice it was painful and ugly. It would be humiliating for anyone to endure, but for Peg it will be bigger and more personal. *'Poor Peg, her whole life has been ridiculed one way or another.'*

Once she was washed and dressed, she went down to wake Hugh with a cup of tea. Alice was getting good at manoeuvring him on her own despite his size. Since he'd been home his weight was steadily going on. The district nurse had said last week he needed to go on a diet. Hugh had made a face. Alice had laughed at him. They had a good rapport these days. Alice soon had Hugh sitting up in bed with a cup of tea and his pillows wedged either side of him for balance. "The carer will be here any time now. We'll soon have you up and washed." She handed him a biscuit. "Just one." He shouldn't have it really, but Alice liked a biscuit in the morning with her first cup of tea and Hugh seemed happy to take one too. Still idly chatting to him, she said. "Millie's coming home at the weekend. That will be nice, won't it?"

It didn't matter to Alice that Hugh couldn't answer. She continued to talk of nonsense things. She filled his head with the Royal romance and the forthcoming wedding. Duncan's baby and the boys. The hilarious story of the budgie having to be re-feathered and the innocence of the boys believing such nonsense. She held back on her worries over Peg James and just when she thought she'd run out of conversation the doorbell rang. "There you go, Hugh. The cavalry has arrived. We'll have you up, washed and dressed in no time."

It was Jackie. Alice knew some of the carers sent out to Hugh from when she herself had worked for West Sussex Home Care. Jackie wasn't one of them. She was young. Not quite twenty by the looks of her. She had a dreadful habit of talking over Hugh's head as if he weren't there, and Alice had to keep saying, 'Did you get that, Hugh? Or what do you think of that, Hugh?' Alice couldn't be sure if Jackie was a bit slow on the uptake or just insensitive and in the wrong job. Still, she was a bright and breezy young girl. Full of fun and conversation, which if truth be told was not really suitable for two oldies like them. Alice felt quite exhausted when she'd gone and told Hugh so. "What an air head, eh? Nice enough but you wouldn't want to be on a sinking ship with her, would you?" Alice laughed as she sat opposite Hugh in the lounge. "Can you imagine it. Hooters all blaring telling everyone to get to the rescue point and she would be saying she'd forgotten her hairdryer." Alice could have sworn Hugh tried to smile. His face twisted up at an ugly angle. Alice went into the kitchen to make his breakfast. Peg was still on her mind, but she had no one to share her fears with.

"Here we go, Hugh. I've done All-bran. Good for your bowels and low in fat. It'll make a change. One slice of toast instead of two because of your morning biscuit." She knew she rambled on these days, but she was good at it. Hugh was like a sounding board.

While she loaded his spoon with cereal, she threw caution to the wind and told him what was bothering her. Peg. The sorry tale she'd heard. How she hoped she had got it all wrong and it was just vicious rumours, but her gut feeling was telling her it was all true. Her nephew wouldn't lie about something like that. She apologised to Hugh for unburdening herself and when he reached out with his good hand and squeezed it, tears fell down her own face. "Look at me. Acting like a silly old woman." Alice retrieved a tissue from her sleeve, leant over and kissed Hugh's twisted cheek. "Thank you for listening."

While she washed up the breakfast things, she felt better, lighter somehow. It was a good feeling to say those things out loud. Also, it felt like Hugh had understood everything she'd said and listened. It made her continuous daily idle chatter worth the effort.

The washing machine, when finished, made an intermittent beep until you switched it off. Alice put the laundry in the wicker basket and took the clothes outside. It had been her idea to get this rotary line fixed in the lawn. Duncan had sorted out the purchase and had cemented it in the ground. Alice was sure Millie's mother didn't know the meaning of hanging washing on a line to dry in the fresh air.

She could see Duncan's blond head bobbing up and down as he hosed down the stable area. She called over to him. "Morning. Another nice one."

He strolled over to her. He was wearing a red t-shirt and shorts that came down to his knees. He was a handsome young man. "What's cooking with you, Alice?"

"Not much. How's the family?" Before Duncan could answer Alice said, "what about the budgie, has the novelty worn off yet with the new feathers." She smiled at her own joke.

Duncan chuckled with her. "You won't believe it. The boys talk to him incessantly like you told them to and he's already saying, 'Billy blue.' It's hilarious."

Alice took the pegs out of her mouth so she could peg Hugh's pyjama top on the line. "I told you he would if you didn't put a mirror in. It must be a young bird too. Keep talking to him and he'll say all sorts."

"I dread to think what he'll end up saying if he mimics us."

Alice didn't want to ask, but found herself saying, "how's Peg?"

"You know. Full of the joys of spring. I shall actually get to meet her fella in a couple of weeks. He's meant to be coming to my birthday bash. I can't believe he's been going out with Peg over three months and I've yet to meet him. You know him, don't you?"

"Of him." Alice fiddled with the peg bag and clothes. She felt uncomfortable. She didn't want to say anything to cause concern like she had done last time. This Sidney seems to have wheedled his way into their lives with a good impression. "I mentioned to you before he works with my nephew, who tells me the work is almost finished. Peg's going to be heartbroken when this Sidney leaves for home or a new job."

"I reckon he'll stay. Go home and see his kids at the weekends like he does now. Or maybe Peg will up and go with him. There's no way she'll let him go. She's besotted with him."

Alice continued to keep busy by pegging the washing on the line. "What about your mother. Peg is sort of carer to her isn't she? Your mother won't cope without her."

Duncan started sorting out the socks and handing them to Alice, so she didn't have to keep bending down. "Peg's a bit wiser to mum's antics these days. She knows mum can do more than she lets on about. Even if she couldn't though, I don't believe wild horses would stop Peg leaving with this chap if it was the only way." He paused as Alice swung the line round a bit. "Mum would just have to go in a home I suppose. There's not the money for us to sort anything out for her like Millie has done for her dad."

Alice was pleased to have the subject changed. "Millie will be home this weekend. Hugh gets so excited at the thought of her coming back. I can't imagine how he survived in that nursing home with all those oldies. It was a setting much before his time. Thank goodness for Millie, that's all I say."

"Do you like caring, Alice. You've always seemed such a free spirit. Now you're tied to an old man, living in too."

"Don't you worry about me, love. No one ties me down. I shall be going to Canada in August. It's all booked. Millie will be home then for good. If not, she'll have to get someone from the agency to live in while I'm away."

"Really? That's sounds amazing. The furthest I've been is to Paignton with the boys last year. I think that's where Charlotte was conceived."

"I don't need to know that thank you." There was laughter. Duncan said on a serious note. "Didn't you want a family, Alice?"

"There was never anyone who I thought I wanted to share my whole life with. I like doing what I want. You could call it selfish."

Duncan spun the rotary line. "I've been with Sindy since I was seventeen. Not lived really. I wouldn't be without the children or Sindy, but sometimes when I see Millie, I sort of wish." He paused for a reaction. Alice was listening in her usual way. Not appearing shocked or casting judgement. "I feel like my life is all about providing and kids. There's no real fun. Does that sound selfish?"

"No, love, it sounds human." Alice picked up the wicker basket. "You love your wife and family, but it's not a crime to wonder."

"I didn't though, Alice. Well not until Millie started coming home."

"Oh, no, love. Don't you start with the wandering eye. That is a crime and a sin. Think of what you have to…"

"Hey, steady on. I'm just saying, Millie makes me wish perhaps I'd lived a bit more. She's planning to leave and travel."

"No, not now. She was until her heart was broken." Alice turned to go back to the house. "You don't want a rebound scenario. I might seem like a silly old woman to you, who doesn't know about love."

Duncan laughed. It lightened the situation. "It sounds like you had your heart broken a few times Alice."

"No, love, just the once. That was enough."

Alice left him watching after her. She was pleased she hadn't said anything about Peg. They weren't her tales to tell.

The Chapter Thirteen

Duncan had brought his little family round to see their nana, Martha and auntie Peg. Martha wasn't keen on the boys running here, there and everywhere, but she was definitely taken with the baby. While she cooed over her, Peg made cups of tea and orange squash for the boys, who were already creating havoc in the garden.

Peg called to Duncan. "Your teas are out here. I'm going outside with the boys. It's beautiful out there." She didn't want to spend a minute longer in Martha's presence than necessary these days. Martha was becoming more and more spiteful to her.

Peg opened up the deckchairs and the boys came and sat with her. "I hear Billy Blue speaks. Is that right?"

Paul full of eager chatter said, "he says his name but he's trying to say Sindy. Mum says her name over and over. He kinda whistles it."

Jack looked up from his glass of orange. "Paul is teaching him to say bum." He lowered his voice at the naughtiness of it.

Paul pushed his brother hard in the arm. "No, I'm not. That's a lie. Take it back."

Peg laughed out loud. "Boys, boys. Enough."

"I'm not Auntie Peg, honest."

"Well, if your mum tells me Billie Blue is saying rude words, I shall know then, won't I?"

Both boys ran off again. There was a long lawn with a huge cherry tree at the top of the overgrown, untidy garden. There were still remnants of aged hutches which housed many rabbits that had belonged to Duncan. A sorry looking chicken run with the roof off the hen house. This was as a reminder of World War Two and its rations. Lots of people kept animals when the war was on for food.

There was a time when Martha kept the garden neat and tidy, but her hands had become weak with arthritis. The painful condition had started when she was in her thirties. Over the next ten years the garden slowly but surely took on the appearance of a jungle. Peg did the bare essentials but waited until Duncan felt duty bound to tidy it up a bit. Still, today with its overgrown bushes, trees, and derelict animal hutches, it made the perfect pretend war zone for the boys to play in.

Duncan came out in the garden with Charlotte tucked snuggly back in her pram. He sat in one of the deckchairs. "Are they behaving?" He was referring to the boys, who were charging around pretending to be Indians.

"Fine."

"How's things with you, Peg. All going well with Sidney."

Peg loved it when she could talk about Sidney. "Yes. He's gone home to see his boys. He'll be back tonight. I'm meeting him in the pub at seven. We'll have a drink and probably go for a walk. It's lovely isn't it." The early spring sunshine had increased. May was a heatwave.

"I hope it's nice like this next week. Sindy's hoping we can hold my birthday bash in the garden."

"I'm hoping Sidney's organised not having his children next weekend. It would be lovely if he could stay and come to your party with me."

Duncan rocked the pram as Charlotte murmured. "I've yet to meet him. You keep him under tight wraps. I'm beginning to think he has two heads or boss-eyed?" He laughed at his own joke. Peg was hurt. "Do you think to fancy me you would have to have something wrong with you?"

Duncan put his arm round Peg's shoulder protectively. "Of course not. I'm kidding, Peg. He's a lucky man. I bet he knows that. Tell me about him. Alice says the building work is just about finished and several of the houses have people living in them already."

Peg felt a wave of sadness. "Yes. Sidney's been looking for work closer to Sussex. He was phoning about a job in Petworth. I'm not sure if he's heard anything."

"How old are his kids?"

"Shelley's ten and Alan's eight."

"Oh, Peg. Not really old enough for Sidney to be living so far away." The disappointment that crossed Peg's face made him tell his news. "Sindy's been thinking. We were going to buy our council house with the six-year discount we've accumulated." Peg interrupted him. "That's a great idea. Will you get a mortgage? Your work isn't that permanent in the winter."

"It is now. Millie's given me a full-time position. Year round. A monthly salary."

"Sindy will be pleased not to have to go out cleaning."

"Peg, what I want to say to you is…" Duncan seemed to falter trying to find the right way of saying what was on his mind. "Sindy thought if you wanted to leave for Liverpool with this Sidney, we would buy this house. Mum's lived here thirty-three years. The discount would be greater. We could…"

Peg stood up. "Are you saying you would look after mum. Set me free to go and do whatever I want?"

Duncan laughed. "Yes, Peg. Yes." He stood and put his arms around her. "Would you like that?"

Peg's voice diminished to a whisper. "I can't believe it. Oh my God. I feel like I've been given wings to fly. Thank you, Duncan, thank you." Tears fell freely down her face. An answer to her constant nagging worry had fallen in her lap. "Yes. Yes please."

The boys ran over to them. "What are you cuddling for?"

"If nana agrees, we will come and live here. Would you like that?"

"Wow! In this garden. On this estate. Brilliant."

Peg put her finger to her lips. "Shush, nana doesn't know yet. Let daddy tell her." The boys cuddled Peg's legs.

Peg looked a little worried. "Where will mum live if you take over the house? I can't see her getting out of her room."

Duncan sat back down. Peg prised the boys off her legs and did the same, listening to Duncan's well laid plans. "Sindy has it all sorted. She says she's happy to see to mum, who'll have the dining room. We'll get it made into a bedsit. She can use the commode until we get the wall knocked down and make the little loo into a bathroom. It will be small but enough. Sindy has an eye for these things. We'll have the house. The boys will have your room, Charlotte can have the box room and we'll have mum's. Sindy has plans to build out so we make the kitchen into a kitchen diner."

"Wow! Oh Duncan. You really are serious. It sounds wonderful. Speak to mum. You tell her. She won't do it if she thinks I want it."

Peg stood up again. Excitement shone in her blue eyes. They were positively sparkling. "I can't wait to tell Sidney. This is perfect. A dream come-true. Thank you, thank you, thank you."

Duncan called to the boys. "Come on lads. We've got to get your sister home. Don't say anything to nana as we go out. Mummy and daddy want to speak to her when the time is right. It can be our secret for now."

He kissed Peg's cheek. "Thanks, sis. This will make a big difference to us."

"No, Duncan. Thank you."

*

When the phone rang at just after six, Peg knew it was Sidney. She closed the hall door. She didn't want her mother to hear their conversation. She sounded breathless as she grabbed the receiver. "Sidney?"

He laughed. "Who were you thinking it was? Have I got competition?"

Peg lowered her voice. "I don't want to meet you at the pub tonight. I want us to meet on the seat by the canal. I have the most fantastic news for you."

Sidney's voice sounded startled when he said. "You're not pregnant?"

Peg ignored the concern in his voice and laughed. "No, no I'm not. It's better than that."

"I can't wait. Give me a clue."

Peg checked the door to the lounge was firmly closed. She still wasn't confident Martha wasn't out of her chair, leaning on her walking stick, earwigging at the door. "Sidney it's top secret at the moment. You won't believe what I have to tell you. I shall be on the seat at the top of the canal at seven." She paused waiting for a response. "Sidney? I love you."

She was relieved to hear him sigh. "I love you too, Peg. I'm just dying with curiosity here."

She laughed down the line. "See you at seven. Don't be late. I am absolutely dying to tell you my good news. No, our good news."

*

Sidney felt uneasy. He sensed Peg's excitement, but couldn't think of anything she could possibly say that would change the fact that he would be leaving for Liverpool at the end of the month. He had no choice. What was more, he wouldn't be accompanying her to her brother's party Saturday. Sidney had to go home. Home to his family.

He'd tossed a coin Friday night in the café he stopped at on his journey home. He told himself *'heads I'll tell her I can't get home because of a tummy bug. Tails I'll say the lads are having a farewell party.'* Tails won. He'd tried the spiel on Saturday. He said the lads were having a bit of a get together, a goodbye boys night. Minnie had been furious that he could even contemplate not going home after they'd been on their own weekdays for the past eighteen months. Minnie had thrown a right hissy fit. She had got on her high horse. The aggro wasn't worth it. Sidney knew he would go home Friday as usual. He'd given in meekly.

He had a shower in the block before meeting Peg. He was waiting for her. He watched her approach. When she hurried like she was now, her limp was always more apparent. He loved her though. Of that he was sure.

Excitement oozed from her. She threw herself into Sidney's arms. Kissing him. He laughed. Hey! I've only been gone for a weekend." Peg's eyes shone with her unshared news. "I can't tell you how much I've missed you, but I have the best news ever."

He sat down and pulled Peg beside him. He put his arm round her. "Let me tell you my bad news, then your good news will lift the situation."

Peg kissed him again. "Nothing you say can upset me today. I feel like a bird eager to try out my wings."

Sidney cleared his throat and put his arm round Peg, pulling her closely into him. "It's your brother's birthday. I really can't make it, Peg. I tried but my son's got into a little local football team he's been trying to play for, for ages. I didn't have the heart to say I wouldn't be there for his first match. You do understand, don't you? He's only eight. This is a big deal to him." Sidney was rambling. Peg looked up at him and said, "it's absolutely fine. My news outweighs a disappointment like that."

Sidney sighed, thinking, why couldn't Minnie be as easy-going as this lovely creature beside him. Peg was a wonderful person and he loved her. He never believed it possible to love two women at the same time, but he did. He knew people sang songs about loving you both, and he'd heard people say, but I love them both. He never believed them. He'd been the first to say it was an excuse for stepping over the forbidden line.

Peg stayed tucked under Sidney's arm. She told him how Duncan had asked if they could move into the house. Buy it. Look after mum and set Peg free. "Oh, Sidney. I can come to Liverpool with you when you go home. I'd get a job there. I'd do anything. Until I get settled I have quite a bit of savings. Oh, Sidney, I am …"

"No, Peg."

Peg pulled out of his hold. Her eyes shone with confusion and hurt. "What, why?"

"Oh Peg. You can't." Sidney took her hand. He was frightened she would up and leave. He needed to explain himself.

Sidney looked at her small hand in his. His eyes strayed to her big boot that poked out of the long skirt she wore. This made him feel worse. "There's no easy way to say this."

Her voice was small. "Don't, Sidney. Don't hurt me."

"Peg I don't want to hurt you. I'm hurting myself and have been for weeks now. Please hear me out." Sidney had rehearsed these words in his head most early hours before the sun came up or last thing at night and had done for the past few weeks. Peg sat very still. Her hand was being tightly held by Sidney's.

"I haven't been wholly honest with you, Peg. My life isn't quite as it should be back home."

Peg's voice sounded small. "You're not married, are you?"

"No. No I'm not." He wished he could leave it there, but now was reckoning time. "I might just as well be. I've lived with Minnie for eleven years. She is my partner." He clutched Peg's hand tightly as she tried to pull away. "No, Peg. Please listen. I do love you. I didn't want to." He paused and looked down. "I'm going to be honest now. Brutally." He took a deep breath. "Back in the very beginning I asked you out for a bit of a laugh, but I promise when I saw you so shyly standing outside the pub on that first date my heart melted for you. When you told me how the children at school had teased you about your leg. I felt terrible. I just couldn't hurt you. I decided to see you again. I liked you Peg. I liked you that first night. Honest I did. I love you now. I love you just as much… no, more. More than I love Minnie. It's the kids. I really…"

Peg stood up. Sidney tried to pull her back down with him, but she stood firm. "Let me go."

"Peg, I'm sorry. I…"

"No, Sidney. I'm sorry." Her voice was flat. Her eyes dull with pain. He hated himself. He watched her slowly walk along the canal path in the opposite direction she arrived. He wanted to chase after her but didn't dare to. He hoped he'd feel better once he got this lie out in the open. Lighter somehow but he didn't. He felt like someone had kicked him in the stomach. 'I'm a lowlife. A rat.' He put his head in his hands and let the tears fall down his face at his own loss. He didn't care who saw him either.

*

Peg went round to the back garden. The door was always left open. She didn't want to be seen so early fumbling for her front door key. It felt like everyone was watching, laughing.

Martha heard the door open and called out. "Is that you, Peg?" She wasn't nervous, the neighbours popped in and out of each other's houses with barely a knock. When there was no answer, Martha called again. "Peg?"

Peg didn't show her face. "It's me."

Martha couldn't help herself. "Ooh has lover boy fallen off his pedestal. Has he come clean and told you he's going home to his family? Or do I detect a little crack in the foundations of this romance?"

Peg said nothing. Martha could hear her moving around in the kitchen. "I don't want my hot drink now. It's far too early. I'll have it at ten thirty."

Peg went into the lounge. There were no signs of tears, but you had to be blind not to sense the sadness around her like a thick fog. Her voice sounded beaten. "Please, mum, can I ask you to say nothing."

"I knew it. Just like your father. They're all the same. The Avon lady was only saying the…"

Peg grabbed the first thing she could lay her hands on. It was a blue glass vase that she'd given her mother years ago for Mothering Sunday. It had come from Woolworths. She threw it in the fireplace. It smashed in the hearth. Martha screamed. She almost leapt out of her chair and would have done if she hadn't been so crippled. "Jesus, girl. What is the matter with you? You are madder than you look."

Without saying a word, Peg turned her back on her mother and went back to the kitchen where she had put a pan of hot milk on to boil.

Martha could hear her rattling about in the kitchen. She wanted to call out again, but the vase still lay in smithereens in the grate. Peg had made no move to clear up the mess. An icy fear had settled in the room, keeping Martha quiet. When Peg appeared again carrying only one mug, Martha remained silent.

Without a word Peg left the room and went upstairs.

Martha felt uneasy. She tried to watch her usual programmes on television, but she couldn't concentrate. The lad, Sidney had let her down somehow. She knew that, but fear had settled in her stomach, a reminder of her time married to Dickie.

Dickie and Martha were married in a registry office when the Second World War was raging. Nineteen forty-two. She was nineteen and he was twenty. They knew of each other from school days. She'd been working on the dairy farm. Dickie was home on leave. They met at a dance in the village, and it was love at first sight. Well, it had been for her. She learnt in time that Dickie fell in love with anything in a skirt.

They married six months after that first meeting. There had been no reception. She'd married in a plain pale blue suit and him in uniform. Plenty of letters came and went through the post, claiming undying love, but the truth was that when he came home, they really didn't know each other. When Susan was born disfigured Dickie had struggled with the deformity. He'd blamed Martha.

Martha was brought out of thought by the stillness in the house. She felt anxious. All was quiet upstairs. She'd never known Peg like she'd been tonight. It had unnerved her.

She sat staring at the television. Not watching it, staring at the screen, and remembering. *I'd been so happy to have a little girl. When they said she had one leg a little longer than the other, I hadn't cared a jot. She was the cutest little thing I'd ever seen. She weighed six pounds. She had my blue eyes even then. We'd been married eight years. Dickie had been thrilled when I first pulled back the shawl to show him his daughter, but the delight turned to shock when he realised she wasn't as perfect as he first thought. I put his first affair down to this adjustment. We might have been married eight years but only lived together for two of them. Dickie didn't come home when the war ended in forty-five. We didn't see each other until May nineteen forty-six. He managed to get a job on the council. Physical work. Digging up and repairing roads. This is where a young girl caught his eye. She worked in the office. Susan wasn't out of nappies and I'd found myself alone with a baby. Six weeks he stayed away. This was a shame to bear back in those days living in a little village where everything is known and gossiped about by everyone. He came back with his tail between his legs and I took him back. I thought it was the shock of Susan and her disfigurement. The next affair there were no excuses. It was with my friend. Beverley. She lived in the same village. Dickie was gone for six months this time. He heard on the grape vine I was seeing someone myself. He hadn't liked this. He came back begging again for forgiveness. I hadn't met anybody. It was just light flirtations from the insurance man. Harmless chatter. Still, it got Dickie back. Susan had been about twenty-six months. Duncan was born the following year. Susan was three. Her limp had been very apparent, and she wasn't made a special boot until she went to school. That is when the name calling started. Peg leg. Peg had stuck. Dickie and I jogged along quite nicely or so I thought. There were other women. I'd learned to turn a blind eye. It was hard to manage bringing up children on your own. I only had a cleaning job three days a week, so when he came home, I was grateful. This is where my bitterness crept in. I secretly despised him and my life. I blamed Peg for being born with a wonky leg. Telling myself things would have been different if she'd been perfect. I was kidding myself. Then he met another girl. A lot younger. I couldn't compete with her. Duncan was six and Peg was nine. I was terrified he'd leave me. There was talk the girl had got herself in the family way and even though we'd rowed about it, I'd begged him not to go. Begged him on all fours. He'd left the house. I prayed to God he'd come home. He did eventually, and only God knows what happened to the girl. I'm guessing the pregnancy was a false alarm or she married someone else. I'm sure there were others, and I swore I'd leave if there were. Then in my thirties I started to notice my feet hurt when I got out of bed in the morning. My knees didn't like weight bearing and walking and gardening became difficult. My hands were stiff and fingers sore. The doctor diagnosed osteogenesis imperfecta. A condition that is inherited. My bones were going to become extremely fragile. I kept this from Dickie for twelve or more months. I was frightened he wouldn't like to think I was going to be a cripple like our daughter. I also knew Peg's condition would mean the blame he'd always wanted to put on me would be clarified in his mind as mine. Trouble was with this inherited bone problem, I believed Peg's deformity probably was from my side of the family. The years went by and I managed to hide my pain with painkillers and prescribed drugs. I told Dickie they were lady pills to help with the onset of the change. Dickie was to start his own trial with health.*

Headaches became a problem for him. They were so bad he couldn't bear the light and lay in a darkened room, sometimes all day, being violently sick. His temper was awful. He stopped going to the pub of an evening, fearing it was the alcohol. The good thing was the affairs seemed to stop too. It was on one such evening as I sat with a cold flannel on his forehead that I told him about my arthritis. This is what I called it. It was easier to understand and I didn't have to mention hereditary. I'd been surprised how he took it in his stride. He didn't realise the seriousness of it. My fingers were already becoming deformed and my toes were turning in and I hadn't yet turned fifty. Dickie's headaches continued and the two of us got closer through illness. At fifty-two he was diagnosed with a brain tumour and shortly after Duncan's wedding, he died at the age of fifty-three. No age at all. I became reliant on Peg.

As soon as Martha had that last thought she was jolted back to here and now. The silence was still deafening from upstairs. It was nine thirty. Martha was ready to have her bedtime drink and go up to bed early. "Peg!" There was no answer. Martha banged with her stick on the hot water pipe that ran up the side of the wall. Still no answer. The broken vase was still in the hearth. "Peg?" Her voice had changed. She had a horrible feeling something was wrong.

Forcing herself on to her feet she balanced herself with two sticks. She called again, "Peg?"

Nothing. Goosepimples had gone up Martha's arms. Something was horribly amiss. She made it to the bottom of the stairs, and leaving her sticks behind, pulled herself up the steps using the double banister. Duncan had put the extra rail on for just this purpose. "Peg?" Martha felt frightened at the silence. She pushed open Peg's door. Walking was difficult without her sticks for support and the sight of her daughter sleeping soundly on the top of the bed made her legs give way. "Peg, Oh, Peg, no. No! NO!" Her voice rose as she did her best to crawl to her bedside. She touched her body and her arm slipped off the bed and hung lifeless. Martha let out a scream.

How she managed to get down the stairs at such speed she'll never know. It was mainly on her bottom. Dialling Duncan's number was difficult with her deformed fingers. He answered immediately.

Before he could tell her off for disturbing the boys by phoning this late hour she was already screaming "Peg's dead. Peg's killed herself."

"Mum? What's going on."

"Come, Duncan. Peg's dead. She's taken something. She's upstairs. She's dead, I know she is."

"I'm on my way."

Duncan put down the receiver and phoned an ambulance.

Sindy wanted to know what on earth was going on. "Is it your mum?"

"No, it's Peg. She's topped herself." A hundred things were going through his mind. "I've got to go Sindy. I'll call you when I know more." His hands were shaking as he grabbed the car keys off the hook.

*

The ambulance was already outside his mother's house as he pulled up on the curb. He leapt out of the car and ran round the back. His mother was sat at the bottom of the stairs by the phone. She was as white as a sheet. "Where's Peg?"

"They are doing something to her now. I don't know. They have been running up and down the stairs getting things. She's dead Duncan. Dead and it's all that Liverpudlian's fault. Ditched her tonight. She didn't have to tell me. I could tell. I reckon he has a family back…"

"Shut up, mum. Now's not the time."

"Excuse us." The ambulance men appeared with Peg on a stretcher. They almost ran down the stairs. "Is she alive." It was Duncan that spoke. "She's critical. Time will tell." Duncan followed them hurriedly out to the back doors of the open ambulance. "Can I come?"

"You can if you want. You can try and talk to her. Keep her with us."

Without saying goodbye to his mother or giving her another thought, he leapt up in the ambulance and held Peg's lifeless hand. "Stay with us, Peg. Please. Come on, there's a girl. God, the boys will be heartbroken if they haven't got auntie Peg." Duncan kissed her hand. Tears from nowhere fell down his face. "Peg. Peg. Peg."

The ambulance chap said, "Keep talking. She can hear you."

The siren seemed to magnify the emergency. They pulled up outside the hospital and the back doors seemed to fly open and the stretcher was off before Duncan could get out himself. He was left watching it disappear through the big double doors. He held his hands together and prayed. He wasn't one for prayer, but seeing his sister so close to death he had to do something.

He sat where he was told, waiting. It was nearly midnight when a doctor said she had come round. Duncan cried with relief. "Can I see her?"

"Not tonight. Her body has been through a huge ordeal. She needs rest. We'll monitor her tonight. Can you leave a number to call if there is any change?" Duncan went over to the desk.

He now had the problem of getting home. His car was at his mum's. He was a good five miles from home. He phoned Sindy.

"Peg's with us but not out of the woods. I'm at the hospital but came in the ambulance. I'm going to get a taxi to mum's. I'll have to stay there tonight. She's in a state too."

Duncan was talking fast. He was in shock himself.

Martha was still sitting by the phone when Duncan arrived. "Come on Mum. Peg's holding her own. Let's get you to bed."

Martha looked up at her son. He was so like his father apart from the colour of his eyes. "Is she alive?"

"By the grace of God, yes. Just, I believe."

Tears fell down Martha's face. "I didn't mean to aggravate her. I just knew this fella wasn't for real. The Avon lady was telling me every week about him going home to his family."

Duncan lifted his mother up like a baby and carried upstairs. "Not now, mum. Let's get you to bed."

"But…"

"But nothing. I tell you, mum, if this Sidney is the cause of Peg's heartache as you say, I'll kill him with my own bare hands."

Martha became scared. "No! Don't talk such nonsense. He's not worth it. Think of the boys, your family. Please don't say that, Duncan. I won't sleep for worry."

"Goodnight, mum." Duncan kissed the top of his mother's head. Something he wouldn't normally do. It seemed like tonight she needed it. She had lost some of her prickliness.

Duncan didn't phone Sindy again. He'd explained his plans earlier. He lay on Peg's bed and despite thinking he wouldn't sleep a wink, sleep came.

*

Sindy arrived at Martha's before seven the following morning. The boys were dressed for school. Paul in uniform. Charlotte in the pram still in her nightclothes and needing a feed. Today was an extra blessing that she was such a contented baby. She was ten weeks old today and sleeping through the night.

Duncan answered the door bleary eyed. "What a night. I must phone the hospital."

The news was that Peg was stable. No visitors until the doctor had done his rounds.

Sindy picked Charlotte out of the pram and gave her to Duncan. "I'll warm her bottle and you can give it to her. I'll see to your mum." Sindy took complete control. The boys sat with books and crayons at the table, having had their breakfast before they left. "Who broke nana's vase?"

Sindy busied herself in the kitchen putting on the kettle to make tea, toast and warm the milk for Charlotte. She grabbed the dustpan and brush and without giving an explanation cleaned up the glass. The boys caught a whiff of the toast. "Can we have some, mummy?"

"Yes, I'll get daddy to do it for you."

"Can we have golden syrup on it?"

Sindy went back to the kitchen where Duncan, still holding the baby, was hovering as if unsure of what he should be doing. She told him. "I'm going to put some toast on for the boys, can you put some honey on it for them?"

Sindy went through to her mother-in-law. She handed Martha the tea. "Come on. Another day. Drink this. Everything seems better once you've had a cuppa."

Martha looked frightened. "I don't know how I'm going to cope. What will I do without Peg? I've been so…"

"Not now. No self-pity. We'll come here until Peg is better and well enough to come home."

"There's not room. Where will you all sleep?"

"It's all organised. I'm going to get Duncan to put your bed downstairs for now. It will be easier on us all. Make a little bedsit for you. Okay?" Martha didn't say anything. She drank the tea but left the toast. "What do you think could have happened that was so bad to make her do that?"

"I'm guessing she and Sidney had a fall out. It will sort. For now, we need to get by best we can. Come on if you don't want the toast, I'll get you to the bathroom."

Duncan had to go to work. The horses needed feeding. There was no one else to do it. He kissed his family goodbye saying he'd be back to take the boys to school for nine. For the first time ever, he drove the car to The Four Willows.

He didn't want to speak to anyone. He didn't know, what was what. The not knowing made him feel uneasy. He couldn't escape. Alice heard his car.

"What brings you here driving instead of cycling that blessed bike? And on such a lovely morning."

"There's been a bit of bother with Peg. I think she's fallen out with her fella."

Alice looked upset. Duncan knew she wasn't a gossip, and her concern and curiosity would be genuine.

Duncan ran his hand through his hair that could do with a cut. "Alice, she tried to top herself. God knows what went on."

Alice paled. "Oh, love. This is terrible news." It looked like she was going to add to it, but Duncan cut her off. "I can't hang around. Sindy's holding the fort at mum's. I have got to get Paul to school for nine and Jack to playschool. It's a mess."

Duncan made his way to the stables. In half an hour both horses were fed and in the part of the garden that had been fenced off for them. He called out goodbye to Alice, but didn't wait for a reply.

As Duncan drove the short distance back to his mother's house, he remembered Alice saying something about Peg's romance. She had clammed up. For the love of him he couldn't remember what it was. He'd had Charlotte with him. Newborn. His head was full of her. Alice had covered up her concerns by cooing over the baby. Duncan was in two minds whether to go back and have it out with Alice, but he had more pressing things to do first. It didn't change the fact that a seed had been sown. The more he thought about it, the more it bugged him.

Sindy was sitting in the lounge with Duncan's mother when he got in. The boys were still drawing and all looked calm. "Daddy's here. Come on boys. Get your shoes on."

Sindy helped Jack into his little trainers and Paul wriggled his feet into his black Velcro school shoes. Duncan asked his mother if she was okay and kissed Sindy. "Any news on Peg?"

"The hospital phoned about ten minutes ago. No visitors. Peg doesn't want anyone. They are waiting for someone to assess her from the psychiatric hospital. It feels to me like she is going to be admitted into Sunnydale's. I'm frightened for her, Duncan. What will become of her?"

Martha looked up. "Get the boys off to school. You shouldn't be talking over their heads about such things."

Duncan's heckles went up. He was already struggling with what happened here. "Such things, mum. Your daughter, my sister, their auntie. Not things. Family."

He grabbed Paul's satchel and handed it to him. "Come on. Let's get the pair of you off to school."

They kissed their little sister, mum, and nana goodbye. Then giggled out to the car. "Daddy's cross with nana. Daddy's cross…"

"Enough the pair of you. In the back." When Paul squabbled to sit in the front, Duncan refused. "The booster seat's in the back. We haven't time to be fiddling with that this morning."

As he drove Paul to school and Jack to his play school 'Little Piglets' he thought over and over about Alice. She had said there were rumours about this Sidney playing Peg for a fool. He was sure of it.

Duncan didn't go home. He drove back to The Four Willows. Alice was over by the horses giving them a few carrot tops. He came straight out and asked her what she knew. Alice hadn't wanted to tell him what she had picked up on the grapevine through her nephew, but Duncan was persistent. "I remember you telling me when Charlotte was born, you were concerned for her. I need to know, Alice. The hospital will want to know if they are going to help Peg."

Alice had been reluctant. She tried to say as nicely as she could, but there was no way it could be said nicely.

Duncan felt his legs go weak. His hands shook and he'd never felt so angry in his whole life. He didn't say goodbye to Alice. He could hear her calling after him. "Now don't do anything silly, lad. Think of your family. Duncan…"

He heard no more. He drove straight to the building site. A young lad was pushing a dirty cement covered barrow. He slowed his car and called out to him from the passenger window. "Hey! Do you know where I might find Sidney?"

Without answering, he bellowed. "Siddo?"

A young man appeared. If Duncan hadn't been so wrapped up in his own pain, he might have noticed the defeated hunched shoulders. The pale face with the dark circles under the eyes and the empty glazed anguished look of a man struggling with emotion.

Duncan got out of his car. It had never happened to him before, but a red mist seemed to fall over his face like a cinema curtain. Without saying a word, he walked up to Sidney and punched him. The sound of a crack was his nose breaking. He fell to the floor. Duncan kicked him hard in the side of his body and Sidney curled up in a ball trying to protect himself. Duncan continued to kick out at the huddled figure that didn't try and defend itself. The next thing he knew was being held back by three other men.

"Jesus, you're a fucking maniac. What's your problem?" Someone was on the floor now helping Sidney up on his feet. Duncan tried to break free and take another swing at him. He was held too fast. He shouted at the beaten figure. "I tell you. If anything happens to my sister, I'll break every fucking bone in your body." He was being dragged away from the scene. He continued to shout. "Do you hear me. I don't care where you live. I shall track you down and…"

One of the chaps that had hold of Duncan said. "Enough. Come on. You're not helping anyone."

Duncan didn't know how long he sat in his car. He couldn't drive. He shook like a leaf. The anger had subsided. He felt like crying.

When he finally got home Sindy wanted to know where he'd been. "Look at you? Is that blood on your shirt?"

There was blood on his knuckles too. It wasn't his own it was Sidney's. "I've let my temper get the better of me. We'll probably have the police here shortly. I gave that piece of shit a kicking he won't forget in a hurry. He asked our Peg out for a laugh. A bit of a joke. Can you imagine how that made her feel?"

Sindy was cross. "What happens to us then? If you're arrested for GBH. Did you think of that?"

Duncan didn't say anything. He was glad his mother was sitting in the lounge with the television on, unaware of the state he was in.

Sindy wouldn't let it drop. "It wasn't your fight. Is the guy okay? You haven't hurt him badly, have you?"

Duncan shook his head. "He was on his feet when I left." He didn't tell her he had to be held up.

Jack had gone to play with a child from playschool and was having tea there. Sindy left to pick Paul up. Duncan had to go to The Four Willows to put the horses away, but he struggled to go. The enormity of what he had done was just sinking in.

"Cup of tea, mum?"

"I know you've been arguing. Is it over me?"

"No, mum. It's just things. Do you want a cuppa or not? Else I'm off to work."

When the phone rang, he guessed it was the police.

"Hello." It was the hospital. Peg was having a few tests to check there was no permanent damage to her kidneys and she would be admitted on Wednesday to Sunnydale hospital. Duncan had asked if he could visit and was told your sister has specifically said she wishes to see no one.

*

Sidney had been admitted into hospital. His nose had suffered a severe break and needed resetting. He had three cracked ribs and an eye that was closed completely with the swelling. The police had been called and despite them urging him doggedly to press charges, he had refused. Sidney felt he deserved every punch and more. What was worrying him was what he thought he had heard Duncan say. Sidney tried to remember. He'd been dazed after the attack. It had happened so quickly and when he was pulled to his feet, he didn't know where he hurt most.

Did he say if anything happens to Peg? Did I hear right? What could be the matter with Peg? She was hurting like him when she walked away, but she was in one piece. What could have happened to her or what might happen to

106

her? Oh Peg. I miss you already. What a bloody mess. I've got to go home in this state too. Jesus, I'm in the Shit and that's for sure.'

Frank had offered to drive him back to Liverpool once his nose had been reset. He'd accepted. Sidney had been eking his work out here in Sussex for the past three weeks, just so he could stay closer to Peg. There was nothing to keep him here now.

When the nurse asked him if he needed anything for the pain, he said, "have you got anything for a broken heart?" She smiled at him sympathetically.

Chapter Fourteen
Sunnydale Psychiatric Hospital

Peg sat staring out of the window. The drugs she was being given numbed the pain but didn't make her want to wake up of a morning. She was tired of this world.

The door to the day room swung open. Peg knew it was Jolene before she caught sight of her. She wore one of those heady perfumes. She'd given a group talk three days ago. It was on assertiveness. Peg hadn't been interested but had been encouraged to go. Today Jolene looked just as outlandish. Her long black hair with streaks of grey through it was tied up in a bright yellow scarf. Her beads were of the same daffodil yellow but her dangly earrings were orange. These matched her long skirt. The jumper she wore was navy blue and far too tight for her ample figure. "Susan?"

Her introduction was a question. Peg nodded. "Everyone calls me Peg."

"I'm Jolene. Would you come with me to the quiet room, please?"

It wasn't really a question. Peg stood and followed like a robot.

Once they were sitting together, Jolene asked why she was called Peg? "Is it a middle name or perhaps a shortened name for Margaret?"

Peg had said quite simply. "I'm called Peg because of my leg. Peg leg."

Jolene didn't show any sign of emotion. She said quite calmly. "I shall call you Susan."

Peg had smiled. "Forgive me if I don't always realise you are talking to me."

"Susan. Why do you think it okay and acceptable for people to change your name from one thing to another without your permission and out of cruelty?"

Peg sat quiet for a while. No one had ever asked her how she felt about anything. She whispered. "You get used to it. It seems to have been my lot in life. I have been called cripple, wonky donkey, limpy lou and simple Sue. I suppose Peg didn't seem so bad."

"Are you happy for me to call you Susan?"

"I wanted to move away. Make a fresh start once. Yes, I wanted to be known as Susan. It didn't happen and I'm Peg."

Jolene spoke softly when she asked. "What about friends. Who was your best friend at school maybe?"

"I didn't have any. I was only used. You know if they wanted someone to hold one end of a skipping rope. Or someone to hide from. I always got the horrible jobs. I didn't mind back then. I was pleased to be wanted."

What about family?

"I have been looking after my mother for seven years now. Since my dad died. She has a form of arthritis. That was when I wanted to leave. Go to Scotland. Start again… as Susan."

Jolene picked up on the care given to Peg's mother. "Are you and your mother close?"

"No. She doesn't like me much either. She mocks me." Peg hesitated. "I have a brother. He cares about me."

Jolene crossed her legs, mimicking Pegs pose. "Susan, is that Duncan?"

Peg nodded.

Jolene said, "he phones every day to see how you are and evenings too. Would you like to see him?"

Peg's voice rose in angst. "No!"

"Susan what do you think you are frightened of?"

"Nothing. I just don't want to see anyone."

"Why?"

Peg sat very still, thinking. She didn't know how to explain. She guessed these pills were making her head woolly. She certainly didn't feel the pain of losing Sidney like she had. "I don't know how to explain it."

"Can you try?"

Peg took a big breath. "When I was just Peg with the short leg, no one bothered me. I worked at the chicken farm locally, collecting and sorting eggs all day. I went home to my mum and helped her until it was bedtime. That was my life. No one was curious about me. It was like I was a closed shop that no one could see or get in." Peg felt a slight emotion building. She fiddled with her skirt. Took a deep breath and said, "then things changed. It was like a window cleaned of dirt. I could not only see out, but I opened it to let people in. They could see me. I was so happy. It didn't last. I realise now, I was just being used. A joke."

"Susan, how can we get you back to feeling happy?"

"I don't want to feel happy again. I want to go to sleep and not wake up. I'm tired of this world. It is cruel and ten times crueller when you're different."

"Susan." Jolene waited until Peg looked up. "Thank you for sharing that with me. I feel we have done some good work this morning. Can I ask that you think about something for me before tomorrow when we meet again?"

Peg stared into the soft grey eyes of Jolene. Her peculiar choice of clothes had become insignificant. Strangely for such flamboyant outfits, she wore no makeup on her face anywhere. Peg nodded. "What?"

"I want you to question why you think if you've opened a window into your heart letting people see the real you, why then would they be happy to see you so desperately sad."

Jolene stood up on that sentence. "I shall leave you now to reflect on what we've talked about. Thank you, Susan. I'll see you tomorrow. Unless of course you wish to join the group therapy session later today. It's at two thirty in the big hall."

*

Being moved down into the dining room didn't suit Martha. The boys were above her and they were noisy little devils and Sindy didn't seem to hear the pandemonium they created, and if she did the giggles were reduced to tears as she beat them with the wooden spoon. Martha had had no idea Sindy was such a disciplinarian. *You never know anyone until you live with them. Well, that's certainly true in this case.*

Martha looked at the clock Duncan had fixed to the wall for her. It was coffee time in ten minutes. Martha felt like she was in a nursing home. Everything that was done here was by routine. Since Duncan's birthday gathering when she'd demanded to go inside because she was cold, she'd been put to bed at eight thirty every night since. She was still allowed to watch the television, but Sindy said the evenings were her and Duncan's time. Martha seemed to have lost her voice in her own home overnight.

"Here you go, Mum." Sindy called her mum when it suited her, otherwise it was Martha and always Martha when she was cross. These days that was more often than not. A mug of coffee was placed on the side with a biscuit. Ten o'clock on the dot. Martha preferred a cup and saucer but didn't complain like she would have a few weeks ago.

Sindy busied herself straightening up the television magazine, "Duncan's going to write to Peg. I thought you could too."

Martha reached over for her biscuit and dipped it in her coffee. "I can't write with my hands. My fingers are so stiff."

"You tell me what you want to say, and I'll write it for you."

Martha's biscuit dropped in the mug before she could get it to her mouth. Her disappointment and annoyance at her own awkwardness caused anger and her voice sounded sharp. "I prefer digestives. They last longer. Peg knows not to buy those shortcake ones with the fruit in."

"No, Mum. No. I won't be putting up with any of your nonsense. If you want something different to what I provide you ask nicely. I am not Peg. I won't be used as a door mat."

Martha clamped her mouth shut. This was a side of Sindy she hadn't seen before. Martha was relieved that once Sindy had had her say, she lightened her voice. "I shall go and put the washing on the line, feed Charlotte and then we'll come through to you with the writing pad. While I'm gone, think about what you'd like to say. I'm busy and haven't got all day to sit while you ponder." Sindy pulled the cushion off the spare chair. "Let's prop you up a bit. You look like you're sliding down."

Martha felt like saying she wasn't an invalid, but she was being made into one before her time. Good sense kept her quiet.

"The boys have made cards and coloured them. So, it doesn't have to be too much. We just need to let her know we are thinking of her." Without another word she left Martha with her thoughts.

Martha heard the back door open. Her eyes went to the window. From where she sat, she could see Sindy walking up the garden carrying the laundry basket that was brimming over with an assortment of clothes. She watched as the long washing line Dickie had put up years ago, once again became heavy with white fluffy terry towelling napkins, and family clothes, telling the neighbours that things had changed at number ninety-nine. Martha couldn't help feeling sorry for her son. Having her daughter-in-law caring for her like this felt like a punishment for all her spitefulness to Peg. Martha covered her face in her hands.

'Oh, Peg. Please get better. I didn't mean to be so difficult. Spiteful. I just envied your youth and health. I ridiculed you like everyone else to make myself feel better. Can you forgive me? Life here with Sindy is bearable but she isn't you. I didn't realise the treasure I had until I nearly lost it. Well, I feel I have lost it. I'd like to speak about your fella, but I don't want to upset you. Truth is Peg, I did like him. I liked his spirit. I could see he was fond of you. More than. I just didn't want it to be the case. Selfish me. I was worried about losing you. Sindy has plans to take our home over. You won't believe what she has in store. I've already been demoted to the dining room. I don't come out. She has taken over completely. The poor boys. I see now why they were always so wild here. Letting off steam. They have the wooden spoon across their bottoms more often than I get a cuppa tea – no, I should say mug. You know how I hate mugs of tea. I'm not to say anything or I'm being difficult, and she tells me over and over 'I won't have it.' I honestly reckon those boys don't know that wooden spoons are meant to be used for cooking. I think she'd whack my bottom too if she thought she'd get away with it. The only one who doesn't get whacked or nagged is the baby. No doubt her turn will come. Still, you know I was always one for sayings. 'What goes around comes around.' Oh, Peg. I wish I could write this to you. Wouldn't you laugh. Or knowing you, you wouldn't. Despite how horrible I've been to you over the years, you would probably take pity on me. I'm praying for you, Peg. Praying you will get better soon. Selfishly again it is for me. I want things back as they were. I'd be more appreciative…'

Martha stopped daydreaming when the door was kicked open and in walked Sindy arms full, holding the writing pad, the baby bouncer chair with Charlotte already sitting in it and the pen in her mouth. She plonked the baby on the floor and the chair bounced up and down of its own accord. She then dragged the dining chair closer to Martha so she could sit and write. "That's it. Ready. Let's get this letter done. Have you thought of something you'd like to say?"

It was awful. Sindy sat opposite her with the pad and pen in her hand. Her foot tapped the baby chair making it bounce. The action was like a reminder that the minutes were ticking away using up precious time. Sindy held the pen to the page, "I've put dear Peg. What else?"

Martha thought she just might cry. So much change in just two weeks and none of it for the better. She almost jumped when Sindy said sharply, "well?"

Martha sounded wistful, "just say I am thinking of her. I hope she gets better soon, and I look forward to her coming home." Sindy quickly wrote the words down. "Anything else?"

"No. No I think that says it all."

"Lovely. That was easy." She folded up the paper. Picked up the baby still in the bouncy chair and left Martha alone with her thoughts.

*

Duncan sat outside with Alice. She'd made him coffee. "How's Peg?"

Duncan shrugged. "It's difficult to say. She doesn't want to see anyone. They say stable. What does that mean?"

114

Alice offered him a bit of fruit cake. "It's a bad business this."

"We've moved in with mum. Sindy is organising everything. She's good at that. Mum's like a different person."

Alice ignored his sentiments and gave him a piece of her mind. "Fancy you going to the building site causing trouble. You could have landed yourself in real bother with the law. You know that don't you?"

Duncan looked down at his feet. Sindy still wasn't speaking to him properly for risking the family security. "I know. It was just I was so angry. I've never felt like that before. It's a good job there were people there to pull me off or I think it quite possible I would have killed him."

"If it makes you feel any better, this Sidney is in a bad way."

Duncan half laughed. "You don't have to tell me that. I gave him a kicking and a half."

"No, Duncan. Not bad in that way. Heartbroken. Torn between two women."

"I don't feel sorry for him. Mum always said if one woman's not enough forty's not too many. There you have it. He got caught out playing games."

Alice became slightly indignant. "It might have started out as a bit of a laugh, but my nephew said Sidney fell for your Peg in a big way. This Sidney didn't want to go home. He could have returned to Liverpool before Easter. He dragged the job out as it was. These past weeks he's been labouring on the site just to stay here. Close to Peg. What does that tell you eh?"

"I don't want to hear it, Alice. Whatever the outcome was. He played Peg for a fool. He played away from home, got burnt with a hiding thrown in for his trouble."

Alice stood up. She hooked the empty mugs through her fingers. "You have a lot of growing up to do, young man. Nothing's as black and white as that. Take it from a wise old lady."

Duncan watched her walk away.

He'd turned twenty-eight at the weekend. The birthday they had planned was cancelled and only a couple of his mates had gone round to celebrate. His mother had been forced into the garden to take part in the celebrations. For the first time in years, he actually felt sorry for her. Sindy had been insistent. Said it would be horrible for Martha to watch the fun from her window. He was ruled by Sindy at the best of times. She always had the last word and what she said went. When he'd tried to defend his mother saying she should be able to choose for herself whether she went outside, he'd got into worse books.

His birthday had been sunny and warm, but the evening turned cool and the blanket Sindy had put over Martha's legs wasn't enough to keep her warm. Her arthritis was always more painful in colder weather and sitting out of an evening in the cool air was not to be advised. At eight o'clock she'd got very anxious and kept on asking to go in. Sindy had been quite cruel to her. "If you go in, you'll go to bed." Duncan couldn't believe how easily his mother had given in to the rules Sindy had made.

*

Alice was pleased to see Millie's little car pull into the drive. Hugh knew she was due home today, and when she was later than usual Alice could tell he was getting anxious. She was at the door to greet her. "There you are. Your dad's been looking for you."

Millie was trying to pull a huge case off the back seat. Alice laughed. "Good God girl, you look like you're moving back home."

"I'm bringing some of my things back. I finish Uni in just over three weeks. It seems sensible to do it slowly." Millie puffed at the effort of lugging the case across the drive to where Alice stood.

"Do you want a hand?"

"No, ta. I managed my end. I'm sure I can lug it this short distance."

Alice said she'd put the kettle on to boil. Millie left the case in the hallway and went through to her father. "Hello, dad. Sorry to worry you. I wanted to bring some things home with me. It took longer than I thought. I should have phoned." She kissed his cheek. "Home now though."

Hugh tried to smile but reached out like he liked to do to express his joy at having Millie home. "I was going to go upstairs with Alice and take the second room but think it best if I take over the old dining room. You don't mind, do you dad?"

Hugh shook his head. "I knew you wouldn't. I'm going to ask Duncan if he can make some wardrobes in the alcove and make me some drawers too . We might as well make the lay out of the house improvements work for us all." Millie flopped in the chair opposite. "I've some good news for you." Hugh's eyes were fixed on his daughter. "Dad. I'm coming home. What's more I'm staying home. I've been offered a part-time position in the local library. You know how I always loved books. I love people and talking with them and learning. I'm so excited. I start at the end of June."

Alice came in at that moment with a tray of tea and slices of cake. "Oh, Alice. Lovely. No wonder dad's gaining weight." She smiled at her father as she reached over to pour the tea.

Alice sat with them. "Did I hear you have a job?"

Millie repeated what she'd told her father. Alice looked a little puzzled. "All that studying so you could be a teacher and you end up going for a job that's only part time in a library. My love, you could have come straight out of school and done that."

Millie moved the cake round her mouth so she could answer. "I know, but for now I like being here. Gives me a break from education. That's unless of course another door opens for me."

No more was said about Millie's job and the conversation turned to Peg and Duncan's fight and the move to his mother's house. Alice said to Hugh. "Sorry. You've had to endure all my worries weeks ago and now you're having to sit through them again."

Millie became animated. "Gosh dad. This is like a daily drama you get on the tv."

Alice made a grimace. "It's horrible. I feel responsible in a strange way. I feel if I'd spoken up earlier, I could have prevented it."

"Do we know how his sister is now?"

"No. Nobody seems to know anything, only that she's in Sunnydale's and doesn't wish to see anyone. I'm wondering if they aren't letting her have visitors just yet. Seems strange Peg would isolate herself from the people she loves."

The talk changed to turning the dining room into Millie's living quarters. Alice didn't say anything but was secretly pleased to keep the flat upstairs as her own.

"When you go to Canada in August, I shall be here to keep an eye on things…" She smiled at her father. "And you." She leant over and squeezed his hand gently. "It's all worked out for the best in the end, eh dad?"

Alice left them to it and took the tray through to the kitchen to wash up the things.

Chapter Fifteen

Sindy had been in a foul mood. Duncan put it down to her hormones. Yesterday she had her first period since Charlotte was born. This time of the month was always difficult, not just for her but for all of them. Sindy could be quick tempered at the best of times but when she was on her monthly, everyone walked on eggshells if they knew what was good for them.

Duncan went into the dining room, which had become his mother's bedsit. When he kissed his mother goodbye he said, "watch yourself today, mum, Sindy's on the warpath. It's that time of the month."

Martha whispered, "any news of Peg?"

"No, mum. Nothing. Only we aren't allowed to address her as Peg anymore. Susan's her name."

"Stuff and nonsense. She'll never get better if they try and brainwash her."

"No, mum, I think they are trying to get her to value herself. That name was given to her through mickey taking. I was called Dunk and Dunkie by you and the kids at school. She should have been Sue or Suzie, not Peg because of her leg. I get it, I really do. I just wish I could visit."

"Me too, but that's out of the question now. I don't think I could even climb my own stairs these days, not even with help. The more I stay on one level the lazier I get."

Duncan sat down with his mother. He sensed she was unhappy. "You do like having us here, don't you? You'd say if it was too much."

He was horrified to see his stern, hard skinned mother with the wicked tongue, cry. "Oh, Duncan. I'm grateful, but I feel I've lost my home. I don't have any say in anything, it is getting…"

Without warning the door opened and Sindy walked in. "Shouldn't you be at the Marlows? Breakfast, mum. Here you are."

It was put on the table that fitted under the chair like you get in hospitals. Martha didn't like the look of the cereal coated in sugar. Without thinking she exclaimed. "Frosties! I'm not keen on…"

"Don't start this morning, mum. Charlotte is unsettled today, and the boys are playing up. I'm in no mood for your whining either."

Duncan gave her a sly wink, trying to lift her spirits. He didn't think he'd ever feel sorry for his mum, but of late he saw her in a different light.

*

Millie made her way to the stable. She could see Duncan's bike propped up against the fence. His head was bent over Champagne's back foot and he was picking at it with the hoof pick. She hung over the bottom half of the opened door and said, "hello."

Duncan turned his head. "Hello Stranger."

She laughed. "Not for much longer. I'm coming home. No travelling. I have a job."

Before he could ask what job, Millie asked how Peg was. "We weren't gossiping. Alice is worried about her, and you."

Duncan straightened up, letting go of Champagne's foot. The horse side-stepped and Duncan gave her a handful of horse nuts. "We're all in the dark really. I have to remind myself she is Susan now, not Peg." He told her about the change and Millie agreed that was right. "I told you that when you first told me about her. Don't you remember? I said back then it was cruel."

Duncan ignored the sentiment, saying, "I'm frightened for her. I feel she's locked up and we can't get to her and I don't think she's going to get better because I don't think she wants…" From nowhere tears fell down his face. Millie could see he was embarrassed. He buried his head in Champagne's mane trying to look like he was comforting the horse. She opened the bottom part of the stable door and entered. "It's okay to cry. God, I've done enough of it lately. Still do." When he didn't turn to her, she put her arms around his waist. She was so tiny to his tall frame that her head only lay between his shoulder blades. "Duncan."

He straightened up. Wiped his nose on his hairy arm. It glistened. Millie fished out a clean tissue from her pocket. "Here you are, give it a blow."

"Sorry about that. It's not just Pe… I mean Susan, it's mum, Sindy and me. It's all getting too much."

"I can imagine it is. How's Sindy coping with your mother and the children all under one roof?"

"Sindy's okay. She's taken on the job like a sergeant major. Mum's unhappy, I know she is. She's lost the fight in her. The boys miss their home too. Sindy constantly telling them to be quiet because of nana. It doesn't work and they end up with the wooden spoon. Trouble is I don't believe my mum cares anymore whether the boys are running amok or not. It's all about Sindy. Then there was the fight I caused with Susan's lover boy. I suppose you know about that if you've spoken to Alice?"

Millie nodded but said nothing. She could tell Duncan needed to talk.

"Sindy is punishing me for jeopardising the family and risking being arrested." He blew his nose in the tissue again. "What was I supposed to do? Stand by and watch him walk away after he nearly destroyed my sister. Well, it looks like he has destroyed her. In just a few weeks my life's turned upside down." He looked at Millie and remembered. "Sorry to be me, me, me. I know that your life's been turned upside down and shaken too."

"It's okay. I understand."

"The thing is it's not just me. I'm responsible for the children too. This is all so silly really. We were planning on asking mum if we could buy her council house with the discount she would have accumulated over the years, and in return look after her. Sindy thought it was a way of getting a bigger house for less money and setting P… Susan free in the bargain. Free of her duty to mum."

Millie stroked his bare arm. "That was a lovely thought."

Duncan drew her into him. Holding her tightly. Her head was tucked under his chin. If she closed her eyes, she could believe she was being held by Simon, only he smelt different. "Sue was so happy when I told her. You should have seen her. It was like I'd given her wings to fly. Then that Bastard ruined everything. It honestly makes me shake with anger when I think about him. I could kill him. Do you know that?"

"I don't believe you could really. Not when you think about what you have to lose."

"Maybe not now, but at the time. I was so wild. A red mist came down in front of my eyes and…"

"Yes, Duncan, but that was then. Like you say this is now. You know what you did was wrong, surely? It wasn't your fight. It sounds to me by what Alice was saying, that this Sidney chap is in a bad way…"

"He is, I broke his nose."

"No, I meant emotionally. I think he does love Susan, but he's trapped in his marriage."

"Well I know that feeling." He kissed the top of Millie's head.

She pulled out of his arms. "You don't mean that. You've just had a beautiful little girl and…"

"I know. I know. It's just things are difficult at the moment. I often feel I'd like to just up and go. Travel, like you talked about a few weeks ago."

Millie tried to laugh. Bring a little lightness to this heavy talk. "Was going to travel. Not now. As Alice said, I'm going to be working in a library doing what I could have done straight out of school."

Duncan wouldn't let his feelings drop. "No, Millie. I've been thinking about being free a lot lately. Wanting to see parts of the world," He paused. Trying to find the right way to say what was on his mind. "You know, before all this trouble. Sindy hasn't been supportive…"

Millie interrupted him. "Not supportive. She's upped sticks with her young family and has taken on the care of your mother. Who, if I dare say sounded quite intolerable for Susan if what Alice said was true?"

Duncan tried to get Millie back in his arms, but she resisted. "Hey, Millie, I'm sorry. I didn't mean that. It's just she's taken over mum's house in not a kind way…" He hesitated at Millie's stern expression. "I'm not making myself clear, but I promise you things are difficult for us at home. When I say, 'us' I mean me, the boys and mum."

Millie didn't want an atmosphere. She placed her hands on his bare forearms and rubbed up and down. In a cheerful voice she said, "come on. Chin up. Let's get these horses ready for riding and blow the cobwebs away. I've got some jobs I want you to do for me."

Duncan jumped when Sindy nudged him. "Penny for them. Come on, up you get. Stop staring into space. The boys need a bath. I've been on my feet all day seeing to one thing or another and not forgetting your mum's care too."

Everything Sindy said or did now irritated Duncan. He asked himself if she'd always been this bossy and he'd not noticed until Millie? He stood up as he was told. "Come on, boys. Up the wooden hill. Let's get you in the bath and ready for bed."

"Can we go into see nana first?" Both boys seemed closer to his mother these days. "Just while I run..." Sindy's voice boomed from the kitchen. "No. Nana's had enough of you for one day. Upstairs in that bath and ready for bed."

Duncan put his finger to his lips. He knew he shouldn't go against Sindy, but she was aggravating him on every level. Duncan tapped on his Mother's door and pushed it open. The boys crept in like mice. "Mummy said we couldn't come in, but daddy said we could." Their voices came out in a whisper. Martha whispered back, smiling. "Get the toffee from the bottom of that cabinet. Quickly." Duncan realised what the attraction was now. "I'll run the bath. Send them up sharpish. We've been given orders not to disturb you."

Martha gave both boys a piece of toffee. Then before Duncan could leave, she asked, "any news from the hospital."

Duncan shook his head. "I'll phone later. I must get these two monkeys bathed first."

Before he could leave the room, Sindy appeared. "Thank you very much, Duncan, override my rules. Your mum's had the boys in already today." She pointed at Paul and Jack. "Out, the pair of you, and upstairs before you feel the back of my hand." The pair of them ran past Sindy, giggling up the stairs with their mouths full of toffee.

Duncan was pleased her tone was softer on his mother. "I'll just feed Charlotte and then I'll bring you in a drink before bed."

With the lighter, warmer evenings it was getting harder and harder for Martha to go to bed this early. She didn't mention this to Sindy, she just smiled and said, "okay. Thank you."

Once the door closed, Martha was left on her own with her thoughts. *'It's so true that you don't know anyone until you live with them.'* She also questioned Duncan's backbone. *'Yes, he overrode her rules, but he jumps to her every whim. I could just see his father behaving like that. He wouldn't be bathing the children either after a day at work.'*

Duncan phoned the hospital once the boys were in bed. Sindy was in with his mother. The news was the same. No visitors, but they did say they'd reduced her medication. He asked if she'd received his letters and was told yes. It seemed like a prison to Duncan. He was convinced his sister would be wanting to see him by now.

Duncan popped his head into his mum's room. She was in bed watching Coronation Street. "The hospital say they are reducing Susan's medication. That's a start, mum. Otherwise, no change."

Calling his sister Susan didn't roll off his tongue like Peg had, but he was making a good effort. He knew it was the only way into that hospital once the doors opened to him.

Sindy made two cups of coffee and sat beside him on the sofa. "Sorry if I've been a bit grumpy. My period has been horrible, and your mum's trying, even though she doesn't play me up like she did Peg."

Duncan jumped on the slip of the name. "Susan! Sorry, Sind, but you're gonna have to get that in your head like I am."

Sindy was sulky. "Susan, then." She wasn't going to give over and added to her gripes. "The boys have been full on. Even Charlotte's been fretful today as if she knew I wouldn't have the patience. I sent the boys in with your mum after school. Then when I called them for dinner, they wouldn't eat it. Said they weren't hungry."

Duncan had a feeling he knew why, but kept quiet. He draped his arm round his wife's shoulders. "I try to do my bit. You're good to hold the fort here, but I think it's telling us that when Susan is better, we won't buy this house. We'll go back home."

Sindy twisted round to face Duncan. Her face held an earnest expression. "Let's not be too hasty. I'm just struggling with a stomach ache and my hormones today. Your mum's not too bad really. Not now I've got her into a routine."

Duncan kissed the top of his wife's head. "I don't think mum's happy though."
Sindy's heckles went up. "Why? Did she say that?"

"No. No she didn't. She's grateful, it's just she misses Susan."

"Bossing her around more like. Being spiteful to her. Making her feel like a second-rate…"

"Not now, love. It's past. It's how we go forward that's important."

"I want this house. It's a better size for the kids. The garden too."

"Let's wait and see then." Duncan wanted to say you'll have to start being a bit easier with mum or she won't want to stay with us long term. To keep the peace, he said nothing.

*

126

Alice called out to Duncan that she'd made coffee. Forecast was rain. They'd had a long spell of sunshine, but June had brought rain. This was so often the case.

She placed Duncan's coffee on the kitchen table. It would be nicer to have it inside today.

Alice picked up the newspaper. She'd looked at the headlines with Hugh earlier. They were full of the forthcoming Royal Wedding. She'd told Hugh how she'd ordered a cup and saucer with the couple's photograph on as a souvenir. He'd smiled crookedly. *'Probably thought I'm a sentimental old fool.'*

She sighed at Lady Diana's lovely young smile and the downcast shy look. Alice guessed seeing such happiness between a pair wouldn't be helping Duncan's sister too much. This was news you couldn't escape. The television, radio, magazines, and papers were full of the young couple. Lady Diana really was an attractive young woman, with a warm look about her. Alice herself couldn't help feeling excited at the romance.

Duncan tapped the door before he pushed it open. "In here today?"

"Yes, come and sit down. How's Susan?" Alice had readjusted to the change easily. It was the young woman's name after all.

"She's okay I believe. They've reduced her medication and they say she's holding her own. We haven't visited yet."

"What about your mother? Is she coping without Susan?"

Duncan unburdened himself with his wife's bossiness. "Honestly, Alice, it's like she's punishing mum for being such a moaner to Susan. I actually feel sorry for my mum. If Sindy doesn't ease up a bit with her strict rules and regulations, mum's going to ask us to leave. She has to go to bed at eight thirty now. Eight thirty! That's horrible at the moment when it's still light outside. Last night

127

Charlotte was fretful and Sindy got up to give her a bottle at three in the morning. Mum called out when she heard Sindy in the kitchen. She needed the commode. You should have heard Sindy. She didn't do it willingly. No, she huffed and puffed about it. Then to top it all she left mum on the commode for twenty minutes while she fed Charlotte, changed, and settled her. I couldn't help but feel that was cruel. I told Sindy I would see to Charlotte, but she wouldn't have any of it. Then Mum tried to get herself back to bed and Sindy found her on the floor. Lucky she wasn't hurt."

"Oh, dear. This isn't good. What about the boys. Do they like having their nana living with them, or I should say living with their nana?"

Duncan took a bit of the fruit cake Alice had put out on the table. "They aren't allowed in mum's room until Sindy starts dishing up the dinner. They get about ten minutes. Talking like this, I know the arrangement isn't working. I'd put mum into temporary care, until Susan's better, but Sindy's set on having the house. She likes the space and the potential it has to offer. Our newbuild is poky in comparison."

"I knew of your mother at school. She was younger than me. It was your father and I that were in the same class. Did you know that?"

"No. Alice I didn't." Duncan gave Alice a hopeful look. "Would you like to visit mum? She could do with some company. The only other person she sees apart from us is the Avon lady."

Alice smiled. "I don't know that I'd like to, but I will. I had more to do with Dickie, your dad, that was until I left school and went my own way."

"Party animal you were, Alice."

She laughed. "Not quite, but I told you before I liked my freedom."

"I would be grateful if you could just pop in for a coffee." Duncan smiled but Alice didn't miss the sigh before he said. "Even mum's morning coffee and afternoon tea is restricted to a set time. Let's hope Sindy makes you welcome and brings in a tray of something if it's outside the schedule."

"Do you know what, Duncan? If she doesn't. I shall go in the kitchen and make it for us myself."

Alice was pleased to hear him laugh before he added, "that's the spirit. I'll warn her though that you are planning a visit. When do you think it's likely to be?"

Alice looked at her watch. "I'm pretty tied up here at the moment. I tend to spend my days with Hugh, not needing to leave the house much." Alice got up and got the homecare rota down. She ran a pencil over the times and dates. "I tell you what, I shall get Jackie to cover for me Friday. That gives me the week to sort it, and also ease Hugh into the change. I'll need to take the afternoon off. I'm not walking." Alice thought about the bus times. Then said, "I'll leave it with you to let Sindy know I shall be calling on Friday – and tell your mum too."

"Thanks Alice. You're a good sort you are. Mum will be dead made up with it. I know she will."

Alice stood up and started to clear away. She needed to start Hugh's lunch. She cooked midday so supper was always a light affair. "I'm not a magician, love, but I'll do my best to cheer your mum up a bit for you."

Friday 5th June

The Visit

Alice shook her umbrella at the door and was greeted by an over excited Jackie. Not only young but such an airhead. Her voice came out fast, "Hugh wouldn't eat his lunch. I've only just managed to get him to have a cup of…"

Alice took off her mac and hung it on the peg behind the door. She felt like the lady of the house these days. "Don't you go worrying yourself, love. Is he still breathing?"

"Yes, but…"

Alice sat down feeling quite exhausted from her journey to Martha's and the emotional drain she'd found there. The last thing she needed was hysterics in what she thought of as her own home. "Love. Hugh is behaving like a spoiled child. He didn't want me to go off this afternoon. It has nothing to do with you. I bet it's just that he's got used to my always being here. I've spent the last seven months at his beck and call and he didn't want things to change. He probably felt vulnerable. You get yourself off now. I'll manage him."

Jackie was off like a shot. Alice made herself a cuppa and walked through to the lounge. "Hello. I hear you've not been in the best of moods. Lunch not to your liking?"

Alice could have sworn Hugh smiled. Her voice took on an air of indignancy. "Yes, you might smirk at me. Poor girl was having kittens just a few minutes ago. She thought I'd be cross with her. I'm not. I'm cross with you."

Hugh raised his eyebrows. Alice sat opposite him. Grateful that the gas fire was on. June had brought damp cold weather and Alice had got wet standing waiting for the bus. "Let me tell you." Alice actually prodded Hugh gently in the arm. "I have not had to

130

kowtow to anyone and I'm too old to start now. I'm off to Canada in August. You won't be able to refuse lunch for two weeks then, will you?" She sat back in her chair and pushed her damp hair back. "This ridiculous behaviour has made me see how settled we have become in each other's company. From today I shall be going out every week, and on my days off someone from the agency will look after you."

Hugh just stared at her. Eyes wide as if he were trying to express himself. Alice had no idea if it was shock, or he was sorry. "It's not just your fault. I've been enjoying the luxury of the flat upstairs, the lovely setting here and the company." Alice's voice had calmed. "I think it's wise though, don't you? It's not good to become too dependent on people." She laughed then. "Especially not a free spirit like me. Don't forget, Hugh. I'm fifty-eight and no one has tied me down yet..." She sipped at her tea. Reached for Hugh's hand. "Now I'm going into the kitchen to write a letter. Something I don't normally do. Interfere, that is. But I feel on this occasion it is necessary." Alice got down on her knees and looked in the cabinet. "Here you are. I'll put on the film Millie recorded for you. Rocky. I can't believe you like this mindless punching. Still, it will give you something to watch."

Alice fiddled a while with the control button. This was a newfangled thing in technology she was still trying to get used to. She had mastered recording BBC while watching ITV, so she was getting there.

Alice went upstairs before returning to the kitchen. She wanted to use her special writing set and Parker fountain pen. She poured herself a glass of water and sat at the table. *'Where do I start?'*

Dear Susan.

I am so sorry, love, to hear you are struggling. Here I am calling you love, and you probably don't really know who I am.

I'm Alice. I went to school with your father. I hear about you from Duncan.
He works for the Marlows like I do. Only I live there.

I don't want to waffle with nonsense. I want to tell you I paid a visit to your
mother today. I know life wasn't easy for you, caring for her. She was bitter
and crotchety. Her disability made her worse. I'm not excusing her. It was
common knowledge in the village she was leading you a dog's life.

I'm going to start at the beginning, Susan. I hope you don't mind me calling
you that, but it's how your mother spoke of you today. I'm going to start by
telling you about your roots.

I went to school with your father. Dickie. All the girls liked him, even back
then. We lived three doors away from each other in the village you were born
and live in today. Your mother as a child lived in the next village nearer the
school. I don't think Dickie took much notice of her back then. She probably
seemed a child to the girls he could have.

Today, I listened to your mother telling me how unhappy she is. You could say
self-pity, but there is more to it.

I'm sure from their letters you know that Sindy and Duncan have moved in to
live with her. It isn't the children that are causing her grief. It is Sindy. I can
imagine you are shocked by that, but I saw it with my own eyes. I know,
Susan, if you had been at home today when I called the first thing you would
have done is make us a pot of tea. Not Sindy. I had to ask. Your mother was
too frightened to. Sindy huffed saying, 'Martha has a weak bladder. I am
getting her into a routine.' All the things your mother told me today about her
strict routine and how she has to be in bed at eight thirty with no nonsense, I
just knew were true. I could tell you more unsettling things she's enduring, but
you are such a lovely natured young woman I couldn't stand you to worry over
her. You need to heal. Your mother is a strong character and will cope. She is
already making plans, and with my help hopefully they will come to fruition.

Your mother told me today she wishes she could tell you how much she loved
you. Not just now but always. Right back to when you were born. She wanted
to say sorry for how she led you to believe that your father's extra marital

132

affairs and absences from the family home were your fault, because of his disappointment in your disability. That was a lie. She admitted to me today that it hid her own poor self-worth and shame at her husband's infidelity. She cried when she told me this. The truth is Susan, your father was having affairs before you were even born. I know that to be a fact because I witnessed it with my own eyes. He was a womaniser through and through. It had nothing to do with you.

This Sidney business. It's a sorry state of affairs. I had heard on the grapevine through my nephew about the silly, cruel prank. I wish I had spoken up before, but it isn't my way. I don't like writing all this gossip to you either. I'm only doing it because your mother wanted to say so many things to you in her letter, but she couldn't because Sindy was doing the writing. Your mother is vulnerable in her own home. That is a shame.

What I do want you to hear, because I believe it to be true, is that Sidney did ask you out for a dare. The lads had been teasing him by all accounts for weeks that he was full of wolf whistles and no guts for the real thing. They gave him you as a challenge. My nephew said what started out as a joke, backfired on him. He fell in love with you. He was taken by you from the first date and over the weeks you grew on him. He didn't want to go home and did everything in his power to stay on the site even when his work was finished.

Your brother gave him a hiding of a lifetime in your defence. Sidney didn't defend himself and even when pushed he refused to press charges. Duncan was a lucky lad. Sidney was hospitalised like you. You were in hospital at the same time. Just a different ward. Losing a loved one hurts, but we heal. I know you will be thinking everyone will be talking about you, laughing. They are not. Of that I promise. You, poor love, have had a lifetime of being the butt of people's cruelty and I understand your fear of seeing anyone at the moment in your frail state.

Believe me, Susan. Your mother is so sorry for what she has said to you in the past. How she's made you feel. She wants you to come home. Not to look after her but to take over the house. Your mother has asked me to look at the new nursing home that has been built. This is to accommodate her own needs.

What is worrying her is that if she goes into a care environment you won't have your family home to come back to, but she knows life with Sindy is not an option she relishes and doesn't know how much more she can take of it. I know this will probably feel all too late for you, but I don't believe it is ever too late to be sorry or too late to tell people we love them. Your mother loves you, Susan. I wish her poor hands could have written this to you, but you will understand it was not possible.

I look forward to hearing from Duncan that you are feeling better. Take time to gather your thoughts. Let yesterday go and think of tomorrow. God bless you.

Alice. x

Monday 8ᵗʰ June 1981

Susan was waiting for Jolene to arrive so they could go into the quiet room as it was called. She had the letter in her hand, which she had read over and over again. So much of it bothered her.

So lost in thought was she that when Jolene called out, "there you are," it made Susan jump. Jolene stood in front of her wearing another of her flamboyant, and if Susan had been judgemental would have said ridiculous, outfits. It was like she got up of a morning and put the most awful combination of colours and items together that she could find. Susan wished she had the nerve to be like that. She had spent her life trying to be inconspicuous. Not noticed. Anything to avoid ridicule.

Susan liked Jolene a lot though. Her personality was peaceful somehow, despite her big wide smiles and uplifting voice. "Let's go, shall we?"

As soon as they were sitting opposite each other Susan said, "I have a letter from a friend of my mother's. She has written a letter for her because she couldn't possibly do it herself, her hands are so bad."

"Is it good news?"

"No. Mum is unhappy. It seems…" Susan faltered and handed over the letter to Jolene. "You read it. What do you think?" She watched Jolene read the pages. Not a sign of shock or emotion anywhere. Susan supposed it was easier for her, as it wasn't her family. Eventually Jolene looked up from the pages and Susan asked, "what do you think? Can you do anything to help?"

"How? What could I do to help this situation?"

"I don't know. It just makes me…" Susan stopped midsentence. After a while Jolene said, "makes you what, Susan?"

Susan put her head in her hands and repeated. "I don't know… I don't know. I just know it makes me feel bad. That's it, that's the feeling, bad."

Jolene sat forward so she was closer to Susan, who was still holding her face in her hands. "Bad?"

"Yes. Horrible in my stomach. Guilty I suppose. I feel I should be at home with her. I know she's difficult, and there were times when I hated her." Susan stopped, shocked at what she had just said. "Well, perhaps not hated…" She tried to find a kinder word. "Resentful. Does that sound better?"

Jolene said quite calmly, "it doesn't matter what it sounds like, it's how you felt or feel that is important. We can't help how we feel. Hate is a strong word. What do you feel towards your mother now?"

Susan looked up. Tears shone in her eyes. "I don't know…."
Jolene let the question hang. The silence had Susan searching for

an answer. She eventually said. "Worried? I feel worried. Not just for mum, but for them all. I don't like to think Sindy is being so horrible to mum, I don't like to think she is hitting the boys and I don't like to think of my brother being bossed about."

Jolene waited a moment. She was letting her absorb the things that she said had worried her. When Susan remained silent, Jolene said, "what about Sidney?"

The tears that had shone in Susan's eyes spilled over. She put her hands over her face. "I can't think about Sidney. It is too painful."

"Would you like to see your family now?"

Susan looked up. "I think I would. Just my brother. No one else."

"Yet it is your mother's letter that has unsettled you."

"I know... but I feel I need to speak to Duncan. He will tell me what's going on. I'll show him the letter. He knows this Alice that has written to me."

"Do you not know Alice?"

"I know of her. She lived in the village. Duncan had talked about her too." Susan was pleased of the change in their conversation. Talking about Sidney was still too raw.

Jolene clasped her hands together and relaxed back in her chair. This was a sign Susan recognised that the meeting was going to close. "We've done some good work this morning, Susan. When your brother phones today he will be told he can visit. You are happy with that..." She looked at Susan for confirmation, when none came, she said with a curious tone, "yes?"

Susan nodded. Almost instantly a ripple of nervous excitement settled in her stomach. "I feel scared already. Silly I know."

"Not silly at all. Perfectly normal."

"It will be good to see a familiar face from home and one I know won't be mocking me in any way."

Jolene always gave Susan a goal before their next meeting. Today she said, "I want you to read the letter again, more than once if you can't find an answer. I want you to tell me why, when it is a heartfelt letter supposedly from your mother, that it is Duncan you wish to see."

Susan stood up. She knew the session was over.

*

Duncan couldn't wait to tell Alice the news. He arrived early at the house and went straight to the back door and banged on it. Alice appeared. "For goodness sake, what's the trouble?"

His face was flushed, and he looked happy. "Sue's agreed to see me. I'm going this afternoon at four. I know it's because you wrote to her. I bet you said all the right things." Duncan had shortened Susan's name to Sue, and it rolled off his tongue easily as if she'd always been called that.

Alice felt goose pimples go up her arms. "I'm pleased, Duncan. Really pleased. We'll talk about it at coffee time. We're in the middle of getting Hugh up at the moment."

Duncan had a real skip to his step as he made his way to the stables. He wouldn't ride today. He'd do the necessaries and put them in the paddock. He missed Millie's company more than he would care to admit. Riding was boring without her beside him and it didn't matter how many times he told himself these thoughts were unhealthy, it didn't stop them feeling intoxicating. Once he'd finished up here, he would go inside and hang the doors on Millie's wardrobes. The time would fly, and he didn't want to arrive late at the hospital.

Over coffee, Alice seemed pleased that his sister wanted to see him. Duncan was shocked to hear Alice had written to Sue about the fight. He hadn't realised that she had put that in the letter. His first response was annoyance and it showed. Alice held her ground. "I told Sue the whole sorry tale. What your mother wanted her to know. It might upset Sue initially, but it will show her that you care." Duncan wanted to say his sister had always known he cared but thought better of it. It didn't lift his mood when Alice said, "the lawns need cutting. Can you do them this morning?"

Duncan resisted. "I can do them tomorrow. I really wanted to get the doors on Millie's wardrobes. She asked me…"

Alice took his mug from him a little too sharply. "No, the weather's nice today. It's grown like billy-o'. Millie won't be home properly for another two weeks. The lawn is more pressing."

Duncan had no choice. He knew Alice was the main voice around here when Millie was away.

He filled the mower with petrol and before long was walking up and down the grounds lost in thought. He switched from worrying his sister might only want to see him because she was angry at him, to thoughts of Millie. As he walked, nice straight lines appeared in the cut lawn. This weekend he'd not seen too much of her, but he hung onto the fact two weeks ago Millie had put her arms around his waist, and he'd kissed her head. It was a simple, fleeting action, but it made him feel good inside. The more he pushed the mower up and down, the angrier he got with Alice. *I could have done this tomorrow. Millie'll be home for good on June twenty-forth. I can't wait. I want to surprise her with the finished job, but with Alice putting her oar in I can't do them.'*

He was being unfair, and he knew it. Alice was a good sort. Her visit had certainly lifted his mum's spirits. It was his infatuation for Millie that was making him irrational. He knew it was dangerous, but it made him feel good. Excited. Young. So, he convinced himself over and over that the thoughts he was having for Millie were harmless.

Duncan went home for lunch at one o'clock. He had to cycle to North Mundham this afternoon. He still worked for Mr and Mrs Bradley in the summer months and their garden would need mowing and a bit of a tidy up. There would be no time for wardrobes today. He would visit Sue and pop back to the Marlow's in the car to settle the horses for the evening.

*

Duncan walked up the long drive to Sunnydale's. He never in a million years thought he'd ever come visiting here. Least of all a member of his family.

He pushed the buzzer on the door and a voice spoke to him through an intercom. *'Jesus, it really is like a prison.'*

"Duncan James to see my sister Susan. I have an appointment at four."

The door clicked open and Duncan went inside. A lady in a pale blue uniform approached him. "Can you sign in the book please, that one there and I'll get one of the staff to show you the way."

A young man appeared. He guessed not much older than himself. He wasn't wearing the uniform. He was dressed in plain beige trousers and a t-shirt. Duncan could have mistaken him for an inmate, but the name badge displayed on his breast told him he was a worker here.

Duncan saw his sister before she saw him. She was sitting on a bench in the grounds. She'd allowed her hair to grow a bit longer since Sidney and today it hung loosely on her shoulders in waves. "Sue?" She turned and stood up."

139

"Oh, Sue. Come here. Let me hold you."

She went into his arms. When she pulled away her first words were, "You don't have to call me Sue. Peg will do."

"No. your name's Susan. This place is right. It should have never been allowed to continue. Even Millie said it was mean when I first told her about us all."

"Millie? Millie as in the daughter of the man you work for?"

"Yes, but Millie's in charge. She organises everything."

Susan sat back on the bench and Duncan followed. "how's things at home?"

Duncan laughed, "bloody awful." When Susan didn't join in with his amusement, he looked remorseful. "Sorry. I shouldn't have said that. It's just the place and things aren't the same without you."

"How's Sindy coping with Mum?"

There were no lies. Duncan told her how things were. Susan listened intently but didn't comment. "I miss you, Sue. We all do. Please get well so you can come home. It's like getting past the gestapo visiting you here."

"I like it. I feel safe. The people are…"

"Bloody loonies. Come on, Sue, you don't belong here. You know that."

"Duncan. No one is mad here. Struggling with society, yes, but that's all. They are like me, human. What I'm finding out is that they're a lot nicer in here than the people I've met on the outside."

"You don't mean that, surely?"

"Yes, I do. I'm happy here."

"Happy?"

"Happy as I can be. Which brings me to Sidney."

"Sue…" Duncan knew he had to be careful. His sister had an air about her that was different. She didn't seem as subservient as she had always been. "Is this going to be about the fight?" Before she could answer, he said, "I'm sorry. I was frightened something might happen to you, and I couldn't let him just walk away. I wouldn't have been able to live with myself. I fought many battles for you at school, don't you remember?" He'd talked fast saying all the things he knew he had to say when this subject came up. "He's okay, though. He's gone home."

"Don't."

Duncan tried to reach for her hand, but she pulled it away and it dropped and rested on her thigh. "I haven't come here to upset you. Honest. You ask the questions and I'll answer. I'm just so happy to see you, that's all."

"Alice says mum's wanting to go into a nursing home. Is that true?"

This was news to Duncan. He knew his mother was struggling but didn't know she felt that strongly. "I…" He faltered on his words. "I don't know, Sue. She hasn't said that to me. Sindy is a bit of a disciplinarian but I didn't think it was that bad."

"You said Sindy wanted the house. Is it working for you?"

Duncan sighed. "I came here to talk about you and how you are feeling. Not the other way around."

She turned to him. Took his hand off her thigh and held it. "I am fine in here. I have no urge to go out in the outside world ever again." Their eyes met and she said, "there I've said it. I'll have to leave one day I know I will, but the thought terrifies me…"

"That's because you aren't well yet, but you will be."

"Duncan let me speak."

"I'm sorry."

"I know and you know mum was difficult for me, but she doesn't deserve to be treated like a child. Her arthritis is getting worse. Getting her upstairs of an evening had become a struggle. How she pulled herself up there to find me, I'll never know."

"Good job she did, or we wouldn't have found you in time."

"I wish she hadn't."

"You don't mean that."

"Don't I? How do you know how I feel? Outside of these walls there is nothing for me. Nothing. Collecting smelly eggs from hens. I'm laughed at because I wear a boot a little larger than my other foot. My lot in life is looking after a mother who can't find two kind words for me…"

Duncan interrupted. He didn't want to hear Sidney's name on his sister's lips. He took hold of her hand again. "I love you, Sue."

Her voice softened. "I know you do. I love you and the children. Sindy too. She's always been kind to me. I love mum as well. I didn't think I did, but in here and reading her letter, I sort of understand how this all came about." Susan took a deep breath, "I ask you again. Do you want to live in mum's house still?"

Duncan dropped his head. He felt weak coming here unburdening himself. "I don't know what I want these days. I love Sindy, but… I don't know. I think things were better when we were in our own home without mum." He paused before adding. "That isn't to say you must come home and look after her. If Alice wrote that mum's wanting to go into some sort of care, then it will be true. Alice is a stickler for the truth."

"Can you go now, Duncan. Please. I've had enough."

"What does that mean?"

"It means I'm tired."

He didn't recognise this side to his sister. "Have I said something wrong?"

"No. On the contrary. Thank you for coming."

"Sue?"

"Goodbye, Duncan." She stood up and for the first time that afternoon he noticed her boot. Not hidden under long skirts or flared trousers but on full view in a mid-length skirt that was all the fashion.

"I'd like to see mum. Can this Alice get her here? I'm guessing she'll need a wheelchair. Jolene said that can be organised through social services. Could you do that for me?"

"I'll bring her."

"No, Duncan. It will be better if Alice does it. Will she?"

"I know she will if she can."

Duncan had no choice but to walk with his sister back inside the walls of the hospital. He kissed her cheek and hugged her. This hadn't been the visit he'd envisaged.

*

Alice was getting the washing in when Duncan pulled up in his car. He tooted at her and Champagne and Truffle neighed loudly and started cantering round the paddock. Alice laughed. "Someone knows it's bedtime."
"Feed time more like."

"How was Susan?"

"I shall come across once I've finished here. I could murder a cuppa too."

Alice was waiting for him when he appeared sometime later. "Let me re-boil the kettle. Tea or coffee?"

"I'll have coffee."

Duncan told Alice about his visit. The change in his sister, and how she wanted Alice to visit with his mother. Alice was adamant. She said, 'sorry but no.' Adding it would be too much of a responsibility. She was happy to do a bit of shopping for her and visit but that was it.

Alice gave Duncan a few leaflets. "Here you go, love. For your mum. There are always flyers like this at the office. Jackie picked them up for me. She said if she fancies Selsey there's a few out that way too." Duncan looked at the top leaflet that displayed a smiling elderly lady being given a cup of something with a slice of cake. Another one had a gentleman smiling in his wheelchair being helped by a young girl to throw a bright green bowling ball. He lay them back down on the table. "How can life tip upside down like this so quickly?"

"You're lucky, lad, you're not being charged for GBH."

"Let it drop, Alice, please. I get it in the neck at home every time Sindy thinks about it."

"I'm not..."

Duncan interrupted her. "I shall get the horses done early tomorrow, then make a start on finishing the wardrobes in Millie's room."

Alice moved over to the sink. "There really is no hurry. I told you earlier Millie isn't coming home for another two weeks. Twenty fourth June. She's swotting for her finals and getting her work ready to submit."

Duncan hadn't taken this in earlier. He'd been too annoyed at having to mow the lawns. His face showed his disappointment. "How do you know?"

"She phones her father. He can't speak so I'm the messenger. I'm getting good at it. I did it for your mum, didn't I?"

Duncan scowled but said nothing.

"Take that look off your face. You look like a child whose just had his sweets snatched out of his hand."

"I was hoping she'd be home this weekend."

"I think you are a bit too fond of Millie's company, young man. I might be an old spinster in your eyes, but I recognise the signs."

Duncan could feel his cheeks grow warm. This was alien for him. He didn't know what to say or where to look. He opted to fiddle with his shoelace trying to hide his glowing cheeks. "I don't know what signs you're referring to, Alice. I like riding. She's good company." He knew his face was still of high colour when he stood up. He guessed it was more apparent with his fair hair and skin.

Alice tapped her nose before warning him. "I'm not one to poke my nose in, love. You know that. But I'll just say one word. Dangerous. You just remember the treasure you have inside your own four walls."

Duncan picked the leaflets off the table and left without commenting.

*

Sindy had got the boys and Martha to bed when Duncan finally got in. He had walked along the canal and stood on the edge and thrown little bits of gravel into the water. The ducks were going crazy thinking he was feeding them with bread. Feeling mean, he'd left telling them 'I'll bring the boys at the weekend and feed you properly.' If Millie wasn't coming home, there was nothing apart from the horses to take him to the Marlow's. He didn't at this present moment feel kindly towards Alice. As he walked back to his car he thought *'don't like to poke your nose in... that's all you've done recently.'* He was being unfair, and he knew it. It was just Alice had been a bit too near the truth for comfort.

Sindy picked the leaflets up. "What's all this?" Before she had chance to sit and read for herself, Duncan told her, "they are homes for mum."

Sindy voice rose with indignance. "What? What's that supposed to mean?"

Duncan felt fed up and depressed. There seemed to be so much going on in his world at the moment that bothered him. He was annoyed at Alice's interference, disappointed to hear Millie wasn't coming home for two weeks and to top it all his visit to his sister had been disappointing. He spoke harshly to Sindy, hoping to make her feel as bad as himself. "It means mum doesn't like being treated like a frigging invalid or a child. This is her house, and your ridiculous rules and bossy behaviour is..."

"Is that what she's been saying? Bossy..."

"Shut up. She'll hear you."

Sindy was up out of the chair. "Hear me. She is going to have to explain herself."
"There you go again. You don't know you do it, do you? Alice said she didn't get a cup of tea and you openly said mum has a weak bladder. That's personal, Sindy. Mum doesn't want people hearing things like that. If we hadn't been here Alice would have gone in the kitchen and made tea for them both and if mum's weak

bladder were a problem, she would either have hauled herself upstairs or gone on the commode."

"Finished?"

Duncan flopped in the chair. "You're being unreasonable. I can see it and so can other people."

"Other people. You mean the precious Alice. If she weren't the age she is I would have thought I had something to worry about with the time you spend at the Marlows these days."

"It's my job, Sindy. It's what puts food on the table AND is going to buy this house if you get your way."

The rowing went on and on. Charlotte slept through the raised voices, but Jack appeared teary-eyed. "Please be nice to daddy, mummy."

Without even a cuddle she demanded he go back to bed at once. It was Duncan who followed him upstairs. "Hey, soldier. Daddy's okay. Mummy and daddy are just clearing the air."

Duncan settled the boys best he could and popped his head into his mum's room. "Alright, mum? Sorry about all this. I will be in to tell you about Sue later, but…" Before Duncan could finish, the door opened and Sindy stood face flushed and eyes flashing. "That's it! Come in here and talk about me to your mother."

The air turned blue as things were said in anger. Both Martha and Sindy were in tears. Sindy left them together, slamming the door behind her as she went.

Duncan tried to comfort Martha best he could. "Do you know what, mum? Sue's doing better than we are."
He was pleased to see she managed a smile. "She wants to see you. She was hoping Alice would take you, but that isn't going to be possible. I did ask her, but she isn't comfortable with it." Not wanting to make Martha feel a nuisance he added, "Alice is really

busy with Hugh these days. Don't worry though, mum, I'll see what I can organise." He leant over and kissed Martha's cheek. "I better go and sort things out with Sindy. Don't go troubling yourself about us either. It will sort."

The rowing continued and all the while Sindy was gathering bits and throwing them into shopping bags. Duncan tried to stop her leaving but she was hell bent on going. "I'm taking the kids home. I know where my efforts are wasted. You can see to your precious mother."

The boys, still in their pyjamas, sat in the back of the car. They were crying but not hysterically like earlier. "Sindy this is bloody silly. Let's sort this…"

"No, Duncan. You sort it out. I'm going home. I've had enough." He watched her put Charlotte's carrycot in the hatch-back, slam the door shut and drive off. He dragged his hand through his hair. *'How has it come to this?'*

Martha was adamant that she could be left alone. "Go to your family. I used to stay here on my own until gone ten thirty some nights waiting for your sister to come in. I shall manage. Go and sort out your marriage. I couldn't bear it if I caused the two of you to break up."

"If you're sure you'll be okay."

"Of course, I will. Go!"

"I'll pop in in the morning, early. I'm quite capable of getting you a bowl of warm water to wash in and help you get dressed. I can even manage cereal in a bowl."

"Go, lad. Go on. Stop worrying about me. Lock the door. I'll be fine."

Wednesday 10th June 1981

Sindy had driven Paul to school and dropped Jack off at playschool. She unlocked the door to number ninety-nine and called out to Martha. "It's only me." She opened the dining room door and there was her mother-in-law sitting in her chair washed dressed and an empty cereal bowl and cup and saucer beside her. "Duncan said he was going to help you up today."

Martha apologised before Sindy could say anymore. "No, Mum. I'm sorry. I got so wrapped up in what I wanted, I forgot about your needs."

Sindy gave Martha the baby. This was something she hadn't done since they had moved in. "Have a cuddle while I put the hot water on to make her a bottle."

Martha was pleased when Sindy came back. Charlotte was just starting to get restless. "She's getting heavy isn't she."

Sindy laughed. "Mum she's nearly four months old. She is starting to roll. She's earlier than the boys were."

While Sindy fed Charlotte, she apologised again and was brutally honest with her mother-in-law. She told her she had made her mind up that if she was going to live here at number ninety-nine, she didn't want to be treated the same way Susan was. So, felt she had to make a stand. Put some rules down. Sindy looked sheepish. "I went over the top. I'm so sorry about being unkind too. The way I treated you the other night when you wanted the loo is unforgivable. It was cruel of me, mum, and I feel terrible. I'm just so embarrassed you told your friend about me."

Martha clapped her crooked hands together at the baby. "Your mum's blowing it all out of proportion, isn't she?"

149

"Oh, mum, I can't bear to think of you going in to a nursing home because of me."

"Now listen to me, girl. I have been unhappy. Not just because of you. I felt you were a good punishment…"

Sindy half laughed. "Well thank you."

"No, I didn't mean it like that. I'd not been fair with Susan, and then when I nearly lost her, I realised just how horrid I'd been. I'm ashamed of myself too. Going in a…" Sindy went to speak but Martha said, "no, let me explain. I think what I would have liked to do is go in a warden assisted place, but I realise that my hands and mobility are getting worse. I don't know if the shock of what's happened recently has accelerated it, or it was always going to be like this. I just know that I need help. I like the idea of company. Bingo afternoons, quiz mornings, having my hair done by the hairdresser. I know it isn't for everyone, but for me, I want to try. I don't want to be a burden on anyone. The house is yours. I'm worried for Susan though. What will she do if you let your house go and buy this?"

"Mum don't be hasty. Let's see how we get on now we understand each other a bit better… Please?"

"It doesn't change the worry of Susan. She will need a home and we are going to be a little overcrowded here."

"Let me show you the plans I drew up. The extensions I want?"

Martha looked at the small bathroom she would have attached to her room. The lay out was impressive and she couldn't lie that a little ripple of excitement went through her at the prospect. It didn't ease Martha's worries for her daughter. She would need a home. "There's still no room for Susan. What will she do?"

Sindy being ever practical. "If she wanted to come here, we would fit her in somehow. It's doable. Being realistic, I don't think she'll

150

want too though. Don't you remember the time she thought she might like to leave for Scotland of all places? Be a companion."

"No! I don't. Did she really? Where did that notion come from?"

Sindy laughed. The tension eased between the two. "The Lady magazine. I can't see her disappearing that far now. She was only in her twenties back then."

Martha sighed. "My poor, poor, girl. Always sacrificing her own happiness for others. She's had a life of it. Sadly, I haven't helped. I hope she lets me make it up to her. By what Duncan was saying this morning, she seems to like it in the hospital. Doesn't want to come out." Martha felt tearful and Sindy touched her arm. The first sign of kindness she'd shown her mother-in-law in just under four weeks. Adopting Duncan's usage of Susan's shortened name she said, "Sue will come out. You will get your chance. Duncan said she wants to see you. I could take you."

"No, love. The more I think about it I know it will be too much for me. My body is too frail. I shall talk to Susan on the telephone. It'll be okay now you and I have cleared the air."

"Oh, mum. You could have spoken to Sue anytime you wanted to. What did you think I was going to do?"

"Earwig at my complaints." They both laughed. Charlotte too. "Look at the baby, mum. Isn't she precious?"

"More than."

*

Duncan felt happier this morning than he had done for weeks. He'd sorted things out with Sindy, and she had promised she'd go to Martha's later and eat humble pie. Duncan had already been to his mother's, he'd gone over early and helped her to wash and dress herself. He had and given her tea in a cup and saucer and All bran with sugar, just how she liked it. When she'd finished her breakfast, she seemed happier than she had done for weeks too. *What was I thinking of? Mooning over Millie in that way. God! Alice was right. Dangerous. Bloody idiotic too.'* He'd made up with Sindy in the early hours of the morning. As they cuddled into each to other, kisses turned to cuddles and cuddles deepened to foreplay. For the first time since Charlotte was born, they made love.

When Alice gave him a mug of coffee at ten, she asked if he was coming in to finish the wardrobes. "No, I'm going to find someone who wants to work here at the stables at the weekend. Do you think that will be okay?"

"What's this then?"

"Alice you were right in many ways. I'd forgotten about my family. It was all about money. I haven't had a day off since Mrs Marlow died. I'm here every day feeding and stabling these horses. It's only a couple hours but it means we can't go off and do family things." He told Alice about the row. How his mum is happier but still feels she'd be better off in care. "You were right about Millie too. Not that there was anything going on. I just forgot myself, and my responsibilities for a while."

Alice smiled. "I know, love. I know. I was worried you were going to risk losing the trust of your good lady for a whim."

"Whim?"

"Yes, if you can't see Millie's heart is with that lad that's about to marry her friend then you're blind. You don't want to be someone's stop gap, surely? You have so much to lose."

Duncan looked down at his shoes. He felt foolish. "I don't know Alice. It felt good for a while. I felt young again."

Alice took his empty mug. "Who are you going to ask to cover for you?"

"I don't know yet. Probably try at the Dimbles. The stables on the top road. I'm sure there is someone there who would love to cover the weekends for me in return for a bit of pocket money and a free ride. Do you think Hugh, Mr Marlow will mind?"

"No. I'm sure not. I don't think you should allow rides though. Let Millie decide that one."

"Do you think I should speak to Millie first?"

No, let's not bother Millie. I'll speak to Hugh. He'll give an indication if he's okay with it. I can't see there being a problem. You need time off and as long as the horses are sorted what difference will it make."

Duncan visited the Dimbles stables on his way home, and they'd allowed him to leave a card asking for weekend help.

Sunday 14th June 1981

Duncan had had no response to the advert at the stables, so set off earlier than usual to sort the horses out. They were going as a family to the park for a picnic. The early sun promised a warm day.

Duncan didn't bother Alice. He guessed she'd be doing the old man's breakfast.

He'd noticed for the past few days Champagne had a bit of a cough but today she seemed more restless than usual. The horses breathing seemed laboured, and the cough had turned quite husky. Duncan was concerned. "Come on girl, what's up?" She pushed at him with her head and left mucus on his arm. Duncan didn't like the look of her. "Steady on, girl." He stroked her side and down her rump. "Let's get you some fresh water." He offered her a handful of hay which she would normally take immediately. Today she raised her head in defiance. He left her in the stable while he saw to Millie's horse and got her in the paddock.

He made his way back to Champagne and could hear the cough before he got there. "There you go girl." He rubbed her nose and fresh mucus oozed out. "I'll go and see if we can get a vet out to see you."

Alice let Duncan wash his hands in the kitchen and after he'd called the vet, he called Sindy to say why he was going to be delayed. She hadn't moaned like he'd expected she would. She said she'd make her way to the park with the children and he was to meet her there when he was done.

Sindy went into her mother-in-law's room. "Are you sure you're going to be okay? I could get Bett round to sit with you for a…"

"For goodness sake girl. Go! I shall be absolutely fine here with my lunch wrapped up like this."

Sindy had put a sandwich and a cheese scone on a plate wrapped in a bit of cling film. There was a small flask of tea and a jug of water. "I'll cook this evening, mum."

Sindy leant over and kissed her mother-in-law's cheek. Something she'd started doing since they had cleared the air. "Come on, boys. Kiss nana goodbye. Daddy's going to meet us shortly at the park."

Jack had his football under his arm and couldn't get out of the house quickly enough. Paul had the cricket set that came in a bag and followed suit. The giggling from the pair of them lifted the simple occasion into one of great excitement. Sindy had Charlotte in the pram, the same pram that had been used for the boys. The picnic underneath bobbed about as she pushed Charlotte along at high speed, trying to keep up with the two excited boys.

The vet's expression was stern. "Where's the other horse?"
Duncan pulled open the stable door. "Truffle is in the paddock."

"I'm afraid this is flu. You're going to need to keep her quiet with
complete rest. That cough has taken hold. Plenty of fresh water. I
think I ought to see the other one. Check her over." Duncan was
pleased the vet seemed to think Truffle was fine. He was told how
contagious it was and that Champagne had to be kept in isolation
for three days. "I shall call again tomorrow, if she's no better I'm
going to have to administer antibiotics."

"What time? I don't live here, but I'll make sure I'm waiting for
you."

"Nine?"

"Yes, that's fine. See you then."

Duncan watched the vet pull out of the drive before he went over
to the house. Alice met him at the door. "What's the matter with
her? Has he sorted her out?" Alice who was normally so calm
looked quite het up. "Flu. I didn't realise it was so dangerous. He
said Truffle might get it too. God that will kill Millie if she loses
her horse as well as all the other things she's lost and had to
endure over these past months."

"Millie will be devastated if she loses her mother's horse too. This
is not good news. Can you tell Hugh for me?"

Duncan wasn't keen. He'd been working on Millie's wardrobes but
didn't go through to the old man. The thought of trying to
communicate with someone who couldn't speak, strangely
frightened him.

Hugh looked up when Duncan stood in front of him. "Good
morning Mr Marlow. I'm afraid I've had to call the vet to
Champagne." He didn't want to say to your late wife's horse. "It

seems she has flu. The vet is coming tomorrow, and I've put Truffle in the paddock away from her. They are to be kept apart."

Hugh waved his good hand at him in dismissal. Duncan took an instant dislike to the arrogant man.

"I've told him, Alice. Not sure if he comprehended it. So…"

"He'll understand. Nothing gets past Hugh."

Duncan wanted to say more, but kept his thoughts to himself. He wanted to be with his family.

It was nearly eleven o'clock by the time Duncan arrived at the park. Paul was preparing to score a goal and Jack looked lost in the middle of the two full-sized goal posts. Duncan called to Jack. "Out on the field, dad's going to be goalie."

The boys ran over to him and he picked them up one at a time and swung them round. "Let's just say hi to the girls then I'm all yours."

Duncan kissed Charlotte's cheek. Sindy was sitting on a blanket with the baby on her knee. Charlotte was chewing the house keys and making them jingle.

"Not good news with the horse I'm afraid. I'll fill you in later, but the upshot is its flu. I'll give these boys a run around then we'll have that picnic. I'm starving already. Alice didn't give me a bit of cake this morning or coffee. She's in a right old dither over the horses too."

The squeals and laughter that echoed round the field as Duncan chased and played with his children were heart-warming.

They finally got home at four o'clock. Sindy went into Martha, who was watching an old black and white film on the television. "Everything alright, mum?"

"Yes, fine love."

Sindy cleared away the tea plate and the thermos saying, "I'll bring you in a cuppa. Do you want coffee or tea?"

"I'll have a coffee please."

Sindy made Martha her coffee in the china cup and saucer she'd always had when Susan looked after her.

Martha looked up and smiled. "Had a nice day?"

"Yes, boys are exhausted. Duncan has chased them round and round. They'll sleep well tonight."

"Where's Duncan now?"

"He's gone back to the Marlow's. The horse is in a bad way. Flu."

This meant nothing to Martha. Flu meant a cold. Something you took paracetamol for, bed rest and fluids.

Wednesday 17th June 1981

It was a worrying fact that by Wednesday, Truffle was showing symptoms of the same strain of flu Champagne had. The vet was not unduly worried about Millie's horse, saying, "it's younger. We have caught it early." He turned his attention to Champagne. "I don't like the sound of this one's breathing though. I'm going to give her an injection this morning and put her on a course of antibiotics. You'll have to give it to her three times a day."

Duncan shook his head. "That's not a problem."

"Do you think the young Miss Marlow should be informed?"

Duncan shrugged his shoulders. He didn't know what to do for the best. He had a gut feeling Millie would be furious with all this going on behind her back and her not being informed, but Alice was determined to keep her in the dark until her exams were finished. He only hoped Alice would own up to the fact it was her idea and not his.

The vet stroked Champagne. "Come on, girl, on your feet." It looked an effort and one which the mare resisted. The vet looked grave. "You have told Mr Marlow."

Duncan nodded. "You can go in and see him if you like. He has a speech problem, but Alice is good at getting him to communicate. He doesn't seem to warm to me. I think it's because his wife took me on. He probably blames me for the selling of his horse."

The vet ignored Duncan's ramblings. "I'm afraid we just might lose her. Do you know that?"

"Go speak to the old man. Tell him that and ask him if his daughter should know. It's Alice that's being the stickler for keeping her in the dark."

Three days later, Champagne was put to sleep, but the good news was, Truffle regained full health. Millie was informed of the details.

*

Duncan spent the weekend washing out the stable with disinfectant on the vet's advice and he brought his boys up to the stables with him on the Sunday and they helped slap paint on the walls. The finished result considering two little boys had helped was quite pleasing. It smelt fresh too.

Martha now had a telephone in her own room. It saved the kerfuffle of relaying messages. Things were working out much better between them all.

With the boys out of the way and Charlotte having her afternoon nap, Martha and Sindy were watching Humphrey Bogart in African Queen. At the start, Sindy was just being kind agreeing to watch the old fifties black and white film, but she had got into it, and when the phone rang, she cursed, "typical, just when it's getting to a good bit." Martha reached for the phone, saying, "it's all good, but this call won't be for me. She picked up the receiver and gave her number before saying, "Hello?"

The voice on the other end of the phone sounded strangely familiar. "Can I speak to Peg, please?"

"Whose calling?"

"Martha! Please don't hang up. It's me, Sidney. I just want…"

The line went dead as Martha put her crooked finger on the receiver button.

Martha had turned quite pale. "Oh, my God! That was him. Wanting Susan. The cheek of him."

Sindy looked concerned. "Sidney?"

"Yes. Bold as you like." Martha looked at her daughter-in-law for approval. "Did I do the right thing. You know hanging up?"

I don't know, mum. Is there a right or wrong?"

"Perhaps I should have heard him out."

Sindy turned her attention back to the television. "Shush this is the climax." They both fixed their eyes on the television as Humphrey Bogart kissed Katherine Hepburn in the last scene of the film.

Martha looked wistful. "So romantic. Not real life at all."

"Were you not happy with Dickie?" Sindy knew about his wandering eye but guessed at the length of their marriage they must have had something.

Martha's mind was back on the phone call. "I should have spoken to him. Told him anyway, you know, the destruction he's caused."

"He'll call again. If he's got something to say. I bet he'll call when he thinks Sue will answer… only it will be me!"

Martha watched the names go up the screen. "I went to see that film at the cinema. My mother babysat for us. Susan was only a baby then. Dickie had already started playing away from home. I guess my mum thought it would do us good to get out as a couple."

"Tell me about Dickie. Duncan always clams up when I ask questions about his childhood."

"My marriage was difficult. He left us a few times. I always took him back. Had to back then. I couldn't afford not to, financially. We didn't get the help they get today. Trouble was I don't think I really knew the Dickie who came home from the war. We married in haste really. We were at the same school, but I was in the year below, so he didn't give me a second look then. A bit like you and Duncan I suppose. It's not until you develop, and they see you as a woman that their head gets turned. Well, I turned Dickie's head, but so did every other female in a skirt. Maybe I would have left him when I was in my thirties had this blessed arthritis not started. I'd had enough of people's gossip and pity. Thing was the doctor told me back then what was in store for me. I guessed I'd need Dickie's income and support for longer than I'd hoped. Trouble was, I hadn't bargained on him having a brain tumour and dying in his forties. You never know do you. I'd sort of hoped he'd be around to look after me in my crippled old age after all the times I'd forgiven his infidelity." Martha could have said more but decided there was no mileage in it.

Sindy was moved by her mother-in-law's honesty. "Oh, mum. I didn't realise it was as bad as all that."

Martha thought of the fear and humiliation of years ago and had the urge to say 'oh a lot worse my love' but just smiled. "I'm okay now. Dickie was a good sort really. When he was ill and needed me, we sort of found something between us that we probably wouldn't have done."

"You're a better woman than I am. I'd never forgive Duncan. Never in a million years. I know I wouldn't. I couldn't"

Martha smiled. Wisdom made her choose her words wisely, "Duncan's a one-woman lad. A family man. You can see it in him."

Charlotte could be heard in her cot. "She's awake, love."

"I know. She never cries. Contented to play in there until I go up. She's a good baby. I can't believe how lucky I am."

Martha said, "the boys are good too, love. Just boys that's all."

"I know, but they really are mischievous. Charlotte is adorable in every way." Sindy noticed the concern that crossed her mother-in-law's face. "I love them all. Boys need a firmer hand, especially mine."

No more was said, and Sindy left Martha to ponder on Sidney's call. It was still bothering her and Sindy knew it.

Chapter Sixteen
The Wedding.

26th June 1981

Stephanie was twenty-six weeks pregnant. She had been of a fuller figure before her pregnancy but standing dressed in a Laura Ashley pink floral skirt with a loose pale pink top and jacket to match, she looked positively radiant. Her red hair had been toned down professionally with low lights and the extra length had straightened out the curls a bit. Pregnancy suited her. Simon took her in his arms. "You look amazing." He rubbed his hand gently over the bump that separated the pleats of the skirt accentuating her condition. "Do you mean that Si?"

Si was reminiscent of Millie. She always called him that with affection. He couldn't help it, but when Stephanie said it, it gave him a sad pang of memories lost. Stephanie prodded him in the ribs. "Surely it doesn't take that long to think about an answer?" Simon laughed. "I'm a lucky man. In answer to your question, I promise. Mrs Few. My wife. Having my baby. Lucky, lucky me." He kissed her long and hard. "Come on, your dad will be waiting at the registry office. We don't want to be late." They hadn't done anything conventionally. They had woken up together, picked the outfits together and were driving to the venue together. He'd invited his dysfunctional estranged parents but had no idea if they would come.

They parked up in the council car park, walking distance from the registry office and paid for the day. They went in together and Stephanie's father was already there waiting. He shook Simon's hand and held the crook of his arm out to his daughter. He looked proud when he said, "beautiful."

The ceremony was over quickly. Simon's mother had come but not his stepfather, his aunt and uncle but that was it. The rest of the guests were Stephanie's family. Once outside, waiting on the pavement were several familiar faces from university. Simon scanned for Millie. He knew it was fruitless and he knew he shouldn't, but human nature had him doing it all the same. "Kiss the bride." The cheers and the confetti being thrown brought him back to the present. He laughed, kissed Stephanie, and stood beside her parents for a few more photos. The sun shone making everything appear perfect. They made their way to the pub on the corner. They'd booked the room at the back and arranged for a buffet to be served. Stephanie's mum had organised a wedding cake as a surprise and Simon was pleased that the day was unfolding well without any hitches. It actually felt like a wedding and he was happy. By two o'clock in the afternoon it was all over, and the happy couple left for a weekend in Lymington.

Simon had his hand resting on the gear stick as he drove. Stephanie stroked the fine hairs on the back of his hand with her finger. "Happy?"

"More than. You?"

"No regrets…" She paused before daring to say Millie's name."

Simon took his eyes off the road briefly. "Till death do us part. Sickness and in health. I love you, Stephanie ." He kissed the side of her head trying to watch the road at the same time. "I loved Millie, but you are twice the person she is… literally."

They laughed. "Honest?"

"My life on it." He squeezed her knee gently. "Mrs Few. Stop being paranoid. You are the mother of my child. I couldn't be happier."

Saturday 27th June 1981

Millie had been home for three days now and Duncan still hadn't seen her, and good sense told him not to keep asking Alice where she was. He was putting Millie's horse in the paddock when he heard. "Morning, stranger. How's things?" It was Millie.

He looked round and despite his good resolve his heart skipped a beat at the sight of her. "Been better. I'm really sorry about Champers. We did all we could. It was…"

Millie stopped his ramblings. "I know. Thanks."

Duncan wanted to cuddle her to him as a bit of friendly support, but it didn't feel right. Instead, he said, "how are you?"

"Feeling relieved my exams are over. My work is handed in and there's nothing more I can do now… but wait."

"You'll pass with flying colours. I know you will."

Millie leant on the fence. "Really? You know that do you? I can tell you I've had eight months of hell. It's been one thing after another and just when I thought nothing else could go wrong, I lose mum's horse and nearly my own."

Duncan wanted to tell her the vet had said her horse was younger, stronger, and never in danger like Champagne, but he held his tongue, saying instead, "it must be good to be home."

"Yes, it is. Dad was pleased. Thanks for my wardrobes. They're great. I've got a new carpet being fitted Tuesday." Millie sighed and leant her head on her arms. Duncan asked, "why the sad face then?"

"Nothing." Millie swung her leg over the gate and dropped down into the paddock beside him. Truffle did a sidestep at the sudden movement. Millie stroked her nose and talked gently into her ear.

"She has to miss mum's horse. They've been together for years. Truffle only knows being here with Champers."

"She'll get used to it." Duncan reached out and scratched the horse's head between its eyes, "have we had any response to my advert for weekend cover?"

Millie shook her head. "No, but I'm home now and I can feed my horse of a morning. You can do the mucking out…"

Duncan acted indignant. "Thank you very much. The dirty work."

Millie laughed and Duncan's heart quickened at the sight. "There's the gardens too to keep up, together with the house, you won't be twiddling your thumbs. I'm just saying you can have the weekends off if it's what you want."

Seeing Millie again had Duncan changing his hasty decision. "Not all weekend, but… perhaps a Sunday?"

"Whatever suits you. I'm flexible." He watched Millie push her hair back away from her eyes and the urge to touch her overcame him again. She was lovely. He was grateful for her constant chatter because there was a tension between them that was electrifying. He wondered if she could feel it to.

Millie was stroking Truffle. "Duncan, Alice says the hall needs decorating. The room next to mine also needs doing up. So you see, as I said, there's plenty to do around here. You won't be scratching around for work. We'll keep you busy."

A wave of sadness swept over him and he couldn't stop himself from saying, "we won't be able to ride together anymore. Now Champers has gone I won't have a mount. I shall miss that."

Millie was serious. "Perhaps that's not a bad thing, Duncan." Without another word, she patted her horse and left the paddock.

He watched her until she was out of sight. All the while he'd been saying to himself, *'if she turns round and looks at me, she likes me like I like her.'* Millie didn't look round once. Back straight she strode across the garden full of her own self-importance.

He went across to the house. He questioned her parting words. *'Why would she say it's a good thing that we can't ride together? Does she know I have feelings for her?'* He argued with himself. *'I don't have feelings for her. I love Sindy.'* He knew he was fooling no one, least of all himself. With a heavy heart that not even Alice's coffee and cake could lift he knocked on the kitchen door. "Is coffee ready?"

*

The boys were playing in the garden. Charlotte was lying on the rug playing quite happily with a penguin that when pushed over, rolled back up again making a jingly noise. She gurgled and talked to it happily. Sindy had blitzed the house and was just flicking round with the duster when the phone rang. "Hello?"

"Peg, it's Sidney. Don't hang up. I need to speak to you. Please."

Sindy was so shocked to hear his voice she just stood and stared.

"Peg? Are you there? Please…"

Sindy found her voice. "Sue isn't here. I'm her sister-in-law. She is in a hospital." Sindy wanted to say thanks to you, but refrained. Without another word she put the receiver back on its cradle. Charlotte had rolled off the rug while trying to reach the rocking penguin and was getting cross with it. Sindy went over and picked her up. Her hands were shaking. The phone call had upset her, and she didn't know why.

Sunday 28ᵗʰ June 1981

Sidney stared at the phone. He pushed the button to get his unused coins returned. *'Hospital? Bloody hell, what's happened to Peg? Sue? Peg said no one calls her Sue. What in hell's name is going on?'*

Sidney put the loose change in his pocket and opened the telephone kiosk door. Somewhere in the back of his mind he remembered that crazy brother saying, 'if anything happens to Peg.' The statement seemed so much more significant now. Sidney's problem was he had no idea how he was going to contact her now. He thought about phoning St Richards hospital, but it was a big place, and he had no idea of the wards or what the problem was, or if there was a problem. Perhaps she'd just taken a job there. He thought of Jay from the building site. He'd seemed to know a lot about the local families. His aunt lived in the village, perhaps she'd know. Trouble was, with the job finished on site, he had no idea where Jay was working now. Sidney pulled his hand through his hair in desperation. *'I have to speak to her. Dare I go back and knock on the door. The thought of getting another hiding from that brother of hers isn't inviting. It's more than seven weeks ago and my ribs are still tender.'* He crossed the road and bought a paper. He didn't want one, but he couldn't think straight. Talking to himself, he said, *'I'm going to have to man up and face the music. There's no alternative. If I want to explain and put this right, I'm going to have to do it - face to face.'* Phoning Peg and seeing how the land lay had seemed such a good idea. He knew he'd have to try and avoid the dreaded Martha and he guessed Peg might hang up a couple of times, but he'd hoped eventually with persistence he'd manage to wear her down and she'd listen. What Sidney hadn't imagined were all these complications.

A car hooting at him made him jump backwards. He'd wandered aimlessly into the road. He stuck his fingers up at the vehicle, but he knew he was in the wrong. His mood was low, making him grumpy at the world. He didn't want to go back to his mothers.

Liverpool didn't feel like home anymore. He wanted Peg. To hear her voice. He never in a million years believed he could miss anyone like he missed her. He thought about trying to phone again. Speak to the sister-in-law. *'She hadn't been very friendly. It must be a requirement if you want to belong in their family unit.'* He almost smiled at his sarcasm and would have done if he weren't so desperate.

After see-sawing with thoughts, he decided he would write. Writing wasn't his strong point. *'Would Peg get it? If she's away will the family give her her post? Surely, they would.'*

Sidney's mind raced. He had a plan. Writing was his only option. Unless he went back to Chichester and risked another hiding. If he thought he'd get Peg back it would be worth it. Tender ribs or not.

He let himself in. His mother was still at church. He rummaged in her side cabinet and found a writing pad and biro.

He sat at the table and chewed the top of the pen. All he'd written was Dear Peg. *'Think about what you'd say to her and write the words.'*

Please don't throw this away, Peg. Not before you've read it. Writing isn't my thing, but I'm desperate for you to understand.

Trouble is I don't know what to say. Minnie has chucked me out. That's not why I am writing. I'm living with my mum until next week, then I shall be in Bognor. There's a big housing development there. I'm going to do the electrics. I could see you, it's only half an hour away from Chichester.

Oh, Peg I'm making a hash of this. I love you. I've loved you from that very first night I took you out. I didn't realise it then, but I do now. Everything about you is perfect. I wanted to stay in West Sussex, but the children. Now I've lost them too. Here I go again, making it sound like I'm only writing because I've lost everything. I'm not, honest. I promise.

When I came home from Chichester, Minnie was horrified at the state of my face. I just told her. I told her I'd been seeing someone. I was grateful to have been behind the sofa, as she threw a cup at me. I dodged and the effort on my ribs had me doubling over. Your brother has a mean left hook, or I should say boot.

Still, I deserved it. I hurt you, and I wouldn't have wanted to do that for the world. The times I wanted to tell you the truth, but I was scared. Then look what happened.

The upshot of everything is. Minnie kicked me out. I came back to live with my mum and Minnie's moved to a place called Eastbourne so as to be nearer her own family. It's about fifty miles from Bognor so I thought it was a good job to take so I could visit the kids, and just as importantly, I'd be able to see you.

Peg. Have I made a pig's ear of this? I wish I could sing to you like I did that night in the pub when you danced with me. I sang into your hair as I held you in my arms. Do you remember? It was an Elvis number. Can't help falling in love and then we danced to Loving you both is breaking all the rules. If you knew how I wanted to tell you that night. I couldn't. It was the night you gave yourself to me. Became mine. I have been playing a record over and over in my room. It is a song sung by Cilla Black. You're my World.

The lyrics capture my feelings. I want to say them to you.

You're my world, Peg. You're my night and day.

You really are every prayer I pray,

If our love ceases to be.

Then it's the end of my world for me.

Peg, if you only knew. I've never written a letter like this to anyone before and I swear to you I wouldn't do this for anyone. Only you. I'm desperate to see you. To explain better. Forgive me for lying.

169

I'm writing to you, not just because I'm on my own now, but I miss you Peg. I love you.

If I don't hear from you after this, I promise to leave you be and I hope you know how sorry I am for hurting you.

My love,

Sidney

He put it in an envelope and stuck one of his mother's first-class stamps on it and went out to post it before he lost heart.

Monday 29th June 1981

Millie was up with the dawn chorus. She'd saddled up Truffle and ridden out to the church. It was a beautiful morning. Once back home she fed her horse and put her in the paddock. She was just getting over the gate when Duncan appeared on his bike. "You're early. I thought you were going to start taking your boys to school first before you come here. There's no need to be early. I can do Truffle. We've had a ride this morning."

Duncan was disappointed and it showed. He was in a bad mood as it was. He'd argued with Sindy over Sidney's phone call. Duncan didn't want him phoning the house. It would only upset Susan's progress. Why couldn't he just leave her alone. Hearing that Millie had been out riding early annoyed him further. He'd have liked to have ridden with Millie. *Why did Champers have to keel over?'*

The ride had blown Millie's hair wild and her cheeks were flushed. Duncan managed to get his feelings under control. "Big day for you today. Good luck."

"I don't start until ten. I'm going in for some breakfast and a shower. I'll probably go early – show willing."

Duncan laughed. "Is there anything in particular you want me to do today?"

"Yes. If you haven't got work anywhere else, I thought it would be good to start clearing out the gutters and painting them. Can you do that?"

He gave her a mock salute. She laughed and pushed him in the arm as she went by. "Get over yourself, you big oaf."

Duncan watched her go, *'if she turns round and looks at me before she gets to the house, she likes me.'* Millie stopped just before she turned the corner. "Duncan, can you mend the puncture on my cycle for me. I might like to ride into work on nice days like this."

His spirits lifted. *'She likes me. I don't want more. Just that we can be friends.'*

Millie was happy when she got home after her first day at work. Alice was just preparing a light tea for Hugh. Poached egg on toast. She looked up. "Had a good day, love?"

"I love it, Alice. I'm going through to dad and tell him about it."

Hugh was dozing in his chair when she pushed open the door. "Dad." He jumped slightly at her sudden appearance, she apologised. "Sorry, I didn't know you were nodding." She sat opposite him and waited until he seemed to wake himself up enough to listen. "Dad I've had a great day. I love the books, the people, and the learning. You won't believe it, but I got talking to a girl who was looking for somewhere to keep her horse. She said she was finding the stabling at Dimbles too expensive. I told her she could have Champers stable. It will be company for Truffle and between us we can help with the care. Duncan is having to

171

spend weekends at home with his family now the new baby is here, and they are looking after his mother. I think it'll work out fine. Don't you?"

Hugh tried to smile as he watched his daughter's animation. She was so alive. He envied her health and youth. Still, he knew he had a lot to be thankful for. His life was a thousand times better than it was this time last year. Alice came in with his supper. "Here you are, love." She was addressing Millie. "Do you want to give it to him?"

"No. I'm going to sort my room. The carpet's coming tomorrow I have to move as much furniture out as I can." She leant over and kissed Hugh's cheek. He used his good hand to squeeze her arm. "Love you, dad." She turned her attention to Alice. "If Duncan's still here I could ask him to give me a hand. Has he gone yet do you know?"

"I'm not sure, love." Alice looked at her watch. "He might be. He's been up on the ladder all day cleaning out the guttering with the hose pipe running. Good job there's not a drought."

"I'll go outside and see. I might be lucky. He said he was going to sort my bike out for me too."

Once outside Millie was drawn to her horse. Truffle trotted over to the gate as she approached. "Here, girl. I've found you a friend. With a bit of luck, we'll sort that out for you at the weekend." Millie lay her head on her horse's nose. "Can't have you being lonely."

Millie opened the gate and Truffle followed her to the stable. Millie had a hand full of pony nuts as bait. Duncan's bike was there, perched up against the stable. She patted her horses rump. "In you go, girl." She was pleased to see Duncan had mucked out and filled Truffle's nose bag with hay along with oats in the bucket and fresh water. "There you go. All waiting for you. He's a good man." Millie patted her horse again and left her to it.

She called out to him, "Duncan!" but there was no reply.

She walked across the garden still calling his name and found him in the top shed with her bicycle upside down. "Here you are. I've been calling you."

The radio was blaring and he turned it off. "Sorry didn't hear you. How was your first day?" Millie filled him in on the great day she'd had and the fact that she'd found a woman to help with Truffle in return for a stable.

"Wow, that's excellent. Will I be able to ride her horse?"

"Let's get her here first. I'm sure it will all work out. She seemed really nice. Grace. Grace Coker. Lives in the village too."

"Grace Coker! Bugger me I know her. I went to school with her brother. Sindy knows her too. She was in the same class."

Duncan dropped the horse talk and showed Millie what he'd done so far to her bike. "I went to Halfords. I hope you don't mind but I used the cheque book and bought new tyres, a bell and some oil for the brakes and chain. It will be like new once I've finished."

Millie was impressed. "No of course I don't mind. That's what it's for. Have you got the receipts?" Duncan fished in his pocket and gave it to her. There you go. I spent just over twenty pounds."

Alice was sitting in the lounge with Hugh watching a programme when Millie went back inside the house. They both looked up, but it was Alice that said, "no Duncan?"

"No, I'm going to do what I can and if there's anything I can't manage he's going to sort it out for me tomorrow."

Tuesday 30th June 1981

Sindy was annoyed to see Duncan was getting ready to leave for work before the boys were even up. "I thought life would be easier for us once Millie was home. What do you have to rush off for? Surely she can see to her own horse?"

"Don't start that now, love. It isn't just horses. I've got the house to work on as well. Then there's Millie's room, she wants me to get that ready for the carpet fitters today and I have to go to the Barkers this afternoon. Their lawns need cutting." He gave Sindy a brief kiss on her cheek. She could have sworn he was wearing aftershave. *'No, he couldn't be. I have to force him to put a splash on if we go out.'* It was a silly thing, but it played on Sindy's mind while she made a cup of tea for Martha and prepared her breakfast tray. The boys appearing in their pyjamas distracted her thoughts, but the first thing they wanted to know was, 'where's daddy?'

"Daddy's gone to work. I'm just popping this into nana. Help yourselves to cereal. It's all on the table. Paul can you help your brother please."

When Sindy returned to the lounge carrying Charlotte on her hip, she was pleased to see the boys had got down from the table and were playing together nicely with the Thomas train set that Jack had been given last year for Christmas.

By eight thirty, Sindy had the boys ready for school, Charlotte in the pram and Martha was washed and sitting in her chair listening to the radio. As she closed the front door behind her she saw the postman just coming out of next door's gate. Sindy called out good morning to him. "Got anything for us?"

The postman handed over what looked like a phone bill and a letter. "There you go, two letters." He gave them to Sindy, saying, "lovely morning, isn't it?" "Beautiful." She noticed the boys had already run on ahead, so she shoved the post in the bottom of the pram and quickened her step.

It wasn't until Sindy had dropped Paul off at school and was waiting outside Jack's playschool that she looked at the envelopes properly. One was for Martha and the other Peg. The postmark was Liverpool. She was more than curious. She had the urge to open it. *'He's not going to give up.'*

One of the mothers got talking to Sindy and was admiring Charlotte, who was propped up in the pram, full of smiles. "She's been an easy baby. So happy. Sleeps all night. I'd have more if I thought I'd get another one like this." The young mother laughed. "You don't though. My first was like that. Good as gold. The second. Ah! I could have smothered him."

The doors opened and the children hurried in. Sindy helped Jack hang his bag on his peg and took his toy out that he'd taken for show and tell time.

"Mummy will pick you up later." Jack was off to the painting table before Sindy could even kiss him goodbye. The letter was back on her mind as she made her way home.

Martha was shocked when Sindy tapped on her door and offered to make coffee. "Yes please." Charlotte was asleep in the pram and Sindy had pushed her round the back under the washing line, which was full of white terry towelling nappies.

Less than ten minutes later Sindy was sitting opposite Martha. "I caught the postman. There are letters. One for you and one addressed to Peg. I think it's Sidney. Look, Liverpool on the postmark."

Martha was concerned. "That's all we need. What are we going to do?"

"I don't know. Shall we open it? You know, see what he has to say for himself. It would be awful if he wrote something to upset her . Especially now she's finding her way a bit."

Martha turned the letter over and over in her hand. "It doesn't feel right. You know, opening her private mail."

"I know, mum, but we wouldn't under normal circumstances, would we?" Sindy took the letter from Martha. "We could steam it. If it seems harmless, then we can send it on to her. If not, we can just destroy it."

Martha still wasn't happy. "Let's see what Duncan thinks."

"Duncan isn't bothered about anything or anyone unless your name is Millie Marlow."

Martha didn't like this reply and said so. Sindy apologised. "I'm just feeling a bit insecure at the moment, and I don't know why." After a lot of deliberation, Sindy steamed open the letter and when they'd read it, they were no clearer as to what action they should take. "I wish now we'd spoken to Sidney when he phoned. It would have been easier I think."

Martha had been shocked at the intimacy. "I knew she'd been with him. Silly girl."

"Mum! She's a woman, not a girlr. Look at me and Duncan. It's human nature to…"

Martha interrupted her. "I don't want to hear what you youngsters got up to. In my day…"

Sindy laughed. "I don't believe you. You have just forgotten."

Martha let her indignation drop and said instead, "I still think showing Susan this letter will stir up a hornet's nest. As I see it, he's left his wife, or she's kicked him out and having our Susan is better than being on his own."

Sindy took the letter from Martha. "I think it's beautiful."

"What all that nonsense. He sounds fed up and sorry for himself."

Sindy didn't agree. The conversation got a bit heated, and Martha was pleased when Charlotte could be heard crying in the pram and Sindy left her in peace, closing the door behind her. Martha had wanted to keep the letter with her and read it again, but Sindy was insistent that it should be stuck down and sent on to Susan.

Duncan came home early. Sindy was delighted. "You can pick Paul up from school. Take Jack with you. He can ride his trike. Burn some energy off." Duncan didn't mind. "Put Charlotte in the pram and I'll take her too."

"No. If you've got Jack on his trike, you're going to have to push him... and watch him." Duncan washed his hands, drank a glass of water, and left. Sindy had kept quiet about the letter but had made up her mind tonight when the boys were in bed, she would show him. She had a strong feeling the decision to send it on to Susan would not sit well with him.

Sindy had promised Martha she would get her in the bath this evening. Getting her in was easier than getting her out, and in the end, Duncan had to come in and assist. Embarrassment went with necessity. It was while Martha was sitting safely on a bath chair wrapped in a towel that she said, "What did you think of lover boy's letter?" Sindy shook her head furiously at her mother-in-law but it was too late.

"Lover boy? Whose lover boy? What letter?"

Martha couldn't back track. "I thought Sindy would have said, but..."

Sindy interrupted. "I've been so busy I forgot. I'll show you once we are settled downstairs."

Duncan looked puzzled. "What am I missing here?"

Martha knew she had made an error. "Sidney. The lad from Liverpool has written to our Susan."

Sindy wasn't ready to explain. "Not now, Martha." Sindy pushed Duncan playfully towards the door. "I'll discuss it with you later. Go back with the boys and finish their story." She could see by the way Duncan's eyes flashed between the two of them looking for clues he was bursting with curiosity, but amazingly he did as he'd been asked.

Martha mouthed sorry. Sindy widened her eyes and shook her head furiously putting her finger to her lips. She rubbed Martha gently with the towel and shook some talcum powder over her. The bathroom took on the sweet smell of Lily of the Valley. Getting Martha down the stairs was easier than getting her up and within minutes she was settled back in her chair, watching Coronation Street, and enjoying a cup of coffee.

Sindy found Duncan in the kitchen. He'd just poured himself a lager. "Let's go and sit in the garden. It's lovely out there. You can read this letter." She handed it to him, and he turned it over in his hand. "You've opened it?"

"I know. We didn't know what to do for the best. It might have been a nasty letter. You know, to upset her."

Duncan slipped the letter out of the envelope. "Hardly. You don't write to someone after you've given them the big heave-ho, to upset them further."

Sindy was rattled. "You've changed your tune. You were…"

"I know, I know. It's just. I think on reflection I acted hastily. Okay?"

"Really?"

He took a slurp of his lager and looked at the scruffily written handwriting. "Yes, really. The ear-bending I got from you was one thing, but I've thought about it a lot." Duncan scanned the letter. It stirred something in him. Envy? This bloke was now free to love his sister. He had to put his own feelings aside and decide fairly on what they should do next. "I think we should phone him."

"How?"

Sindy had missed the telephone number under the address at the top. Duncan pointed it out to her. "I think we need to let him know how she's struggling. He just might be the answer to her wanting to come out of thar godforsaken place and into the real world again."

"What about us? If Sue comes home, where will she go? And he'll know we've opened her letter."

Duncan knew that was easily explained under the circumstances, but he was annoyed with Sindy always thinking of herself. "We'll just have to go home. It might be temporarily. You can still come and help mum if you want. Show willing. That might give Sue some time to find her feet and we can decide then if this situation is what we really want."

Sindy was upset now and said sulkily, "you don't have to be nasty. It's just you know I want this house."

"I know you do, but what about what I want. I want my life back. You and the kids. Just us. If I'm honest I don't like this situation. I love mum but living like this isn't for me."

Things got heated between the two of them. Sindy felt put out for all the effort she'd made of late with Martha. Their relationship had improved immensely and although Duncan agreed, wouldn't budge. This was the chance he needed to take his family back home.

Sindy brought the conversation back to the letter. "I think we should just seal it back down. Take it to Pe… Sue and let her decide."

Duncan stood up. "Why ask me then? You've already made up your mind."

"I wanted to know what you thought. Of course, I did."

"Really? Well, if you really want to know my thoughts, I shall tell you. I think you're nosey. You opened Sue's letter because you were curious. That was wrong. If you feel she should get her letter, then…"

"Shut up, Duncan. You always have to play the high and mighty. Like you punched the poor guy without explanation because you wanted to protect Sue, well I opened the letter because I was worried about it. Maybe it was wrong."

Duncan stood up and drained his glass. "You were being nosey. I know it and you know it. That's why you're so angry. Guilty conscience. I'm going in to get another lager." His body looked tense as he walked away. "Do what you want. I'm not being part of this."

Sindy sat staring after him. She felt troubled. Things between them had changed since Charlotte had been born. Why? She didn't know. Charlotte was such a good baby, so it couldn't be her. *'Perhaps he's right, we need to go home.'*

*

Duncan got another lager and went back outside. Sindy had gone and he guessed it was to sit with his mother and gossip about him. He didn't care. The letter had unsettled him for different reasons, and he was pleased to be alone.

He sat back in the deckchair, staring into his glass, thinking. *What a soppy letter.'* Duncan wanted to mock the sentiments, but something stirred in him. An understanding. *'I get it though, even the music. Torn between two lovers. That's me, only Millie isn't giving me an inch. It doesn't stop these feelings of wanting what I can't have.'* Duncan took a long swig of his lager and didn't stop to breathe until the glass was empty. His head was full of Millie, and he couldn't change that. Deciding to mow the lawn he went over to the shed and pulled out the petrol mower. *'I hate myself. I know if Millie was willing, I'd be the same as Sidney, play away from home too.'* The petrol mower came to life with the pull of the cord. *'It's the kids though. Their my Achilles heel. I wonder how this guy really feels now he's lost his family... and his home. Maybe that's why he's wanting Sue.'* Duncan walked around the overgrown, weedy borders, cutting the lawn best he could, thinking all the while. *'I reckon this guy has it really bad for Sue. He's probably glad to be free of his ties. If I could just have Millie, just the once, I'm sure I could get things back on track with Sindy. I married her too young. I probably wouldn't have if she hadn't gone and got pregnant. If only...'*

Sindy called out to him, bringing him back to the present. He stopped the mower. "What's up?"

"Sidney's on the phone. I said he could speak to you seeing as you seem to have all the answers."

Duncan wiped his hands down his shorts and went inside. *What am I going to say?'*

He picked up the receiver that Sindy had left on the telephone table. "Hello?"

"I'm sorry to call. It's just I sent a letter. I was hoping…"

"It's okay. Your letter arrived but Sue's not here. There's no easy way to tell you this, but when I do, perhaps you'll understand why I gave you that hiding." Duncan paused slightly expecting a comment but when all he got was silence, he said quietly, without blame, "my sister tried to take her own life. She's in a psychiatric hospital and it's only this past week that she's allowed anyone to visit."

"Can I see her?"

"I don't know and that's the truth. You have to phone and make an appointment. She's no longer Peg, we have to call her Susan, but I call her Sue. I think they are right, after all that's her name."

"I wanted to call her Sue when she told me about her nickname, but she said I wasn't to. I wish I had now. I feel terrible. How can I reach her? Will you be able to get my letter to her?"

Duncan was feeling mellow with the alcohol he'd drunk, "I'll see what I can do. My wife opened the letter. She said she just wanted to…"

"No worries. Just please get it to P…Sue for me please. I know you don't believe me, but I love her. I love your sister. I really do. I feel a right bastard for hurting her, it's just…" He paused and in what sounded to Duncan like defeat, added, "I thought I had no choice."

The words were out of Duncan's mouth before he had chance to think. "What about your wife and kids, what are they…"

"I wasn't married. We lived together. They are my kids and yes of course I'm worrying about the hurt I've caused them, but Minnie, that's my partner, she will be fine. She's moved nearer her mother. So it makes sense for me to take work nearer Sussex and nearer Sue." Sidney was already thinking of Peg as Sue. Could I just come down this weekend and turn up at this hospital and surprise her?"

Duncan's voice rose. "No! You have to do things by the book in there. I'll make enquiries for you." The panic left his voice. "Let me start by giving Sue your letter. She's the kindest most forgiving

182

person you will ever meet. I'm sure she'll see you, but you might have to be patient."

They said goodbye and when the phone went dead, Duncan felt worse than he did while he was mowing the lawns. *'How could I have nearly kicked the guys brains out? He seems really genuine.'* When Duncan went back through to the lounge Sindy was on at him immediately asking questions. "What did he say? Is he coming to see her? What…"

"I'm as confused as you. I've told him we'll get the letter to Sue and take it from there." Guilt had him pulling Sindy into his arms. "I'm sorry about earlier. I'm tired, that's all. This situation is getting to me. I shouldn't have said all that stuff about being nosey. I know you wouldn't hurt Sue for anything. It just felt wrong seeing the letter open. I understand. I really do. I just wish we were back in our own home. You do know that don't you?"

Sindy looked tearful with his heartfelt apology. "I shouldn't have opened the letter. You were right. It was curiosity that got the better of me and I feel bad now. As to moving back to our poky house… I don't want to. I like it here. I think it would be better if we just let our house go now, then you would stop thinking about it. This would be home." When Duncan didn't say anything she said, "it's all working out now. I'm fine with your mum. She's a doddle really. I don't know why I got so bossy initially. Laying down all those silly rules and being cruel. I suppose I'd seen what she could be like to Sue and I didn't want to be used in the same way."

"I don't know. Maybe if…"

Sindy was terrified his response would be negative so stopped him midsentence. "Can we just see what happens when Sue gets her letter. Please? Make decisions then."

Duncan took her in his arms. He was weakening. "Let's leave it for now and we'll decide when Sue gets her letter and tells us what she wants. Does that seem fair." She giggled as he kissed her ear. "What time will you manage to get mum to bed? I fancy an early night."

Sindy gave him a playful dig in the ribs. "Go and put the mower away. I'm sure she'll go at nine if I ask her. You go and tell her you want an early night because you're bushed."

Laughing he said, "like she'll believe that old line."

The atmosphere had lifted and Duncan chastised himself once again for these horrible mixed feelings towards his wife. *'God, man. What are you playing at? I've got to get myself together. I'm behaving like an irrational teenager.'*

Chapter Seventeen
Thursday July 2nd 1981

Things were easier between Duncan and Sindy the following morning, and when he left for work he felt happier with things at home and told Sindy he would do his best to get back early and take the boys over the playing field with the football and have a kick around. Yet this happy mood was short lived.

Disappointment outweighed any thoughts of home or playing with the boys. When he arrived at The Four Willows, Truffle had been fed and there was no sign of Millie. He walked her horse into the paddock so he could muck out the stable. This is how Alice found him when she put her head over the stable door. "Morning, Duncan. Message for you."

He stopped raking up the dirty straw and gave Alice his attention. "Yes?"

"Millie wants you to plane the door of her bedroom. The new carpet has made the door stiff to close. She also said you can take Truffle for a ride if you want. She didn't have time this morning."

"I would have done, Alice, but I have a busy day today. I've got three gardens to mow in the village this afternoon and I've promised Sindy I'll be home early. Can you tell her I'll come back later this evening if it's desperate?"

"I think it is, lad. She was in a right old strop about it. Made her late for leaving here this morning. I haven't seen that side of her before."

"Women! They're all the same." He laughed to himself, pleased to know Millie wanted him back later.

Duncan didn't get back to the Marlows until six thirty that evening. He had managed to get home early and play football on the green with the boys, but Sindy was hoping they would have another early night together when Martha went to bed. He left Sindy under a cloud. She shouted after him, "why don't you move your bed round there. It would be a darn sight easier for you." Duncan ignored her.

When he cycled into the drive of The Four Willows, Sindy, the kids and his mother were all forgotten because there was Millie picking flowers from the front garden. "Hello. Seeing you like that amongst the blooms would make a perfect picture on a chocolate box." She smiled and ignored his flattery. "It's good of you to come. I hope I haven't ruined your evening?"

He was instantly concerned by the tone of her voice. "Are you okay?"

She pushed her hair out of her eyes with her forearm. "Feeling a bit low. Nothing for you to worry about. Come on let me put these flowers in a vase and get this door sorted. It drove me crazy trying to push it open and closed last night. The silly carpet fitter said it will loosen in a couple of days. I think not."

Duncan had the door off and planed in no time. He swung it backwards and forwards. "Perfect. What do you think?"

"Lovely, thanks for that. It drove me mad yesterday trying to push the door open," Millie offered him a bag. He looked puzzled, "what's this?"

"Just a few old things of mine. I thought your boys might like them. Nothing that exciting."

Duncan pulled out a game of Coppit. "I used to play this with Sue. She always beat me. Who did you play with, you know being an only child?"

"My mum and dad. We always played board games together."

"Were you never lonely?"

Millie shook her head. "Never!"

Duncan was reminded of her earlier low mood. "What was eating at you when I arrived? You looked like you'd lost your best friend."

Millie's eyes watered. "I lost more than that."

"Oops, sorry. Me and my big mouth. Wanna talk about it?"

Millie held her head in her hands. "I'm being silly, I know I am. It's just I saw a photo of Si's wedding in the paper. Someone local must have put one in. So, you see you were right, I have lost both. My best friend and my first love, the love of my life."

"You're overreacting a bit, no?"

She shook her head. "No. No I'm not. Simon WAS my first love, and Stephanie became my best friend at Uni three years ago. All gone."

Duncan looked incredulous. "Didn't you have boyfriends at school? You know when you were growing up."

Millie shook her head again. "No. I wasn't interested."

"Didn't you play kiss chase, postman's knock or just kiss the boys behind the bike sheds?"

"Maybe the other girls did, but not me."

Duncan laughed at his own memories. "I was always kissing the girls. Walking home holding a girl's hand. I'd have only been nine or ten. I thought it was part of growing up."

"I suppose being an only child I didn't need affection like that from anyone else. I was adored here. I loved Marble, that was my first pony. He wasn't much bigger than a Shetland. He was a lovely creamy colour. Mum and dad bought him for me when I was eight. Then at thirteen I was bought a bigger one. Black and white.

I called him Domino. Then at sixteen I had Truffle given to me for Christmas. Mum and Dad tied a big red ribbon round her neck. It was the best ever. So, you see I didn't need to look for love outside my home. I always had a pony and my parents."

Duncan was fascinated. "Didn't you have friends at school?"

This made Millie laugh out loud. Her mood seemed to have lifted. "Of course, I did. I was popular. Everyone wanted to get round here with the horses we had then. Mum and Dad always rode."

"How the other half live." Duncan pulled another game out. "What's this."

Millie laughed again. "You wouldn't believe me if I told you about that one."

Duncan was intrigued. "Go on. I'm all ears."

She pulled it out of the box. It was a circular disc the size of a dinner plate and she stood a plastic pole in the middle. Hanging from it was a piece of string with a what looked like a plastic coin at the bottom. "You swing the rope round like this." She held it out and let it go. It swung round and round for a few turns and as it slowed it was pulled to the word YES. "See, it's a magnet. I understand now, but when I was younger, I used to ask it questions and it would tell me the answer. Like… will I get what I want for Christmas. Silly isn't it. Back then though I thought it was a good way of foretelling my future."

"What about if it landed on this disc, make a wish. What then?"

"Well, I'd believe I would be granted a wish."

Duncan was amused. "I can't believe you really believed in all this."

"I did. I believed in all those things. Santa Clause and the tooth fairy. Didn't you?"

"I suppose I must have done at some stage. Too far back to remember. The boys do though. You should see the excitement when they hang up their stockings."

She started to put the game back in its box. She said in a very matter of fact manner, "well, there you go then."

Duncan took the game before she completely dismantled it. "Let me try." He spun the disc and the two of them watched like excited children full of anticipation. 'WISH'.

"What do I do now?"

"Make a wish."

The words were out of his mouth before he could stop them. "I'd wish I could kiss you."

She moved off the bed and put her lips to his. "There you are. It's not nonsense."

He was so taken by the moment he hadn't had chance to grasp the fleeting meeting of lips. "No, not like that, like this." He drew her to him and for a few glorious moments she melted into him. Both seeming to want the same thing with the same need.

When Duncan let her go his voice was husky, "and what would you wish?"

Millie stood up. She grabbed up the game and started stuffing it hurriedly in the box. "I wouldn't know where to start. Too many things."

Duncan noticed her hands were shaking. He grabbed hold of her arm. "It was only a kiss. We haven't done anything wrong."

"If you believe that then you are sillier than you look."

Duncan let her go, hurt. "Thank you. I was trying to make you feel better."

"I don't feel bad. I was just wondering if that is how it happened with my best friend. Just a bit of fun." Millie looked straight at him and he could see her eyes had watered. "It's dangerous fun. Like playing with fire. Someone will get burned. I don't want to be the cause of hurting your wife like I've been hurt and then there's your children."

He couldn't fail to see how strikingly lovely she was. He wanted to relive the moment, hold her, move his hands over her lovely body. He said instead, "kids are resilient."

"Well wives aren't." Millie bundled up the bag and handed it to him. "Thanks for what you've done. It's great."

"Millie?" Duncan didn't want to go. Not like this. He wanted reassurance that she liked him. Had enjoyed the experience in the same way as he had done. "Didn't you feel the connection between us?"

Millie sat back on the bed. "Duncan." She paused as if thinking for the right words. "I like you. Okay. I think – if - and obviously, it's irrelevant because there is… but maybe if there were no Sindy I'd be tempted."

Duncan knew he should leave it there while he was winning, but he wanted more. "We wouldn't be hurting anyone. No one would need to know, we…"

"Do I look like the sort of girl that takes second best? I've been number one all my life. Special. Don't insult me to suggest it. What you don't realise is that when you kissed me that second time and I closed my eyes and leant into you I was imagining I was in Simon's arms. Just once more. To feel loved like he loved me. Please don't give yourself airs as to thinking it meant anything more."

Duncan felt breathless. The pain of her words made him feel like he'd been kicked in the stomach. He took the bag from her and said, "thanks for these." Without a backward glance he left.

As he passed through the lounge, Alice was sitting watching television with the old man. "Cheerio, Alice, Mr Marlow. See you tomorrow."
Alice made to follow him out to the back door.

He held up his hand. "It's okay. I can see myself out."

Despite June's warm light evening his insides felt cold. His bike was still where he'd left it nearly three hours ago, perched up against the gate.

*

Millie stayed in her bedroom. She couldn't face Alice or her father. She felt quite wretched. Lying to Duncan was one thing, but she knew she was lying to herself. Her feelings for Duncan were dangerous and the last thing she wanted to do was give him any encouragement. If he only knew Simon, he'd know she couldn't possibly have closed her eyes and thought it was her ex-boyfriend holding her in his arms and kissing her so passionately.

Both men were about the same height, but Simon's hair isn't shoulder length and wavy, it's spiky, short, and prone to stick out at all angles, which makes him look like he's just got out of bed. When she'd held the back of Duncan's soft, wavy hair it wasn't only the length of it that told her who she was kissing it was the smell of him. Boyfriends were something Millie had little experience of, but she would have known Simon's kiss blindfolded. Millie let her tongue sweep over her lips where she could still feel the tingle of Duncan's presence. Millie was startled when her door was tapped. Alice pushed it open. She swung the

191

door back and forwards a few times over the new carpet. "That's better. Duncan's made a good job of this, hasn't he?"

"Yes. He's only just gone. Did you see him?"

"I did. He called out but didn't want to chat. Probably needed to get home to his family. It took longer than I thought, probably longer than he thought too?" Alice kept playing with door admiring how smoothly it now glided over the new carpet. "Still it was worth it, it looks really nice in here, love. I bet you're pleased."

"I am. I have a few things I want still."

The subject changed. "I'm just making some tea. There's a film just starting. 'Somewhere in Time'. It's got Christopher Reeve in it and my idol Christopher Plummer. It was on at the cinema last year. I've told your dad and he seems to want to watch it. I thought you might like to sit with us too?"

"Give me a minute. I'm just going to have a quick shower. Then I'll come through. No tea for me though, I'm going to open a bottle of wine and indulge myself with a few glasses."

Friday 3rd July 1981

Sidney had packed the last of his things to take to Bognor. It was his thirty-fifth birthday today and for the first year ever he hadn't received a card from either his daughter or son. He'd guessed Minnie wouldn't bother but had secretly hoped she might have reminded the children. To add to this disappointment, it had been three days since Sue's brother had phoned to say they'd received his letter and as yet he'd heard nothing from her. He was sure by now she would have read it and got in touch. What they'd had together was real, he couldn't possibly have imagined it.

"His mother's strong accent broke into his thoughts. "Gerra move on luv. Ere's yer ciggies. You need ta miss the busy traffic. Yer give us a call, like, lerrus know yer there. Good lad. An keep yerself arrar mischief."

Sidney kissed his mother's weathered cheek. "Let me know, mum, if a letter arrives for me."

"Now how canna do tha, lad? Yer gonna av to phone us."

He lugged his case down the steps and threw the case in his Bedford van. He hugged his mother and kissed her again. "I'll be in touch. Promise."

As Sidney pulled away from the curb, he gave a toot. He wasn't worried about his mother; she would be fine. It wasn't going to be him that she missed, he'd worked away from home since he'd left school at sixteen. It was the grandchildren that would leave a big hole in her daily life.

Minnie's family came from Eastbourne. His infidelity had given her the perfect excuse to up and leave Sidney's hometown.

The journey was tedious. He'd made it so many times this past year he was sure he could do it blindfolded. His radio was playing but he wasn't listening to it, his mind was on Sue.

After three stops at roadside cafes, he finally arrived in Bognor. It was seven thirty in the evening and the keys to his new digs were left under the stone by the front door as promised by the landlady. Sidney was used to living like this and had stopped at the shop and bought a few provisions, but he was pleased to see there were teabags and milk already in the fridge, it felt like a nice touch.

The flat was ground floor and spacious, situated on the outskirts of the town centre. Opposite him was the cinema and next to that a fish and chip shop. It all seemed the perfect setting. He usually lived in caravans while he oversaw jobs, but this arrangement suited him better now he needed more stability. Sidney knew he would stay in Sussex. Not necessarily in this flat, but a thought had crossed his mind that maybe he'd buy around these parts, who knew? The starter homes he was going to be working on, you could buy half finished. You had to paint them yourself. He'd worked on several estates like this. They were normally only two-bedroom properties, but that's all he would need… that's if he was ever going to be allowed to have his children overnight. The more he thought about it the more he liked the idea. Minnie was taking the equity in their Liverpool home. He'd walked away from it. Leaving her with the kids, it seemed only fair to leave her with the assets. He knew he'd make his way. Sidney had taken this flat because it was furnished, but there was no bedding. Not even pillows. Luckily he'd brought his sleeping bag with him. He'd go into town tomorrow and buy some bits, cheap in Woolies. The television was one of those you had to wiggle the aerial on top of the box. He would have to sort that out. If he was going to spend lonely nights here, he wanted a good TV and sound system.

*

Martha was in hospital. She'd gone by ambulance. She'd fallen in the early hours of Friday morning. Sindy had been annoyed with her for not calling out for help, but seeing the agony her Martha was in, it was fruitless.

She had broken her hip and arm in two places. They were serious breaks, and the hospital were waiting for the swelling to go down before they could reset them under anaesthetic. Her arthritis was going to be an issue for her chances of healing and the consultant said they would need a consultation before and after the operation to see how they go forward.

Susan's letter from Sidney was still on the mantlepiece. Martha had decided yet again she couldn't make the journey to the hospital and it was in Sindy's mind to go visit Susan alone, only the accident had put pay to the plans. She'd phoned the hospital to let Susan know. She hadn't come to the phone even though Sindy hung on just in case she'd wanted to speak to her. The lady on the other end of the line had told Sindy quite politely, 'Sue understands. She wishes you to send her mother her best wishes and hopes she gets well soon.' That was it. The phone went dead. This is a Susan that Sindy didn't seem to recognise or know anymore.

Sindy was pleased to hear the back gate open. Duncan was home. He would pick Jack up from nursery school while she prepared lunch. Charlotte was asleep in her cot, so she didn't have to be disturbed either. Duncan came straight in and washed his hands. "Any news on mum this morning?"

"No, only what I said earlier. Comfortable but nothing is happening as yet. I phoned Sue, but didn't get to speak to her. She sends her best, but we really should get this letter to her. Shall I post it?"

Duncan picked it up off the mantlepiece. "We'll have to stick it down again and write a card or something to her. Explain a bit like."

"Why? She need never know we opened it. We could just redirect it." Sindy was still put out by her sister-in-law's rebuff earlier. It had hurt her more than she cared to admit for not even bothering to come to the phone to say hello.

Duncan flopped in the chair. "Whatever you think."

Sindy hit him playfully round the head making his hair sweep across his eyes. "Don't get too comfy. I want you to pick Jack up from nursery. I'll do you a sandwich for when you get back."

As Duncan stood up again, she asked him what he had planned for the afternoon. "I'm back at the Marlows. I'm in the middle of digging over a border. Why?"

"One of us ought to visit your mum. Take her a few things. I bought some squash this morning and a Woman's Own. She'd like to see a familiar face, I'm sure."

Duncan kissed Sindy briefly. "I'll go this evening. Can you find out the evening visiting time for me. Unless I babysit and you go?"

"No. I'll let you."

While Charlotte was asleep this morning Sindy had had a good clean in Martha's room. She'd put everything artfully arranged in there like it was an everyday sitting room and not a place where someone with a disability spent their days. Even the commode had a medium sized teddy bear perched on a cushion which matched the curtains. Sindy loved the end result. It made her feel happy. She felt freer too. Martha had only been gone for the morning, but already Sindy could feel the release from her daily chores that she'd learnt to take in her stride.

Sindy made Jack Marmite soldiers and Duncan a round of cheese and tomato sandwiches, together with a packet of crisps. She made herself one of those 'Slimfast' flavoured milk drinks that were meant to help you lose six pounds in a week. She swallowed it quickly, thinking to herself it looked more appetising than it really was. Still, she was determined to persevere. Her clothes were still too tight from carrying Charlotte and she was spending her days slopping around the house in baggy t-shirts and loose jogging bottoms that were proving too hot and heavy for the warm weather.

She made a pot of tea and left it brewing under a tea cosy. She'd normally do a tea bag in a mug, but she wanted to get organised so when Duncan came in with Jack they could just sit and have their lunch together and she could concentrate on feeding Charlotte. She was having solids now, but most of it ended up on her bib where she'd spat it out in disgust.

Hearing the rattle banging on the side of the cot told Sindy that Charlotte was awake. She went upstairs to get her. "What a good girl you are." Little chubby arms and legs waved frantically with the excitement at seeing her mummy's face appear over the cot. Sindy lifted her up and blew a noisy kiss on her neck making her squeal. "Come on, Poppet, let's change your nappy." She lay her on the changing mat and gave her the lotion to hold while she folded the terry nappy. "You've got carrot and tomato waiting for you downstairs. It looks delicious, but probably tastes as bland as mummy's milkshake." Sindy leant over and blew another raspberry kiss, this time on Charlotte's tummy. She gurgled with laughter. "Ooh mummy loves you."

Duncan and Jack were already at the table eating their lunch when Sindy appeared carrying the baby on her hip. "Here you are. There's your brother, look, he's eating his lunch too." Charlotte smiled. Jack was full of his morning at school, which dominated the conversation.

Chapter Eighteen
Susan James

Susan re-read Sidney's letter that Duncan had re-addressed and posted on. She folded it in half and put it in the pocket of her shorts. Then a few minutes later she pulled it out and read it again. The pain that ripped through her had her slowly tearing the pages, watching the words become unrecognisable.

Michael, a patient like herself, broke into her thoughts as he called out to her. She shoved the torn pages into the envelope and put it in her pocket and went over to the potting shed. She liked Michael. He was recovering from an alcoholic binge and had a history of self-harming. "What's up?"

"Give us a hand, Sue. I want to prick these seedlings out into these bigger pots. If I don't get help, I'll be here all day."

Michael was a patient at the hospital and loved being outside. He'd taken on the garden project, which Susan was also involved with. She went into the shed not feeling in anyway embarrassed by her big, soled boot exposed by her bare legs. Her shorts were shorter than average, and the other foot was in a school like plimsole. She would never have been seen by anyone dressed like this at home. Here, people had a better acceptance of individuality and differences. Susan felt comfortable amongst them. Jolene helped this a lot by the outrageous clothes and jewels she wore to everyday meetings and her one-to-one sessions. Susan had begun to think this was the reason behind Jolene's terrible dress sense. Not that she'd ask her such a question.

Sally, one of the girls from the B block, popped her head in the greenhouse. "There you are. There's a phone call for you. A Sidney. Do you want to take it?"

"No. No thank you."

Susan continued pricking out the plants not looking at either Michael or Sally. Michael teased her when they were alone. He gave an exaggerated whistle, "who's Sidney?"

"I don't take calls from anyone. It's easier that way." She knew she hadn't answered his question, but she had no intention of discussing Sidney with anyone.

Susan ate very little lunch. Her mind was spinning with the news the letter had held and the fact that Sidney phoned to speak to her. *'How did he know where to find me? He must have phoned home and Sindy told him.'*

"Susan?"

Susan would recognise those dulcet tones anywhere. Jolene had one of those voices that held the same key. Never rising or sinking. Always questioning calmly. Susan stood up and followed her through to the quiet lounge.

Susan sat quietly, not wanting to open the discussion up. Jolene spoke first. "I hear your mother's had an accident and you have had a phone call from Sidney."

"Is nothing private here?" Susan knew her outburst was uncalled for and ridiculous, but she was feeling vulnerable again, which was alien to her lately and she didn't like it.

"Susan. You can pick up your life whenever you wish, but while you are here, I need to be part of your world."

"I'm sorry. I just feel mixed up."

"Mixed up?"

"Yes."

"Let's think about your mother's accident. How do you feel towards her?"

"Well, I didn't want her to fall, obviously, but Sidney's letter and his phone call has overshadowed that."

"You didn't wish to speak to him when he phoned?"

"No…no I didn't."

"Why?"

"What would I say? I'm in here because of him. If I had my way, I wouldn't be here at all."

"Do you still feel that way?"

Susan shook her head. "I don't know. I feel safe in here. I don't think I want to venture outside and certainly not with Sidney."

"But you loved him."

Susan nodded. "Completely."

"Do you want to read the letter to me, or explore some of its content?"

"No." Susan took the letter out of her pocket. She opened the envelope and showed Jolene the tiny pieces of torn up paper. "You see I couldn't read it to you if I wanted to. I've destroyed it."

"How does that make you feel?"

"What, destroying the letter?"

"Yes."

"It makes me feel I have done to him what he did to me. Does that sound silly?"

"No. It's how you feel." She paused for a few seconds letting her words hang. When Susan remained quiet, Jolene said, "do you wish you could read it again?"

"I guess with time… and if I was patient enough, I could put it together again like a puzzle, but I'm not inclined to do so at the moment."

Jolene placed her hands on her knees. A sign the session was coming to an end. "Susan, I want you to think about what you have said this afternoon. I want you to ask yourself if you could put yourself together again just like you said you could do with the letter; would Sidney be part of the new building?" On that question Susan knew the meeting was over. Always a question hanging to make her think.

*

Sidney had phoned the hospital several times now. Each time he was told Susan did not take phone calls. How he was going to see her he had no idea. He thought about phoning her mother's home again, but he resisted.

He tossed a coin from his pocket. *'Heads I phone her again, tails I leave her alone.'* It landed on tails. *'Best of three.'*

Sidney phoned the hospital. He knew in his heart it was foolish to bet against the toss of a coin. He was given an appointment for today. Friday evening at seven o'clock. He couldn't believe it. Excitement and nerves played a big part of his mixed emotions.

He had so much to tell her. He'd got his eye on one of the part build houses, which would be ready next year, at the beginning of January. They were going for fourteen thousand pounds, but he'd seen the site manager and been offered a discount bringing the price down to twelve thousand five hundred. He just had to get his mortgage approved. On the family front, he'd sorted out the access arrangements for having the children on a weekend, and if he could just get Susan back in his life it would feel perfect.

Sidney had a shower and put on a pair of light-coloured cotton trousers and a sports t-shirt. He splashed his freshly shaved face with Karate aftershave. The evening was warm and he'd driven with the windows down. He checked his hair in the rear-view mirror like an excited teenager on a first date. He'd been so keen to see Susan he had a good twenty minutes to kill before he could visit. He parked in the town and had a pint in the pub before walking the short distance to the hospital.

His heart was going nineteen to the dozen as he waited at the door to be buzzed in. He had so much to say to her. He couldn't wait to hold her to him tightly and say how sorry he was. The door opened and a tall thin lady stood in a blue uniform. "I've come to see Susan James. Seven o'clock?"

"Yes. She's expecting you. Jay will take you to the quiet lounge."

A man who he guessed was around his own age, said, "this way." Sidney followed without saying a word. This place felt cold and unfriendly. White walls, lino tiles on the floors and high ceilings. It was all very clinical.

He saw her before she saw him. She was talking to an elderly lady who was knitting. He cleared his throat nervously and without thinking, the familiarity of her face had him saying, "Peg." He wanted her to jump up and leap into his arms, but she didn't. She stood up and said softly, 'Sidney.'

They went out into the garden at her request and sat on a bench overlooking a pond. They were alone. Sidney had dreamt of this moment but found himself tongue tied.

Susan broke the silence. "How are you?"

"Oh Peg, I…"

She corrected him. "I'm called Sue. That is my name."

"I know. I'm sorry. It's just you are always going to be Peg to me. Not because of your silly leg, but my Peg. The Peg I fell in love with, but if you really want me to call you by your name then I will. I wanted to if you remember. First night I took you out."

"I know you did. Things are different now. I'm trying to start afresh."

Sidney saw his chance and the words were out before he could stop them. "I'm doing the same. I'm lost without you though. I can't bear it. I was hoping to persuade you…"

Susan interrupted him and took him completely off his guard. "Sidney what are you expecting of me?"

Sidney felt in his pocket. He pulled out a little black box that held a single solitaire diamond ring. He'd bought it in anticipation of this moment." He held it out to her. "It's for you. I want you to marry me."

Susan stared at the ring that shone from the little cushion. How she'd dreamt of a moment like this. She said instead, "now is not the time for promises."

Sidney hesitated. Not so sure of himself. This was not going how he planned. "You do still love me, don't you?"

Susan fiddled with her long skirt. She'd put it on specially for the visit. "I don't know. That is being honest with you. You hurt me. I had such dreams and plans, and all the while you were living with someone else."

"I never married Minnie. I never ever asked her either. Not even when the children came. It wasn't until I met you that I ever thought I could make such a commitment."

Susan turned her attention to the pond and stared at the water. Her voice was calm, giving no clue to the emotions she was struggling with. "I know you say you weren't married to Minnie, but you had children with her, and you were still living with her while you were leading me on, and all the time you were lying to me. Having me believe you were parted. Living separately. I loved you. I loved you with all my heart. When you told me that Sunday evening about Minnie, I realised you were no different from everyone else. You made me, and my life, look foolish."

Sidney felt sick. "Please look at the ring. I bought it for you. I bought it with plans for our future. Together."

Susan smiled at him and he was reminded of his Peg. The Peg he fell in love with. She dashed the moment by saying, "please put the ring away. I'm not ready for commitment or plans. I take one day at a time."

Sidney sounded desperate. "You don't have to now. I'm free. I'm all yours. I'm about to buy a house for us to…"

"No, Sidney. Not for me. I'm not yours anymore. You destroyed me. I'm broken. You did that to me. I don't know if I can trust you again, or love you like that again. I am still…"

"Didn't you read my letter. I told you my life is over without you, I meant it."

"Sidney…My life ended when I left you sitting at the canal after you told me you were going home to your common-law wife and family. The future and the dreams I thought I had, were never mine."

"You're wrong. I'm here. All for you. Please don't do this. I need to…"

"For now, Sidney, there's no us. If you're serious about me, we need to start again. Slowly. I'm not promising anything. For now, I don't know how I shall ever put one foot outside the security I have found in this old building."

Sidney thought before he spoke, using her real name as a start to show her he was listening, "Sue, my letter. It should have told you everything. I did my best to explain. Don't you…"

"Here's your letter." She handed him the envelope that held tiny pieces of torn paper. He opened it.

The shock on his face was evident. "Why did you do that?"

Tears slid down Susan's face. The first tears she'd shed in weeks. Her voice came out in a whisper, "because that is what you've done to me. So, if you are serious that you want to rebuild a friendship, you can start by visiting me on Fridays at seven."

"It's not the best day. I have to…" Sidney saw the look on Susan's face and back tracked. "No, that's fine. I shall be here next Friday. I'm sorry, really sorry. I made a mistake. I should have been honest at the start. I can see that now."

"Yes, Sidney, you did make a mistake. You thought because I looked like a freak, I wouldn't have the same feelings as everyone else. You were wrong."

Sidney stood up indignantly. Disappointment made him cross. He sounded angry when he said, "never! Never ever have I thought of you as a freak. That's unfair of you to say that. What I felt for you was true. I was just tied up in another relationship. That's where I made my mistake."

Susan stayed sitting. She ignored his desperation and anger and said quite calmly, "it's time for you to go now."

"Tell me, Sue. Please just tell me. Do I stand a chance?"

"One thing I've learnt in here is don't waste today, tomorrow might not arrive."

Sidney pulled Susan to her feet and for the first time this evening he held her close. "Think about the fun we had, the love…"

She didn't pull away, but rested her head on his shoulder and whispered, "no, Sidney. I can't relive yesterday. I'm looking forward. Maybe we do have an us, but at the moment my heart is in pieces … and… as I said, you did that to me."

*

Duncan soon realised the wall Millie had put around herself to protect her from the attraction between them had crumbled the night of their first stolen kiss. She was difficult at first but slowly he had wheedled his way into her affections. She more than liked him and he couldn't be happier. The secrecy in it made it all the more exciting. He couldn't remember ever feeling like this.

Stolen, secret kisses came easily and often between them both. There was only one problem, the kisses were no longer enough. Both of them wanted more.

Martha was still in hospital and it looked like she would be there for a long while yet. The consultant had told both Sindy and Duncan that she would need to go to the rehabilitation unit before she came home. Sindy was still very much enjoying the freedom of the bigger house without the restrictions of caring for her mother-in-law. They had given notice on their old council house and had removed their furniture. Sindy had spoken to Martha and she was happy for them to clear her stuff out if they didn't need it. A removal van had arrived the following day taking lots of things to the second-hand shop. Duncan had gone along with everything. Guilt at his feelings for Millie meant he was more than compliant at home. They were now in the throes of buying Martha's house, cashing in on the maximum discount for her thirty-one years of residency.

Saturday 11th July 1981

Duncan was up early and leaving the house before seven for the Marlows. He'd told Sindy he had to help Grace settle her horse into the spare stable. It wasn't a complete lie. Grace was moving her horse, Tallis, into Champers old stable today, but Duncan wasn't really needed, and he knew it. Both he and Millie thought of every excuse under the sun to be together these days. They hadn't made love yet, but Duncan had roamed his hands over every inch of her body and knew it as well as his wife's. He ached to have more and could feel the want in Millie too.

Guilt no longer had the power to hold them back, it was lack of opportunity and courage that stopped them stepping over the next line.

Duncan had fed and put Millie's horse in the paddock before she appeared. It seemed the most natural thing to do to shut the stable door and fall into each other's arms. They had just over half an hour together before Millie had to leave for the library. "Good luck with Grace. Don't let her put Tallis in with Truffle just yet. He needs to be in the separate paddock. He draped his arm around her shoulders. "I know, I know. You've told me a million times." Words were lost as lips met urgently again. "I'll miss you."

Millie pulled out of his arms. "I must go and get changed for work. Try and come back later. Say we have a leaky tap or something."

Duncan pulled her back for one last kiss. "I'll try."

Late morning a land rover pulling a horse box appeared. Childhood memories had Duncan feeling at ease with Grace. "Well look at you, going up in the world." He was referring to the land rover.

She hopped out of the truck and laughed. "Not me. Borrowed and at a price. It's good to see you again. I see Sindy occasionally at the school but not to speak to. She seems to be in a hurry. How are you?"

"I'm good thanks. Sindy's in a hurry as she has to get Jack to nursery once she's dropped Paul off. She sends her love though."

Duncan hadn't seen Grace since he had left school years ago but would have recognised her anywhere. Perhaps she looked a bit plumper than he remembered, but then her nickname had been 'thunder thighs' and nothing had changed on that front. Her hair was straight and still the same brown colour. It was shaped in a pageboy style, which made her face look fuller too. The cute dimple in her cheek was still apparent when she smiled. Large straight white teeth dominated her face, the metal braces were long gone. They chatted easily as he showed Grace where she'd be keeping Tallis and when she smiled her face lit up making her look attractive.

"What's the story on you then? Millie said you were divorced."

She told him she had one daughter, Emily, who was six. Her marriage failed because of an office affair, and that she now lived with a useless live-in lover.

"Who's the live-in lover, do I know him?"

"Pete. Pete Weller. I doubt if you do. Didn't go to our school."

Duncan shook his head. "No, doesn't ring a bell. What's wrong with him? Why's he useless?"

"He likes a flutter on the horses. Well not just the horses. Anything that moves."

"Is that so bad?"

"It is when he doesn't pay the bills or raids your child's money box or if needs must, steals out of your purse or…"

Duncan was genuinely horrified and interrupted before she said more. "Blimey Grace, you can pick em." Duncan moved over to open the horse box. A beautiful black stallion horse's rear stared him in the face. "Bloody hell, this is a beast. You're lucky to be able to keep him with all the things you've just said."

"I know, my mum helps, but that's why I don't kick Pete out. He works hard and brings in a tidy penny. It's just a shame he loses most of it."

The two moved around each other getting Tallis out. He was a beauty there was no mistake in that. "You can ride him if you want. It would help me too."

"Oh wow, Grace. Yes please."

Duncan was curious about her split marriage. He seemed to have Millie and their future on his mind all the time these days. "Does your ex see Emily?"

"Every weekend. It's our time. Pete and me. I don't think we would have survived as a couple if we didn't have that breather."

"Why do you say that? Sindy and I have the kids all the time, no one takes ours for a weekend."

Duncan witnessed the sadness flit over her face. "That's the thing with broken marriages. It seems your new partner can never love your children like the couple that made them. Emily is in the way. Not my way but Pete's. He's quite mean to her really."

Duncan was shocked to hear this. "Don't you tell him off? I couldn't stand it if anyone upset my boys... or Charlotte for that matter."

"We row all the time and Emily gets caught up in the middle. If she's reading at night with the light on, she's in trouble because she should be sleeping. If she doesn't eat her tea, she's wasteful. If she's playing with her dolls, he tells her she's too big for dollies, if she's watching TV she should be doing something constructive, and the list goes on. I know Emily hates him."

"Does she say that?"

"No. I'm frightened to ask her. I know though. She's not the happy little girl she used to be either. There's a nervousness about her when Pete's home."

Duncan didn't say any more. Just thought to himself, *'Millie would never be like that.'* He'd witnessed her with the boys. She was brilliant with them. What Grace had told him still played on his mind. While he moved around helping Grace with Tallis his thoughts were with Emily. *'Poor kid. I can't believe anyone could be like that to a child. What a bastard.'*

Nothing more was said about partners or marriages. Duncan didn't have to tell Grace to keep Tallis separate from Truffle, she'd already made up her mind to leave him stabled today. "Let him settle," she said. "I'll hopefully catch Millie later. What time will she be home today? She only works part time at the library, doesn't she?"

"Yes. I think she'll be home about threeish."

Duncan left Grace to it. He went off to tidy up a few things in the garden. He wanted to mow a lawn in Mundham this morning too, and now Millie had said she was hoping to see him later he needed to spend the afternoon with his family. It didn't matter how many times he told himself, *'you're walking a dangerous line.'* It didn't stop the excitement, craving and wanting. Millie was like a drug to him.

Duncan didn't get a chance to say he had to go back to the Marlows that evening. Sindy was insistent that he visit his mother. He toyed with the idea of pretending to make the visit, but it was all too risky. His mood was irritable, and he snapped at the boys when he was trying to watch the news, and then Sindy annoyed him further when she asked him to help with the washing up. This was totally out of character, but he couldn't help it. At six o'clock he walked into the hospital carrying a few magazines the neighbour had sent round for Martha, and a bunch of flowers he'd picked up from the garage. He leant over and kissed his mother's soft cheek. "How are you?"

"I'm in a lot of pain, but they monitor me." It was on this visit that Martha told Duncan she wouldn't be coming home. "I'm too much for Sindy. She doesn't complain and things have been great between us lately, but I'm getting worse. I have been talking to one of the physios and she is arranging a meeting with a social worker. It looks like I'll qualify for sheltered accommodation. You know, like the ones they built over the back of us. Council. I'm hoping to get one of them. If not there's always Chichester. They are all warden assisted. It will be for the best."

Duncan was about to comment, but Martha stopped him. "No, love. I've made my mind up. Your family is growing, and you need the space. You don't want to be wasting money having a toilet and bathroom built downstairs just for me. Put the money to good use. Have a conservatory, that seems to be the thing these days. Or just extend, make the third bedroom bigger for Charlotte."

"Mum…I don't know what to say. It's so good of…"

"Don't." Martha reached out and touched her son's hand. "I want you to have it." She pulled herself up in the bed a bit and winced at the effort and the pain it caused. "Have you heard how Susan is?"

"Yes, she seems brighter. She doesn't say a lot but she's making friends and Sidney's been. He went yesterday."

"Really? What was the outcome of that visit or don't you know?"

Duncan couldn't help laughing, "I don't know. I haven't seen her since. Stop worrying. She seemed fine." He fiddled with the flowers he'd bought for her, arranging them best he could in the vase. He then went over to the washbasin and filled it with water. "Sue's working on some garden project with a guy called Michael. He's an alcoholic and…"

"Jesus wept boy! Surely not."

"Mum, Sue's in a special hospital for the mentally ill. Theres all sorts in there. She's okay. She's made friends and she seems to like this Michael. Like, mum. That's all. I wouldn't lose any sleep over it because I still believe she's in love with Sidney. I don't know if she's punishing him for hurting her so badly or she really doesn't want to hurry into anything."

"Good. Good. I'm glad to hear that. Not that I have anything against him but…"

"But nothing mum. He's left his family for our Sue. Give him some credit."

"I don't believe him. She kicked him out more like."

They begged to differ and talked about the royal wedding at the end of the month. "You'll watch it in here, won't you? Sindy's joining in with the neighbours and they're having a bit of a do after the event on the green. Alice at the Marlows is full of it too and is planning a bonfire party in the garden, weather permitting."

Martha scoffed. "Weather permitting! What with all their bloody money. They could afford a marquee if the weather's bad. It's the likes of us on the council estate that will get washed out if it rains."

"A marquee with a bonfire." Duncan laughed.

Martha took him off his guard, wiping the smile off his face when she said, "and whose party will you go to?"

"I'll be with my family of course." Duncan grabbed his sweatshirt off the back of the chair, making out it had got chilly. "I'll be off now, mum. Sunday tomorrow, we might not get in to see you tomorrow." He hesitated and added, "unless of course there's something you need."

Martha seemed to forget her question. "No. I'll be fine. Don't tell Sindy about my move. I'll do that. It will give us something to talk about when she next visits. I do have some furniture left though, don't I? I'm going to need a few bits to furnish a little flat."

"Mum, there's heaps. Sindy has squashed all sorts of stuff into your room just in case you wanted it. You'll be fine and if there's anything you need that we've sold, we'll sort it." Duncan kissed his mum goodbye, pleased the conversation had steered away from the Marlows. He didn't feel comfortable at his mother's observations.

Once outside he knew he should go straight home but with the evening still warm and light The Four Willows was like a magnet. He steered his car into the drive. Millie met him at the door. She'd been waiting for him. "I'd given you up."

"Sorry. Sindy insisted I go to the hospital and visit my mum." He didn't tell her about his mother's comment, but he did tell her about the housing situation. "It all helps if I have to leave. You know, knowing mum is settled away from my family home. That could have been difficult."

Millie walked with Duncan over to the stables. They closed the door on the tack room and fell into each other's arms. Without planning, sex just happened. Their kisses increased, clothes got removed and hands wandered. Their pleasure increased as they explored each other's bodies. The two of them lay in the straw exhausted and sated from the release that only making love can fully bring.

Millie was the first to speak. Her voice a whisper, "are you planning on leaving Sindy for me?"

Duncan traced his finger over her tiny breasts. "I guess something will happen. Don't you want more than this?"

"Of course, I do. I just wasn't sure where 'this' was going."

"I've fallen in love with you Millie. Really fallen in love. I don't want this to be a passing fancy. Don't you feel the same?"

She nodded. "I never thought I could. Not because of you, but I loved Simon so utterly and completely I thought I would always crave what I couldn't have."

Duncan held her to him tightly. "I shouldn't say it, I know, but I hate that bloody guy. Not because he hurt you, but because of the way you love him."

"Jealousy. You don't hear me say that about Sindy, do you?"

"I know, but I'm choosing you over my family. I have a feeling if Simon were around, I wouldn't get a look in."

Duncan was fishing for reassurance, but none came.

Half an hour later Duncan left for home. He knew Sindy was going to be furious. Daylight had gone and he was very late. Sindy would know he'd not been with his mother at the hospital all this time. He had no idea what he'd say as an excuse, but the stolen time in Millie's arms had been worth it.

What he didn't realise as he pulled out of the drive, the person who had sussed them out was watching from the window behind net curtains. Alice.

Chapter Nineteen
Friday 24th July

This was Sidney's third visit to the hospital. He now not only called her Sue but thought of her as such. He'd wanted her to be his Peg, the old Peg, but she was a different young woman to the one he'd first started courting. He signed the visitors book and was told Susan was in the garden. He didn't need an escort anymore, he knew his way. He could see her down at the pond. She was wearing shorts and her boot stood out on her bare leg. It told him of her growing confidence.

"Sue!" he called out and waved. She stopped what she was doing and waved back. She said something to the girl she was helping and walked towards him.

"Sorry, I forgot the time." This hurt Sidney. It proved to him that her days weren't waiting with bated breath for his visit. Her words were so painful he had to say something. "I can't believe you have just said that. I can't wait for Fridays. Seven o'clock is our time. How could you forget?"

Susan shrugged her shoulders and walked up to the seat with him. "Every day is the same in here. It's nothing personal."

He told her about his children and that last weekend they went to the beach and then to the cinema opposite his flat." She smiled and said that sounded nice. He told her about the house he'd got planned for them, and the fact that his mortgage had been approved. She seemed interested but didn't say one way or the other whether she wanted to be included in his plans.

"Sue, Wednesday is a bank holiday. It's the wedding of Prince Charles and Lady Diana." She just stared at him. He said again, "The Royal wedding! Surely, you've been following it. It's like Di mania out there. Every paper, magazines and news are full of them. Or her I should say her."

"Of course, I've heard of them. It's lovely. A fairy tale. I'm looking forward to watching it. We all are. I think we will have a little party here. Do you want me to see if you can come?"

This was the first time Susan had offered him a visit outside his Friday. He wanted to say yes but he wanted to take her away from this place more. "I was hoping you would come to my flat. Watch it at mine. I'd bring you back whenever you wanted." Susan didn't say anything. Sidney took her hand and held it tightly. "Please… it would be just us. You know a bit like old times, only now I have a flat and not a shared caravan." His attempt at a joke had fallen on deaf ears. "Well?... Yes?" He watched her, waiting for a reaction.

Susan pulled her hand out of Sidney's desperate grip and wrung her fingers together. "I'll think about it."

He tried to hide his disappointment. "How will I know?"

"Phone me Tuesday and I'll let you know then whether you can pick me up, or if not, you can come here. We'll definitely watch the wedding together. That's all I can promise at the moment."

She let him kiss her goodbye. He savoured every moment. His eyes were glassy with unshed tears. "I love you, Sue. I've never stopped loving you. Don't you forget that."

Susan looked up at him. "I know you do. I think I'm only just starting to realise that."

As Sidney walked back to his car, he wiped a stray tear from his cheek. These visits were so wonderful but so painful. There had been no reassurance from Susan that she still loved him. Telling himself, *'Don't hurry her. Give her time.'* Didn't help much at all.

Chapter Twenty
The Royal Wedding. Wednesday 29th July 1981

There was going to be a party later today after everyone watched the wedding between Prince Charles and Lady Diana Spencer. Paul and Jack were full of beans and driving Sindy crazy. "Take them out with you this morning, Duncan. I've got to make cakes for the tables."

Duncan pushed his feet into his trainers. "Come on, boys. Let's get you out of your mum's hair. We'll go to Millie's, you'll see Emily."

"Whose Emily?"

"Emily Coker. She goes to your school, Paul. You'll know her when you see her. Also, Millie's rescued a Shetland pony, it's called Scuttle. If Millie's there you'll be able to have a ride." The excitement increased as the boys hurriedly pushed their feet into shoes that weren't suitable.

Duncan didn't comment or make them change. He was eager to go. Getting to The Four Willows to be near Millie was becoming an obsession. "Come on then, let's go."

He remembered to kiss Sindy on the cheek. Affection between them was waning. She seemed happy to read a few pages of her book when they got into bed as he lay beside her thinking of Millie and wishing life were different.

When he pulled into the drive there was no one to be seen. He knocked on the door and Alice answered. Her voice was impatient and hurried, "what do you want? We're watching the procession. This is history. I don't want to miss the first glimpse of the bride."

"You go back and watch. I was just giving the boys some fresh air. They're driving Sindy crazy indoors."

"Millie's gone out with Grace for a ride." His disappointment didn't escape Alice, and her heart ached for what she believed lay ahead for Duncan's family. She could smell trouble. She looked at the two little boys. Their eager little faces full of anticipation, and she spoke with a softer voice. "There's a little pony out there. Here you go." Alice grabbed the tops she'd cut off the carrots earlier and gave them to the boys. "You can give it these." They ran off clutching the vegetable tops, giggling. Paul was faster but Jack did his best to keep up.

Before Duncan went with his boys to see Scuttle, he asked Alice where Emily was.

"I expect she's with her dad, or maybe her nan. I don't know if I'm honest. I'm fixated on the television. I've been up since six making food. The care team are coming later. We're having a party. I expect you'll be popping back again for that."

Duncan shook his head. "No, they're having a bit of a do on the green. Sindy wants to be part of that."

Alice didn't pass comment. "I'm going back in. I don't want to miss anything. You should see the crowds…"

Duncan turned away and made his way across to where Scuttle was kept. His mood was flat like a deflated balloon, making him irritable. "Don't hang over the fence like that. It'll break and then I'll have to fix it. Your mum moans enough about the amount of time I'm here as it is."

His ranting was falling on deaf ears. They still leaned over scratching the pony's head and grabbing handfuls of grass trying to get it to feed from their hands.

Duncan's eyes kept straying to the drive, hoping the girls would return before he left, but it didn't look like it was going to happen. Paul and Jack were bored and wanted to do something else. "Can't we go to the park, daddy. You said Emily would be here and we could ride the pony. There's no one. It's boring."

Duncan tried to delay them a bit longer, but he couldn't. "We can't ride the pony without Millie saying it's okay. That would be a bit cheeky." He found a ball in his car and the three of them had a kick around for a few minutes. He was just thinking he'd have to go when he heard the sound of hooves trotting on the tarmac. "Millie's here. You might be able to ride after all."

Two confident boys ran towards the two horses trotting side by side. Duncan felt jealous but forced a smile. "Morning ladies. I thought you'd be glued to the TV like everyone else is."

Millie laughed along with Grace. "We're going to be now. We've been over Dell Quay. It's beautiful this morning. We had a lovely ride."

Duncan spoke to Grace. "Where's Emily. The boys were hoping to ride Scuttle and play with her."

"She's with her nan. I'm going there in a minute to watch the wedding. They'll see Emily later. We're coming to the green for the street party."

Duncan brushed the top of Paul's hair not daring to look at Millie. "See boys, you'll see Emily later."

Jack jumped up and down, "Millie can we ride the pony please. Daddy said we could if you were here."

He blushed at the confidence and the insinuation that he'd given permission if Millie were here. She didn't seem put out. "Come on, quickly though. I want to see Lady Diana marry the prince. Don't you?"

Both boys screwed their noses up. Jack copying Paul. "No way."

There was laughter as they made their way over to the field. Duncan was left with Grace to put Millie's horse away. They chatted easily, leaving it that he'd see her later with Emily.

Duncan stood against the gate watching Millie walk Jack around the paddock with no saddle. He was hanging on to his mane for dear life. Millie called to him, "not coming to Alice's little do here then?"

He could tell she was put out. "I'll try, but I think I'm going to have to celebrate this wedding on our green today." Without thinking of the implications, he added, "you could come to ours."

"Paul spoke up excitedly. "Oh yes Millie you can do that. You'd see baby Charlotte and mummy. Or maybe we could all come here."

"No not this time. You enjoy your party and I'll enjoy mine."

She didn't look Duncan's way and he was left wondering what she was thinking. This always made him feel uneasy. She was so free, and he was always frightened she'd tire of the restrictions their relationship held. How he dreamed of being free.

"Come on, boys. Let's get you home for lunch." He wanted to kiss Millie, but it was too risky. He looked around thinking on his feet for a way to distance himself from the boys just for a moment. Millie was addictive. The more she gave of herself the more he wanted. It was no good. Grace was in the stable and the boys were right beside him. They didn't miss a trick. He gave Millie a wink. "Might see you later. See what turns up." She squeezed his hand and he leant in making it look like he was telling her a secret. "Love you." He whispered.

His heart felt heavy as he took the boys home. Torn, that's what he was. He realised how foolish he'd been to have beaten his sister's bloke up for the same sin he was committing. *'Perhaps this is my punishment for being so self-righteous.'*

*

Sidney had kept in touch with Susan's sister-in-law, Sindy. She was always pleasant when he phoned and through this communication he knew all about Martha's fall, and the plans to buy the council house with the sizeable discount. These were all things he'd been able to discuss with Susan on his visits, making him feel part of her family circle. Sindy had also invited them to their street party on the village green, but he had refused. Sidney had his own plans.

As he stood on the steps of Sunnydale hospital, he still couldn't believe Susan was going to come out with him today. He'd cleaned the flat best he could and bought in a few nibbles to enjoy while the wedding took place.

Sidney felt excited to be taking Susan out at last, away from this blessed hospital. He had so much he wanted to say to her and show her. He kept telling himself *'One step at a time. Watch the wedding and try and show her what I've accomplished and what I'm wanting to share with her. Things are moving in the right direction now. I can feel it.'*

Susan let him take her hand as they walked the short distance to the car park. She was wearing one of her long frocks. Her hair looked fluffy like it was freshly washed, and she'd clipped it up off her face. He thought she looked wonderful and told her so.

As they made their way to the car it was hard to believe he had Susan to himself at last. She laughed with him, just like the old days. He told her about his work on the new builds and the pranks that were being played. He was amazed too when she agreed to see the house, he'd put a deposit on.

"First stop is here." There were cement mixers, rubble, and half-built houses everywhere. It looked like a derelict bombsite. Sidney opened the car door and offered her his hand. "Here's ours when you're ready." She burst his hopeful bubble. "Not ours, Sidney,

221

yours. I'm not promising anything. She walked towards what would be the path that would lead to the property's front door.

"I know, love. I know. I'm just pleased you're here with me. I can't help dreaming and hoping though, can I?"

The walls of the house were up, but it was a dusty shell. You could see downstairs would have a kitchen and lounge diner. The staircase was wooden and covered in brick dust and dried bits of cement. Upstairs there was an airing cupboard, and you could see where the bathroom would be and the two bedrooms ."What do you think?"

"I think it's great. Definitely new." She paused before adding slowly, "maybe…it's possible… it could be a new start for us."

Sidney picked her up in his arms like a baby. "I do hope so, Sue. I want to marry you and carry you over this doorstep. Our first home together." She didn't correct him this time for referring to this place as our home but said instead, "can we go now? I don't want to miss seeing Lady Di emerge from the carriage."

Sidney's flat was less than fifteen minutes away and once they were home he turned on the television. He'd bought a new one with remote control. The picture was crystal clear and didn't need any aerial fiddled with. Susan kicked off her shoe and undid the lace on her boot. She curled herself in the chair, watching the crowds waving flags in anticipation of catching a glimpse of the carriage. Sidney couldn't believe how confident she seemed. He loved it.

"Shall we have champagne. I've bought some?"

"No. I'd like a cuppa though."

Sidney made tea and took some of the goodies in he'd bought. When he sat on the sofa, putting the tray down on the coffee table he said, "come and sit with me. Let's watch it together cuddled up."

He couldn't describe how happy he felt when she leant forward and took a marshmallow, stuffed it whole in her mouth and literally plonked herself beside him. "This is great. My favourites." He laughed. "I love you; I love you with all that I have, Sue. Come and live with me here. Marry me. Let's move to our new home together."

"Shush! Look there she is." There on the television was the first glimpse of the soon to be Princess Diana. She was smiling at the crowds from the carriage, giving an occasional shy wave. "She's just beautiful. He's such a lucky man."

"You're beautiful to me. I'm a lucky man."

Susan pushed him in his ribs, and he winced. They were still fragile. "Quiet I want to watch this."

They sat curled up together, wrapped in each other's arms watching as the crowds went crazy as the carriage passed by.

Sidney didn't mention the family party in Hunston they'd been invited to. He didn't want to share her with anyone. He wanted Susan all to himself. He didn't ever want to take her back to that weird hospital either. This could be her home. He wanted to take care of her here, forever.

*

Sindy took a tray of cakes out to the pasting tables that had been put up and were now laden with sandwiches, pork pies, sausage rolls and other delights that people had made for the street party. The ceremony was over, but the television was still showing the highlights of the day. It was full of the slight falter of Princess Diana's vows where she'd stumbled over Charles's name and the kiss on the balcony that the public had been waiting for.

223

Sindy caught sight of Duncan. He looked hot and sweaty. He'd set up a game of cricket for the children and was fielding on the green. The cheering and laughter echoed round the estate. The day had been glorious and as Sindy took in the gathering of people, the food, and the excitement on the green, the day seemed extra magical. "Sindy, there you are." It was Grace with Emily.

"Oh, Hello. Wasn't it wonderful? She looked absolutely beautiful." Her eyes strayed to Grace's daughter. Hello, it's Emily, isn't it?" The child nodded. Sindy called out to Duncan. "Emily's here. Can she join in?" Emily didn't need any encouragement; she ran across to the boys without hesitation.

Grace handed Sindy a bag. "Sorry, not one for home baking. A bag full of crisps, twiglets and cheese puffs."

Sindy took them gratefully. "Perfect, just what the children love."

"Where's this new edition to your family? Duncan tells me all about her but I've yet to see her. School mornings look busy for you. Always in a hurry."

"I am. I see Paul into the playground, then have to get to the nursery school for Jack. I don't suppose it would matter too much if he was late, but I like to try."

Grace looked around for the pram. "Well! Where is she?"

"Charlotte? She's in her cot. She's a bit off colour. Didn't sleep too well last night which isn't like her, and today she's eaten precious little. I think she's catching up on lost sleep."

"I bet it's her teeth. Emily was a terror with teething. You name a symptom and Emily got it. Sore bottom, diarrhoea, sore chin from all the dribbling, even a high temperature, and when those back molars tried to push through..." Grace groaned at the memory. "Nightmare days."

An easiness settled between them. "I've made a few other bits for the table too. Can you help me take it out?"

Grace followed Sindy into her home. Her eyes widened in surprise "Blimey, you put me to shame! Three children and you've prepared and baked all this."   There were little squares of cheese on cocktail sticks with a small pickled onion poked on the end. Scotch eggs cut into quarters, and three homemade large quiches on the side cooling.

"I love doing it." They walked out to the tables, both of them carrying food.

Sindy asked Grace about the stables at the Marlows and how her horse had settled. "Duncan says he's a beauty."

"He is. Tallis. I've had him eight years. I was lucky to get talking to Millie at the library or I'd still be struggling with the stabling fees. Grace sat on one of the chairs that had been placed near the tables and Sindy followed suit. "It must help now Duncan doesn't have to do every weekend. He said it was getting too much."

Sindy looked wistful. Her eyes strayed to her husband who had just caught one of the children out and there were cheers and clapping from the bowling side. Her voice was soft and incredulous in disbelief, "did he say that?"

"Yes, why?"

"He practically lives at the Marlows. He can't get there quickly enough of a morning and then again of an afternoon and evenings too if he can wangle it."

Grace looked puzzled. "I suppose it goes with the job, caretaker stroke gardener. He probably feels he has to be at their beck and call. You don't seriously think you have anything to worry about with Millie, do you? And if you aren't worrying about Millie there's only me and Alice, and she's got to be in her late fifties or even sixties."

"What about all those young carers that see to the old man?"

Grace shrugged her shoulders. "Yes, there are girls but no one you have to worry about or not that I've seen."
Sindy felt foolish, but her fears of Duncan's behaviour of late were out of her mouth before she could hold her tongue. "You might think I'm crazy, Grace, but he wears aftershave when he goes round there. He used to hate putting it on his freshly shaved face, said it stings. Not anymore. I get a whiff of it every morning. He seems to worry more about his appearance too. I caught him trying to pluck out nose hair the other evening. He always has an answer for me too if I question him, making me feel paranoid."

Grace laughed. "Nose hair! Are you serious? Honestly Sindy, Duncan's steady. Steady as a rock. I went out riding with Millie the other day and I tell you her heart is with some fella that betrayed her at university." She thought for a moment. "Millie and Duncan having an affair, no way."

Sindy sounded sulky. "Well maybe they aren't, but I feel Duncan wishes he could."

"That's in your head. You probably feel a bit mumsy having had three children before your thirty. I think you're amazing. I'm sure Duncan does too."

Sindy looked across at her husband. He had Jack on his shoulders and was charging across the green with the children trying to catch him. She couldn't help smiling. "Look at him, he's just a big kid really. I guess I am being silly. He said Alice was having a bit of a do at The Four Willows and we were invited. I refused to go initially but perhaps I should. Meet this Millie. It might make me feel better."

"We could all go. Go later. The care staff Millie uses are invited too. It starts about seven tonight. Alice is doing hot dogs and burgers. Duncan's built a bonfire at the far side of the garden, well away from the horses and I think they're having a few fireworks. The boys would love it. I'm taking Emily when I finish up here. She's really taken with the place. She's also fallen in love with the little Shetland pony."

Sindy wasn't convinced. "The boys were there this morning with Duncan. I really think they'll need an early night. It's been a long day too."

"One late night won't hurt them. They can come with me if you like."

Sindy looked across at the boys racing round the green. "I'll see."

Grace beamed and slapped Sindy playfully on her thigh, taking her slight hesitation as a yes. "Excellent. We'll have some fun." She stood up. "Now let me see this little girl of yours, or I'll think she's got two heads or something."

The two of them went into the house like old friends. Charlotte was sleeping. Grace peeped over the cot. "She's gorgeous. Sorry to tell you this but she's another Duncan look alike." Grace brushed her hand over the baby's head. "She's boiling. Has she got a temperature?"

"She always gets like that when she's teething. Look at the red cheek."

"I'd get her out of the cot. Cool her down a bit. It's a hot day and you've got her all cossetted up in a blanket."

Sindy took Grace's concern as interference. "She's only got a vest and a nappy on."
"Oh! I was only suggesting. I just thought she looked a bit hot,

that's all. It was instinct. I'm sorry. Come on let's take her downstairs and get her some fresh air."

Charlotte opened her eyes when Sindy lifted her from the cot, but she didn't cry. Grace was amazed. "She is good isn't she. You couldn't have done that to my Emily. She'd have screamed blue murder."

"Can you take her for me?" Without waiting for an answer Sindy passed the baby over. "I'll make a bottle up and see if I can get her to take a feed. She's not eaten a thing today. Just fluids."

Grace could feel the heat radiating from the child through her t-shirt. She kissed her warm cheek taking her downstairs, leaving Sindy fiddling around with things in the bedroom.

Sindy found Grace sitting at the table trying to get Charlotte to eat a crust off one of the sandwiches. She was showing no interest. Sindy held out her arms. "Give her to me, she'll take this." Children were grabbing paper plates and filling them with all the sugary goodies off the table. The noise was deafening but Charlotte seemed to take it in her stride. Sindy was pleased to see her drain the eight-ounce bottle of milk eagerly.

Duncan came across at that moment. "Hi, Grace, Sindy, alright?"

"Yes. Charlotte isn't best. Grace thinks she's got a temperature, but I think it's just her teeth. Look at her red cheeks. She's taken her bottle, so that's something."

Duncan took Charlotte and held her in the air above his head. "You're okay aren't you sunshine?"

Charlotte started crying inconsolably and Sindy was on her feet at once taking her from Duncan. "She isn't one of the boys who likes aeroplanes and rockets. She's a little girl." Grace laughed, "Emily loved all that rough play. Her dad used to roll her up in the rug and throw her on the sofa."

Thank you, Grace, not helpful!" Sindy felt Charlotte's feverish brow. "I'm going indoors to give her some pain relief." Sindy placed her in the pram and rocked it gently. "This isn't like you, darling."

Grace was apologetic.

"It's not you, it's me. I'm just a bit worried if I'm honest. This is so unlike her, isn't it Duncan. She's not been a day's trouble since she was born." The awkward moment of Sindy's outburst was forgotten. Duncan put an arm across Sindy shoulder, and she apologised again. "Grace has been trying to convince me to go to the Marlows later. Would you like that?"

Duncan shook his head. "Nah! The boys were there this morning, they're tired after the run around here. Let's just get Charlotte settled, I might go…"

It was Grace who interrupted him. "Go on, come. A party needs children. Emily will love it with the boys there."

Duncan wouldn't be budged, not even when Sindy said "I'm happy to go. Charlotte can sleep in the pram." He shook his head. "No. Not today. I might have to pop back later to check the bonfire is out properly and anything else that needs attention."

When Grace went to say something, he interrupted her. "No Grace, it'll give Sindy and me a chance to have a night in together." He moved over to the tables, took a plate, and started filling it with food. The conversation closed.

Grace winked at Sindy. "Well, he's hardly having an affair with anyone is he. He wants to be with his family."

"He's going to go back later though. Did you hear him."

Grace laughed, "Sindy! Listen to yourself."

"Oh, you're probably right, I'm being silly."

Grace wouldn't give in. "So, you'll come?"

"No. We'll have an early night. The boys will be tired. Jack's only four and they're up with the dawn chorus these days. It's so light and warm."

Stephanie Few

Stephanie felt quite emotional watching the royal wedding. Her hormones were all over the place with her pregnancy, her moods were irrational, and she was arguing with Simon more and more of late. He was always the first to apologise, making Stephanie despise him for his timidness. She asked herself the same question frequently, *'how could Millie have been so in love with him? He's so boring.'*

The wedding today was so romantic. True love. It really was a fairy tale. It made her realise how lucky Lady Diana was to be marrying her prince. Someone who'd chosen her. He must feel so lucky too. She was young, looked virginal, and was truly beautiful. Stephanie rubbed her stomach. She was heavily pregnant, and today's wedding had made her own marriage seem even more of a farce.

Everyone apart from herself and the professionals believed she was nearly thirty-one weeks pregnant. Just how far she was gone she couldn't be sure. She'd been lying now for so long she'd forgotten the date of her first missed period.

'Was Rafi the father?' Stephanie glanced at the television where they were showing Lady Diana getting out of the carriage, the dress was so creased it looked like she'd slept in it, but everyone was saying how beautiful she looked. 'A butterfly emerging from a chrysalis.' *'If I'd worn a dress like that, I'd have been pulled to bits for it.* Stephanie stroked her tummy like she did now from habit. *'What have I done? Millie had taken herself off the scene. Her father's needs had taken priority over university, her love life, and parties. Simon had become fair game. He'd fallen for me easier than I'd ever imagined. When I missed my period, I had a*

strong feeling it was Rafi's. Simon and I had only just started sleeping together, but when I'd thought about prospects, Simon was the better bet. Rafi was good fun, but he liked the drug scene. I'd enjoyed a dabble with the hard drugs at times, but I'd been happiest with a joint.' Stephanie focused on the television again. The crowds, the noise, the flags and flowers, it was amazing. As the carriage made its way to Saint Paul's Cathedral, the music they'd put on for the journey gave you goose pimples. Tears pricked Stephanie's eyes. They were showing Diana's father getting out of the coach; two bridesmaids were on the steps trying to gain control of the veil. Stephanie had never seen such a long train. The Princess turned and giggled in that shy way of hers and gave a wave to the crowd. They went wild. Her veil blew across her face uncontrollably. She'd seen this clip three times now and each time it made her want to cry. *'Jesus, what have I done?'* She felt anxious. Her blood pressure had been up on her last antenatal visit and she knew why. She'd bumped into Rafi last week. He'd made a joke that the baby could be his. She'd laughed a touch too loud and said, 'in your dreams.'

There it was again. That beautiful scene where Lady Diana took her vows and became the Princess. Stephanie rubbed her tummy gently, feeling sorry for herself and terribly mixed up. *'I miss Millie. What was I thinking? I didn't have to marry anyone. I could have lived with Millie. She'd have stood by me. There would have been room in that fancy house of hers, I know she would have helped. Now I spend my days rowing with Simon and wishing things were different. What a mess. What a bloody, bloody mess.'* Stephanie continued to rub her stomach as it contracted in a Braxton Hick spasm. *'Don't come yet little one. Three more weeks at least.'*

Stephanie had a thing for Chinese food at the moment and the sound of the key in the door told her Simon was back. "Sweet and sour pork balls and spareribs. Just as the lady ordered." He kissed the top of her head. "Here you go. Just what you fancied."

"I could eat that all to myself."

"I don't mind. You're the one eating for two, not me."

His kindness made her feel apologetic. "Sorry for earlier. It's just my hormones. I don't mean to snap."

"Don't worry about it, my skin's thick." He took the food through to the kitchen. "I'll put this on plates. Did you put them in the oven to warm?"

"No, sorry. I'm keeping my feet up like the doctor ordered."

Simon scoffed. "Bollocks! You were watching that rubbish again."

"It's not rubbish, it's lovely. She looked beautiful."

"So did you on our day, and you didn't have all that paraphernalia. You were just natural, and I loved you even more for it."

"I don't believe you, even then I looked like a beached whale. Just go and dish out my dinner, I'm starving."

*

Alice had watched the Royal wedding as it unfolded with Millie and her father. He'd cried. Alice and Millie had teased him, but he'd seemed to take it well. The crowds, the military, the music, it made you feel proud to be British. Alice had said so to Hugh. The day had been pleasant, and they had drunk a bottle of fizzy wine between.

"What time is Grace coming over with Emily?"

Millie shrugged her shoulders. "I'm not sure, but I'm going to take Truffle out for a ride first. I expect she'll be here when I get back. I don't know if she's staying for the party, but she'll definitely be here to feed and stable Tallis."

"Is Duncan coming back this evening with his family?"

Millie shrugged her shoulders again. "Who knows. Your guess is as good as mine."

"I hope so, the boys will love it here. What with the fireworks and the bonfire?"

"Duncan said they're having a party on their green. I think Sindy wanted to do that one." Without a backward glance Millie strode off towards the paddock.

Alice watched her go. *Have I been imagining a situation between her and Duncan when it's not so?"* Without further thought she went into the kitchen to prepare for the party. She had sausages to cook for the rolls and the cakes to ice with red, white, and blue icing. Two of the girls from the agency were coming this evening with their families. They were going to get Hugh in the new wheelchair he'd been measured up for and get him outside in the garden. Alice could tell he wasn't fussed, but he'd gone along with it to please her and Millie.

*

The boys were in bed and asleep by eight o'clock. "They're absolutely bushed." Sindy handed Charlotte to Duncan. "Here you are. You can try and get her to bring her wind up. I'll make us a coffee."

Charlotte laid her head on Duncan's shoulder. He patted her back gently, "you really aren't yourself, are you darling." He kissed her soft cheek and called through to the kitchen "she's still warm, Sindy. Do you think she's going down with something?"

"She has a few spots on the top of her leg. I'm thinking it's either teeth or she's got chicken pox."

"Really? Why her and not the boys."

"I don't know. These things are airborne."

Duncan laid her across his knees and patted her back. "She cried briefly then lay as if lifeless. She certainly wasn't the wriggly little thing she normally was. Do you think we should call the doctor?"

"What's he going to do? Tell me to give her children's paracetamol and plenty of fluids."

Duncan sat her up on his knees and her chin dropped to her neck. "I don't like this one bit. I'm going to phone him. Just for some advice."

Sindy was up and out of her chair like a shot. "No, you won't, I will. What is it with everyone? Grace accused me earlier of overheating her and now you don't believe me when I say she's just sickening for something. I've brought up two little boys and they're healthy. I think…"

"Sindy! Listen to yourself. I'm worried that's all. You're great with the kids, you know I think that. It's just she seems listless… or I should say lifeless."

Tears sprung to Sindy's eyes. "I'm worried too. I just don't want to make a fuss. I'll take her to see the doctor in the morning."

The tears made Duncan all the more determined. "No. I'll phone now. For advice. If he says plenty of fluids and pain relief then at least we know."

Sindy was cradling Charlotte when Duncan returned. "You were right. Give her Calpol and plenty of fluids and take her in to the surgery tomorrow if you are still worried." Duncan didn't sit down again. "Would you mind if I popped to the Marlows? I won't be long but I ought to check the bonfire's out properly and that there's nothing Millie wants me to do."

Sindy didn't want him to go anywhere. She was still worried about Charlotte. "Please stay in. I'm sure there's enough people there today to sort out any problems. She would have said earlier if she needed you to go back this evening. Surely?"

Duncan was pulled between loyalty and desire. He couldn't get enough of Millie. "I'll just go and check. I won't be long. Promise."

Tears fell down Sindy's face. "I can't believe you. It's nearly nine o'clock. You told Grace you wanted a quiet night in with us. What's changed your mind?"

"Nothing." He shook his head. "You're exhausted, Sindy. Charlotte kept you awake last night with her crying and what with all the cooking you've done for today's event, you could do with an early night. Why don't you go on up to bed? Get some sleep while Charlotte sleeps. I'll be back before you know it."

The front door closed leaving Sindy alone. She put Charlotte over her shoulder, and she didn't stir. "Come on, sweetheart. Let's do as daddy says. Sleep while you sleep, eh?"

Charlotte still didn't murmur when she was placed in her cot. This was nothing out of the ordinary, but she would usually bang around and play with the cot toy attached to the sides, talking to it. Sindy had a quick wash and got herself into bed and read for a bit. Her eyes were tired, and she settled down to sleep it had been a long day.

Alice was pushing Hugh into the house just as Duncan arrived. "Evening, lad. We didn't expect you at this hour. Grace said you've been having quite a party."

Duncan smiled at Hugh but got no response. "We have, but I just thought I ought to check on things here before I settled down at home."

Alice's voice softened as she recalled the day. "Did you see the wedding, she looked…" Hugh started making noises which Alice had learnt meant he was unhappy. "Okay Hugh. We're going in. You men aren't as romantic as us women."

Duncan made his way across to the bonfire thinking, *'bloody old misery. How does Alice cope with him?'* As he reached the paddock a child running full pelt nearly knocked him off his feet. "Whoa there. Where's the fire?" She instantly bobbed down as another child appeared running in the same fashion. Her young voice was high and excited. "That's your last bob down and then you have to run for your life." The child that had nearly knocked Duncan off his feet stayed crouched down on the ground getting her breath. Then Emily appeared. She screamed with excitement when she saw the two girls and took off in the other direction. Duncan smiled at the fun they were having, but was still pleased he'd made the decision not to bring his family. He was sure it would have been too much.

He could see a few people gathered round the bonfire, sitting in deckchairs. The only person he had eyes for was Millie. The chemistry between the two of them made her stand out from the others. He sauntered over towards the fire trying to look relaxed and uninterested. He called out, "all okay here?"

Millie waved. "Come and join us." Her cheeks were high in colour. He wasn't sure if it was down to the warmth of the bonfire, the consumed alcohol, or his presence. There's food in the kitchen if you fancy anything and plenty of wine here." There was laughter from the gathering, and he couldn't help thinking it all looked very schoolgirlish. Grace smiled at him. "It was a great day earlier. Sindy is amazing. All that food prep. I don't know how she does it.

I was more than impressed." She stood up. "Did you see Emily as you came over?"

"Yes, she's playing some form of chase and catch me."

"I must go and get her and make tracks home. She must be exhausted. It's been a great day though." She patted the back of the deckchair, "Here you are you can have my seat." She thanked Millie for a great evening and waved at the other three women. "Oh, Duncan, how's Charlotte? She looked proper poorly earlier. I'd take her to…"

"Yes, she's fine. They're all settled for the night." Duncan didn't want to be talking about his family in front of Millie.

Nothing more was said, and he was pleased to see her leave and even more pleased to see the other three women stand up. It seemed his arrival had been the cue to break up the happy gathering. Millie said her goodbyes and smiled at Duncan. "It's good to see you. Thanks. I didn't think you would make it. Grace said you were having some family time."

"God, Millie. Don't let's talk about my family. I miss you every minute I'm not with you. I know it's wrong, but I can't help it. You're driving me crazy."

Millie changed the subject. "Today was beautiful wasn't it? Did you watch the wedding?"

"Nah. I've seen a few highlights. I kept the kids happy on the green. It's been a long day though, but I couldn't settle indoors without coming to say goodnight."

"Are you going to stay for a while?" She held up an empty bottle of wine. "There's plenty more where this came from."

"Can we just have a few minutes together on our own somewhere. I really must get back." He forgot that only minutes earlier he had not wanted to talk about his family. "Charlotte's ill. I know I made light of it to Grace, but I phoned the doctor before I came out. I think she's got one of those illnesses like chicken pox or measles. She's not herself."

Millie stood up and folded the deckchair. "Can you fold those up too and carry them over to the tack room for me." He followed like a lamb.

It was less than half an hour later that the two of them stood half dressed, picking straw out of their hair. He hated leaving. When he was with Millie, he felt young again. Alive and happy. The feeling was intoxicating. Duncan took her hand as she walked with him to his car. He knew he shouldn't, not here, not like this, but desire had him pulling her into his arms and kissing her full on the lips. After the intimacy shared moments ago, it felt the most natural thing to do. He brushed her hair back from her face and said, "you're beautiful. I love you with all my heart. I've got to have you, Millie, no matter what the cost." She melted into him. "I love you too. I really do."

Neither saw the curtains twitch from the upstairs flat. There was no doubt in Alice's mind now. She knew.

*

Duncan's heart missed a beat as he turned into the estate and saw blue lights flashing outside his house. Sindy was at the side of the car before he had chance to get out. "Duncan! Oh, thank God. I'm going with the ambulance. Can you get Sheila from next door to sit with the boys and then come and meet me at the hospital?" Sindy ran back to the house not waiting for an answer. Duncan was out of the car like a flash, following her in. Charlotte was being carried out on a small stretcher by two ambulance men. Her tiny face was swamped with an oxygen mask. "What's wrong with her?"

The taller of the men briskly answered. "She's in good hands. We'll get her to the hospital and then we'll know more." Everything seemed to have a matter of urgency to it. Sindy was crying. Duncan gave her a quick hug and helped her into the back of the ambulance. "I'll be right behind you. Give me a minute to sort out the boys."

He was pushed aside as the back doors were closed. "Time is of the essence here."

Those were the last words he heard as the siren started up and the ambulance disappeared out of view. Duncan felt physically sick.

Sheila came out of her house before he got round to her. "Is everything okay, love? I'm not being nosy but I …"

"No, Sheila. Everything's not alright, Charlotte's ill, very ill. Could you please sit with the boys while I go to the hospital? I'll be home as soon as I know she's settled and things are under control."

Sheila placed a hand on his shoulder. "You drive careful, love. I'll be here waiting for you. No hurry."

Duncan's hand shook as her tried to turn the key in the ignition and his feet were behaving in the same way on the pedals. He felt like jelly. He'd never been overly religious but as he drove to the hospital he prayed. *'Dear God, don't punish me like this for my foolish behaviour. Please, please let Charlotte be okay.'* He drove as if the devil himself were after him.

He ran into accident and emergency and up to the desk. He was frantic to find Sindy. "Where's Charlotte James? She's…" He hesitated as he thought about how old she was and instead of saying she's five months old he said she's just a baby." They brought her in in an ambulance. Her mother was…"

The lady on the desk said in a quiet voice, "she's with the doctor now." She stood up and pointed, "follow the blue dots until…"

Duncan was off before he'd truly grasped where he was supposed to be going. "Sindy!" he called her name every time he passed a drawn curtain or a closed door. The place looked like a warren. "Sindy!" He darted down one aisle of dots only to come back to find another one sporting the same colour. "Can I help you?" A nurse had pulled back the curtain. Duncan told her hurriedly who he was looking for. The nurse stepped into the corridor and said, "shush. Everyone here is poorly or in shock." She gave him clear directions and Duncan listened properly this time. He followed the dots to the end and turned right and took the red dotted corridor and there was the room. He could see her through the window. "Sindy." He pushed open the door and she went into his arms clinging to him for dear life. "She's ill, Duncan, really ill. The doctors are doing some tests on her. She's having what they call a lumbar puncture."

They sat together, both ashen faced with their own terrifying thoughts of, what if? A nurse appeared asking them if they wanted to use the kitchen for a warm drink, but they shook their heads. Duncan couldn't bear this not knowing. "How is Charlotte. Do you know anything yet?"

"The doctor will be round as soon as he has some news." Sindy looked at Duncan, her eyes still red and glassy from the tears she'd shed and her face was as white as a sheet, showing the signs of exhaustion and worry. "I'm worried for her, Duncan, she's so small. What if she…"

"Don't even think about it."

They sat in silence again. Sindy drifted off to sleep with her head resting on Duncan's shoulder, but he stayed awake fearful of what Sindy had dared to mention. What if? It was nearly eleven o'clock when the door opened. Sindy stirred instantly and was up on her feet. "How is she?"

The doctor looked grave. "Charlotte has meningitis. She's stable and seems to be holding her own, but she's not out of the woods yet. The best thing would be for the pair of you to go home and get some sleep. There's nothing you can do here. We shall phone you if there is any change."

Sindy refused point blank to leave. Duncan said he'd have to go because of their neighbour. "She's looking after our boys. I said I wouldn't be long."

The doctor tried to encourage Sindy to go too, but she would have none of it.

It was eleven thirty by the time Duncan got home. Sheila had just made herself a hot drink. She turned as he entered the kitchen. "Oh, love, any news?"

Duncan shook his head. "She's got meningitis. That's serious, but the doctor says she's stable. I'm frightened for her, Sheila. Frightened for us all."

"Now, now. Come on. The little one is in the best place. She'll be fine. I'm sure of it."

Duncan didn't feel so confident. "Sindy wouldn't come home she wanted to stay. I feel I ought to be with her." Sheila put her hot drink on the coffee table. "I'll just pop back next door and get my little dog, grab my duvet and pillows and sleep on your sofa tonight. You go back to the hospital with Sindy. She needs you, lad. Go on. You're right, you ought to be together."

Duncan didn't argue and by the time Sheila came back with her arms full of bedding and her yappy little dog trotting by her ankles, he'd made up Martha's bed in the dining room with a bottom sheet. "It's clean. Mum's still in hospital and we haven't got her settled anywhere yet. Please sleep in here. It will be more comfortable."

"Go on off you go. I'll be fine. Don't you worry about anything back here."

"The boys…"

"Go! The boys will be fine."

Duncan got back to the hospital shortly after twelve-thirty. Sindy wasn't asleep she was pacing round the room in circles. He took her in his arms, and she cried all over again. He spoke gently to her as if she were a child and stroked her head. "I'm so frightened, Duncan. I've got a horrible feeling this is worse than we think."

"She'll be okay, Sindy. Yes, she's ill. She's got to be ill or she wouldn't be in here, but she's in the best place, and the doctor said she's stable."

They eventually fell asleep in the chairs, but they'd had less than a cat nap before they were woken with the offer of breakfast in the staff canteen. Sindy said she couldn't eat a thing, but Duncan pulled her to her feet. "Come on, love, we could both do with a cuppa."

It wasn't until seven thirty that the doctor appeared. "Sindy, Duncan." The formality of Mr and Mrs had gone, making the situation feel more serious somehow. He closed the door behind him. They were both on their feet now. "How is she?" Sindy looked as desperate as Duncan felt.

The doctor spoke slowly and clearly. "Everything that could be done was done."

"Can we see her now?" Sindy looked so hopeful, but Duncan had made sense of the terminology. Goosepimples spread over his body and he thought he might be sick. He reached for Sindy. "Love…"

The doctor said in the same quiet, clear tone. "Charlotte died at six forty-eight this morning. I am so, so, sorry."

242

The room seemed to shake with Sindy's scream of denial. She tried to run, but Duncan had hold of her. His own arms and legs felt weak and holding onto Sindy took all his strength. "Can we see her?"

Sindy was hysterical now. She was shouting, "No! No! No!"

The doctor spoke softly to Duncan, "I can give your wife something for the shock if you think it might help."

Duncan shook his head. He didn't know what to do for the best. He couldn't believe what had happened. The only thing he was sure of was that Sindy was in no fit state to see Charlotte. The doctor reassured them there would be another chance to say their goodbyes.

They drove home together in eerie silence. The pain was indescribable.

Chapter Twenty-One

Alice told Millie the sad news and witnessed the colour leave her cheeks. "I've told Duncan he must take all the time off he needs. I hope I haven't spoken out of turn there, love. It's just he'll have to come back sooner rather than later. He has a mortgage to pay now."

Millie nodded. Her voice was quiet. "That's fine, Alice. Fine." Alice shut the bedroom door and went back to the kitchen. Her mood was low. *Just when I thought nothing could be worse for Sindy, this happens. How are they going to cope?'* Millie appeared, breaking into Alice's thoughts. She was wearing jodhpurs. "I thought you were working today, love?"

Alice could see she was close to tears. She moved closer to Millie, not sure whether to give the girl a cuddle or not. Instead she placed a hand on Millie's arm offering comfort. "Now, now it's no good upsetting yourself. Going to work will take your mind off it."

"No, Alice. I can't. I'm going for a ride. I need to think. You don't understand."

Alice thought to herself, *'I do understand my lovey. Oh, you won't know what I understand.'* But again, Alice chose her words carefully. "You have had lots of shocks of your own of late. I expect this has brought it back. You go and blow the cobwebs free of your mind if you think it will help."

Alice watched the small, slim figure stride across the lawns. *'The poor girl is tormenting herself with guilt. I can see it written all over her face.'*

*

Millie galloped over the fields, blinded by tears. Thoughts kept haunting her. Not just her affair with Duncan, that was still all too beautiful in Millie's mind, but she'd convinced herself that she had fallen in love again. How things were going to pan out now for a while she had no idea. She stopped by the trees. The very same trees she'd first stopped at with Duncan on their first ride out together. She'd been heartbroken then over Simon's deceit. Now she was the one being deceitful. Millie knew she was the bigger bitch, Duncan had a family.

Millie rode slowly back to The Four Willows. She had to talk to someone. The trouble was who could she really trust? The minute she let her secret leave her lips it was at risk of finding another pair of ears and onwards.

*

Alice looked up from mashing Hugh's food so he wouldn't choke. "There's plenty here would you like some. Steak pie and baked beans. Not overly exciting." Millie shook her head. "No Ta." She was pleased Alice had let their earlier conversation drop. "I'll feed dad for you though."

Millie's mind was racing. Her father had eaten well, and she was just scraping out the dish when she found the courage to say what was on her mind. "Dad…" Hugh looked at his daughter, puzzled. Had Alice told him why she wasn't at work? Did he wonder why she was feeding him? Millie had no idea. He was the perfect person to unburden herself with. He could tell no tales.

"I'm sure Alice has told you about Duncan's little girl. It's terrible isn't it." Some of the remains of Hugh's dinner dribbled down his chin. Millie wiped it away with the serviette. "I don't know how to tell you this, but I have to tell someone." Millie took a long deep breath. Tears threatened at the release of having a sounding board.

"The thing is, dad, I love Duncan and he loves…" Hugh reached out with his good hand. Millie thought he was going to stroke her cheek like he so often did. She screamed in pain as he grabbed her hair and tugged it as if his arm had gone into a spasm. He twirled his hand round best he could in her wavy shoulder length locks. Alice came running in from the kitchen. "Help me, Alice. Dad's going to pull my hair out at this rate."

Alice spoke gently to Hugh, but something was wrong. He didn't seem to be able to use expression to communicate at all. She prised his fingers loose so Millie could go free but there were strands of her hair still stuck between his fingers. "Hugh… Hugh can you hear me?" She tapped the side of his face gently. Millie was just going to call for an ambulance when Alice said he was looking better and more aware of his surroundings again. "I think he's had a minor stroke, love." The doctor said he would be prone to them."

"Well shouldn't we get the doctor to look at him then?"

"The district nurse will be in at two. He's having some blood tests. I shall mention it to her."

Millie took Alice at her word and went through to the kitchen. She didn't want to see her dad, not yet. His behaviour was terrifying. She wondered if he'd even heard her.

Alice followed her. "I'll make us all a cup of tea."

Millie slumped in the chair. "Alice…" Millie wrung her hands in front of her. "Alice… I feel so wretched. You won't believe what I'm bottling up. I…"

Alice placed her hand on Millie's shoulder. "You won't believe what an old lady like me sees, understands and doesn't judge."

Millie's eyes widened. "You know?"

"I know there's an attraction between the two of you and I'm not saying I approve, but yes I know."

"It's more than an attraction. Oh, Alice. I've been so wrong, but I couldn't help it. It just happened."

"I've been your age, love. I know what temptation is like. I know how thrilling it feels and God knows what it does to your hormones because it makes you positively shine from the inside out. Trouble is, someone always gets hurt."

"Do you think Charlotte dying is…"

Alice stopped Millie before she could utter her foolish fears, "No. No it isn't anyone's fault. Things happen. Do you think your dad had a stroke because he'd done a misjustice somewhere? Or your mother had said something out of turn so she was kicked by her horse? No, love, no. It doesn't work like that. Some believe these things are sent to try us. Others just know the world is full of good things and bad. This sadly is one of the bad things. I'm hoping as a family they will find the strength needed. This is a heartbreaker for sure."

"Am I a bad person for saying I'm hurting too? I'm scared Duncan won't be able to bring himself to carry on seeing me because he'll feel guilty. I love him, Alice."

Alice took a deep breath. "You know, just a few months ago you loved Simon. There was never going to be anyone else for you like him…"

"I know, Alice. I know, and I do love Simon. I think I always will, it's just the finality of it was so real when I knew Stephanie was pregnant. Loving Duncan has helped me."

"No, love. Duncan put a plaster over your pain. I don't know how things will go between the two of you, but I do know you're a good girl. You'll do the right thing."

"Say I don't Alice? Say I can't let go."

"Time will sort everything out, you'll see. Now go and see your father. Make your peace with him."

Millie moved towards his chair hesitantly. Hugh looked up at her and his face twisted in a strange fashion as he tried so desperately to speak. "I'm sorry, dad. That was wrong of me to try and unburden myself. I didn't mean to worry you."

Tears fell down Hugh's face. His good leg twitched up and down and his hand flapped at her. He was still trying to say something, but Millie had no idea what. "It's okay, dad. It's okay."

*

Millie had a restless night. Her agitated mind made for fanciful dreams. They seemed so real while she was in them and troubled her when she woke, leaving her mind reeling with questions.

She made the decision to go to work that morning. It was a short day and she finished at two in the afternoon. She had a plan now of what she would do. The more she thought about it the more determined she became.

She'd asked the librarian if she could use the telephone in her break and phoned the nursing home, Rose Cottage. The matron was hesitant to give out the information. Millie stressed how important it was to speak with her father's mother, her grandparents. The voice was firm. "I can give you a phone number, but I don't feel comfortable giving out their address." Millie was delighted.

When Millie finished work, she went to the nearest phone box. Doris Marlow answered. "Yes. Who is calling?

"It's Millie, Millie Marlow." There was a brief silence.

"Yes, and what can I do for you?"

"We got off to a horrible start. I just wondered if I could come and see you?"

"Is Hugh alright?" Doris's voice rose with concern. Millie assured her he was as well as can be expected. Better than he was when she last saw him.

"I'm sorry, Millie for the things I said on that afternoon. It has played on my mind. I was wrong."

Millie relaxed. "It was a difficult time for us all, but I would love to come and see you." Before Doris made an excuse Millie reassured her. "I'm happy to meet you somewhere or come to your home. Whatever suits you best."

Doris gave in easier than Millie could ever have imagined. Their home address wasn't far, and Millie reckoned by car she could be there in under an hour, traffic willing. "Would it be okay if I come on Sunday? I work all day tomorrow." That is how it was left. Millie would meet her supposed grandmother at two o'clock this Sunday at her home. *'Maybe, just maybe she will be able to answer some questions for me. Clear my muddy thoughts.'*

*

Sunday 2nd August

The only explanation Millie gave her father and Alice as to where she was going after lunch was 'out'. She supposed they thought she was off to meet Duncan in secret. This saddened her. *'surely they could not believe me to be so shallow?'* Once Millie was in her car singing along to her favourite love songs, she wondered if she really would have had the strength to refuse Duncan if he'd asked to see her. Pushing the what ifs from her mind she concentrated on finding Doris Marlow's home and getting the answers to her many questions.

An hour later Millie was lost. She pulled over and asked a pedestrian if they knew where Church Lane was? She was told she'd missed a turning about half a mile back. Millie did a u turn and headed back to the Red Lion pub, which she remembered seeing earlier. After taking a sharp left, down an un-made-up road, she found herself on a country lane with sheep in the surrounding fields. The dried mud that made the road was bumpy and the car seemed to shake from side to side which forced her to ease her foot off the accelerator and change down to first gear.

She checked her watch; she'd arrived with fifteen minutes to spare. Millie waited at the church. Her grandmother's house was opposite a pond. Ducks and moorhens were swimming on the water. The house looked huge and the gardens well-kept and spacious. Millie tried to imagine herself playing there as a child. *It might have been lovely to have had grandparents and play in that beautiful garden with the duck pond running alongside the grounds. I might have had a little boat or picnicked with friends on the bank. It would have been fun to come here and play in the church grounds.'* Then catching sight of the many gravestones. *'Perhaps not.'*

Millie looked at her watch again. She didn't want to be late nor too early. She had allowed enough time for the possibility of getting lost and that had paid off. Locating 'The Gate House' had been easier than she originally thought. Situated by the church, opposite a duck pond and next to a farm meant it was well known.

At exactly two o'clock Millie pulled an iron bar that made the door chime. It was opened immediately. She was greeted with a smile. Doris was so different from the angry sour woman Millie had met nine months ago. "Hello."

"Come in. I hope you found us easily?"

"Yes, just one hiccup. I'm here now."

The conversation was nonsensical, but it eased Millie's entrance. "Would you like a drink, tea or coffee?"

Millie was hot. "Could I have something cold please…orange?"

"Yes of course." Doris pointed to a room. "You go through there, dear, and sit in the conservatory. I'll bring the drinks through in just a minute." Millie's eyes scanned her environment as she walked through a lounge which was tastefully decorated and void of clutter. It opened up to reveal a beautiful hexagonal conservatory. A man could be seen through the glass. He was working up the top of the garden. Millie wondered if it was her grandfather or the gardener. *'Surely no one worked in gardens on a Sunday.'* She watched him pulling at a particularly stubborn bush. He was on his knees and his back was bent over with the effort. It looked like hard work. A full head of grey hair blew in the light breeze and as he stood and glanced across, Millie could see no likeness in the man and her father. Her father was nearly bald. "Here you are." Doris appeared carrying a large tray that not only held her orange juice but a pot of tea, a jug of milk, and a sugar bowl. The cups and saucers were rose patterned china and it all matched. A beautiful cake stand was adorned with a small variety of little cakes. Doris answered Millie's curiosity when she glanced at the window. "That's my husband, John. He'll be in in a minute."

The orange was freshly squeezed, and a slice of lemon floated on the top with an ice cube. It went down easily. Millie hadn't realised how thirsty she was.

"Would you like another one?" Millie shook her head. "No, that's fine." A tea plate was then offered. "Cake?" Millie refused again. This was all small talk. Neither of them knowing where to start. Millie was grateful when Doris broke with the niceties, "what's troubling you, dear? You haven't come all this way to drink orange juice and stare up the garden."

Millie cleared her throat. "You said my dad wasn't my father. He married my mother when she was pregnant. I wanted to know if that was true."

Doris had the decency to look ashamed. "I don't know what to say. I'm so sorry for the way I behaved. I was just so angry at your mother. I felt she'd let him down. He'd stood by her when she needed help all those years ago, then when he was struck down with that devastating stroke, all she gave him was two days a week of her precious time. Two days! It felt cruel to me. I took it out on you. It was wrong of me. The trouble is, when you appeared looking so like her, I just exploded. All my pent up hurt and anger was directed at you and I've been furious with myself ever since."

Millie's voice was quiet. "So, you're telling me the man I've thought of as my dad for my entire life, isn't my dad?"

Doris fiddled with the napkin that she'd laid neatly on her lap moments earlier. "My dear girl, the way you've treated him since your mother died and the way I watched him respond to you at the home, he is your father, and you are his daughter. I have no doubt about that."

Millie wanted clarification. "But what you're saying is he's not my biological father."

Doris shook her head and looked down in her lap. "No. No I don't think he is." When Millie said nothing, Doris went on to explain. "Hugh was a shy boy and when our friend's daughter was left a widow, I pushed Hugh into a relationship with her. It worked. They seemed happy and an engagement followed. Then out of the blue he came home one evening with Davinia. Back then she looked just like you do now. The only difference is she already had the early signs of pregnancy protruding through her tight skirt. Hugh told us he wouldn't be marrying Sylvia…that was his fiancée's name, he would be marrying your mother." Doris paused as she recalled the moment and Millie thought for one horrible moment Doris might just cry. "Sylvia was the daughter of a long-time friend of mine. I didn't and couldn't believe Hugh had got your mother pregnant. I believed he felt sorry for her. She'd turned his head with her youthful beauty and style. We both, John and I, tried to talk sense into him, but he stood his ground. This had been a first for Hugh and so out of character. He was easy to bully and bend. I'm ashamed to say we'd bullied him into going into the family business and he'd followed like a lamb. But this, he stood firm and things got heated between us all. John said some unforgivable things about your mother, which led to Hugh striking his father. John still has problems with his jaw, even today. It wasn't just John though, we all said unforgiveable things. It was the hurt and anger talking, but Hugh left this house with your mother under a cloud and never crossed our doorstep again."

Millie sat quietly. Stunned at what she was hearing. Doris spoke softly. It felt to Millie, Doris was fearful she'd said too much as she tried to backtrack a bit. "You might be his daughter. Who knows? Without proper tests it's a guessing game, but my intuition is he was infatuated with your mother and he helped her when he found out her predicament."

Millie's mind was racing. "How did you know dad had had a stroke?"

"The lady who cleans for me. Her sister is the Avon lady that takes the orders and delivers in your village. She hears all the gossip. It might take a while but eventually I hear everything. When I heard my son was in a nursing home, I found out which one and phoned them. They told me Davinia visits twice a week. I started visiting on a Tuesday. It caused huge rows between me and John, but I stood my ground. I couldn't turn my back on him any longer. He's my son. I couldn't bear to think of him in a nursing home, it broke my heart. Especially with him still being a relatively young man." Doris removed a tissue from her sleeve and blew her nose, but there didn't appear to be any tears. She got her thoughts together and continued. "When I first saw Hugh again, mute, dribbling and unable even to reach for his beaker I went ballistic. You know what my tongue's like when I'm upset. My ranting didn't help any. I was told they leave his drink on the table to encourage him to use his good hand. It was ridiculous. I tell you he struggled to lift his hand off his lap, let alone feed himself. I think if he got anything out of my visits it was just the fact his thirst was quenched."

"That's sounds dreadful. I'm sure you're wrong, he always looked well cared for when I went in."

"I hope I was wrong, but I'm his mother, I wanted more. When I set you that challenge of taking Hugh home, I never in a million years thought you would do it, or even believed it was possible, but you did and I've heard on the grapevine you've done wonders, even renovating the house so he can have live-in care and organised help from an agency."

Millie told Doris about the physio Hugh had had for twelve weeks and how his good hand is much stronger. "He's never going to walk or communicate, but Alice is very good at understanding his needs. She's been a godsend."

"I know, dear, I hear it all."

The next revelation came when John appeared. He seemed pleasant and sat opposite Millie while Doris poured him a cup of tea. His voice was deep and despite his late years he was a good-looking man. Close up, Millie could see Hugh looked more like his mother in every way. "Now, Millicent, has my wife managed to swallow that humble pie she's been choking on since the last time she saw you?"

Doris was instantly annoyed with him and it showed. "It's Millie. She likes Millie. Everyone calls her Millie, don't they?" Doris looked for confirmation and Millie smiled. "You really do hear everything, Doris."

John's voice took on a more serious note. You want to hear about Hugh? Hugh punched me, struck his own father. Anger, grief, disappointment? You can call it what you like but it does that to you and we both said unforgivable things to each other. Doris is right, I've been awkward and stubborn, but it was years ago now and I'm only just seeing that life's too short." He took his tea and two of the cakes Doris had brought in on the tray. Doris smacked his hand playfully. "One is sufficient. Anyway, Millie wants to know about her real father." She glanced quickly at Millie, frightened she'd said the wrong thing. "I know Hugh's your dad, dear, but you want to know about your biological father."

John took a bite of cake and swigged his tea before he said anything. "From what I can remember, your mother was a lively soul and that is being kind. I first met her at a hotel. We were doing a big extension at the back of it. She was having a bit of a fling with an Italian lad who worked at the bar. She was there most lunchtimes, flirting. She knew what she was up to, she could turn heads that one. We used to whistle as she walked to the bus stop wiggling her pert little bottom."

"Shut up, John. For goodness sake, the girl wants to know who her father is, not what a trollop you thought her mother was."

Millie couldn't help being upset and embarrassed by John's description of her mother. This definitely didn't sound like the mother she'd known. Millie held her tongue. It was in her best interest to say nothing, because it was here that she would solve the puzzle to her many questions. John apologised, and so did Doris. Then her world crashed with John's next revelations.

"Before we'd even finished that extension, your mother had already moved on to someone else. Dickie James. That was his name. He was married, two small kiddies and one was disabled. Used to wear one of those funny boots I believe. You know the type with the big sole. I knew of Dickie, he worked on the council." Millie heard no more. A darkness clouded her vision and she struggled to breath. She came to, to the sound of Doris's concerned voice. "Are you alright, dear?" John was patting her hand. "Get the girl another drink, Doris. Put something a bit stronger in it. She looks like she's seen a ghost." Millie was trying to breathe, the conservatory had got horribly hot, and she could hear John trying to make peace with the bombshell he'd dropped. "Sorry about that. Me and my big mouth. Too much for you to take in in one go, eh?" His voice sounded echoey and distant.

Millie stood on shaky legs. "I need to use the bathroom." She only just made it to the toilet where she was physically sick. She splashed cold water on her face and rinsed her mouth, but nothing helped. Once back in the conservatory she told them she had to leave. "I have to get back. Alice likes to go to church on a Sunday and I do tea for dad."

Doris looked pale too. Her voice was gentle. "That's the spirit, dear. He's your dad. He always will be."

Millie tooted the horn of her car as she pulled away, managing to hold herself together, but once she was out of sight of the house she pulled over. *'Oh my God! I never saw that coming.'* She clutched her stomach for fear she'd be sick again. It all made sense. Her father's distance towards Duncan. His grumpy rudeness that he managed to display, and then the anger at Millie's own revelations. *'He must have been terrified at what the future would hold for us if we got together.'* Millie felt scared. *'What now? How do I tell Duncan this? Will he feel as dirty as I do? It was always wrong, but now…'* Millie wiped her eyes and blew her nose. *'I've got to get away. That's what I'll do. It's the only way.'*

The journey home felt long. Millie didn't play any music. She sat in silence letting her thoughts unravel the months of mystery. Everything had fallen into place, and she could see it all so clearly. *'Did mum know Duncan was this Dickie James's son? Is that why she employed him?'* There were always going to be questions. Questions that couldn't be answered. Tears clouded her vision again making driving impossible. She pulled over again, the last thing she wanted was to be the cause of an accident.

*

Alice was instantly concerned when she saw Millie. "Are you alright, love?"

"No. No I'm not, but I don't want to talk about it."
"Now might not be the best time, but I have to tell you, love, Duncan was here earlier. He came to see you. I told him to go home to his family. I'm sorry if I spoke out of turn. I just felt… "

"No, Alice, that's fine. That was the right thing to say."

Alice reached for the kettle. "Let me make you a cuppa. You go through to your dad. I'll bring it in."
"No, thanks. I'll have a cup of tea, but I need to get my thoughts together. You're going away on the fourteenth and will be back on the twenty-ninth. Is that right?"

Alice nodded, but her concern was for Millie's wellbeing. "Whatever's the matter? Sharing will help. Promise."

Millie put her head in her folded arms and her shoulders shook as she sobbed. Alice sat beside her, draping her arm across Millie's tiny frame. "Come on now, nothing can be as bad as all this, surely."

"It's worse. Honest. I don't know where to start."

After what Millie had been through these past ten months it looked like it was about to take its toll.

When the tears eased, Alice stood up. "Now I promised you a cup of tea. You get yourself together and then you can tell me what has brought this angst on."

Millie stared vacantly into the mug of tea, but words stuck in her throat giving no explanation for her tears.

"This is about Duncan. Am I right?"

Millie nodded slowly. "In a fashion. Only it's so much bigger. I know what I've got to do, but it means leaving you to deal with the care while your away on holiday."

"Oh, love, please. Can't you wait just until I get back? I'll only be gone a fortnight."

"No, Alice, I'm really sorry but I can't. I shall have to give an explanation to dad…" Millie paused and added "and Duncan, but it doesn't change the fact that I have to get away."

Alice sat opposite Millie and took her hand. "If that's how you feel then so be it. You will have to speak to your dad though. He'll worry about you. I understand love, it's your way of doing what's right by Sindy. You're a good girl at heart. I knew you'd do the right thing."

When Millie didn't say anything, Alice believed she'd guessed right.

"Thanks for listening, Alice."

"Any time. I make a good sounding board.

*

Millie called out hello to her father as she went through the lounge to her room. She didn't get close as she didn't want him to see her tearstained face. Millie refused to think of Hugh as anything but her father. She had to hang on to the fact that he was her dad. Her earliest memories included him loving her. He'd been the very best dad ever and she loved him as much as she believed he loved her.

She stripped off naked and stood in the shower letting the water pour over her trembling fragile body. She scrubbed vigorously at herself with the bath brush. *'How can I clean myself from Duncan's kisses, Duncan's touch, and the fact I've had Duncan's body inside my own. We'd been one.'* Millie had to breathe deeply as the urge to vomit again swept over her with the spray of the shower.

*

By the time Millie felt strong enough to speak to Hugh he was in bed. This suited her. She didn't want Alice to hear what had to be said.

Tapping the bedroom door gently, she pushed it open. "It's only me, dad." She pulled a chair across so she could sit beside him. Before she said anything, she brushed her hand over his balding head. *'You weren't blessed with your father's head of hair.'* She lay her head close to his and whispered, "I love you, dad. I love you so much." Tears threatened and she hadn't spoken a single word of importance yet.

He reached out from the covers with his good hand. Two big eyes stared at her. Eyes that strangely were the same colour as her own. She took his hand and pressed it to her lips. "I'm going away, dad. I have to." He started to make verbal noises, but Millie had no idea whether he was protesting or understood already the predicament she was in. "Dad, I don't know where to begin, so I'll just be as honest as I can and if it comes out in a jumble, or in the wrong order we will unravel it all as we go. It's just I'm in such a turmoil I don't know whether I'm coming or going." As soon as she admitted that statement tears did fall, and Hugh became agitated. He tried to comfort her by squeezing her hand encouragingly. Taking a deep breath Millie said, "I know why you behaved so vehemently towards me when I told you about my feelings for Duncan." She stopped and looked for a reaction, but all she could fathom was sadness. "He's my brother... or I should say half-brother." The hand that held hers lost a slight grip and she tightened her own. "It's okay, dad. I get it now. Everything. Your

259

distance towards Duncan and your obvious dislike of him. You are wrong though, Duncan's a really nice guy. I don't say that because I love him, but he's a good man." She watched as tears trickled out of her father's eyes. He was always emotional, but tonight it was more. Millie squeezed his hand again and gave it a little shake, hoping to remind him there were things to be said. "What you did for mum was amazing. I don't care who made me." She shook his hand again and whispered, "you are my dad. You always have been, and you always will be. I love you and I know you love me. The problem is, dad, is that I love Duncan too. It's not right and I know it can't be for many reasons, but I can't just switch off my feelings. I now know why when I confided in you, you behaved like you did to me, it was because you knew the connection between us. I understand." She leant forward and kissed his cheek, moving closer to him. Her knees were pressed against the side of his bed. "This is why I have to get away. What has happened to Duncan's family is horrible. I can't begin to imagine how they are coping, but I must leave here. I would have had to distance myself anyway but knowing what I know now has taken away my freedom of choice." She paused again. "You do understand, don't you, dad?" He made his usual grunts. He sounded in pain and Millie guessed he was. This in itself was painful. She took a tissue from the side of his cabinet and wiped his eyes and then blew her nose in the same tissue. "Look at us. A fine pair." She sat beside him on his bed. There wasn't a lot of room. Hugh was curled in a disfigured ball, but Millie still had to tell him about her visit. She laid her hand on his still body. "I went to The Gate House today, dad. I met my grandparents. They were nice to me." The noise that came from the bed had Alice running to his aid. When she burst in the door Millie said, "it's okay, Alice. I'm here."

Alice looked pale. Millie thought perhaps she'd been asleep. "Love I didn't mean to eavesdrop but the monitor. It's on all the time so I can listen out for Hugh."

Millie had forgotten. Alice put her hand on Millie's shoulder. "I think you've said enough for one night, love." Hugh was still making the most horrendous noises. Alice took complete charge. "It's alright, Hugh. It's alright. Millie's home. No harm's done. She understands everything now. Everything." She looked across at Millie. "And he's still your dad, eh."

Millie was still in shock at forgetting about the monitor. Everything she'd told her father, Alice had heard. The situation was getting worse. "I'll leave you with him." She bent over and kissed his cheek. "You did hear me, didn't you, dad? I liked your parents. My grandparents. Doris and John. I liked them very much."

Monday 3rd August 1981

The following morning Millie woke early. She saddled Truffle up and rode over the fields towards North Mundham. She was there before six o'clock. The sun was promising a glorious day. She pulled Truffle to a halt under the tree she had first sat under when she'd ridden with Duncan all those months ago. Not wanting to get into thinking about him she gently kicked her horse in the ribs and galloped across the field.

When Millie finally got back to The Four Willows, Grace was there feeding her own horse. Millie hadn't seen her since the night of the royal wedding. Grace turned at the sound of Truffle's hoofs clopping on the concrete. Millie slid off the saddle and patted Truffle's nose. "Morning, Grace. How are things?"

"Good. You're up and about early. Where have you been?"

"Just riding." Millie took the saddle off Truffle's back. "Grace…" She paused not quite sure how to say what was on her mind. Grace anticipated it was about Duncan and said, "I know, Millie, it's tragic. I can't believe it. Little Charlotte. She was such a beautiful baby." She quickly corrected her foolish outburst. "I didn't mean it like that. It would be awful whatever the baby was like. I don't know how they'll get over this, do you?"

Millie shook her head. "I know. It's horrible. I have a problem of my own though. Something's cropped up and I'm going away. Today I shall be sorting out work and giving in my notice at the library and finding lodgings elsewhere. Please don't ask why, I don't want to explain. I know for a while Duncan isn't going to be around so often, so can I leave it with you to look after the horses until he's able." Millie was talking fast. "Scuttle is easy. She's a hardy little thing, but Truffle needs to be stabled and exercised daily. Can you manage that?"

Grace nodded. "Of course, I will. Where are you…"

"Please, Grace, I don't want to talk about it. I just need to know you can do that for me. Alice will sort out dad. She's away for two weeks in August but she'll get carers in."

"Millie…"

"No questions. I'll be back when I can."

"Please just tell me you aren't in any trouble. I'd help you if you were."

Millie shook her head. "No not trouble. I just need to get away. Gather my thoughts." Without another word, Millie turned her back on Grace and walked Truffle over to the paddock. She knew Grace was puzzled but Millie had no intention of offering any explanation. Everything felt confused and muddy. Her feelings were more than fragile, and guilt was starting to find its way into her conscience. *What have I been playing at of late and to think I even had thoughts of Duncan leaving his family for me.'* She sighed as she told herself, *'This is my comeuppance.'*

She had a letter to write. She'd imagined in the early hours of the morning what she would put on paper, and it seemed so easy. She had got up and sat at her desk, pen in her hand and the words had failed her. Instead, she'd gone out for an early ride and had ended up having to deal with Grace's curiosity. Still at least she had manged to sort out the care of Truffle and Scuttle.

Once indoors she made breakfast and left for the library. Her shifts had been changed around recently and she'd been given more hours. Millie was anxious at having to say she needed to leave as soon as possible. Just thinking about it made her feel sick. *'This is all your fault Simon. You ruined all our plans. This would never have been an issue if you'd not messed around with Stephanie.'* Thinking about Simon and what they'd had together made her feel worse. *'What have I done to deserve all this grief?'* These were irrational thoughts, but she couldn't feel any other way at the moment. Her world felt like it had been hit by a tornado.

By lunch time Millie felt a little bit better. Things were looking up slightly and falling into place. She'd not had to leave her job and find work in a school but had managed to get a transfer to another library in Midhurst. Full-time as well. She was just waiting for a phone call to say she could view a flat above a newsagents set in the middle of the town. Knowing Duncan was her half-brother had added an urgency to the situation. Their relationship had to stop right now. The death of Charlotte added to the finality of this foolish situation. *'How did I get caught up in this in the first place? Doing to Sindy what Stephanie did to me. I must have gone crazy for a while.'* Telling herself this, didn't ease her bruised heart, and she knew she'd miss the familiarity of home and leaving was going to be a wrench.

*

It was late when Millie got home to The Four Willows. She was pleased with what she had been able to accomplish. As of Monday week she would be working fulltime in the Library at Midhurst. She had written a cheque to secure the flat above the newsagents, which had been small but perfect for her needs and what was more if she provided two references by Friday she could move in this Saturday. It felt as if things were finally coming together for her. The problem she hadn't addressed of yet was Duncan. The relationship had to be closed down leaving no loopholes for hope or possibilities. *'I'm sorry, Duncan, but I'm going to have to be brutally honest with you. I'm going to have to make you feel as sick as I do. There is no easy way of saying we're related. Related by sharing the same father.'*

*

Wednesday 12th August 1981

It was the day of Charlotte's funeral. Alice had never witnessed such devastation, not even when her own parents had died. The sadness at the loss of such a young life filled the air like a choking smog. The church was packed, and the sound of sobbing echoed in the high-ceilinged building. It was heart breaking. The music, the hymns and the speeches made the occasion harder to bear if that was possible. Sindy looked terrible, as did Duncan. Alice had heard of people looking ashen, but the only word Alice could think of that came to mind was they looked yellow, yellow with grief. She was pleased the boys were absent from their sister's send off. She hoped they were with friends. Why she was thinking such things, she had no answer to. The wake was a little brighter, but Sindy still looked empty, void of life. Alice gave her a hug, "I'm not going to say how are you, love. I just hope you can find strength to pull together as a family and find your way. It will be difficult, I'm sure."

Sindy didn't answer or respond in any way. Duncan appeared, he put his arm round his wife's shoulders. "Thank you for coming,

Alice. It means a lot." Sindy said nothing. Alice reached out and touched his arm. "Take care, lad. Don't hurry back to The Four Willows. Millie has sorted out the horses until you feel able." She paused and when he made no response she added, "there really is no hurry." Alice chose that moment to move away. She filled her plate with a few sandwiches and crisps and getting a cup of coffee found a seat. Her eyes were watchful of Sindy and Duncan. *Thank God Millie's gone. That's one complication this family doesn't need. Especially now.'* She quickly chastised herself for judging on what wasn't her business. *I'll be glad to get away. I've been around these people for far too long. I'm beginning to feel like they're my responsibility. It's like they've become the family I never created for myself.'* She thought of the letter she had to give Duncan when he finally came back to work. That will be another blow for him, or maybe it won't. A quiet voice broke into her thoughts. "Hello. It's Alice, isn't it?" Duncan's sister stood before her. "Sue!"

"Oh please, you don't have to call me that."

"I do, love, because that's your name, and I don't have to ask how you are, because you look absolutely lovely."

"I'm getting there. This tragedy has been a life changer for us all. Mum's heartbroken. I do though want to thank you for visiting mum, you know, while I was away."

"That's okay. It was good to chat with her. Come and sit down here with me for a while." Alice patted the spare chair. "Where's your mum today? I thought I might see her."

Susan shook her head. "No, her arthritis has escalated which has caused a problem with the healing of her new hip. I offered to put her in a wheelchair, but she's still in a lot of pain when moved. The hospital was against it too. I fear she might never walk again. If that's the case, it means she won't manage in the retirement flat she was so looking forward to either."

Alice found the subject too depressing on top of the funeral and lightened it with positivity. "I'm sure she'll get there with time."

"I'm seeing Sidney again, did you know?"

Alice patted Susan's arm. "I did. I'm delighted for you. Where is he?"

Susan smiled. "He's working. That trouble with Duncan and all, he felt it would be better if I came alone. I've moved in with him now. He keeps asking me to marry him. I will, just not yet."

Alice laughed. "I can tell you, love, things have changed from when I was your age. No one turns a hair at living together these days, but I'm pleased for you, love, really pleased."

"I'm going to move back home for a while. Just until Jane, Sindy's mum can sort out coming to stay. Sindy isn't coping, which was bound to be the case, but I'm worried about Duncan too. He hasn't shed a tear yet. He's bottling all this emotion up and it's not good, Alice. I'm frightened for him."

"I know, love, I know." Alice patted Susan's hand. "Things unravel. You'll see. It's time that's needed."

Susan stood up. "I'm going to get a coffee." She looked at Alice's empty cup. "Would you like another one?"

Alice shook her head. "No, I shall be going soon. I have to get back to Hugh. I'm off to Canada on Friday for a fortnight."

Alice watched Susan walk towards the buffet tables. There was hardly a limp. She had been honest with the young woman, she did look lovely, happy. There was a confidence about her that hadn't been present before. *'She's a good egg that one. She deserves happiness.'*

Chapter Twenty-Two

Stephanie had been taken into hospital with high blood pressure a week ago for complete bed rest, and when the doctor made his rounds on Thursday, he'd made the decision to induce the baby tomorrow morning. Stephanie had been delighted, but when Sunday arrived she'd had enough. Two days of pessaries, probing and internals was just too much. All this intervention was making her sore below and giving her a niggly backache. She couldn't walk around as her blood pressure was too high, and she was strapped up to a monitor so they could hear the baby's heartbeat. Brenda walked on to the ward at eight o'clock ready for night duty. Stephanie was delighted to see her. Brenda was a mature midwife and Stephanie had bonded with her. She was pleased now she hadn't gone into labour earlier. Brenda gave her a winning smile. "Hello my lovely. I didn't expect to see you in one piece still." Stephanie warmed to the way she spoke to her. It made her feel like she was six years old again. It was just what she needed to calm her fears of the unknown that lay ahead. "I've had enough. I just want it to happen now."

"It will, my lovely, it will. Now let's just pop your legs up so I can see how things are progressing." Stephanie felt herself tense as the gelled glove found the opening between her legs. "It's softening. You're in the early stages of labour, my lovely. Three centimetres."

Stephanie was sure the weekend had been just as long and boring for Simon, but she had to give him his due, he'd sat with her all day on Friday, arrived early on Saturday and did the same on Sunday. Brenda said, "where's that lovely husband of yours. Have I missed him?"

"Only just. Do you think I'll have the baby tonight?" Now Brenda was back on duty, Stephanie was desperate for the baby to come. The pain in her back was becoming more than niggly, and she really was beginning to feel uncomfortable. "Should we get Simon back? I don't want him to miss the birth."

"No, no, my lovely. Let him have a rest. He'll probably get a call from us in the early hours." Stephanie could quite easily have burst into tears. "Can I just go to the bathroom. I feel like I need the toilet."

"No, my lovely. I need you to stay on the monitor. I'll get the bed pan."

As Stephanie's pain started to increase her blood pressure rose and so did the colour in her cheeks. All the while Brenda fussed over her, listening to her stomach, prodding it gently, and feeling inside her for progress. "Would you like something for the pain? It will help you get some rest before the birth."

"No. I don't want to sleep. I want the baby to come now. I want Simon with me. Can you phone him, please?"

Brenda lay a cold damp flannel on Stephanie's forehead. "The baby will come whether you have pain relief or not, my lovely. I'd sleep while you can, it will help you cope later."

"No. I want Simon."

"Okay. I'll phone him and tell him to make his way. Then will you have a little pethidine?" Stephanie nodded. The fight had gone out of her. Stephanie did drift off to sleep but was woken shortly after with a searing pain going down her back. She tried to roll on her side, but the wires from the monitor restricted her movements. Simon was sitting in the chair beside her. "I didn't want to wake you, Stephanie, but you're alright I'm here now." She grabbed his hand just as another pain ripped down her back. She screamed out in agony. Brenda appeared from nowhere. "Hang on my lovely. Let me have a look what's happening."

Stephanie had to endure yet another internal. "Almost fully dilated. I'm just going to see if I can break your waters. Then things really will accelerate. It was uncomfortable for Stephanie and she complained throughout. "I don't want to do this, Si."

"Come, on, you're doing fantastic." He looked at Brenda, wanting backup. "Yes, he's right, my lovely. You're doing just grand."

The birth was long despite the breaking of Stephanie's waters and it wasn't until six thirty Monday morning that a little boy was born. He was placed in Stephanie's arms. Simon cradled her, looking down at his son. "You're wonderful, Stephanie. Look at him, he's perfect." Brenda spoke softly. "Well done my lovely. Let me just clean him up a bit and weigh him, then you can have him back." She lifted the baby into her arms. "You're a real beauty aren't you. Just like your daddy. I can see it already." It was true. Even though he was only minutes old you could see the baby born was Simon's. The shape of the face and eyes. He even had the wild spiky hair, but maybe that would change. "I love him already, Si, he's the best thing I've ever done."

"Me too. I love you, Stephanie. I love you with all my heart. You were amazing." Stephanie glowed with the praise and the joy of motherhood. "Here you are." Brenda placed the baby back in Stephanie's arms saying he weighed six pounds and adding, "that's a good weight for an early baby. Now let me take your blood pressure again." Stephanie held out her free arm, still looking adoringly at the new arrival. Brenda pumped the pressure bulb. "That's a bit better already and now babe's here it should settle down again quickly."

Stephanie passed the baby to Simon and tears fell down his face as he kissed the tiny soft cheek. "Oh my God, he's so perfect, I can't believe he's ours."

Brenda smiled and said in a much more mature voice. "Every baby is perfect, and every baby is a miracle. Now have we chosen a name for him or shall I call him baby Few for now?"

Stephanie shook her head. "I thought Ben. What do you think Si?"

"Ben! Where did that come from? I thought we were going to call him George if it were a boy." Stephanie reached out and brushed the top of the baby's head. "I think he looks like a Ben."

"Ben it is then." Simon's eyes shone with pride. "Hello, Ben. Your daddy loves you."

Brenda wrote the name clearly on the little blue band and clipped it round the baby's tiny wrist.

*

Grace had already seen to the horses when Duncan arrived at The Four Willows. It had been a week since the funeral. "Morning, it's good to see you." Grace reached out to touch him, but he moved back, and her hand hung foolishly in mid-air. "Duncan, I'm so sorry. I don't know what else to say." It was as if he wanted to look too busy to talk. Grabbing the hay fork, he said, "it's okay. There's nothing anyone can say. I don't want to be rude, but I really don't want your sympathy or kind words. It doesn't help. I'm sorry to be blunt, but I'm doing my best to hold myself together... for Sindy."

Grace wanted to say more but chose to talk about Scuttle. "Did you know Millie's gone to work in Midhurst? She's got a transfer. She says the kids can ride Scuttle whenever they want. Emily loves him. Tallis is far too frisky for her."

Duncan didn't look surprised by the offer. "That's good. I might bring the boys round. It'll do them good to get out of the house or off the village green. I'll be glad when the school holidays are over

270

and there's a bit of normality in their lives. Jack starts in September, which will hopefully help Sindy too."

Grace asked tentatively, "I could have the boys for you of an afternoon if it helps in any way."

"No. No ta. My sister's helping out and Sindy's mum's coming to stay at the weekend."

The conversation turned to the house. "Alice has laid out good plans before she went on holiday. I have to say the care team are arriving and leaving like clockwork. She's a good sort. Shame she never married, isn't it?"

Duncan was keen to mow the lawns. He had done precious little here of late and when Grace tried to engage with him about Millie and her sudden disappearance his reply was sharp. "It's good for her to get away. There's nothing here for her. All that time at Uni then to find herself working in a library part time…" He paused wondering where his ramblings were leading and shut the conversation down by saying, "well, it was a waste of all that education."

Grace wasn't going to give in that easily and defended Millie. "Librarian work is highly thought of. I'd like to see you do it. All those books under all those subjects, and in alphabetical order too. Anyway, she's still working in a library. This position came up and it's full time. I reckon, knowing her, she'll end up running the show in the end."

Grace couldn't lighten Duncan's mood and she guessed it would be that way for a while. After all, how would she cope if she lost Emily. Emily was her life. She watched him pat Truffle and lead her to the paddock before getting out the mower.

*

271

Susan was up early. She was going home to Sidney this evening. Sindy's mum, Jane, would be here later today. Susan wanted to strip the bed and make the room nice for her. Duncan had left for work and Sindy was sitting in the lounge holding a cup of tea staring into space. The boys were at the table dipping biscuits into their mugs of tea one after the other. They were giggling unaware of the vacant look on their mum's face. Susan came in briskly with a smile. She was carrying the laundry. "Now now boys. I think you've had enough biscuits. Go and clean your teeth and get dressed. That will help auntie Sue and mummy." Susan was amazed how the boys had accepted her changed name easily and never referred to her as auntie Peg anymore. When Paul grabbed another biscuit and shoved it in his mouth whole, she attempted to sound stern. "No more! Off you go. Up that wooden hill. Scoot."

They did as they were told, but Sindy didn't flinch or help to enforce her instructions. "Do you want another cuppa? I'll make us a fresh one. Let me just put these sheets in the machine and I'll do that. Would you like a piece of toast?"

Sindy shook her head negatively but said nothing.

Susan wanted to say you have to eat something, but kept quiet. Hopefully Jane would be able to cajole her into eating properly again.

Susan went back into the lounge carrying a mug of tea and a slice of toast smeared with marmalade. The boys were back down again dressed. "Look at you, Jack. You've got odd socks on and by the colour of that blue one you must have worn it yesterday." Susan left her breakfast on the table and took Jack by the hand. "Come on back upstairs. Let's sort you out."

By ten o'clock both boys were out playing on the green with the other children. Susan had cleaned through and remade the bed ready for Jane. "What time's your mum coming, Sindy? Do you know?"

Sindy shook her head. "No. I don't need her here. It's not necessary. We can manage now."

Susan wanted to put her arm around her sister-in-law's shoulders but was unsure of herself. She took a deep breath. "Do you want to talk about it? I'm a good listener." Susan thought about the way Jolene had spoken to her when she was struggling, but Sindy shut that route down before it was opened. "No! No – I - don't. I know you mean well, but what on earth can you or I say to make a penny worth of difference? My little girl is dead. Gone. Nothing can bring her back and without her I have nothing. I am…" Sindy paused. "I don't know what I am." Susan wanted to say she had a husband and two little boys who loved her and needed her, but knew from experience when you felt low like this nothing anyone said helped. Angered, yes, but not helped. So, choosing to keep quiet, she got up and went into the kitchen to peel vegetables. She planned to get the boys fed their main meal at lunch time so the evening would be easy for Jane. They could just have a boiled egg and soldiers or cheese on toast. Something quick that they'd gobble up without arguing.

*

"Morning, Duncan." Grace turned her attention to the boys. " Emily's in the stable with Truffle. Go and tell her you're here." Duncan had started taking the boys with him to The Four Willows, it all helped things at home. The three children played well together and seemed happy leading Scuttle round and round the field, feeding it carrots, and having a ride when Duncan or Grace finished what they had to do. It was normally Grace that had the job of saddling up the little pony and taking them one at a time round the grounds.

Duncan still wasn't working weekends. He'd heard through Grace that Millie had come home last Sunday to see her father, the last

273

thing he wanted was to bump into her. There were no emotions spare for worrying about Millie, Sindy was in a bad way and still needed him. He was pleased with how, all things considered, he was coping. It was easier now with Jane's help, she didn't seem to sense his struggle the way Susan did. His sister had a way of knowing how he was really feeling, and he couldn't hide the pain he was in from her or the fight he was struggling with to stay strong. Sindy seemed more comfortable with Jane too and it helped a little knowing when he left for work Sindy wasn't on her own. All these small things made life a little easier.

"Look at me, dad." Duncan could see Paul riding Scuttle without being led. The child's sudden excitement seemed to spook Scuttle and the horse did a little trot. Duncan couldn't help smiling as Paul lent forward and grabbed the pony's neck in fear.

Grace was laughing. She waved. Duncan made his way over to where they had gathered. "Morning. This looks like fun."

Emily was jumping up and down beside Duncan. "I can ride too. Mummy put me on Truffle, and Millie said I could ride her when I felt I could handle her."

Duncan ruffled the child's hair. She was a cute little thing. Excitable. Loud and squealy. Nothing like the boys, they were noisy on a different level. It was strange how they had just accepted Charlotte's death with a few tears and then it had become the norm. How he wished it could be like that for him too. His stomach felt full and heavy all the time, like he'd swallowed a boulder. He woke in the early hours of the morning and had to tell himself to breathe slowly to stop his heart racing. He hadn't slept a whole night through since the night Charlotte had been taken ill. He'd never experienced pain quite like this in his whole life. He guessed it was the grief and loss of Millie. Alice would be back Friday. He probably wouldn't see her until the Monday, but he was looking forward to her return. There was something comforting about Alice's presence.

*

Midhurst library was a listed building and Millie thought it was a really beautiful place to find herself. It had been a good move for her, and she loved working here. She watched the locals daily going about their lives and felt she knew them, not personally, but by their regular habits and style. First thing every morning she saw a gentleman. She called him this because of the way he walked. Proud. He wore a Stetson style hat and a light blue jacket. Impeccably smart and always bought a paper from the newsagents below her flat and lit a cigarette as he walked up the street.

About an hour later a lady would pass by pushing one of those posh silver cross prams with a toddler strapped to a seat on top. A little girl would trot alongside the pram trying to keep up. Then there were two boys racing along the pavement on scooters. They looked like twins. Millie couldn't be sure if the woman was still carrying her pregnancy weight or was having another baby. Then there was an elderly lady who walked with a trolley on wheels. Every now and then she stopped as if to catch her breath. She seemed to be well known as people stopped and spoke to her. Millie had seen her in the library last week but hadn't spoken to her as she'd been upstairs putting the returned books back on the shelves. Millie saw lots of life living above the newsagents. Millie had become a people watcher wondering what sort of life they all lived and what it was like for them. The weeks flew by and she looked forward to going home at the weekends when she wasn't working.

It was Friday and Millie had just finished work. She'd been working the late-night opening. She'd normally go home Saturday morning but tonight, she had the urge to go sooner. She guessed

Duncan would have gone home by now and questioned if she was secretly hoping to catch a glimpse of him. She still missed him and wondered if he missed her too. When thoughts like that filled her head, she shut them down immediately. They had no future together and no amount of dreaming would change that. Alice was due home tomorrow and Millie was looking forward to seeing her.

*

Millie woke early on the Saturday and was out grooming Truffle when Grace arrived. "Morning Millie." Millie looked up. "I've seen to Truffle. Where's Emily?"

"She's with her father for the weekend. You'd think the free time would be good for me and Pete as a couple, but he isn't interested in 'us' anymore." Grace put her fingers either side of her head when she said the 'us'. "I wish sometimes I'd never hooked up with him. Lazy sod. He's got no time for Emily. In fact, I think she hates him, and I don't blame her. The only time he smiles is if he's managed to back the right horse and won a few quid. Doesn't treat us to anything though. I dread to think what she tells her dad of a weekend about him." Millie's laughter was short lived when she realised Grace wasn't laughing with her. Millie changed the subject. "Have you seen Duncan? How's he faring?"

"I'm amazed. Duncan's doing great. Oh, and…" Grace put her hand on her forehead and did a fake swoon. "Emily is in love with him. He's here every day and brings the boys too. Sindy's in a bad way by all accounts. Lost, that's how he describes her."

"That must be hard for him." Grace seemed to be enjoying filling Millie in on the day-to-day gossip. She didn't realise how much pain her words were causing Millie or she would have stopped there.

"Hard, Millie. I think it's incredibly hard. I thought he was going to cry the other morning . He loves her so much. It breaks my

276

heart. I've never had that adoration; my husband ran off with the first bit of skirt that flashed a knee after Emily was born. Then I get lumbered with a lazy oaf like Pete."

Millie had to ask. "Does Duncan know I'm home weekends? Is that why he stays away?"

"Blimey, Millie, don't be daft. I'm sure it's nothing personal. The idea of me being here remember was so he could have the weekends off with his family. I thought you agreed that."

Millie fiddled with her horse's bit so as to distract from her embarrassment. "I know. Of course, I know. I just would have liked to have offered my condolences. I didn't go to the funeral, did you?"

Grace shook her head. "I couldn't. There was no one to have Emily. Alice went. She'll be back later today, won't she?"

"Yes. I'm looking forward to seeing her. So is dad."

Duncan was forgotten. Grace told her all about Susan and how she'd been helping Sindy with the boys and that she was now living with her boyfriend. "Think there's talk of an engagement. Who'd have thought it. Sue. We always called her Peg Leg at school. Kids are so cruel, don't you think."

"I do. Adults do a good job too."

With both horses saddled and ready to ride Grace cocked her leg over the saddle. "I know. You've had your fair share of heartache of late."

'If you only knew' Millie kept her thoughts to herself and kicked her horse in the ribs and trotted off going quickly into a canter. Grace caught her up easily on Tallis. He was not only bigger and stronger, but a faster horse than Truffle by far. As she drew alongside Millie, she shouted, "Duncan loves riding Tallis. I'm

always riding Truffle these days." Jealousy made Millie's next words sharp. "His job is to exercise my horse, not yours."

Grace took the raised volume of Millie's voice as a way of being heard in the saddle and not annoyance because she shouted back in a so what kind of manner. "I guess it doesn't matter who rides who's horse as long as they're getting fed, watered and exercised."

Millie had the good grace to bow down and shout back, "absolutely." She was still rankled and couldn't wait for Alice to come back home and shed some light on how Duncan had reacted to her heartfelt letter. The letter she had taken ages to write and had sobbed over when she'd reread it. *'Was he tormented like me by what he'd found out? Does he feel the same way as I do – desolate? Does he ache to see me even though he knows it can't be?'* Millie's thoughts turned to the other side of the equation. *'Does he feel dirty? Incest. It makes what we shared feel so horrible and shoddy.'* Millie had Truffle in a gallop now and had left Grace behind doing a steady canter. The faster she rode the more she thought. *'How can our relationship have felt so good, so right and yet been so wrong? So wrong on so many fronts.'*

Millie could still hear Grace calling after her. It felt good to ride like this. Exhilarating. For a while she felt happy. Then 'CRASH' back down to earth. *'Family always wins.* She had to accept. *'Simon left me because Stephanie got pregnant… family. Duncan has left me, unbothered by my pain because when it came down to it… his family won. I won't be anyone's plaything anymore. Next relationship, I'll call the shots.'*

"Are you okay?" Grace seemed to have picked up on the fact that Millie wasn't quite her usual self.

"Course I am. Rub Truffle down and put her in the paddock?" There were no pleases or thankyous and she didn't wait for an answer. Truffle was left with her reins hooked over the fence post while Millie walked away. She knew Grace would do it, after all that's what she was here for. Millie was behaving like a spoiled brat, and she knew it. Duncan's absence and the fact he didn't seem to care about her had hurt. Millie chastised herself for expecting more resistance. *'He had no choice. Neither of us did. Alice will shed some light on the matter.'*

*

Alice got home at seven thirty in the evening. What a relief it was to drop her bags in the entrance hall of the little upstairs flat. *'It's good to be home.'* She'd been surprised to see Millie was here. The arrangements were when Alice left for Canada, Millie would be giving Duncan some space. How she hoped the relationship between them hadn't started up again. *'Surely not, not with what Millie now knows. It's not even legal.'* The thought was quite shocking even for Alice, who tried not to have an opinion on people's welfare or behaviour.

When Millie tapped on Alice's door less than half an hour later, her concerns were eased. Duncan had been true to his word. He'd let Millie go. When he'd said it was for the best, Alice had taken it upon herself to keep hold of the letter Millie had written to him, believing under the circumstances it was for the best. Seeing Millie's eager eyes as she said, "did you give Duncan my letter?" Alice wasn't so sure it had been the right decision. Millie looked thin and pale faced and Alice's heart ached for the girl. It was obvious she was struggling with what life had delivered. *'Well, who wouldn't. It's been one thing after another for her.'* Alice didn't want this conversation tonight. She'd been travelling for fourteen hours one way or another. She didn't have the energy for any form of emotion. " Love, I'm absolutely exhausted. I'm going to pop down and say hello to your dad and then I'm having a bath and getting into bed. I'm dead on my feet. We'll speak tomorrow."

The disappointment was apparent on Millie's face, but Alice was pleased she didn't argue. "Tomorrow, love. Let me have a good night's rest and I'll bore you with my holiday and you can ask me about Duncan. I don't know much, but I'll do my best. You know I will."

Alice was pleased to see her leave. It was pitiful. In situations like this, there was always pain. Alice had had a horrible feeling at the time, it was going to be Sindy's loss. Sindy's pain. Never in a million years had Alice envisaged the pain would be caused by the death of a baby. Sadly, they all lost something, and they all hurt.

She wondered how Duncan was holding up. He'd looked in bad shape two weeks ago. She'd been worried for him. She couldn't possibly have given him the bombshell she knew Millie had put in the letter. It had felt better at the time to hold on to it. The news of Millie's biological father had shaken her, and she wasn't directly involved. *'How much more though can that young girl shoulder. There has to be a straw that breaks her.'*

*

Millie lay on her bed, curled up in a ball. *'What did I expect? There was no way forward for us, even if we wanted it. Perhaps this is how he's feeling.'*

Thoughts spun round Millie's head. How she'd hoped to speak to Alice, but even she could see the older woman was beaten. Tomorrow. She would have to wait until tomorrow. Then she would go back to Midhurst. She just had to know how Duncan had taken the news. *'Perhaps he blames me.'* She dismissed that idea as soon as it entered her head. Duncan loved her. He'd told her over and over. There was a time when he was more desperate for that reassurance than she was. Now she seemed to be the needy one. *'What can Duncan offer me now? Nothing. Friendship? Be the sibling I never had. We would both want more, surely. Even though I know, it doesn't stop me wanting what we had.'* These thoughts tormented her, but she forced herself to go down to her father where she knew Alice was saying hello and hearing from the carers how they had coped.

Alice had made egg and cress sandwiches and a few cheese scones along with one of her delicious Victoria sponge cakes filled with butter icing and strawberry jam. Millie and her father had eaten well. "Alice you aren't meant to be working until tomorrow. This is awfully good of you."

"I couldn't have you going back to Midhurst on an empty stomach. Anyway, I don't call baking, working. I always loved making teatime treats for my mother and father when they were alive."

Hugh reached out for Alice's hand and she took it. "Someone's pleased I'm home." She brought the hand to her lips and kissed it. Millie was moved by the moment. Her father seemed so relaxed with her. The thought crossed her mind that perhaps her parents hadn't had the marriage she thought they had. Maybe Doris, her supposed grandmother was right, her mother was selfish. Millie pushed these thoughts away; grateful Alice was home, and her father was happy.

Millie packed the small vanity case ready for her return back to the flat. She stripped the bed and looked around her room. Duncan had completely fitted it out with shelving and cupboards. She pushed open the double doors into what used to be the conservatory and sat in what had been made into her sitting room. It was a shame when she looked around her that she'd had to leave all this behind. *'If I'd known Duncan would have coped with our separation like this I would have stayed.'* Taking one last look around her she made her way up to Alice's abode. She'd heard the carers arrive and knew they would be seeing to her father. Now was a good time to catch up see what Alice could tell her.

*

Millie couldn't face driving home. She went back to her bedroom and sat in her sitting room staring out at the garden where she could just see the outline of Scuttle in the distance, grazing. *Duncan was pleased I'd distanced myself. How could he be so cruel. Alice said she could see the relief on his face that I'd gone. Was I nothing to him at all? Surely, I couldn't have imagined the want in him. It's like I thought earlier – family always comes out on top.'*

Millie tore open the letter that Alice had felt was unnecessary to deliver. *What gave her the right to decide whether Duncan should know he's my half-brother or not?'* The anger she couldn't vent on Duncan went to Alice. Millie was furious with her. Without reading the painstakingly difficult letter Millie had written, she tore it into tiny pieces. *Never, never ever am I falling in love again. Bastard! That's what he is. Beat his sister's fella up for the same crime he committed, only what he did was worse because his sister's fella wasn't even married. Damn you Duncan James. You're a bloody hypocrite and I hate you.'*

A tap on her bedroom door had Millie on her guard. "Yes?" She knew no one could get in. She'd locked it.

"It's me... Alice. Please open the door?"

"Not now. I need some time."

"Please, Millie. I just want to say..."

"No. Not now."

"Millie I'm not going until you let me in. I'm worried about you. Open this door now... please." Alice's voice had become stern. "I won't ask again." She put her ear to the door to listen for movement. When there was none, she said, "Have it your way. You want your father to hear the upset between us, do you?"

The door opened slowly and Millie walked back to where she'd been sitting. Alice looked at the tiny pieces of paper littered on the floor. She guessed it was the letter. Millie's face was wet with tears and her eyes were already red and swollen. "Love, love, love. Come here." Alice held out her arms and surprising her, Millie went into them. Her slim shoulders shook as she sobbed. Alice spoke softly. "I didn't mean to upset you. Honest I didn't. I am sure Duncan misses the fun the two of you had. I know he was smitten with you, love. I could read him like a book, but we both know now even if he wanted to; he couldn't have you, or you him for that matter. Be sensible, love. It's best this way. Surely the least people that know about the situation between your parents and your parentage the better. Don't you agree?"

Millie was slowly beginning to see the reasoning behind Alice's actions. Her voice was hindered by her sobs. "It's just I feel so worthless, Alice. First Simon, then Duncan. What is it with me?"

"One thing you aren't, love, is worthless. You are a treasure and I bet my life on it Simon misses you too. Even if he doesn't admit it to himself, your memory will be in the back of his mind. He'll…"

"No, Alice, you're wrong. The baby will be here by now. He'll be wrapped up in it. I know he will."

Alice stroked Millie's hair. "Do you want to know what I think?" She didn't wait for an answer. "I've told you before. I think you are still in love with Simon and as I said, Duncan helped you in your hour of need. He would never have been your choice, but served as a plaster over a wound. You are from different worlds. You will marry a scholar like yourself, have a lovely home, not a council house that was bought with a discount…"

"You're wrong Alice. I don't care for any of that stuff. I just want someone to love me for me. Really love me. Not…"

"Hush, hush, hush. You will. You will and you will be all that I say you will. You are destined for great things. I can see it in you."

Tears fell again down Millie's face. Alice was more than concerned. "My love, it wouldn't hurt for you to see a doctor. I think you ald do with some help. You have had more to cope with in these past few months than some people cope with in a lifetime. Even if it's only a bit of bereavement counselling. It will help you...you know, with your understanding of your dad and all." Alice let her advice sink in before saying, "please, love. Go to the doctor for me." Millie didn't respond to her advice said that it was time she made tracks back to her flat. "Stay here the night. Go in the morning." Alice didn't want her driving in this frame of mind.

Millie shook her head. "No. I did think about it, but I have an early start. It's best I go tonight. There's nothing here for me."

Alice took Millie by the shoulders and waited for her to look up at her. "Oh, yes there is. There's your dad, there's the horses, your home..." Alice paused. "And there's me. I love you, Millie. I didn't want to admit that, but you and your dad have become the family I never had." Alice let go of Millie's shoulders. "There - I've said it. I love yer girl. And that's the honest truth. I'm more than fond of your dad too in a strange way."

Millie kissed Alice's cheek. "I believe you." And she did.

Chapter Twenty-Three
Thursday 3rd September 1981

The weather was still warm and Sindy had the boys dressed in grey shorts and white polo shirts. Duncan had polished their new shoes hoping to help with the toe scuffs. Jack looked so grown up standing in his school clothes with a satchel on his shoulder. "You be a good boy, and Paul you look out for your little brother in the playground, won't you?"

"Mum." Paul dragged out the mum as if it went on forever. Sindy gave him a look. "Oh mum, Jack will have his own mates. He'll be fine." Both of the boys had had their birthdays in the holidays, but little was made of them. Paul seemed so much older than his seven years. Sindy guessed they had had to grow up over these past five weeks, what with losing Charlotte and having to fend for themselves so much more. She had been too absorbed with grief to care. Five weeks on though and things were a little easier. She'd found a lady who was helping her. Mrs Maxwell. She came to the village hall of a Friday evening and gave talks. Sindy had never been religious but this wasn't the normal stuff. It was helping. This lady had a strong connection with the afterlife. At the hall Sindy felt connected to Charlotte in a way she couldn't at home. Duncan looked after the boys and seemed pleased she was going, despite the cost. He'd refused to go himself, calling it mumbo jumbo stuff, but she didn't care. Her lifted mood had meant her mother had been able to go home last weekend and not return. Sindy did feel she was coping again.

"Come on boys, we don't want to be late on your first day."

Jack put his hand in Sindy's and the three of them started out on the two mile walk to school in the next village.

There were no tears as Sindy left Jack in his new classroom, and she wasn't surprised. This was another sign that the tragedy that had hit their home had hardened them both up. He had a peg with a picture of a rocket stuck above the hook and it was here he hung his P.E things. "See you this afternoon. Have fun." She didn't remind him to behave, she'd already done that at home.

The walk back to the village was enjoyable and Sindy had a spring in her step. Mrs Maxwell had said she could go round for a coffee. This in itself made her feel better.

Mrs Maxwell lived on the canal on a boat called The Billing. It was an impressive size and seemed comfortable. Sindy called out to her from the bank. Mrs Maxwell appeared. " Sindy! I'm so pleased you took me up on the offer. Did the boys go back to school okay?" "Yes. Even Jack. No tears. I had terrible trouble with Paul. Took him a good week to settle and for him to grasp that he had to go Monday to Friday."

Mrs Maxwell laughed. "Children, they are funny." Sindy felt Mrs Maxwell was looking to check she'd brought her handbag. These sessions didn't come free. She took Mrs Maxwell's outstretched hand and was guided on to the boat.

Once they were seated with a mug of coffee in what had been made into a lounge area, Mrs Maxwell got out the money tin and took Sindy's three pounds and perched it back on the shelf. She told Sindy how she knew her own husband's presence was still here on the boat. Sindy was all ears as she heard that Mr Maxwell's walking stick would fall as she walked past or that she could smell his aftershave before she drifted off to sleep and how he came to her in her dreams. Sindy was agog. "How will I know Charlotte is near?"

"I know she is. I can see her."
Sindy's eyes grew in her head. "You can? Where is she?" This was amazing to Sindy. "Does she know her mummy loves her?"

Mrs Maxwell put her hand on Sindy's. "Of course she does."

Sindy was told about the process of grading. "When someone dies, they make their way slowly to the other world. While they are travelling it is easier to communicate, but the higher up they go the more distant they become. Now is the best time to communicate with Charlotte as she is in what we call phase one. That's why I asked you to come here today. I feel we can let her know her mummy is really here, wanting to speak to her."

Tears slid down Sindy's face. "How can I communicate with her. She couldn't speak. She was just a baby."

"I can feel her presence. She's here now. She's trying to find her way to the next level. Someone has held out a hand and lifted her up. A guide."

Sindy was so full of mixed emotion she couldn't speak. "You are welcome to come every day if your finances stretch to that? We can follow your little one's path until she reaches her destination and until you can be together again in years to come."

Saturday 5th September.

Millie wasn't going back to The Four Willows this weekend. She had to work and wouldn't finish until six this evening. If Alice had still been away, she might have pushed herself to make the journey home, but these days her father was in good hands and she didn't have to worry about him.

Millie was on the front desk today stamping the books out and checking the dates as people returned their borrowed ones. Her stomach rumbled. She had a quarter of an hour before she was on her lunch hour. She had several things she needed in the chemist's and was going to grab a readymade sandwich and a bag of crisps from the supermarket.

She smiled at the middle-aged woman as she handed her her chosen books. "I've read that one. It's brilliant. There's a real twist at the end."

The woman dropped them in her bag. "Well don't tell me about it. I want to read it for myself." Millie had no intention of telling her but apologised all the same and smiled. "I know what you mean. It's like a film isn't it. People ask you if you've seen it and then tell you what it's all about." Millie's friendly acceptance of the rebuff eased the situation and the woman smiled. "I'm pleased I've picked a good book. I shall seek you out when I bring it back and tell you what I think."

With the woman gone and her desk void of a queue, it seemed the perfect time to get Bridget to take over from her.

The summer was fading fast but Millie was still able to go out without wearing a coat. As she came out of the chemist clutching her purchases in a carrier bag, she heard a shriek. "Millie! Oh my god, It's you." Millie recognised the voice instantly. It was Paula the girl she'd shared a house with at university. "How are you? What are you doing in Midhurst?"

Millie's shoulders relaxed. Her hunger forgotten. "I work here. What about you?"

"Really? I work in Guilford. I'm a sales manager for Tandy's Fashions. I love it." Paula looked Millie up and down. "Look at you, you look fab. Any new man in your life?"

Millie attempted to laugh. "Come on, there's a lovely café over there. I have an hour." She checked her watch. "Well, three quarters."

It was over coffee that Millie heard all the news. Paula didn't seem bothered that Millie was working in a library and not teaching. Paula was full of Rafi. "We're an item now. We got together a couple of weeks ago."

Millie took a bite of her roll and chewed it at the side of her mouth while saying, "what is it with the college set. Stephanie takes my boyfriend. You take Stephanie's." It was said in jest but there was a hint of sarcasm to be heard in her voice. Millie then had to listen to the latest on Stephanie. Paula couldn't help telling her all about the new baby. How he was a miniature Simon. How Rafi thought the baby would come out looking like him.

"I don't know why he thought that. I always knew it was Simon's."

Paula's eyes widened. "You did. How?"

"Well, Rafi is always stoned or high. I don't believe his sperm could swim let alone find an egg." She was being catty, but she couldn't help it.

They hugged goodbye with the promise of getting together again soon. Millie knew it wouldn't happen. They'd shared a house for their last year at university and Paula had been supportive when her relationship with Simon fell to pieces, but there had never been that spark you get when you know you're going to hit it off with someone.

*

Millie was pleased when the library closed. Her mind had been on Paula, Simon, Stephanie and the baby. She hadn't wanted the news to have had an impact on her, but it had and it hurt like hell. She climbed the steps up to her flat and pushed it open.

'Only Stephanie would fall on her feet like that. Why couldn't the baby have been Rafi's. That would have tipped their world upside down.' She wasn't sure which but one of Rafi's parents originated from Pakistan, but he'd inherited the permanently tanned skin and dark velvety brown eyes. *'Yes, that would have taken some explaining. No! Only Stephanie could get away with pulling a stunt like that. I wonder what Simon would think if he knew Stephanie had been unsure who the father was or maybe he*

wouldn't have cared.' Millie grabbed an apple and flopped in the armchair. *'Stop thinking about them, it's not my worry, I must move on.'*

Millie's thoughts didn't stop. She was envious of the life Paula had described. New home on the Sterling's. Paula had said it's the first semidetached one as you go into the estate past a row of terraced houses. She didn't know whether Paula told her this because she, herself was genuinely happy for the life Stephanie had created, or she was enjoying being spiteful. Whatever the reason behind the tales, she'd certainly given a good description of how happy Stephanie and Simon were. How perfect it all was. The new carpets and furniture. When Millie had made a snidey dig that Stephanie would miss the social life she so enjoyed, Paula had shot that gloat down in flames. It seemed Stephanie's mother and father loved babysitting, which meant they could still go out as and when. Paula had said excitedly that Stephanie still threw parties regularly, mainly dinner parties, and Paula had given a pathetic giggle at what fun they were. Millie couldn't see Simon in this scene, but she hadn't seen him cheating on her once her back was turned either. How wrong she'd been on that score. *'Ben, the spitting image of his daddy. Well he had to be, didn't he.'* Millie tried to shake off the jealousy, but the news had more than hurt her.

The next day Millie woke early. She put on a track suit and was out running before ten. She'd never done this before, but she felt restless and needed to move. It was while she was running round the pond avoiding the dog walkers that she spotted the gentleman with the Stetson who bought his paper from the newsagents below her flat. Only this time instead of wearing a jacket he had on a long beige mac as if he expected rain. He was sitting on the bench with his legs stretched out in front of him. He had a takeaway coffee in his hand. The white polystyrene cup with the red top told her he'd bought it from the café she'd visited yesterday with Paula.

Millie called out good morning as she jogged towards him. There was no real speed to her steps, so she saw him smile. She didn't know if he spoke, it was a fleeting moment, but she was sure she sensed his eyes burning into her back as she jogged away. She didn't turn around. She felt a little spooked.

Monday 7th September

Millie found herself reading stories to the children in the morning. Mrs Fairbandly had called in sick and Millie had volunteered.

The lady who passed by Millie's flat of a morning with the silver cross pram was there with three of her children. Millie could see clearly now that she was pregnant again. *'Poor woman.'* Millie couldn't imagine why anyone would want so many children.

When the area filled with little eager noisy faces, Millie introduced herself. "Good morning. My name's Millie and as Mrs Fairbandly is off today you have me reading the stories. Our first book is about a bear with a special cake. It has five cherries on the top." Millie held up the colourful book. "Can you see him. He is looking for somewhere quiet to sit down and enjoy it." Millie's teacher training had given her good experience of expression and voice volume to different characters and the children were as quiet as mice while the story unfolded.

After she'd read several stories finishing on George, the loud-mouthed fisherman, she invited the children to pick their own books to take home with them. It was while the children were looking in boxes and shelves that the pregnant lady with all the children spoke to her. "I do like Mrs Fairbandly, but I have to say I have never known the children so absorbed before."

She spoke really nicely, and Millie could see close up that she was well to do. Her nails looked salon painted, and her hair was highlighted and cut into a neat style. It was obvious money wasn't an issue, even her baggy maternity clothes looked quality. It was the swollen pregnancy legs and the waddle that had given Millie the impression she was old and frumpy. Millie was flattered by the compliment she'd paid her and thanked her for it. The woman held her hand out to the little girl who stood beside her with a book. "This is Amy. She's four. You enjoyed Millie's stories today, didn't you?" The little girl hid her face in her mother's dress not saying anything. Millie smiled and said, "I think you've gone all shy like Emily Jane in the story I read to you."

The lady introduced herself as Julie and told Millie she live in Cocking. "It's just outside of town." Millie knew where Cocking was as Bridget lived there too, but let Julie ramble on. "My husband's a solicitor. He has an office not far from here. Just round the corner actually."

It turned out the gentleman who always wore the hat and dressed in a suit was Julie's husband. His name was Bradley. Millie didn't ask why he was out alone on a Sunday morning drinking coffee from a polystyrene cup, when he had a wife at home who must need help with such a large family and in her condition too. She felt foolish now for having been spooked by believing his eyes had followed her. *He couldn't possibly have the energy for any such thoughts, sexual or violent.*' Millie was snapped out of reverie when Julie said, "I really do hope you share the reading from now on with Mrs Fairbandly. I thoroughly enjoyed the morning." Millie smiled but didn't promise anything. She started to clear away when another mother approached and said very much the same thing, and so did three other parents. Millie felt good about herself. Bridget, the librarian also told Millie there had been some pleasingly positive compliments about her morning's readings. "Perhaps you and Mrs Fairbandly can share the activity. I feel the mothers will be expecting to see more of you on the seat and disappointed if you're not."

Millie was delighted. "I don't mind. As long as I don't upset anyone. I did enjoy it."

Bridget changed the subject and asked if Millie fancied going to the quiz night at the Greyhound pub on Thursday. It's a curry night. For three pounds you get your meal and a quiz. It's a bit of fun. Carol's up for it. Go on, say you'll come."

"What time is it?"

"We've got to get there for seven. The quiz starts about seven thirty and at half time we have food and do a picture round. It really is good fun."

"Oh alright. Go on then, I'll come."

Thursday 10th September

Millie left her flat on foot at about six thirty. She called for Carol on her way and the two of them called for Bridget who lived a stone's throw from the pub. They'd all walked into The Greyhound together and Millie bought the first round of drinks. Walking and not driving meant they could all have not only a proper drink but a good few.

They paid their money over to join in the quiz and called themselves the Bookies, which seemed apt seeing as they all worked in the library. At half time they were fourth out of seven teams. Millie was poring over the picture round while she ate her curry. "I think that's a young Humphrey Bogart." Bridget twirled the paper round, "No, no way. It looks more like Edward. G Robinson."

"Give it here, let me look." It was Carol who grabbed the sheet and looked next. "God! I don't know. It's not Humphrey Bogart though. I loved him. Go with Edward G if you think so, Brid?"

That was how the picture round went. The three of them making wild guesses at the faces. James Stewart was put down when in fact it was Trevor Howard. They really didn't have much idea. Millie got the young Michael Jackson. He was her idol. "It's definitely him."

While they ate their meals, the door opened and in walked Julie's husband, Bradley. The gent who until Monday, Millie had called the gent with the Stetson hat. Tonight, he was wearing a leather flying jacket and a pair of beige trousers. He took his hat off and placed it on the bar as he waited to order a drink. His hair was dark brown, a bit ruffled from the hat and it had a gentle kink in it. He turned to scan the room as if looking for a seat. His eyes met Millie's and he seemed to hold eye contact for a little longer than was comfortable. Millie looked away.

Bridget noticed him. She was thirty-five and married with three children all in their early teens. She leant forward and whispered, "look what's just come in. What a stud." Millie whispered back indignantly, "his wife's heavily pregnant. I met her on Monday at story time. She's the lady with all the children. Julie. She has five already. He must be a right randy old goat." Carol laughed out loud. "He's old. He doesn't look like he has it in him."

Bridget ignored Carol's remark and recalled the woman Millie had described. "I know who you mean, Millie. She was the lady who liked your story telling. Well, she's got herself a dish of a husband there. He's not old either. He's lovely."

Carol laughed again, "That's because you're old too. He's old enough to be my dad and Millie's for that matter."

Bridget grabbed the picture round and turned her attention to the last few pictures they hadn't put a name to. "Less of your cheek. I tell you he's a good-looking man. What do you think, Millie?"

"Not my type. As Carol said, he's too old for us, but I know his name's Bradley and he's a solicitor."

Bradley stopped at their table. Millie hadn't seen him approach. "Well hello ladies. How are you doing?"

Bridget went a bright shade of pink and showed him the picture round pointing at the faces individually. "We know those. We're completely stuck on these and we've guessed those two."

"Can I join you?"

Millie grabbed the picture round. "No! You have to pay to join a team. We're midway through."

He straightened up quickly and held his hands up as if he were being threatened with a gun. "Whoa! I only wondered. Fine. No worries." He moved away and Bridget told Millie off for being rude.

"I don't want to encourage him, he's married. His wife's lovely. He should be at home helping her. Anyway, he gives me the creeps. I saw him when I was jogging on Sunday. He was sitting in the park on his own…"

"Since when has there been a law against that?" Millie knew Bridget was miffed with her. The moment was forgotten when the bell rang, and the quiz master told them to pass their papers to the opposite tables. The picture round was bad for them. They only got four out of ten. Millie wanted the quiz to be over. Every time she looked up Bradley seemed to be staring at her. She didn't say anything to the others. She'd already made herself look silly by her earlier outburst. It didn't change the fact that he seemed too interested in their table, and Millie felt she was the prime attraction. *'Surely he can't be looking at me when his wife's about to have another child? Bloody men.'*

The last round went badly for them too and they dropped to sixth place or second to last, however you wanted to view it. Still, they giggled about the evening as they walked home. Bridget was first to leave them. She lived just over the top of the hill on the estate there. Carol and Millie walked on. They talked about Bridget fancying Bradley. Millie who had drank too many Bacardi and Cokes laughed. "I don't suppose she was serious."

Carol said, "I bet she was. I'm sure if you get married and sleep with the same guy day in and day out it gets a bit boring, don't you think?"

The drink had made Millie's tongue loose. "I don't know. I fell in love with someone at uni and it never entered my head to look at anyone else. I loved him. Three years we were together."

Carol was also more than tipsy. She pushed Millie in the arm. Her voice was too loud for the still of the night. "Dark horse, you. Where is he now?"

"Long story."

Carol stopped outside her house. "Want to come in for a coffee?"

"No. I'll get home." It was only a short walk to Millie's flat from here, but daylight had gone, along with the full moon, which had been on Sunday. It was dark and Millie felt unusually nervous. She quickened her step and welcomed the town where the streets were lit. She could see her flat and she already had her key in her hand ready to open her front door. She hesitated for a split second before entering the dark alley that led to the steps at the back. Holding her breath she practically ran up the stairs. Her hands shook as she opened the door. She slammed it shut and put the bolt across. Her heart was beating fast, and her hands were still shaking as she flicked on the lights. Slowly she calmed down and got herself together. *What was I thinking? Letting my mind run wild like that.* It didn't stop her going round the flat closing all the curtains and filling the flat with music and lights. It wasn't until Millie had had a shower and a hot drink that she felt calmer and able to turn off her music and think about settling down. It was then that she heard something. It was coming from the shop below. *'Was Mr Fisher doing a stock count downstairs?'* Millie checked her watch it was gone eleven o'clock. *'He couldn't be, surely.'* Millie put her head to the floor trying to hear if anything was amiss. It was quiet and she convinced herself that she'd imagined it. Just as she was about to get into bed, she heard another noise from the shop below. There was no mistake in it. She got out of bed with the intention of phoning Mr Fisher at home. It was a bit too late to phone someone, but she felt sure he'd like to know if the shop was being burgled and she didn't like the thought of being above such activity either. Just as she was about to dial the number, she heard the shop door close. She ran to the window and peeked through a gap in the curtain. There was Mr Fisher. Mr Fisher, himself, with the lady that works with him behind the counter. Millie couldn't believe it. They were giggling like teenagers. Mr Fisher had to be at least fifty, maybe more and there he was a married man with a fancy woman. *'I wonder what he's told his poor wife he's up to. 'Jesus! These men. They just can't be trusted. And by the looks of Mr Fisher, you never get too old either.'* Millie slid into bed. She felt cold and wrapped herself in the duvet. *'It's a good thing Duncan and I are no more. It was wrong.'* She didn't know why she had suddenly thought this, and it wasn't just because he was her half-brother. It was like for the first time she really realised just how many lives she would have shattered. *'Our relationship was a ticking time bomb.'* On this thought Millie turned off her bedside lamp and sleep came easily.

*

September was slipping by and Millie's birthday was looming. She would be twenty-two on the thirtieth and was going home at the weekend. She'd not been home for four weeks and was planning to stay for the week. There was a new man in her life, Adam. He was just what she needed. Two years older with no complications and his easy-going nature reminded her of Simon. When she asked him to join her at The Four Willows for her birthday on Wednesday and to meet her father, he had readily accepted the invite. She met him at the library. He'd been coming in on a regular basis, taking out books on cycling. He would bore Millie with the content. He seemed obsessed with the sport. When he'd finally got round to asking her out, they'd gone to the cinema in Guilford . There was nothing flash about him. They'd driven there in his father's works van. Their first kiss had been when he'd picked her up, it had been hesitant and had left Millie feeling a bit embarrassed and awkward. Adam hadn't given up and had taken her hand when they walked to the cinema. He continued to show affection throughout the film. The conversation was easier and flowed on the journey home. Millie hadn't said much about the horror of the year she'd had but spoke about her father's stroke and finishing university. He'd accepted when she invited him up to her flat and after hot chocolate and digestive biscuits, kisses became more relaxed and had deepened. Millie had felt the warmth and excitement that you get with a new romance. She liked Adam. She liked him a lot and told herself it was a start.

Millie said goodbye to her work colleagues Carol and Bridget on Friday afternoon. "I'll see you week today." She drove home that same evening. She knew she'd see Duncan on the Monday, but she was ready to face him again. There were things that needed saying, but she would keep their family connection a secret. She knew that no good could come out of telling him he was her half-brother now.

Alice met her at the door, "It's lovely to see you, love. Your father will be delighted. He had another little turn on Wednesday. Nothing to worry you about, but just to let you know now you're here."

Millie was instantly concerned. "Alice, I want to know of any changes in future. Especially when I haven't been home for a while. I'm an hour away at most, I would have come home."

"That was my point, love, there was no need. Your father is fine now and as I say he'll be chuffed to bits to see you."

Millie said no more and went through to see Hugh. He was sitting in his recliner chair and turned as she went in. "Hi, dad. Been a while I know. I've been busy." She kissed his cheek. "There's a new man in my life. He has his own bike business and runs it with his dad. He's coming here Wednesday to spend a few days with us. I'll be twenty-two. Twenty-two, dad. Where have those years gone?"

Hugh patted the side of Millie's face. "You'll get to meet him. He's really nice. Fun. No complications."

She didn't know if he understood or remembered what she was getting at, but conversation was difficult to make when it was one-sided. Alice was better at it than Millie.

Alice entered the lounge carrying a tray of tea and cakes. "Here you are. A nice cuppa. I bet you could do with one after your journey. She sat with them, and Millie noticed the tray had been set for three. "Oh, Alice, are you joining us?" She hadn't meant it to sound rude and luckily Alice didn't seem to take offence. "Yes, I always do of a morning, don't I, Hugh. We do the crossword together. The easy one." Millie could see Alice was wonderful and felt cross with herself for speaking so curtly to Alice earlier regarding her father's health. "Alice tells me you were having an off day on Wednesday. Still, you're in good hands here with Alice, eh dad." This was Millie's way of an apology.

Hugh smiled lopsidedly and lifted his good hand. Millie thought he was reaching out for her, but instead he took hold of Alice's hand and she smiled at him warmly. Millie felt a bit in the way and to lighten the moment she told Alice about Adam. Then Millie heard about Grace and the arguments she'd been having with her partner. Alice lowered her voice as if she feared someone might overhear her. "He has a problem with gambling. I think there's been quite a to do about it. She's moved in with her mother for the time being. Too small there though, so she's looking for a place for her and Emily. Poor girl and the poor child. Emily's such a sweet little thing. Having a father you only see once a week is bad enough but then thinking you have a stepdad as a replacement and it's snatched away from you in an instant must be unsettling. I don't know. These things didn't happen in my day. You made your bed and you had to lay on it."

Millie laughed, "Alice! Thank God times have changed. That chap Grace lived with sounded horrible. Duncan told me he was mean to Emily and Grace told me a thing or two about him, honestly, he's ghastly. I should think Emily's delighted to have left and moved in with her nanny."

Alice poured out more tea. "Oh, I don't know. It's just not the way it was in my day, that's all."

Millie stood up. "I'm going through to my own room. I want to unpack my bits and put some washing on. I'll come through to the kitchen a bit later and make myself a sandwich if that's okay."

Alice was up on her feet. "Good grief, girl. I'll make you a sandwich. You sit with your dad."

"No, you stay here. I'll come back later. I'll eat it in my own sitting room." Millie went through to her bedroom and pushed the double doors open that led out to what was the conservatory. It was her space. She'd made it like a sitting room complete with her mum's old writing desk. Within minutes she heard a tap on her door. Alice entered. "One sandwich. Ham and tomato."

"Thank you, but you shouldn't have." Alice smiled and left her to eat in peace.

Saturday 26th September 1981

Grace arrived at The Four Willows to find Millie tacking up Truffle. "Hello stranger. Long-time no see."

Millie was startled and Truffle sidestepped at her sudden reaction. "Jesus! you made me jump." She stroked her horse and spoke gently to her. "Steady girl. There you go."

Grace apologised. "I didn't mean to creep up on you. I thought it was Duncan."

"How's he doing, how are they all coping?" Millie didn't want to sound too interested in just Duncan.

"I think they're okay. Emily and Paul are in the same class now. It's good because they became quite close here over the holidays. Jack's settled into school too."

Millie had to ask. "What about Sindy?"

" I believe she's seeing some religious nutter." There was a pause. "I shouldn't say that, but it all feels like mumbo jumbo to me. I reckon this woman plays on people's emotions. Duncan says it's helping her though, so that's the main thing."

"What sort of mumbo jumbo?"

"I don't know, he doesn't say. What worries me about it all is the money it costs for the meetings. I think if it's about helping people and religion, it should be free. After all, it doesn't cost anything to go to church of a Sunday, does it."

"As you say if it's helping that's all that matters. Duncan obviously doesn't worry about the cost."

"No, he's just grateful that Sindy's coping again. I think for a while she didn't even look after the boys properly. His sister came to look after them and then Sindy's mum. They are back being a family again. Martha, Duncan's mum's in a care home too. Her hip didn't fix with the arthritis, so she's gone into that new home in Chichester. Loves it by all accounts." Grace paused waiting for a response from Millie. When none came, she said, "listen to me, gossipmongering. I'm only filling you in on what's been happening."

"I know. It's fine, but what about you?"

"Fine. I'm living with my mum again. Story of my life. Always pick the wrong buggers."

Millie didn't let on she'd heard. "I'm sorry to hear that."

"Don't be sorry. Emily's a different child. I hadn't realised just how she struggled with Pete. I just need to find somewhere we can afford to live on our own."

Millie walked Truffle out of the stable and pulled herself up into the saddle. "I'm sure it will all fall into place. I'm going for a ride over Dell Quay. I'll catch you later." Without waiting for a reply, Millie kicked her horse gently and headed for the drive.

Monday 28ᵗʰ September 1981

Millie was surprised to see Duncan's car pull into the drive. She'd expected to see him pedal in on his bike, leaning over the handlebars and his hair blowing all ways, but when she saw the two boys jump out of the car, she realised.

She pulled the brush through her hair one last time, pinched her cheeks, and licked her lips that shone with the natural gloss she'd applied. Checking her appearance in the mirror, she told herself over and over it wasn't important what she looked like, but it was, and she'd made an effort. She was wearing a clean pair of jodhpurs and a navy jumper with a red stripe across the front. A checked collar framed the neckline and when she pulled on a wax jacket and slipped her feet into short, polished riding boots, she looked striking, and she knew it. Holding her head high she strode across to meet Duncan. The boys ran at her full pelt. "Millie, Millie. We've been looking after Scuttle for you, and Emily. She rides Truffle but we just ride Scuttle. Can we ride your horse too?... Please?" It was Paul who was asking, but both boys stared at her waiting for her consent. "If daddy thinks it's okay then I'm happy."

They jumped up and down saying thank you. Duncan hadn't said a word as yet. Millie brushed her hand over the boy's heads, "Go on you two. Go and get some pony nuts and feed Scuttle. I need to speak with your daddy for a minute." The two boys didn't need telling twice, they were off like little rockets.

Duncan said before Millie could get a word in, "I want to thank you for putting the distance between us. I was grateful."

"It was the right thing to do. How are you all?"

"Millie, I…"

"Duncan, I've met someone else. I'm happy. Properly happy. No complications. Just us, Adam and me."

Did she see an emotion flicker across his face? It was too quick to read. "So, how are you all?"

Duncan's eyes stared at her. It was intense. She didn't want to feel anything for him, but it was difficult. He sounded defeated. "Getting there. The boys are resilient. It's like Charlotte was just ours on borrowed time. The acceptance of her disappearance was almost immediate. Sindy struggled for a while, obviously, but she's coping now. Her mum went home a few weeks ago, and she's manging to run the house again. It's a start."

Millie was being truthful. "I think that sounds amazing." She paused. "And how are you?" She couldn't fail to see he'd lost weight. His eyes had lost their sparkle and were dulled with dark shadows. He looked older. "I'm okay. Now Sindy's coping it's easier for me. She's joined some sort of religious group. It costs us a tidy penny."

"Really? I didn't think religion cost money. It used to be a collection bag at the end of the service if you wanted to put anything in."

"No, this is a group. I don't know what to make of it if I'm honest. The lady lives on a houseboat on the canal. I'd never noticed it before. I'm not sure if it's hers or not but she runs this group at the hall. She's convinced Sindy that our little girl, who wasn't even crawling let alone talking, is telling Sindy she's making her way to heaven. I don't get it, but it is definitely helping Sindy. I just worry what will happen when this lady tells her Charlotte has accomplished the journey and she can't speak to her anymore."

Millie had the urge to reach out and touch Duncan to offer some sort of comfort. "Let's hope by the time Charlotte's made her final journey Sindy's in a better place and able to stand alone without this lady's foresight."

"How are you, Millie. I'm sorry about…"

"I'm fine. Honest. You don't have to be sorry. We needed each other for a while, but it's over." She pushed her hair out of her eyes. "You'll meet Adam on Wednesday. He's coming for my birthday and staying until the weekend." There it was, the same flicker of emotion again. Millie recognised jealousy. It was as clear as your reflection in a polished mirror. It was brief but it was there. Duncan's voice was husky. "Does he ride?"

Millie laughed easing the tension. "No! He's scared of horses. He rides bikes. His father has a cycle repair shop. They run it together. It does well."

"Millie…"

"No, Duncan. There's nothing else to say. I'm going for a ride now. Take care." She turned and walked towards the stables. Her eyes were stinging. She still had feelings for him, she couldn't fool herself and she knew he still had feelings for her too. If she hadn't known about their genetics, she might have felt pleased and maybe weakened her resolve to keep away. Not now. It wasn't to be. Life was easier with Adam.

*

Duncan had never been so pleased to see the weekend arrive. When the boys pleaded to go to The Four Willows to ride, he'd been quite sharp with his refusal. "But dad, we can't ride after school, it's dark in the evenings, and weekends is the only time. Millie said we could ride her horse, you heard her."

"You'll have to wait for half term then." When the boys protested hoping to wear him down, he'd told them the subject was closed, but he'd take them swimming instead. It was then that Sindy said she needed some money for Mrs Maxwell. She wanted to see her today. "It's only three pounds."

"You went to the group yesterday. What can you possibly want to say to her?" The row that followed was horrendous. Both of them were screaming unforgivable things at each other. Duncan sent the boys upstairs, but they sat on the steps crying as the row blazed. He accused Sindy of ignoring the fact that Charlotte was ill for the sake of the street party. "You just wanted to show off with all your baking and boast about how capable you are."

Sindy vented her own anger. "How dare you! You! All you did was race around the green with the kids, acting like a bloody fool and not caring that Charlotte was running a temperature."

"Oh really? Wasn't it me who said that we need to call the doctor? Me that picked up the phone against your better judgement and got advice. Even then you said you'd see how Charlotte was in the morning."

"That's unfair. The doctor said see how she goes. Give her paracetamol and plenty of fluids. It was me who called the ambulance." Then it was said. The real core of the animosity. Sindy was crying bitterly. "And where were you when I had to call an ambulance? Come on Duncan. Where?" He didn't say anything. "I'll tell you where you were. With Millie bloody Marlow. Millie, Millie, Millie. I was absolutely sick of the name and the place."

The colour drained from Duncan's face. The pain her words delivered were breath-taking. "You've changed your tune. That's not what you thought when you knew working at the Marlows would enable you to get your mitts on this place, was it? Oh no! Even my poor mother went through hell because…"

"Your mother was a bitch, that's why Sue…"

"For Christ's sake, shut up." Think of the boys. Can't you hear them?" The sobbing coming from the hall had Duncan going to them. He picked them both up and took them into the lounge and sat in the chair, one either side of him. They were too upset to speak. He kissed the side of their heads. "It's alright. Daddy's sorry. I didn't mean all those things and neither did mummy. It's just…" he couldn't finish. His voice trembled and he started to cry himself. The boys became inconsolable and Sindy tried to intervene, but Duncan was lost. He'd been holding himself together for so long now and letting go of his pent-up grief was tidal. It was as if someone had opened the floodgates, and nothing could close them.

The four of them clung together, trying to find comfort. Sindy seemed to be the stronger of them all. She stood up and made a mug of tea for Duncan and switched the television on for the boys. They didn't move off Duncan's lap and stayed huddled up close to him. They'd never seen him cry before. Duncan manoeuvred them on to the floor so he could sort himself out. "Come on, boys. Dad's okay." He blew his nose and wiped his eyes on his sleeve trying to pull himself together. "Ask mummy for a biscuit, or some jam on toast. You like that." Before they could ask, Sindy said, "there's nothing. Not an egg, bread or butter."

"Why? What have you done with the housekeeping?" The air was becoming tense again. Neither of them were strong enough for another row.

"Leave it now, Duncan. I'll get some bits on Monday when I draw the family allowance."

"Monday. What are we going to eat today?" Duncan looked at her with red swollen eyes. "Sindy…This woman is bleeding us dry. She's playing on your emotions. Even Grace says she shouldn't charge and Millie…"

"Have you been telling them things about me?" The boys climbed up onto Duncan's lap, sensing another argument. When he didn't answer she raised her voice. "I don't want you discussing me with anyone, least of all, them." She almost spat, 'them'. "Do you understand?" Duncan could sense tempers were rising again and he didn't have the strength for it. The boys were still upset, and he was aware Paul had his fingers crossed in his lap and Jack was sucking his thumb. Duncan feared what was going through the little mite's heads. "Sindy, I'm sorry. Please let's draw a line under this. I don't gossip about you anywhere. People care and ask how you are faring. They are worried for you." He put both boys on the floor and stood up, cradling Sindy in his arms. "Can I please have some money so I can go to Mrs Maxwell's and I'll pick up a few things from the shop."

"I've only got a fiver. I was going to take the boys swimming with that. You could come with us…"

"No. I want to see Mrs Maxwell, and food is more important."

Duncan didn't want to fight again. He gave her the money. "Come on, boys, let's go for a bike ride. Go get your shoes on. They were up like a flash. Not a single complaint about not going to Millie's or swimming. The argument had so obviously unsettled them.

The tightness had gone in Duncan's chest. The row and the tears had been painful, but it was a relief to release the grief and anger that he'd been bottling up inside him. He knew some of his anger was down to losing Millie and last week was painful watching her with the new boyfriend. Adam. He had a flash Claud Butler bike and when Duncan had tried to excuse his old Raleigh as just an old run-around that had belonged to his father, Adam had said they were good bikes. There really were no airs to him, and he seemed a genuine guy. This hadn't helped Duncan either. Nor did hearing the two of them laughing in the stable like school children. Millie had tried to get Adam on Truffle and he'd slipped off the saddle and was left with one foot caught in the stirrup. Duncan would have laughed too under different circumstances, but seeing them together hurt. He was pleased he didn't have to go to The Four Willows until Monday. Millie and her fella would be gone.

Sindy sat with Mrs Maxwell and was told Charlotte had almost completed her journey. "Our work is almost done. We've guided your little one into the hands of our Lord and angel. When the time is right you will be reunited with her, but until then she is in good hands."

Sindy was entranced. It was this belief that helped her cope and keep her sane. The argument between her and Duncan had upset her more than she cared to admit. She wanted to share this with Mrs Maxwell, but she was ashamed for not realising Charlotte was ill, and ashamed for being so caught up with the royal wedding and the preparation for the street party she hadn't sought medical attention for her. Duncan's accusations had stung.

"Did you hear what I said, Sindy?"

Mrs Maxwell had touched Sindy's arm. Sindy stared at her, appearing completely lost. "I'm sorry. I was miles away."

"I said I shall be leaving here shortly. I'm being called further afield. I'm needed elsewhere to help with grief." Sindy was unable to say a single word. Mrs Maxwell spoke softly. "As I said, our work is nearly done. Your little one will be in good hands by the time I leave, and you will be able to concentrate on your living family. Here."
"No! no. Please. I need to speak to Charlotte. I have to reach her through you."

Mrs Maxwell kept her voice calm and continued to speak in the same soft tone. "In a few weeks I shall not be able to reach her myself. She has been on a journey just like I told you, and we've helped her arrive. I can do no more."

Tears slipped down Sindy's face. The row she'd had with Duncan this morning had taken its toll. She wanted to beg, but knew the subject was closed. Sindy handed three pounds to Mrs Maxwell and left to buy a few groceries from the village shop with the change.

Sindy was so lost she passed by people without seeing them, nor hearing their greetings. Depression clouded her thoughts. She crossed the road on autopilot without looking. A car hooted at her but she didn't seem to notice. Sindy was desolate. Her little girl was going to be lost to her forever. The pain was too much to bear.

*

When Duncan got home with two excited boys, pockets full of conkers, they found Sindy sitting at the kitchen table with a cold cup of tea in front of her and the few bits of shopping she'd bought, still in the bag. Duncan touched her shoulder. "Alright, love?"

She looked at him, but her eyes were glazed. Duncan remembered this look from when she'd fully realised Charlotte had died. "What's up, did you not go to your meeting?"

The boys interrupted. Full of excitement. "We've got conkers. Dad's going to put strings on them. Can you bake them mum?" Sindy said nothing. Duncan shoed them towards the back door. "Outside, boys. Go and put them in the shed and we'll do them after lunch. "I'll make us a sandwich. Do you want jam?"

This would normally have got a reaction from Sindy. She didn't like the boys having jam on white bread. She said it was bad for their little teeth. There was still no response. Sindy stood and walked slowly into the kitchen. She poured the cold cup of tea down the side of the washing up bowl, leaving splashes on the work surface. Not bothering to wipe them up she went through to the dining room where Martha had slept and lived for a short while. Duncan prepared lunch. He was hungry himself. While buttering the bread, he worried that Sindy's low mood had been caused by his outburst this morning. *Perhaps my accusations have hurt her more than I intended, and we're back to square one again. Maybe she aired our argument with that weird woman she visits. Perhaps she told her I was in the wrong, and Sindy's cross with me. Maybe all the accusations she threw at me have made her think more into my absence. Perhaps she guesses there was something between me and Millie?'* The boys wolfed down the sandwiches, even Duncan's share. His appetite had disappeared.

Wednesday 7th October 1981

Sindy was still not responding to her family or everyday life. Duncan was worried about her. There was nothing he could say to reach her. He'd phoned Jane, his mother-in-law and asked her if she would come and stay again. He was pleased she'd agreed to come back for the half term. Duncan was relieved. *However, would Sindy have managed here on her own when the boys were off school?'*

"I'm off now, love. I'll pop home at lunch time. Are you okay doing the school run?" Duncan had the boys washed, dressed and ready, but Sindy was still in her dressing gown. When she didn't answer he touched her arm and said, "shall I drop the boys at number forty-two. They can all walk to school together?"

He'd hoped suggesting that would get a response from her, but she stared up at him with that same familiar vacant expression. . He was still relieved when he heard her defeated voice. "No. I'll do it. I need to go out."

He tried to kiss her goodbye, but she turned her face away.

*

Without washing, Sindy slipped on a track suit. It was a bright canary yellow. It was far too bright for the dismal day outside. This was of no importance to her. Jack had been trying to hit Paul's conker and the strings were tangled. "Come on. We haven't got time for that. I need to walk along the canal."

"But we want to go…"

"You'll do as you're told. Now hurry. We haven't got long."

Sindy grabbed the satchels off the coat hook and practically threw Paul's anorak at him to put on. She helped Jack into his. "Come on. Put your arms in." She zipped him up and caught his neck and when he cried, she scolded him for not lifting his chin up. They hurried through the back of the estate, Paul and Jack were trying to keep up with Sindy's fast pace.

"Oh my God!" Sindy forgot about the boys little legs and the fast pace changed to a run. There was someone on Mrs Maxwell's mooring. "What are you doing? Where are you going?"

There were three men trying to manoeuvre the boat. "Hello!" Sindy waved and shouted. "Hello! Where's Mrs Maxwell?" The boys had caught up with her and were instantly fascinated with the movement on the water. One of the men hopped on the bank. "We're gotta tow this boat up to the basin. Jerry 'ere 'as a crane waitin' to move it to the Grand Union Canal."

"No! No you can't. I need to speak to Mrs…"

"She's gone, me duck. Long gone. You missed 'er. Went yesterday."

Sindy grabbed hold of Paul and Jack and marched them to the road. "I'll see you over this road and I want you to walk to school. You can cross with the lollypop lady. Do you hear me?"

The two boys were excited to be walking on their own to school. They had never been allowed to do this before. "What about you, mummy. Where are you going?"

"Home. I've things to do."

Sindy walked aimlessly back home. She had no idea what she was going to do. Once inside she picked up the telephone directory, but of course there was no number for Mrs Maxwell. Who could she ask? The members she'd met of a Friday were not from the village. This had appealed to Sindy at the time, and she had enjoyed the anonymity of the group. She felt safe if no one recognised her, safe from the village gossip. Not knowing anyone had meant she hadn't had to talk to anyone either, only Mrs Maxwell, and that had suited her perfectly. Sindy's heart was hammering in her chest. *'How could she up and go like that. All the times we've sat together. All the money I've given her.'* Sindy didn't want to think about Mrs Maxwell's warning, warning her she'd be leaving. *'Charlotte, Charlotte, Charlotte.'*

Sindy stayed where she was, holding the telephone book, willing someone's number or a name to come to her. When Duncan came in at midday that's how he found her, still clutching the telephone book with the same vacant look on her face. The breakfast things were still strewed across the table and if he'd gone upstairs, he'd have seen the beds were still unmade, and pyjamas were left screwed up in a heap in the bathroom where the boys had had a wash and left them.

Duncan was at a loss. Who was this woman? This wasn't the Sindy he'd married. For a while things had been a little easier, but since their row she'd slipped back so far he felt he couldn't reach her.

"Do you want a cuppa?" She said nothing. "Sindy, what is the matter? Is it me, have I done something to hurt you? Oh, Sindy, listen to me. Please. I didn't mean those things I said, I'm sorry. Okay. I just think I needed to explode. I'm so angry at losing Charlotte. I'm hurting too just the same as you are." He tried to reach out and hold her hands, but she resisted, clutching the telephone book as if it were a lifeline. "Sindy, you have to pull yourself together, if not for me but for the boys."

Sindy stared ahead. Her eyes shone with tears that framed her eyes. Her voice sounded as lifeless as she looked. "Charlotte's gone. I can't speak to her anymore. She's in heaven. Too high up to contact. Mrs Maxwell has gone, she's…"

"Jesus, Sindy. Listen to yourself. The woman's a crank. A fucking lunatic. She's ripped you off, playing on your emotions. I wish I'd said no you couldn't go. Charlotte's dead. God! I miss her. I loved her too. It was no one's fault, not mine, not yours, but she's gone. Where? I haven't a clue, but I don't think for one minute you or anyone else has been guiding her any bloody where. If there's a heaven, she went there the day she was taken from us. She was a baby. No sins committed. An innocent…"

"Shut up, Duncan. You don't know anything." Sindy got up and went upstairs still clutching the telephone directory.

Duncan didn't know what to do. He was at his wits end with her. She was the one he felt was slipping away, not Charlotte. His wife was becoming harder and harder to deal with.

After lunch, Duncan would have to go back to The Four Willows. There were jobs to do in the house for Alice. He didn't want to leave Sindy, but his presence didn't seem to help either. He felt useless and out of his depth. He called to her from the hall, "I'm going back to work. I'll be home at four. Get the boys, won't you?" *'of course, she'll pick the boys up.'* He was just going to open the door to leave, but the silence unnerved him. "Sindy! Did you hear. Pick the boys up?" When he still got no answer, he went upstairs to find her sitting on the floor in what was Charlotte's room. He kissed the top of her head and squeezed her shoulders in comfort, she made no response or acknowledgment that she'd felt the affection. He didn't pass comment about her sitting in the redundant bedroom either. There seemed no point.

Duncan spotted Grace leading her horse into the stable. He called out to her. "Hello, alright?" She looked round concerned by the tone of his voice. "I am, what about you?"

Duncan needed to talk. He unburdened himself. He told her all of his concerns. The row they'd had at the weekend and the way Sindy had withdrawn again into herself like when Charlotte first died. "I'm frightened for her. For us. The boys as well. She's like a different person." Duncan was close to tears. Once he'd let go of his pent-up emotion at the weekend, tears were never far away.

Grace shut the stable door on Tallis. "I don't want to tell tales or say anything out of turn, but this morning Paul and Jack walked to school on their own."

"What! Are you sure? How do you know?"

"The lollypop lady told me. Said she was surprised to see them on their own. Paul told her his mummy had seen them across the road, but…"

"Bloody hell. She can't be trusted with them. Jesus, Grace, what am I going to do?" He pulled his hand through his hair. I'm at my wits end with her. Her mum's coming in the half term but that's not for another couple of weeks yet."

"She'll get herself together. Like you said, the row has probably unsettled her."

"I'm going to have to finish up here early and pick the boys up myself. I made a comment when I left not to forget them, but I didn't really think she would. God they could have got picked up by someone or played around on the…"

Grace put a hand on his forearm. "Duncan. They didn't. They arrived safely, in one piece, together. Just like we used to remember. Our mum's never walked us to school."

"I know but times have changed. They're always asking to walk with the other kids, but Sindy's protective of Jack. Or she was." Grace looked a bit embarrassed at telling tales. "Look, I'll be at the school at three. I'll check she's there and if she's not I'll pop them home for you. Give her some trust. I'm sure she'll be fine."

Duncan realised he hadn't asked how Grace was coping. Life wasn't easy at the moment for her, what with being a single parent again and living with her mother.

He knocked on the back door and called out to Alice. She was there. "Do you want a cuppa? You look tired love, are you okay?" Duncan swallowed the lump that rose in his throat. Alice was full of wisdom, and he was sure she would have some good advice and answers, but he'd just aired his problems with Grace, he didn't feel able to speak openly again without tears. He excused himself and took the tools into the lounge where Hugh was sitting watching some afternoon programme. Duncan spoke to him and he sort of grunted a response. Alice breezed in behind him. "Hugh! It's Duncan. He's come to fix the door. You've been anxious about the catch." He made the same grunt at Alice. Duncan guessed it was his disability that made him sound grumpy and unapproachable, and his behaviour was nothing personal.

*

Duncan got home at four as he'd promised. Both boys were sitting watching television, but leapt up as he entered the room. "We're going to stay at nanny Jane's tomorrow. Mummy's taking us."

"No, no you're not. Nanny Jane is coming here in the half term."

Sindy appeared from upstairs. She seemed better. Brighter somehow. "What's all this the boys are saying? It's been arranged that your mum's coming here in the half term."

Sindy busied herself with the dish cloth. She wiped the same spot over and over. "No, she's not. I'm taking the boys tomorrow. They can have a few extra weeks off school."

316

"They can't, Sindy. Jack's just settling in and Paul is learning to tell the time. No. You can go in the half term. I'll take a week off with you and we'll make a family holiday of it."

The boys punched the air, excited at the prospect. Sindy burst their excitement. "We're not a family anymore. Our…"

"Don't even say it." The tension was building, and the boys had gone quiet. Duncan ruffled Jack's hair. "Come on you two. Let's go upstairs and see if we can put that train set together." The two boys scrambled up the stairs on all fours. Duncan paused before following them. Sindy was still wiping the same spot on the table. He didn't know what had got into her. His voice sounded tired. "Sindy, we'll sort this out later, but one thing's certain, you're not taking the boys out of school and that's final."

The smell of boiled cabbage gave Duncan just the excuse to go downstairs and close the adjoining doors to the hall. Sindy knew Duncan hated cabbage and wouldn't think anything of the action.

He went into what was Martha's domain and made a phone call to The Four Willows. Luck was on his side and Grace was still there with Emily enjoying tea with Alice. "Grace, I need a favour. Can you take the boys to school for me in the morning? They'll be at The Four Willows with me. I'll do Tallis for you."

"Of course I will. Is everything alright?"

"I can't explain now. Speak tomorrow. Thanks, Grace. I owe you one."

Once the boys were in bed the rowing started again. Sindy would have none of his compromises. He'd even said on Friday he'd bring the boys to her mother's and they could have the weekend together. This hadn't been good enough and she only backed down when Duncan said he was going to phone her mother to see why she couldn't come to theirs as planned and what was so urgent that the boys had to be taken out of school. They went to bed in silence and lay back-to-back with a good three inches of space between them. Duncan had never felt so helpless.

Duncan woke with a start in the early hours of the morning. Ignoring the fact that they had gone to bed not speaking, he whispered, "there's someone downstairs." He realised it was Sindy. Her side of the bed was empty. It was when he heard the boys protests that he leapt out of bed calling to her as he ran down the stairs. The boys were huddled together in their dressing gowns, looking blurry eyed. Duncan stood in a pair of boxer shorts. "Upstairs both of you."

"No!" Sindy shouted. It seemed louder at this ungodly hour. Her eyes were fixed on him like that of a wild animal. "Get in the car, boys."

"You can go, Sindy, but I told you the boys stay. We'll see you Friday at about four."

The boys didn't need telling twice. They hurried up the stairs. It seemed even they didn't want to go with their mum in the state she was in. Duncan grabbed Sindy by the arms. "What in hell's name do you think you're playing at? You're acting crazy, like you need to be sectioned. Is that what you want? People to think you are stark raving bonkers."

Her voice was quieter. She broke free of Duncan's hold. "I'm sorry. I just want to take the boys with me. You can bring them home with you on Sunday if you come up for the weekend. That way they'll only miss a couple of days of school."

"Sindy. Not now. I've made arrangements for the boys tomorrow. I might have gone with that idea if you'd…"

"Made arrangements, have you?" Her heckles were up "Since when have you been so in charge? They're my children and I say what and where they go."

"Jesus, you really have lost the plot." He pulled at his hair. "They are our children. If you must go at this silly hour to your mum's then I suggest you go now, before the traffic gets busy. I'm taking it that that was the method in your madness and not just deceit."

"Deceit! Listen to yourself. You think I didn't know what was going on at The Four Willows with that bloody Millie. Millie this and Millie that. Even if you did nothing, it was there, in your head. You talk in your sleep remember. It wasn't mine or the kids names on your sleepy breath, but hers."

Duncan felt like he'd been kicked in the stomach. The fight went out of him, like flames doused in iced water. "Go to your mum's. I'll see you Friday with the boys." He turned and left her to her own devices. The boys were cuddled in bed together. Duncan had never seen them do this and he could have cried at the sight. Paul had the pillow over his head and one arm round his younger brother. Duncan went in and sat with them. "It's okay. Mum's not well at the moment. Nanny Jane will sort her out. We'll go up on Friday and she'll be much better. Sometimes no one can help but mum."

Jack said in a sleepy voice, "I wanted to go with mummy. I wanted to see Nanny Jane. She's got a swing and climbing frame for us. It's in the garden."

Duncan didn't know how this could be. Jane's garden wasn't big enough to have much more than a washing line. It was the size of a postage stamp, all lawned with a table and a couple of chairs placed in the middle. The boys always played out the front. He didn't say anything to this effect. "You'll see it all on Friday. Grace is taking you to school later. Now get some sleep or you'll be dozing off at your desks tomorrow."

He heard the car start up and knew Sindy had left. Duncan didn't go back to bed. He was fearful she'd come back and steal them while he slept. Instead, he washed hurriedly and pulled on his tracksuit bottoms and a woolly jumper. A terrible combination but he didn't care. He went downstairs and made himself a coffee.

*

Millie couldn't believe it. Three times this week she had encountered Bradley. He was always browsing books where she was working or stationed. Bridget seemed to love him and almost fell over herself to help him, but it was obvious he was only interested in Millie. Millie tried to ignore him but she could feel his eyes watching her. *What is his problem? Surely he can't for one minute think I'd fancy him. His wife's having their sixth child and he's old. Do I look desperate?'*

When he walked in the library again at three thirty, Millie's heart skipped a beat. She felt ridiculously nervous. He walked straight up to her counter where she was stamping out books and checking dates on the returns. He was third in the queue. Her hands were trembling when he stood in front of her. He had no book to return or take out. He just said, "Millie... isn't it?" She was wearing a name badge but didn't point this out. "Can I help you, sir?"

He just came out with it. "Is your mother's name Davinia." Millie almost collapsed. She stared at him. *'Was he having an affair with my mother? Julie's husband. Is that why my father was put in a home and only given one or two visits a week?'*

Millie stopped staring and cleared her throat. "My mother is dead. Now if you'll excuse me, I have customers waiting to take out books...Unless of course you have something you need to take out or bring back?" She knew he didn't, and he stood aside but didn't leave. Millie got Carol to cover the desk on the pretence of needing the toilet. She had to get away from him. She stayed in the staff loo letting her mind imagine horrible things that her mother had been getting up to. Her supposed grandparents accusations never far from her mind. She wondered if her parent's marriage was as idyllic as she'd believed. When Millie reappeared, Bradley had gone, "Thank you, Carol."

She gave Millie a look. "What was all that about? Are you okay?"

"Yes. He asked about my mother."

"Your mother! What does he want to know about your mother for?"

"He knew her name. He said Davinia. It's not a common name, is it?"

Carol didn't say anything. There were no answers. Millie whispered. "How would he know I was her daughter? Did he recognise the name, Marlow on my badge? Or perhaps he recognised the likeness between us. People always said we looked alike. It was a long shot though, don't you think?"

"I don't know what to think. Weirdo. Weirdo with a capital W."

Millie couldn't help laughing. "Stop it. I live in that flat on my own, and he seems to know a bit too much about me these days and is far too interested."

"Not in you Millie, in your mother. I'd want to know why if it was me. I'd want him to answer some questions.?" Carol was called away by Bridget to help a customer. Carol raised her eyebrows before leaving Millie, and scooted off.

Millie thought about what Carol had said, and she made her mind up that yes, she did want answers. The thing that was troubling her was that if her suspicions were right and her mother was having an affair while her father sat in one room in a nursing home unable to communicate, was she going to be strong enough to shoulder another blow to her already fragile life. *'God! If that's true, no wonder Doris and John don't like her. After all my dad did for her.'*

When Millie left work at six, she expected to see Bradley loitering outside hoping to catch up with her and she gave a sigh of relief, when was nowhere to be seen. She opened her front door and could hear the phone ringing. Throwing her bag over the chair, she ran to get it before the caller rang off. She grabbed the receiver. "Hello?" Millie sounded breathless.

"Is that you, Millie." Millie recognised Alice's voice. Her heart skipped a beat. "Is everything okay with dad?"

"Yes, love." There was a definite pause. "Millie…are you sitting down?"

"Alice what has happened? Tell me please, my mind is racing."

"Sindy has died, love. She's had an accident this morning…"

"Oh my God! I must come home."

"No. There's nothing you can do. Everything is fine here. I just wanted you to…"

"Alice don't be daft. Of course everything's not fine. I need to sort out the horses. I need to speak to Grace. I shall have to…"

"Millie everything can wait until the weekend."

"No, Alice. I wasn't planning on coming home, I'm working this weekend. I shall come this evening. I need to." Before Alice could argue further Millie hung up and phoned Adam. "I've got to go home tonight. Duncan… the stable hand at The Four Willows, you met him remember?" Before Adam could answer, Millie said, "His wife's dead. There's been an accident. I need to sort some things out, I'm so sorry, but I have to go home." They had planned to see a film tonight at the cinema. It wasn't going to happen.

"It's fine, Millie. I understand. I shall come with you. I'll bring dad's van, so you don't have to drive."

Millie felt the sting of tears pricking the backs of her eyes. "Thanks. That means a lot to me."

As she replaced the receiver, she thought how lovely it was to have someone to support her and look out for her again.

Millie wasn't quite ready when she heard Adam's voice calling to her through the front door. "Millie… It's only me. I came round straight away."

*

When Millie pushed open the door at The Four Willows, she was greeted with what looked like a family scene. Her father was at the kitchen table sitting in his electric wheelchair and Emily was next to him reading her schoolbook. Grace and Alice were standing by the hob having a whispered conversation. Millie greeted them as cheerfully as she could under the circumstances. "Dad, it's wonderful to see you in your electric chair. See it was worth the money." Millie leant over and rubbed her hand down Emily's hair. "What story are you reading my dad?"

"The tale of Tommy Tickle and Mr Mole." Emily showed Millie the pictures. Millie gave a good show of being interested. "My dad used to listen to me reading stories, didn't you?" She nudged Hugh and he attempted a smile. Millie said, "I bet you're loving listening to Emily, eh dad. I bet it's bringing back memories of my early reading days."

Alice and Grace moved over to the table. Alice offered to make them a hot drink. "I'd love one, would you Adam?"

Once they were settled, Hugh went through to the lounge with Emily in tow. Alice then told Millie how Sindy had wanted to take the boys to her mother's, but it turned out she had no intention of doing so. She'd bought three bags of builders sand the day before and put them in the boot of her car. She had driven along to the Chichester Canal and went straight over the edge into the water. Millie was horrified. She thought it had been an accident. "Poor Duncan. How is he?"

"We haven't seen him. God knows how he'll cope, his own mother can't do anything, she's wheelchair bound and living in a nursing home now."

"What about his sister, can't she help?"

"Sue. No, she got married on the quiet last week and is still on her honeymoon."

Millie forgot the horror of the day. "Oh! That's wonderful news. Did she marry that builder chappie?"

"Electrician, but yes. It's lovely news isn't it. Sue's a lovely girl… or I should say woman."

Adam sat quietly not really knowing who they were talking about. When Emily entered the kitchen, bored of being with Millie's father, he asked her to take him outside to see the horses. She couldn't get her little shoes on quickly enough. "I can show you how I ride Scuttle. It's only a small horse. I can ride her without a saddle."

Grace raised her eyebrows at Millie. "She loves it here. You giving her permission to ride your ponies has been a godsend. Especially with the upset of late and having to live with my mother again."

Millie aired what she'd been thinking about for a while. Now seemed a good time to share it. "Grace, with Duncan off work and I don't know when he'll be in a position to come back, would you like to move in here? You can have the apartment I've made for myself. Sleep in my bedroom and use my space. Emily can have the study. We'll have to clear it out. It's got mum's clothes and personal bits in." Millie looked at Alice to see her reaction. "It won't interfere with you, will it Alice? They'll be using my little sitting room."

Alice shook her head. "What about you though? Where will you stay when you come home?"

"I can stay upstairs in the flat with you. There's room."

Alice smiled broadly. "That's an excellent idea. I was worried you wouldn't come home as often. It would kill your dad if he didn't have that pleasure to look forward to."

Millie ignored the sentiment and looked for Grace's reaction. "Would you like that, would it help?"

"Like, Millie. I can't believe it. It's perfect. I'm going to love it. So will Emily. Thank you so much."

"You'll have to do the horses pretty much seven days a week unless of course I'm home."

"Millie, it's fine. I'm ecstatic. There isn't room at mum's for us. That's why I spend so much time here."

"Right, that's that settled. I'll just get Adam and say cheerio to dad, and we'll make tracks home. Can I leave it with you Alice… or you Grace to inform Duncan that he's on full pay until he feels well enough or organised enough to come back to work?" Millie hugged Grace. "You can continue to use the house until you no longer need to. You can be an extra pair of hands for Alice."

Alice held out her arms to Millie. "You're an absolute treasure. Come here girl."

Millie paused. "Can I leave you to empty mum's stuff out of the study. Put her clothes in that shop in Chichester that buys second-hand things, but I don't want any money for it, just donate the lot. Any personal bits like photos, keepsakes or jewellery that you think I might like, can you put them to one side for me."

Grace looked a bit hesitant. "Millie?" Her face went a shade of pink. "Can I have first pick of the clothes? Not for me but for my mum. She was roughly about the same size and I'm sure your mother's clothes are top quality."

Millie laughed. "Mum was the worst dresser. She wore odd things at times. Things that were far too young for her, but of course. You take what you want. We're going to head off now. I won't be home at the weekend. I'm working Saturday and then we're off to a concert in Brighton." Alice hugged Millie again and so did Grace.

When Adam came in with Emily, the prospect of living at The Four Willows had the child leaping around like a frog. "I'm so excited, mummy."

*

Millie opened her front door and Adam went through to the sitting room. She called out to him. "Do you want a lager or a coffee?"

"I'll have a lager." Millie carried in two bottles, reminding him to say please. "I didn't think you'd want a glass."

"Nah that's fine." Before taking a swig he said, "who's Doris and John?"

"Oh! You nosy Bugger. Reading my mail."

"It was here on the coffee table. I just peeked to see who the card was from. The picture caught my eye."

Millie snatched it out of his hand. "Doris and John are my grandparents."

"Really? Why don't they write from nanny and grandad then?"

"Long story. In a nutshell I've only recently found them. Mum and dad fell out with them before I was born. I'm just getting to know them. They want to see dad again. It's just I don't want any hysterics from dad, and I never seem to be home long enough to organise it. Although I do want to sort out a meeting before Christmas."

"Your dad couldn't be hysterical. He can hardly communicate. I bet he'd love it."

Millie put her lager down on the table. "Don't you be so sure. My dad can make himself pretty well understood when he's upset or doesn't want to do something."

Millie switched on the television. "Shush! It's 'Only Fools and Horses'. I love this programme."

Adam downed his lager and stood to go. "I'll make a move then."

"No! Stay. It's just I don't want to talk about family stuff. I'll turn this off."

He moved over to the sofa and the programme was forgotten, along with Millie's family.

Adam went home in the early hours. Millie tried to cuddle him into the duvet so he'd stay, but he wanted to go home. He had been upgrading a road bike and he had a few bits to finish off and deliver in person to Portsmouth tomorrow. He'd promised it would be there before midday.

He kissed the top of her head as he rolled out of the double bed. "I think it's quite possible I could love you, Millie."

"Don't force yourself. There's plenty that would like to be in your shoes."

She heard him laugh as he went through to the lounge picking up his clothes that had been strewn over the floor in the heat of the moment.

Millie woke early despite her late night. She didn't have to be at work until eleven. She made breakfast, toast and coffee. The card caught her eye. Adam had propped it up on the windowsill. She decided she'd phone Doris today. Millie hadn't seen them since she nearly threw up over their carpet and made a fool of herself. They write to her often, telling her their news and how they hoped she would visit soon. She knew they wanted to heal the rift, and Millie had made her mind up she would do this small thing for them before the New Year. She just needed to find time at home to speak to her father and smooth over any fears he might have. Millie hoped, when he saw her acceptance of them and theirs with her, he would soften towards them as she had done. She found herself questioning her mother's behaviour more and more. Millie had always thought of her childhood as idyllic. Brought up by a mother and father who loved her and each other. The more she thought about it the more she could see the flaws. Yes, Millie knew without doubt that Davinia loved her, but she wasn't so sure Davinia loved her husband. Millie found herself questioning again the decisions made on her father's care. *Would she have left him in a nursing home and not visited him if she felt anything for him? It had always been dad who read the bedtime stories. When I rode at the weekends it wasn't as a family, it was always with one or the other. Yes, I'd been showered with love, but I'm not so sure they loved each other.'* One thing Millie was not letting go of and that was, Hugh was her dad and always would be.

At ten o'clock she phoned Doris. Millie could tell by her voice she was delighted to hear from her. "We're desperate to see Hugh. Even John has come round now. Please see if you can organise it for me, Millie. We don't want to upset anyone."

"I know, Doris. I'm sure dad will come round. I just need a weekend off when I'm on my own with him. I have a boyfriend now, and we tend to spend our free time together. I don't really want him to be in on this little venture."

"I understand, Millie. In your own time. Don't leave it too long though, will you love? It's been too long already."

Millie ran her finger down the calendar and looked for her next weekend off. "I'm off again at the end of the month. I'll go home on the Friday night and perhaps you can come on the Saturday. Does that sound good?"

"It's on my calendar already. Saturday thirty-first. Thank you, Millie. Thank you."

Millie replaced the receiver. Nerves jiggled in her stomach at the thought of what she'd just arranged.

Chapter Twenty-Four
Saturday 10th October 1981

Millie dressed for warmth. It was an undercover concert, but she knew it wasn't a hall. When Adam tapped at her door it was eight o'clock. She was wearing a pair of dark brown cord trousers with a beige checked shirt. A chunky heavy knit brown and cream cardigan with red buttons. She loved this outfit. It wasn't only warm but striking. Her brown cowboy boots set it off a treat. She threw a scarf around her neck and grabbed her beret. "Oh, look at you. You look like a model advertising autumn clothing."

"Thank you kind sir. I'll take that as a compliment. I wish I could say the same for you."

Adam always wore jeans and t-shirts. "What's wrong with this. It's going to be hot in there especially if we dance."

"Is there dancing?"

"I don't know. I guess there might be. It will still be warm. People create heat." They were going to see a Debbie Harry take-off. Adam had been raving about this for weeks. Millie kept telling him she wasn't the real thing. When he'd accused her of being jealous, she'd not mentioned it again. They could hear the throb of the music before they got to the marquee. At nine thirty Blondie came on. Her first song was 'Denis, Denis' and the crowd went crazy joining in with the singing. Adam was on his feet waving his hands above his head and his enthusiasm was catching. Millie, with more than a few drinks in her, got into the swing of things too and sang along with 'Hanging on the telephone.' Her arm draped over Adam's shoulder, the pair danced side by side. Millie was boiling hot and could feel the sweat running down her back. She shouted in Adam's ear. "I'm going to find a loo. I need to cool off." He stuck his thumb up in acknowledgment that he'd heard her.

The cold air outside of the marquee felt good. She could still hear the music and was tempted to sit on the ground and listen out here, but the grass was damp from the rain earlier. Just as she joined the queue for the portaloos she heard her name on a squeal, "Millie! Oh my god you're here. It's brilliant, isn't it?" It was Paula. Millie agreed it was good and asked, "Where's Rafi or are you on your own?" Paula stood beside Millie in the loo queue. "No, I'm with Rafi but he's in the marquee with Stephanie. Simon should be here too, but the two of them had a right old barney and Simon refused to come. I thought Stephanie would stay with him, but she didn't. She's in there now bopping like a teenager. You know how she likes a party." Millie felt sickened for Simon. She didn't want to care but she couldn't help herself. Her mood changed from feeling all fireworks and stars to a depressed blue. *Poor Si. I bet he knows he's got her.'* Millie used the smelly loos and went back into the marquee. Adam was still bopping and waving his arms around. His hair was stuck to his head with sweat. Millie couldn't lift her low mood and found herself wishing it were over so they could go home. She caught sight of Stephanie's wild curls bouncing up and down as she jumped with the music. She'd always been heavily built and since she'd had a baby, she looked larger. This pleased Millie. Rafi was with Stephanie now. He had an arm draped across her shoulder, just the same as Adam's had been across her own earlier. It looked too friendly to Millie. She looked for Paula but couldn't see her. This added to her concerns for Simon, and this brought her mood lower. Millie caught hold of Adam's arm and tried to shout above the music, "how much longer. I've had enough."

"What! Are you for real? This is brilliant."

"I'm tired. I want to go home."

"You can't be serious. Go and get another drink. Jolly yourself up." Every minute that passed was a minute too long. When the Blondie look-alike had sung her final song and everyone was calling for more, Millie started pushing through the crowds to get out first. She didn't want to come face to face with Stephanie. Millie got back to the van before Adam, and when he appeared, she was leaning against the door with her arms folded, annoyed.

Adam was full of himself and didn't seem to notice. "She was brilliant, wasn't she?"

"If you like that sort of thing." She knew she sounded churlish, but Paula's conversation had upset her, and she didn't like herself for caring.

"Millie! What's wrong with you? She was fantastic."

"If you like that sort of thing. It's not for me."

"Well, if you looked like her, I'd marry you tomorrow." This was too much for Millie. She was sick of these silly comments he came out with about his feelings. In the mood she was in, she didn't let it go over her head or joke back with him. She snapped. "Why do you have to do that?"

"What?"

"You know very well."

"No I don't. What?"

"Say stupid irrelevant things like you could fall in love with me if… or if I looked like that you could marry me."

Adam unlocked the van and pushed open the door for Millie. "I'm only joking. It doesn't mean anything."

"Too right it doesn't. You need to understand that I don't want you to fall in love with me. I don't want to marry you, not now, tomorrow or in the future. I couldn't be persuaded to marry you or love you even if you looked like Patrick Swayze…" Adam put his hand on her arm. "Whoa! Where's all this coming from. I was joking. Okay?"

"It's not funny. It's boring. In future don't say you could love me, because even if you could you'd be wasting your energy. I could never love you. Not even if you were dripping in diamonds."

The journey back to Millie's was spent in silence. When Adam pulled up at the front of the newsagents, she got out without inviting him up, kissing him or even saying goodbye. She slammed the door and didn't look back as she went through the alley to the steps that led to her flat. She knew she was acting like a spoilt, moody bitch, but she couldn't help herself. Her eyes pricked as she put her key in the front door. She knew the relationship was finished. It had been fun without the complications of real romance and the clingy need of two people in those early days of loving. It didn't stop the empty feeling of knowing she was on her own again though. *'Oh Simon. Things could have been so different.'* She made herself a Horlicks. She'd had a lot to drink tonight, and the evening had started early. The events of the evening had sobered her up completely. *'I could write to Duncan. Offer my condolences. Nothing more.'* Thinking of Duncan made her feel sad too. She had for a while believed she was in love with him. She questioned these feelings now, and thought it was possible it was just a case of wanting the unattainable. The excitement of living on the edge.

Millie didn't write any condolences to Duncan. She finished her Horlicks, cleaned her teeth and got into bed.

*

Millie woke late in the morning to the sound of someone ringing the doorbell. She leapt out of bed, dragged her hands through her hair and grabbed the dressing gown off the back of the chair. *'Who calls on a Sunday at this hour?'* She glanced at the clock before she opened the door, it was gone ten. *'Maybe not so early.'* Feeling vulnerable in her night clothes she called, "Who is it?"

"It's me, Adam. Please, Millie, let me in."

Millie opened the door to be greeted by Adam carrying a bottle of wine and a box of Milk Tray. He held them up with a silly grin on his face. "I'm not very good at this, but it's a peace offering."

Millie opened the door wider to let him in. "Want a coffee?" She took the gifts and put them in the kitchen. When she'd made two mugs of coffee, she went through to the lounge to find Adam sitting in the chair wringing his hands together like a worried little boy. "Adam…"

"No, Millie. I'm sorry. Really sorry. Can we say it was the drink talking?" Millie handed him his mug. "Adam, you and I both know you had minimal on the drink front. If anyone should be blaming the drink it's me."

"Can we say I'm forgiven then. Back to as we were?" Millie put her mug down and took a deep breath. "Adam…" The pause in her speech had him saying, "please, Millie."

"No, Adam. It's not just because of last night or anything you said, it's because…"

"Millie I only said those things because I wanted you to protest. You never say you love me or talk about a future together. We were always just uncomplicated fun. I want more with you. I hoped when I said those things you might start saying you were…" It was Millie's turn to interrupt. "I said those things because I did want uncomplicated fun. Friendship."

"Jesus, Millie. We've been sleeping together."

"I know. We are in the twentieth century. I'm on the pill." She laughed trying to lighten a heavy situation. He was having none of it. "Millie, I want you to come to Sunday lunch with my family today. I've told mum I'm coming to get you. Please say you'll come. My brother will be there and my auntie Prim and Uncle…"

"No, Adam. No. I'm going to pop home. I want to sort out something with my dad."

Adam wouldn't give over. He wanted Millie to reassure him they were still a couple. This was too much for Millie. She took another deep breath and said in a soft, defeated voice, "I'm not in love with you Adam. My heart belongs to someone else. I thought I was over…"

"It's that bloke from your stables. The one who sees to your horses whose just lost his wife. I could see it in his face he liked you. Now his wife's dead you…" Millie was quick to defend herself. "No, Adam!" She spoke emphatically. "No-it-is-not. If it makes you feel better to think it's him, that's fine, but if you want the truth, then yes, the man I love IS married. Not just married but he's married to what was my best friend and they have a baby. I can't have him, and it hurts like hell. I hoped having fun with you would help. It hasn't. I can see that now."

"But…"

"No, Adam. I don't want your love. I wanted your friendship. The friendship you were offering. Remember. No complications. How many times did you say that to me? Let's have a bit of fun. I liked that in you."

"I know, Millie. I just want more now. I like you a lot. Really like you. No, Millie… I love you."

"But I don't love you. I'm sorry."

"Can we go back to being friends then?" He hesitated. "Please." Millie shook her head. "I think the time has come when we call it a day with no hard feelings."

"But…"

"It's no good, Adam. My mind's made up. I'm going to have a bath and go home. I need to speak to my dad."

Millie walked with him to the door. He gave her a hug. She pulled out of his arms. "Hang on." She popped into the kitchen and gave him back the wine and chocolates. "Give them to your mum for the Sunday lunch. She'll love the gesture." He didn't argue and left holding the peace offering he'd hoped was going to heal their squabble. The relationship was over and they both knew it.

*

Millie got to The Four Willows at three o'clock. She pushed open the kitchen door and there was Alice. "Hello, Alice. How's dad and where's Grace and Emily? Have they settled in okay?" Alice got up and hugged Millie. "Slow down. Everything's fine. Grace is at Duncan's helping out with the boys. Sindy's mother's in no fit state to help, poor woman, and his sister's still on her honeymoon. Grace was over there yesterday as well, even though Emily's with her dad. I'm sure she could have done with the free time to recharge her own batteries. She's a good sort that one." Millie sat at the table pleased to be home. "I'm sure she likes helping. I know I would." Alice patted her hand. "I know. You're a good girl too, but I really don't think it's wise, do you?"

"I know, I'm just saying, that's all. I need to speak to dad today, Alice. I'd like you to be with us if that's okay?"

"Ooh this sounds exciting. Is there a wedding on the cards?"

Millie laughed. "No, Alice, quite the contrary. I've finished with Adam. He's…"

"Oh, love, no. I liked him. He was a lovely…"

"Yes, Alice he was. Only he wasn't for me." Millie changed the subject. "I need to talk to dad about his parents. They want to visit. I haven't said anything, but I've been keeping in contact with them. I like them and they like me. I think it's time to bury this horrible hatchet."

Millie was just getting ready to leave The Four Willows when Grace came home with Emily. Grace said things were pretty grim with Duncan and told her how he's only just taking on board the enormity of what happened, and how if he hadn't caught Sindy sneaking out in the early hours, just what he would have lost. "I think it's only the boys that are keeping him going. Honest I do."

Millie felt sad for him. "Do you think she would really have driven that car in the canal if the boys were in the back."

Grace nodded. "Sadly, I do. She had it all planned. The verdict is suicide, but they reckon it was down to a nervous breakdown. She needed professional help not some bloody religious freak taking her money and filling her head with nonsense."

"That's so sad. Tragic."

Alice appeared at that moment and handed Millie the personal bits that they'd cleared out of the study. Bits that had belonged to her mother. As Millie drove back to Midhurst, she was pleased she'd been able to get her father to agree to the meeting. There had been a little resistance from him, but Alice had eased his stubbornness when she'd said, 'it's time, Hugh. How would you feel if you upset Millie and she held a grudge and never spoke to you again?'

Millie had got down on her knees and taken her father's hand in hers and spoke softly, telling him how she liked his parents. She told him how they write to her and vice-versa. Eventually he'd bowed his head and squeezed her hand. A sign of acceptance. With tears on both sides, she'd kissed his cheek and told him she loved him. She did love him.

*

Millie lugged the three bags of her mother's things up the steps to her flat. Once inside she threw them on the table and made herself a cup of coffee. The three bags looked like rubbish, but Millie was determined to sort through them properly. Find a few sentimental pieces that she could keep. She hadn't intended to do it this evening but when a photo album of her young years fell out first, she was lost in memories long forgotten. There were photos of her sitting up in a silver cross pram and later in a pushchair, some of them were of mealtimes where she was in a highchair with food all round her face or photos of her propped up smiling on the sofa with cushions behind her, and in them all she was dressed beautifully in knitted jackets and cardigans.

She smiled at her first birthday cake. It was covered in pink icing with a number one in the middle. Her mother had never been very creative in the kitchen. The photos were lovely. Millie was mesmerised by the many events that had been captured on film. There was a holiday to Cornwall. Millie had been photographed on the sand with her mother making sandcastles. She couldn't have been more than three or four. Somewhere in her distant memory she could vaguely remember it. There were no photos of her father, it was as if this box had been her mother's memories.

Photos and more photos. Millie was lost and captivated by nostalgia. She sifted through them trying to find a picture of herself with her father. There were none. Millie was puzzled. There were lots of photos at home in albums of them all as a family, so why would her mother have separated them like this? The more she thought about it, Millie realised the photos at home were mainly of herself with her father or with friends or just Millie on her own. It seemed now that any photos with her and her mother had been stashed away… for what? Millie had no idea. She was still enjoying looking at them.

After a while she placed the photos in neat piles and popped them back in the box. *'I'll do one more then I must get ready for work tomorrow.'* Millie was curious to see a large brown envelope that was sealed. Opening it felt sneaky and nosy. *'Oh my god! Who's this? Is this what dad looked like as a young man.'* He was smiling at her from the photograph. It was a seaside shot and he was wearing swimming trunks. Tight-fitting ones like speedos. Millie would laugh if she saw anyone wearing anything like that today. She picked it up and studied it. There was something familiar about him, but it was such a small black and white photo that had faded with time. There were more. Millie stared at the photo of the same young man. This one was clearer. She could see he had a thin boyish body but he was handsome, and it definitely wasn't her father. Her hand shook at the realisation of who it was. She stood up and took it to the lamp. *'Oh my god it's him. Bradley. My mother with Bradley.'* She looked at some more, the envelope was full of him and her mother together. Her mother could have only been about nineteen, twenty. Millie's age. Millie could see the likeness between them. *'You'd think this one was me. No wonder Bradley's so interested in me. He doesn't fancy me. He's remembering my mum through me.'*

Fascinated, Millie decided to open more envelopes. Then she saw the connection. The puzzle was complete. There in writing was a few lines scribbled on what looked like school paper to her mother. Her heart thumped painfully in her chest, her hands shook, and her eyes glazed over as she read the faded scrawl.

Dear Davi

A little girl. Thank you for the photo. She's beautiful. This is difficult for me as I miss you and can't bear to think of you with that old codger. Yes, I shall be at the fountain, one o'clock.

love B XXX

The realisation that Duncan was not her brother was like a cold shower, but it took second place to the shock of finding out that Bradley was her biological father. *'Urgh, Bradley'* Her whole existence had been built on lies. Anger quickly replaced shock as she realised her mother had tricked her dear father into believing she'd got pregnant by a married man. A married man with children. One of them disabled, which meant he couldn't possibly leave his wife. Millie held her sides as a wave of nausea swept over

her. *'Oh dad. You fell for it. Finishing your engagement to take her on…
and me. She spun you a line so there was no way you could expect the father to
marry her.'* Millie looked at the photo again of Bradley in his
trunks. There was no way he was married back then. He was just a
boy. *'What was going on. Why didn't they set up home like Stephanie and
Si?'* Millie wanted to find Bradley this moment and ask him
outright what this all meant, but there was no need. Millie knew.
Her mother was a liar. She'd used her father as a meal ticket. She
became more enraged when she thought of Bradley referring to
her father as 'the old codger'. The more Millie understood, the
more she realised how cruel her mother had been to put her dad in
that nursing home and not visit. Perhaps it was her fault he'd had
the stroke in the first place. *'No wonder Doris and John hated her and
wanted nothing to do with me. I don't know if I like her myself anymore.'*
What Millie had done for her father was proof enough that he
could have stayed at home. If her mother had organised it, he
could have been looked after by carers. It was all so clear now. *'She
just didn't want him. How long had she felt like that? Did they row when I
was away at university. Did the marriage fall apart with my coming of age?
Was it just a marriage of convenience for her? Did my dad give his life to her
for her to wait until I'd flown the nest?'* There were so many questions
she wanted answered. *'Thank God for you, dad. Thank God for you.'*

Millie gathered up the photos and paperwork. She was too angry
now to do anything logical. She would sleep on this, but tomorrow
she would catch Bradley when he bought his paper and cigarettes
and get some answers.

*

Millie didn't see Bradley the following morning. Ever since she'd
moved in, he'd bought a paper and smoked a cigarette out the
front as regularly as waking up and eating breakfast. *'That's just my*

340

luck. When I want him, he doesn't turn up! Good father he would have made.' Millie had slept badly, her mind troubled.

She wanted to drive home to The Four Willows and hug her father. Thank him for all the wonderful years he'd given her and the sacrifices he'd made, but now wasn't the time. She had to go to work. The bills on this place needed paying and now she'd given her space over to Grace and Emily, home was a little cramped these days.

Once Millie got to work she found herself watching for Bradley. Not a sign of him. She had been given the job of putting the library books away and tidying up the shelves. The children's stories were being read by Mrs Fairbandly. Despite the parents' requests for Millie to do the children's session it was seen as Mrs Fairbandly's job and she'd taken the criticism badly, even giving Millie the cold shoulder for a while. "Hello Millie." She was so lost in thought she jumped. "Oh, Si." Green eyes stared at her expectantly. His wild spiky hair had been gelled down and he was wearing a grey suit and a navy-blue tie. He not only looked smart but mature. He smiled. "Paula told me you worked here. I'm doing the accounts today for the card shop across the road and I couldn't resist coming in to say hello to you." Millie could see he looked nervous. He'd lost weight too. Her legs felt quite weak and her heart had quickened at the sight of him. She sighed. "You're actually a blessing. I couldn't wish to see anybody better." His face lit up with the compliment. "Really? I nearly chickened out. I wasn't sure if you would want to see me."

"Oh, Si, hopefully we've moved on from all that bitterness. I'm more than pleased to see you. How are you?"

"Don't ask."

"Oh, dear." Millie instinctively touched his arm and Bridget who must have caught the action said in hushed tones. "Millie can you get another trolley from the back please. There are still three more to empty."

Simon whispered, "I'll go. Can you meet me for lunch? Coffee…" He hesitated and Millie could see he wasn't confident. She wheeled the empty trolley towards the stockroom door and smiled encouragingly. "I'll be waiting outside for you at one o'clock." She didn't witness the spring in his step as he left.

Over lunch Millie heard all Simon's news. She could see he loved and was proud of his little boy. She could tell things were difficult between him and Stephanie, even though he played it down. Millie couldn't help but feel secretly pleased. He'd tried to apologise for the way things had turned out, but Millie closed that train of thought down. He listened when she'd told him she'd had a couple of relationships, but nothing serious.

Millie looked at herself in the cloakroom mirror, the side of her face still tingled where Simon had leant forward and kissed her goodbye. She pulled a comb through her hair and put on a bit of lip gloss. Talking to her reflection. *I really loved you, Si, and you loved me. What have you done? What a mess you've caused through a moment of seeking…'* Millie paused as she recalled what Simon had told her happened. *'It was a moment's madness. Weakness at not being able to refuse what was being offered. He said he'd wanted to blame it on the drink, but the truth of it was I hadn't been around. He'd got lonely and fell for a moment's sexual release.'*

*

Simon called out to Stephanie as he opened the front door with his key. "I'm home."

"I'm in the lounge. Rafi's here." This annoyed Simon. Rafi was becoming a too frequent visitor. He forced a smile on his face and entered the lounge. Stephanie was feeding Ben a bottle and Rafi had a mug in his hand. It looked a bit too cosy. Simon spoke first. "Where's Paula and what brings you round here again?"

"I got the sack today. Stoned on the job. I've got to move back home. Can't pay the rent if I haven't got work. I'll get something else though. If not, I'll run one of dad's laundrettes."

Stephanie started flirting. "Don't you just love him?"

"No, not really." They both laughed at Simon's comment, but he was annoyed at Rafi's presence. "What about Paula. What does she make of all this?"

"I've yet to tell her. She isn't as easy to talk to as Stephanie." Simon saw the look shared between them and jealousy spiked. "I suggest you make tracks now. Sort out your problems rather than air them. I'm home now and I want my dinner with my family."

Stephanie stood up a bit too quickly and fell back with the baby in her arms. Ben started crying. "Now look what you made me do, Simon. How rude you are. Sorry Rafi for my husband's behaviour. He thinks we live in the dark ages and…"

"No I don't. I just don't expect to find a cosy little twosome and no dinner cooking when I get home after working all bloody day to bring in a wage for us, not out smoking dope and getting the sack."

Stephanie didn't try and stand up again, and Rafi was already up and putting his coat on. He looked uncomfortable. "Sorry mate. I just didn't know where to go. Stephanie and I go back…"

"Yeah, I know all that." Simon's voice sounded sarcastic and bored. "Still, it's time you went. Go and find Paula. Cheerio." Simon left the room and went upstairs to get out of his suit and into something more comfortable. He heard the front door close and knew Rafi had left. The bedroom door flew open and there stood Stephanie with her hands on her hips. Ben could be heard downstairs protesting at being left alone. She was oblivious to the crying. "What was all that about?" Simon chose to play ignorant. "What was all what about?" Stephanie was so angry she spat as she shouted. "Rude! That's what you were. Bloody rude."

"Rude, was I? I don't take kindly to coming home from work to find you fraternising with your ex-boyfriend. Someone who you seem to find more fun to be with these days than me."

"Oh, too right I do. Boring. That's what you are. All work and no play… Do you know the saying?"

"Yes, I do. There should be a saying that goes all play and no work doesn't provide for a family."

"Get a life, Simon." She picked up his shirt that he'd thrown on the bed. "This goes in the wash bin." She waved it at him aggressively, "I'm not your skivvy." She buried her face in his shirt and sniffed. "Millie. You've been with Millie." Simon couldn't believe it. He felt his armpits moisten. "Oh, let's pass the buck. Caught in a corner so you…"

"Don't fuck with me. I can smell her perfume. Necking with her, were you?"

"You're going mad. I reckon you've been slipped something dodgy by Rafi. Hallucinating."

"You don't fool me. I know what you've been up to." Stephanie's face was screwed up in anger. She looked ugly. Simon couldn't believe he'd ever fallen for her charms. He quite disliked her. "I don't know what you're talking about."

She poked him hard in the chest. "Yes you do. I can see it written all over your face. Guilty. Talk about the pot calling the kettle black. You're a hypocrite. As of now, Rafi will come here as and when he wants, and you won't say a bloody word about it."

Simon rubbed his chest. "Oh won't I. We'll see about that. You're off your trolley, you are. I haven't seen Millie. You're paranoid. It must be one of the girls in the office."

"Bloody liar. I'm not stupid. You can't fool me. You've been with Millie Marlow. I know you have. I'd know her perfume anywhere. It's old fashioned. No one wears that anymore. It stinks. It gives me a headache …"

"Go downstairs and see to Ben. You're really pissing me off now."

Stephanie pushed him with both hands. He lost his balance and fell back in the chair. She pointed her finger at him again and said aggressively, "you go downstairs. You see to Ben. I've had him all day." She grabbed her dressing gown. "And while you're down there make yourself some dinner. I'm going to have a shower and go out."

"No you're…"

Stephanie waltzed out of the bedroom and into the bathroom. He heard the bolt go across. Stephanie sang loudly and her voice echoed into the hall. His shouting fell on deaf ears. He went down into the lounge and picked Ben up out of his little bouncy chair. "There you go, big fella. Daddy's got you."

Monday 26ᵗʰ October 1981

Millie pulled back the curtains in her flat. It was still dark outside. The rain wasn't helping and the sky looked dark and angry. She flicked on the lights as she went through to the kitchen to make coffee and toast. She stood at the window and watched the world go by as daylight arrived. She didn't have to be at work until eleven. It was her turn to work the late shift.

It was over two weeks ago that she'd brought home her mother's photos, jewellery, and memory box and she still hadn't seen

Bradley. She wondered if Julie had had her baby. Millie hadn't seen her walking the children to school or the younger ones at the library for story time. *They could be away on holiday, but I doubt it. The baby had to be due by now by the size of her.'* When she'd first found out that Bradley was her biological father, she'd been set to attack him on sight. Now her temper had cooled she didn't feel so brave. *'Say I've made a mistake and it isn't him in the photo.'* She was kidding herself and she knew it. She'd studied it long and hard and knew without doubt it was Bradley. He hadn't changed that much either. Then there was the letter. It all pointed to him. There were questions she wanted answers to, but she had no idea how she would approach him or broach the subject. *'I'll wait until he starts haunting me again, and then I'll ...'* Millie bit into a slice of toast. *'I don't know what I'll do, but I have to do something. I have to know.'* Then she saw him. Mr Hat, Bradley, her father, walking towards the newsagents below her. She jumped back from the window, not wanting to be seen. Her heart quickened in her chest and the toast she'd bitten seemed to stick in her throat. She swallowed a mouthful of coffee to wash it down and dared to peek at the window. He'd gone inside the newsagents. She knew his routine and he'd be out in a minute with the paper, lighting up a cigarette. She had to speak to him. *'What can I say? How am I going to engage with him when normally I avoid him, or give him the brush off?'* There was so much going on in Millie's life at the moment, she felt weighed down. This weekend she was going home. Her grandparents were coming to be reunited with their son and Millie guessed it was going to be her job to act as peacemaker. She also wanted to tell Alice about Duncan. That he wasn't her brother and although what they did was wrong, it wasn't incest. She really was pleased now that Alice hadn't given Duncan her heartfelt letter. At the time she'd been angry and felt Alice had been unfair, but with this new knowledge, the secret kept had been a blessing. *'Shall I tell dad the truth?'* She didn't know. *'One thing at a time.'* Millie had to speak to Bradley first and then tackle the reunion.

Millie's eyes went to the pavement below. There he was. Just as she knew he would be. She took a deep breath and opened the window. "Bradley." He looked up, surprised. Millie said the first thing she could think of. "Has Julie had the baby?" A look of genuine delight could be seen on his face. "Yes. Another girl." Without thinking further Millie called down, "can I have a word with you?"

He threw his cigarette on the ground and stubbed it out with the toe of his shoe. It was obvious he was looking for a way up to Millie's flat. She hung out of the window and pointed to the alley at the side of the shop. "Go up the steps. I'll have the door open."

When he stepped inside, she offered him a drink. He refused.

"I want to show you something." The photos were easily accessible. Bradley almost lost his balance when he realised what Millie had uncovered. His hand shook. "I wanted to speak to you about this. Honest I did. That's why I've been hanging around the library. You see you look so like your mum. I wanted to know for sure, or if I was just letting my imagination run wild."

"Say I didn't know. You know about my parentage?"

"That's why I was careful with my questions. Why I asked you in the library about your mother. When you said she'd died I was prepared to leave well alone."

The words were out of Millie's mouth before she could stop them. "Why didn't you marry her?" It was a blatant accusation.

"I was in my first year at university. We'd met in the New Year. I didn't see her again until I got a job at the sports club for the Easter holidays. In the summer of that year, we spent all our free time together. I was a lifeguard. She was on the desk. She was fun. Lovely." He paused, looked at Millie and said quietly, "so like you are today."

"So?"

"Well, you know… She got pregnant." He looked at his hands. He was trying to be honest; she could tell. "I tried to get her to have an abortion. She wouldn't."

Millie said nothing and he continued.

"There was this guy. Hugh. He'd joined the club earlier in the year and had started swimming in the evenings. We both knew he liked her. She… we mocked him because he was older. Shy and awkward looking. Old fashioned too. Wore funny clothes from another time, he…"

"Don't laugh at my father please. I want to know how it is that you dodged your responsibilities and my dear dad shouldered them."

Bradley had the decency to look uneasy. "Sorry. I was just remembering. I suppose I was jealous of him if I'm honest. He'd taken your mum out for a drink one evening. I could tell she liked him after that. She was impressed with the fact he worked for his father, their own business. He talked properly too. You know with a plum in his mouth…" Bradley stopped again before apologising. "Sorry, Millie. I guess when we knew Davinia was pregnant we panicked. She didn't want me to give up my career and the truth is I didn't want to be a father either, not back then. It was easier to go along with Davinia's idea. She'd earmarked your dad. He was obsessed with her, you see. We could tell. Between us we spun a story that she'd got herself into trouble with a married man who…"

"I know all that." Millie was annoyed with Bradley. "Does Julie know about me?"

"No. Not you exactly. She knows I got a girl pregnant and someone else took the baby on. She doesn't know any more than that. I haven't mentioned that I noticed a likeness in you and your mother, or my suspicions. I don't think Julie would mind though."

He paused. "Well… she might, but not if it was you. She raves about you at home. The kids do too."

Millie ignored his little speech. "Did you continue to see my mother after I was born? What I'm really asking is, did my mother cheat on my father?"

"I wanted to see you. We met a few times.   In the first six months of your life." His face coloured. "I sort of moved on. I'd met someone else. Not Julie, but a girl studying law like me. We were close. Very close for about four years."

"I'm not interested. I just feel sorry for my father. Betrayed, lied to and…"

"Your mum stayed with him, didn't she?"

"Yes. Enjoyed the good life. Then when dad had a devastating stroke and needed her, she dumped him in a nursing home. Everything I thought about my idyllic childhood was fabrication. A figment of my imagination. I don't think she loved my father at all."

"You're upset. I understand. You have to remember your mother and me, we were young. We did what we thought was best at the time."

"Oh, you did, did you? Did you know my father was engaged to a lovely woman of his own class? He ditched her for my mum. Married her because of her predicament. For the pair of you to be laughing at him behind his back and then sneaking around when I was born, probably laughing at him again."

"Millie, I don't want to get annoyed with you, but you need to grow up. Your dad was leering after your mother for weeks. Weeks before we told him she was having a baby. It was obvious he wanted her. In fact, he was so desperate to have her, he took her on knowing you were on the way too."

"Well thank God he did."

"Did they have any more children?"

Millie didn't want to share any more information about her parents' marriage. "Can you go now. You have answered all I needed to know. Thank you."

"Millie, I…"

"No more. I want you to leave me alone. Goodbye."

When Millie was alone, she let his confession wave over her. She felt like her life really had been built on a pack of lies.

Chapter Twenty-Five

Friday 11ᵗʰ December 1981

It was eight o'clock when Millie left the Wheatsheaf. She'd gone for a drink with Bridget and Carol after work. This was something that they'd started doing a few weeks ago and it seemed to be becoming a habit. Despite the dark gloomy weather, the streets were festive with colourful lights, showing signs that Christmas was on its way. The shop windows were lit up with colour and the book shop had a waving Santa Claus who was smiling and holding a sack brimming with toys. A clockwork train was going round Santa's feet on a track and pretty baubles hung from invisible thin wires. The sight made Millie feel happy, along with the alcohol.

Millie was going home for the weekend tomorrow. She hadn't been home since the reunion had taken place between her father and grandparents five weeks ago. Work kept her busy and it was easier to stay at her flat than trek back to Hunston for the day. She'd seen Simon three times since their initial meeting and they'd enjoyed coffee together on each occasion. The last time she'd seen him, he'd brought Ben with him. Millie wasn't really a baby person, she preferred it when they were toddling around and you could play with them. She had to agree with Paula, he did look like a miniature Simon and she'd told him this. He'd glowed with pride.

Millie had seen Adam too. He'd managed to persuade her to go to a firework night in Stedham. It was excellent and they'd had fun together. No strings attached. He'd asked her to go to a Christmas party on the nineteenth, but it was the same evening as her works Christmas party. They had parted with the promise of getting together in the New Year. She was so lost in thought that when a figure emerged from the darkness of the alleyway and said her name, her heart thumped in her chest with the scare. When she recognised who it was, relief had her saying, "Jesus, Simon. You made me jump. Don't you ever do that again."

"I've been waiting for you. I thought you said you finished at six."

"I do… did, but we've been for a drink. "What's up?"

Simon followed her up the steps to her flat, uninvited. "I had some time to kill. I just thought it would be good to see you. Now it's a bit late, I really ought to be going home."

Millie opened her front door. "Cheerio then."

"Millie?"

"What, Si. What do you want? You're married. You need to get home. Go."

"I wanted to see you. I just…"

"Well, you've seen me now, so bye bye." She waved her fingers at him in a silly fashion. She knew she was being mean, but the drink helped her say what she would normally hold back in thought.

Simon stepped into her flat.

Millie started taking off her coat. "Look, Si. It's all very flattering but these visits are going nowhere. I'd rather you went home."

"A quick coffee?" His face looked like a child begging to stay up for ten more minutes.

"Quick one. Then you must go. I want to pack a few things for the weekend. I'm going home. I'm hoping to be on the road by seven."

Simon sighed with relief as Millie filled the kettle. "Tea, coffee?"

She made two mugs of coffee and sat with him in the lounge. Millie could tell he was unhappy; she'd known him too long. She didn't probe into his feelings, or life with Stephanie. She kept the conversation basic. "What are your plans for Christmas?" She told him about her works party on the nineteenth and how she was going home to spend Christmas with her dad including her grandparents and Alice. "I expect Grace will be home in the evening and we'll play those crazy childhood card games…" She paused. "Do you remember, Si, the ones we played at mine that first year at uni. You came home with me to the Four Willows and had Christmas with us."

"I do, Millie. It was the best ever. I'd never been involved with a family like yours before."

Millie thought, *'if you only knew'*, but said instead, "well the faces will be different this year, but I'm sure we'll be playing Old Maid and Fish at the table."

*

Millie pulled into the drive of The Four Willows at nine fifteen in the morning. Much later than she had planned, but getting Simon to leave had been difficult. The ten o'clock news coming on had him deciding that he really did ought to be going. Millie couldn't begin to think how he had explained himself to Stephanie. Millie knew they'd done nothing wrong, but she knew it wouldn't sit well if Stephanie knew he'd been with her. *'Perhaps it's as Si says, she's so wrapped up in Rafi these days she doesn't miss him.'* Millie didn't think so somehow.

Alice was making bread in the kitchen and was kneading the dough ferociously on the work top. "Gosh, Alice, you look like you're taking your anger out on that bread." Alice stopped kneading. "Oh, love, it's lovely to see you. Go on through to your dad, he'll be delighted." She rolled the dough up and plopped it in the bowl and covered it with a tea towel and left it in top of the warm oven to prove. Alice shooed Millie with her hand like an unwanted fly. "Go! Go on through. I'll make you a cuppa."

"No tea thanks." She looked out across the garden. "I see Duncan is here with the boys. I'm going to have a word with him."

Millie caught the concern go across Alice's face. Millie ignored it. She didn't want to share her discoveries just yet. She left the kitchen and went through to her dad, who she knew would be sitting in his chair. She got a surprise when she entered the lounge. He was in his electric chair and she guessed he'd manoeuvred himself across to the window. He jumped slightly as she entered. "Look at you. What's caught your attention." Millie moved over to the window. She draped her arms around her father's neck and kissed the top of his head. "Oh! You're watching the boys." Duncan's boys were playing in the field with Scuttle. The pony had on a bridle and Jack was leading him round the field. Paul was waiting on the fence and Millie guessed he'd jump on as Jack went passed. "I'm home for the weekend, dad. I'll have to go home tomorrow but I'll stay the night." She noticed he tried to move the lever to reverse the chair. "Can you move yourself around now?" She watched as he jerked the chair backwards. At that moment Alice came through to the lounge. She'd overheard Millie's question and answered for him. "Yes, he does. Knocks the table over and runs into the chairs, but he can get around now."

Millie couldn't help laughing. Alice and Hugh were like an old married couple. "I'll leave you two together for a moment. I'm going to take my things upstairs." She held up her little overnight bag and said to Alice, "I'll only be in your way for the night."

"Nonsense, girl, I shall love having the company."

Millie left the two of them.

Millie went out into the garden and opened the top stable door. Duncan looked up and she smiled at him. "Hello, Duncan."

"Millie." He looked pleased to see her.

Millie entered the stable and closed the door behind her. "It's cold. There was ice on my car this morning. I'd hoped to be here earlier." She was waffling and knew it. Then taking a deep breath she said, "I'm so, so, sorry for what happened… you know with Sindy."

Duncan kicked at the straw beneath his feet. "I know, Millie. Thank you for your support. It meant a lot." He looked at her and his eyes looked so earnest when he said, "I'm sorry about us, Millie. I really did…"

"I know, Duncan. You don't have to say anything. I think we needed each other for a while."

Duncan reached out for her. "No, Millie. I really cared for you. I wanted you, but…"

"It's behind us now though."

"Adam?"

"No. Adam and I have finished. It didn't work out. I think there's something wrong with me and relationships." She tried to laugh but it didn't work. Duncan had the saddest look on his face, it made her feel tearful for what she'd lost. She touched his hand, the one that had taken hold of her shoulder and said, "I did care about you… a lot." Millie stopped. "No. I do care about you. Still."

"Really?"

"Always. It was special, but I know what we did was wrong. It was very much needed at the time, but I know for now my heart belongs elsewhere. It won't always, but I need to heal. I must let myself grieve for what I've lost, as must you."

Duncan let go of her shoulder and took her in his arms. She seemed to melt into his embrace willingly and as she laid her head on his chest, she could smell the scent of him. It was so familiar. She felt his breath on her head as he said ever so quietly, "Simon."

355

Millie felt her eyes water. "Silly, aren't I?"

"No, no you're not. He's the silly one. I would have given my right arm to have you love me the way you loved him."

She felt his lips kiss the top of her head and she moved out of his embrace. "The boys are having fun out there."

She brushed at her jacket as she got her emotions under control. "I hear Grace is being a godsend to you?"

"She is. She does the school run and picks them up. Between us we do the horses. It works well. She'll be here in a minute. She's taken Emily to her dad's and calling in on her mum."

The boys were calling, 'Dad'. Millie opened the stable doors. The cold air swept in cooling the emotion. "We're in here." She smiled at Duncan, "I'm home for Christmas. Might see you then."

The two boys ran at her. "Millie! We've been playing cowboys with Scuttle." She laughed. "I know, I saw you from the lounge window. My dad was watching you too." She brushed her hands over their heads. "I hope Father Christmas comes. What are you hoping for?"

"Paul wants a football but I want Grace to be our mummy."

Duncan picked him up. "Jack, we've been over that a hundred times. Tell Millie about the dog you've been going on about."

Millie picked up on the awkwardness of the mummy business and went with the change in conversation. "A puppy. How wonderful. You must have been good." She looked at Duncan and raised her eyes in question. He nodded and winked. Millie wasn't sure if that meant the puppy was going to be delivered or a good distraction from the mummy – Grace situation. Millie didn't wait to hear one way or another. She felt sorry for the child. He was probably enjoying having Grace around. Picking him up from school and being in the home. It must be hard for him. Hard for them all.

356

Poor little Jack. He's barely five years old. Too young to lose his mummy.

*

Millie went back inside and plonked herself at the table. The bread was in the oven now and the smell was delicious. The phone rang in the hall. "I'll get it, Alice." Millie stood and went to answer it. She waited until the pips stopped and the money dropped into the phone box. "Hello?"

"It's me, Millie. Simon." He sounded frantic. "I need your help. I've killed Stephanie. I've strangled her. She's dead. I…"

"Jesus, Simon. What are you saying?"

"Simon!" When he didn't answer she said in firmer tones, "Simon. Simon listen. Tell me what has happened."

"Millie, I didn't mean to. She just goaded me and goaded me, and I grabbed her. I couldn't shut her up and I must have had her by the throat because she fell lifeless on the floor. Help me, Millie. I'm going to be done for murder."

"Simon, calm down." There was silence. "Simon listen to me."

"Oh Millie, what have I done?"

"You're going to have to go to the police…"

"No! I can't Millie I can't."

"Simon you are going to have to. It's better if you give yourself up. I shall come home now. I'll find you. Please, I…"

"Millie, I can't. I'm scared."

She lowered her voice. "I know. I am too." She repeated herself over and over again willing him to listen. "Simon? You must phone the police now and give yourself up. You are going to need a solicitor. I want you to ask for Bradley Thorpe. Have you got that? Bradley Thorpe. Tell Bradley you know Millie. Millie from the newsagents. He'll know." She was talking fast. "Have you got that Simon?"

"Millie, I…"

"No, Simon. You need to do as I say. I'll be in touch…Simon?" There was no answer. "Simon I know you're still there."

"Oh, Millie."

"I'm not listening to you anymore. I'm hanging up. You phone the police and I promise you I'll be on my way home."

Millie replaced the receiver. Her heart was hammering in her chest and her legs felt like they wouldn't hold her up. Getting herself together, she went through to the kitchen and told Alice that an emergency had taken place and she had to go home. "I must tell dad. I'm sorry Alice but I have to go."

Millie went into the lounge and knelt down by Hugh. "Dad, you remember Simon." There was no response. Just a silent stare. "He's in trouble, dad. He needs me. I must go."
Hugh's hand reached out for hers. This was his way of saying *'I understand'*.

Millie hurried upstairs and grabbed her little overnight case. Alice met her on the steps. The disappointment was obvious. Millie spoke before Alice had chance to ask questions. "Not now, Alice. I'm sorry but I have to go. I'll explain later."

"But…"

"I'll be home for Christmas." Millie instinctively kissed Alice's cheek and thanked her. "I've really got to go. I'll be in touch."

Millie drove straight home and walked into the newsagents below her flat. She asked her landlord, Mr Fisher if he knew where

Bradley Thorpe lived. She explained he was a solicitor and he bought cigarettes and a newspaper in the shop every morning. She didn't have to say anymore, Mr Fisher knew Julie. "I know him. He has his own practice in the town. It's Thorpe's. He lives just on the outskirts of Midhurst. There's a big house on the main road called The White Cottage. You can't miss it, it's the only one with a thatched roof."

"Thank you." Breathless, she hurried out of the shop and headed for Cocking not bothering to go up to her flat. Mr Fisher was right, the house was easy to find. Her insides were all of a tremble as she rang the doorbell. One of the boys answered. "Is mummy or daddy in?"

"Mummy!"

Julie appeared almost at once. "Millie! Hello. How nice to see you? Do come in. Have you come to see the baby?"

"No. I need to speak to your husband."

"You've just missed him. He had a call from the police station. He's been called in on a case."

Millie almost collapsed. "Thank God. Oh, thank God."

"Come and have a cup of tea. You look like you need one."

"Thank you, Julie. I really can't. I must go home. I might be needed."

"Is everything okay?"

Millie felt close to tears. It sounded like Simon had listened to her and given himself up. "No. No it's not. A friend of mine's in trouble. I'm hoping it's him Bradley has gone to help. This is serious, Julie, I'm so scared."

"Come on in, love. Come and sit down, you can't go anywhere in this state. See our new addition. Georgia. She's as good as gold. Best one so far."

Millie couldn't settle. She drank half the tea and left. She hadn't said a word about her fears for Simon or what Bradley had been called out to and was thankful Julie wasn't one for prying.

Millie drove too fast back to her flat and once home she paced around unable to settle. She couldn't believe Simon had hurt Stephanie or anyone else for that matter. He was the gentlest person she knew. Every minute that passed by seemed like an hour. She continued to walk round in circles like a caged tiger. Intermittently she would look out of the window, hoping, for what, she had no idea.

It was five o'clock when she heard footsteps. She had the door opened before anyone had chance to knock. Relief swept over her when she saw who it was. "Bradley! Where's Simon?" Millie couldn't help herself. She reached out and pulled him into her flat as questions spilled from her mouth. "Is he okay? Is everything sorted?"

"He's been given bail, and he's staying with a friend."

"Friend, what friend?"

"You used to share a house with her… at university?"

"Paula. That will be Paula. Why can't he go home?"

"He isn't allowed to, that's the conditions. He's to have no contact with the victim either, or his son."

"That's awful. Poor Simon. How is he coping?"

"He's lucky his wife's alive, Millie. He didn't kill her. She was just unconscious. Thank God he had enough about him to phone for the ambulance. If he'd left her on the floor and run, leaving her with no help, she could well have died, and I would be dealing with a murder charge."

Millie was speechless. Her arms dropped by her sides with relief and Bradley asked if he could sit down. Millie got herself together and poured him a large scotch, leaving the bottle on the coffee table so he could help himself. "Oh, Bradley. I'm so pleased he gave himself up." She was desperate for positive news. "It will have helped, won't it?"

"He's got to report to the station on Friday. I'll go with him and we'll know more then."

"Friday! That's a week away."

"The police need to investigate the case. They need to speak to the victim. Find out if there are any witnesses."

Millie flopped in the chair; her legs could no longer hold her up she was emotionally exhausted. "Can you tell me what happened?"

"If what he says is true, it was an accident. An argument that started about you, Millie. Stephanie accused him of sleeping with you behind her back. It got out of hand and I believe Stephanie said some rather hurtful unforgivable things. One thing led to another and he grabbed her. Tried to shut her up."

Millie let his words sink in as Bradley poured himself another scotch. "I wasn't having an affair with him. We were an item at university. I thought we'd marry, but Stephanie ruined all those dreams when she set her sights on him. It was while I was dealing with the death of my mother and getting my father…"

"I know, Millie. I've heard the whole sorry tale. My instincts tell me he's still in love with you though. You might not feel the same way about him anymore, but he married this Stephanie out of duty. I can tell he feels terrible for what he's done today and is blaming himself completely."

"What will happen to him?"

"Time will tell. I'll do my best to support him and act for him. It's as I said, it depends on the charges brought against him. Friday we'll know for sure."

Bradley left Millie's just after eight o'clock, three scotches later. She didn't think he should be driving but said nothing. The drink had loosened his tongue, and as he was leaving, he said, "I know you don't think of me as your father and I don't deserve the title, but I want you to know I think of you as my daughter, and you are my daughter." He was rambling and Millie didn't want this conversation right now, it had been a long, tiring day, but she didn't want to be rude, not when he'd helped her in her hour of need. "You might not like it, Millie, but I see a lot of myself in you. Your intelligent. I'm not saying Davinia was stupid, but the confidence and drive you have reminds me of myself."

Millie was moved, but her answer was honest. "Bradley... I can't think of you as my father. I'm sorry. My father is at home. The man who brought me up gave me a childhood to cherish. I wanted for nothing. I didn't question the lack of family members around me, I was happy being just us. Now I realise just how flawed my existence was. In just over a year, I have found out about grandparents who spent their lives hating my existence. I am just getting to know them and them me. We have no blood ties at all, and yet we seem to be becoming a family. Now I find out I have six half-siblings that are more related to me than anyone else I know, and yet I have no feelings towards them one way or another. Then there's you. A biological father who up until today I couldn't stand the sight of." Millie stopped. She'd said enough, Bradley looked close to tears. His voice was husky. "I understand." She watched him as he walked slowly down the steps into the darkness and home to his family. She closed her front door.

*

Millie looked for Simon all day, she'd expected him to come into the library and tell her how he was. Nothing. At seven o'clock she ate a hurried dinner and met up with Carol. They went to the village hall where they were showing the film Arthur on screen. Afterwards they went for a drink. Millie told her friend the history behind herself, Simon and Stephanie and the mess they had found themselves in. "I shouldn't care. It's nothing do to with me, but I seem to have got caught up in it. I'm trying not to, but I'm worried for him."

"You obviously do still care, and he does too by the sounds of it. Do you think you'll get back together?"

"No! He's married to Stephanie, and he has a family now."

"So?" Carol couldn't see the problem.

"I know Simon, and family will always come first. He had a hell of a life at home as a child."

"Children adapt and they're resilient. My mum always says 'marriage is a long old road.' And I'm sure it would feel even longer if you're sharing it with someone you don't love. Especially if the woman you want to be with is still out there and single."

"None of that matters now. Simon might serve time. I feel scared for him."

"So... if there was no Stephanie would you want to get back together?" Millie shrugged and Carol said, "okay, put it this way. If Stephanie thought you were having an affair with her husband, did she have grounds for such thoughts?

"No to both. I wouldn't want to get back with him as I don't think I'd ever be able to trust him. I just wonder why she thought we were having an affair. I can only guess she was angry at how late home he was on the Friday. Simon had come round to my flat. He'd been waiting for me when I got back after having a drink with you and Bridget. It was already quite late when I got home. I shouldn't have invited him in, but I felt sorry for him. He was freezing so I made him a coffee." Carol was about to ask more but Bridget came into the pub. The subject changed and the attention diverted to buying drinks and shuffling chairs around to make room for Bridget and her husband. Millie was pleased. No more about Simon was mentioned and they stayed in the pub until last orders were called.

Thursday 17th December 1981

There was still no sign of Simon. Millie began to think he had been told to keep away from her too. Then at lunchtime, there he was standing outside the library waiting for her. "Millie?"

She was delighted to see him at last. "Si. How are you?" Annoyance was temporarily forgotten at his distance and for not letting her know how things had gone.

"Stephanie phoned me at the office today. Millie, she told me she's dropped all charges. I've spoken to Bradley and he says we'll have to go to the station tomorrow for the bail appearance, but without a charge it will just be a case of tying up the paperwork."

Millie hugged him. She was so relieved. "That's great news. Are you going home now?"

"No. Bradley says I'm still under the bail conditions. Probably Friday night. Millie I really want to thank you for talking sense into me. I was that frightened Saturday I didn't know whether I was coming or going."

Millie's heart sank. His excitement at the thought of going home was too real and she found it painful. She tried to smile, but her voice betrayed her. "I'm pleased for you." Millie looked at her watch. "I don't want to seem rude, but I'm meeting someone for lunch. Cheerio." She walked away. Tears stinging her eyes. *'Did I think he'd leave Stephanie for me now? Did I like the fact that he needed me? He didn't though. He'd even chosen to go and live with Paula when he'd been bailed. Paula of all people. He'd phoned me though. When the chips were down and life was at its worst, he'd phoned me. Not Paula.'* This made her feel slightly better. Millie bought herself a sandwich, only to throw half of it in the bin. Her hunger had diminished. *'What's up with me? Feel pleased he's off the hook.'*

Bradley came into the library late that same day. She hadn't seen him either since he'd poured his heart out to her. Millie was just about to lock the doors to the public. "Millie wait! Have you heard?"

"I have, Bradley. Thank you so much for what you did for him…me as well."

"He'll be fine now. Charges having been dropped. It's just a case of sorting and tidying up the paperwork." He looked awkward and uncomfortable. "Millie…I took it upon myself to explain about you to Julie. I thought she'd show some resistance, but quite the contrary. She's delighted. She wants you…"

"Thank you, Bradley. Not yet though. Do thank Julie for me." Millie hesitated. She chose her words wisely not wanting to hurt anyone further. "Tell her I'm moved to think she would want to welcome me into the family so easily."

"I want it too, Millie. I want to move you into our family."

Millie didn't want or need this sort of pressure. She made it obvious the library was closing. "Excuse me please, I have to bolt the door. Happy Christmas, Bradley. Goodbye."

Thursday. Christmas Eve 1981

Millie gave Duncan two Christmas selection boxes for the boys. "Thanks, Millie. That's kind of you." It felt formal. "My sister's having a baby. Its due in the spring. They're absolutely delighted." Millie hugged him. "I'm delighted to hear that. You won't know how I need happy news." She felt him stiffen and she dropped her arms and stepped back. "Are you okay?"

"Yes. Yes of course I am. It's just..." Duncan had never looked so uncomfortable with her. Millie for one millisecond thought Alice had told him she was his half-sister and that they were related. Millie had never got round to telling Alice what she had revealed through her mother's memory box. Duncan quickly apologised. "Sorry, Millie. I don't know how to say this..."

"What?" Millie nearly dropped her guard and told him they weren't related.

"It's Grace. We've sort of come together. We go back a long way...school."

Millie forced a smile on her face. "That's lovely, Duncan. I'm pleased for you...Jack too. He got his Father Christmas wish!" Millie smiled. She was getting good at hiding her feelings.

Duncan relaxed. "We aren't quite at the mummy stage, but we're sort of seeing each other. I like her and she likes me. It's a good start for me and the kids and it seems to be working." Nerves made him talk fast, but Millie gave him a hug. "Duncan's it's fine. It's a good thing. Grace is lovely. I hope it works out for you. Bye for now. I must catch up with Alice." She didn't turn round as she walked away.

When Millie went into the kitchen Alice was full tales. "To think of Sue, having a baby. I'm that chuffed." She became hesitant when Millie mentioned Grace and Duncan's relationship. "I'm sorry, love. I didn't know if you had any ideas of..." Millie

366

snapped. "Ideas? I wouldn't have had ideas for Duncan if I thought he was my half-brother. I was disgusted at the thought. I went to hell and back over that discovery. My whole life is flawed with lies. Do you know that? I feel like a patchwork quilt. Only put together with unwanted scraps."

Alice put down the tea towel. "You're being over dramatic. You are loved, Millie. Loved by so many."

"Really? It doesn't feel like it." Millie told Alice what she'd found out about Bradley. The whole sorry tale. Alice paled. "I'm sorry, love. I don't know what else to say." Millie stood up to go and Alice made a move to stop her. "Millie." Millie turned. "Not now, Alice." And she left the kitchen.

*

Doris and John came early Christmas Day. Alice was making the dinner with all the trimmings. They all ate together and the jokes in the crackers were giggled at despite being corny. No one took any notice of Hugh struggling to put his food on his spoon with one hand. Alice helped where necessary and sat next to him. The atmosphere was jolly and Millie forgot for a while how out on a limb she'd been feeling. When she went to bed that evening, she thought about all that had happened. She was restless. A big part of her wanted to go back to her flat so she could be alone to dwell. A lump came into her throat. It felt like she was going to choke. She had another six days to kill here and no excuses to leave.

Millie was going back to Midhurst on Thursday. She needed to go into Chichester to buy herself an outfit for Bridget's New Year party. All the staff had been invited. Millie toyed with the idea of phoning Adam and asking him to join her, but she didn't. *'I expect by now he's already doing something.'*

Chichester was busy. Everyone seemed to be enjoying buying up the early sale items. Millie had just bought herself a pale beige dress with a navy trim on the waist. She was so busy making sure she had all her bags that she collided into someone. Millie couldn't describe her feelings when she realised it was Stephanie. She was alone. There was no Simon and no baby. They stood looking at each other for what felt like minutes but was in fact seconds. Stephanie spoke first. "Millie…I'm sorry."

"What for?" She wasn't going to make this easy for her old friend.

"Everything. I…"

"It doesn't matter now. You're married to Simon, you have a baby and the whole messy court case thing is cleared up too. Happy New Year." She went to walk off, but Stephanie grabbed her arm. "Please, Millie. Simon and I are parting. We…"

"So? What do you want me to do about it? What Simon and I had between us is gone. You killed that. We can never be. Not now. He's all about Ben and family. You knew that. That's why you latched on to him when you found out you were pregnant."

Stephanie had the decency to look embarrassed at the truth. "I'm everything you say and more. I'm sorry. Sorrier than you'll ever know, but you're wrong. It's always been you, Millie. Even when Ben was born, he always…"

"No, Stephanie. It will always be family with Simon. I know him."

Stephanie raised her voice. Desperation, anger? Millie couldn't be sure. "I've been so jealous of you. Always. Simon didn't want me. He wanted you."

Millie looked bored. "Really? Is that why, when my back was turned, he jumped into bed with you?"

"It was foolish on both sides. I didn't really want Simon. I wanted…"

"A father for the baby. I know. Well, you got one. Lucky for you it was the right one."

Stephanie lost patience with Millie's self-righteousness. Her voice had a catty edge to it. "You were always the same. Spoiled. Never had to share your toys. Had new everything. Only child. Well..."

"Well, I certainly didn't intend to share my boyfriend's with anyone if that's what you mean." People passing were starting to stare at the raised voices, but neither cared.

"It's up to you, Millie. Let Simon go if you want. Let your silly pride get in the way of your feelings, but I know you, and I know you still love him, and he loves you."

The fight went out of Millie. She was tired of the anger. "Stephanie. It wouldn't matter how I felt, it's as I said, I couldn't trust him anymore. If every time we have a blip in our relationship, or something happens or I have to go away for a while, I don't want someone in my life who falls to pieces and finds himself another woman for comfort."

"You're wrong, Millie."

"No I'm not. It's as you say. I've never had to share my precious things and I don't intend to start now."

Stephanie was bored of the conversation. They were going round in circles and getting nowhere. "Have it your way, Millie. What you don't realise is, yes he loves Ben and I think he tried to love me too. He probably did in his own way, especially when the baby came, but that was the closest we ever got to loving each other." Stephanie stopped. "You're not listening to me, are you?"

Millie went to leave but Stephanie grabbed her arm. "Look at me Millie, look at me." Millie met Stephanie's stare. "Millie it isn't my photo he carries in his wallet, nor Ben's, it's yours Millie. Yours. It's always been you." Stephanie hunted in her handbag and Millie thought she was going to bring out the photo. Instead she'd found a pen and quickly scribbled a number on an old receipt. "Phone him." Stephanie walked away.

*

Millie sat in her car and looked at the crinkled bit of paper in her hand. The number was smudged but she could still read it. Millie's mind spun with yet more revelations. She was worn out and looking forward to seeing a new year start.

She hung her outfit up as soon as she got back to her flat, and before she could talk herself out of it, she made the call. The ringing seemed to go on forever as if willing her to change her mind. Then he answered, his voice so familiar. "Si… It's me, Millie."

"Millie!" She could hear the pleasure. "Millie, I wanted to come and see you. I've been meaning to, honest. I guess I was frightened, unsure of myself. I knew you'd be at home for Christmas. I'm on my own. Stephanie and I have…"

Millie couldn't help laughing. "Stop rambling. I know everything. I bumped into Stephanie in Chichester."

"Really. And you spoke to her?"

"Yes. Things were frosty at first, but we got there in the end. We're never going to be bosom friends again, but we just might have to tolerate each other."

His voice lowered. He was trying not to get too excited at what he hoped was an indication of a rekindled friendship. "Are you telling me there's hope for us?" Millie was quiet. "It was never going to work between Stephanie and me. It was all about Ben. I didn't want him to have the same childhood I had. I felt I owed him that… and I do."

370

"You owe me one too remember. It was me who sorted out your brush with the law."

Not feeling quite as confident and fearing he might have misunderstood her reasons for calling. "Millie I'd do anything for you. What's up?"

"I'm going to a party tonight and could really do with some company. I need an arm to escort me in."

The excitement returned. "Millie Marlow. Look no further. I'm your man."

Millie was silent on the other end. She couldn't believe this was happening. Simon's voice was barely a whisper. "Did you hear me, Mills. I'm your man. I'm all yours. I always have been and I always will be."

THE END

Acknowledgements

Firstly, a big thank you to Irene Campbell for checking this book for me and finding my many errors and overuse of the dreaded commas.

Irene is a huge supporter of my writing and the encouragement she gives keeps me tapping the keys.

Wendy Devonshire. Thank you, Wendy. She has cast her eyes yet again over my work, looking for errors and giving good feedback.

Always a big thank you to Keith, my husband, who patiently watches television while I lose myself in my world of fantasy without a single moan. Then when the book is finished, he sorts out the whole printing set up and print run for me. He is also the first to tell people about my success at finishing another book. The praise he gives is embarrassing, especially as he has only ever read my first novel! But he will be the first to tell you he's listened to the chapters as they developed… which is the truth! Thank you, Keith, for always believing in me.

My dear mum. She never fails to tell anyone and everyone about my books… and always asks if they would like to buy one!

My daughter, Christe. I miss her every day.

FIRST EDITION

The Author

Sharon Martin

Lives in West Sussex with her husband, Keith.

Sharon has two children. Christie Ann Finnegan and Mark John Checketts.

Five grandchildren

Amelia Grace Finnegan

Josephine Ann Finnegan

Evania Rose Checketts

Jensen George Checketts

and

Ottilie Rose Martin